The Departing

The End Time Saga
Book Four

Daniel Greene

For Jen. You've rescued me more times than I can count and you're more amazing than you'll ever know.

MAUSER
West Coast of Michigan

A perfect clear magnified circle formed around the man below. The man inside the scope's sight picture smiled, unknowing of the projectile violence about to explode his existence in a fraction of a second.

A cross with small hashes on each arm hovered over the man's tattoo-covered head. The tattoos ran down his neck and disappeared beneath his clothes. He raised a beer to his lips and took a long swig between laughs. A black eight of spades tattoo ran from the middle of his skull down to the center of his ear so that it would look like he had it wedged under a ball cap even when not wearing one. *Nice artwork.*

Mauser shifted the M24 sniper rifle to the man next to him, letting it rest on each individual as he scanned them in search for his elusive prey.

The small town crawled with bikers, each club displaying different patch-laden leather vests. Motorcycles roared on side streets. Civilians in their mismatching gear appeared almost leisurely as they came in and out of buildings. They smiled and laughed as they drank and ate in the streets like they were throwing an apocalypse block party. Their ignorance disgusted Mauser. They had no idea of the wall of humanity that marched their way nor of the firepower that could be brought down upon them at any moment. Two things that they should respect but were too ignorant to know any better.

He slowed his sweep and reversed back where he had just scanned. His crosshairs settled on a single man in the town below. "Bingo," he said under his breath.

He knew it was him because of the scar running along his head. The man would stick out like a sore thumb anywhere with that nasty, puckered, shoddily treated wound. His beard had grown longer, making him look almost like a castaway on a forgotten island. His shoulders were still strong. His gaze showed little exterior emotion. He knew the man always held his cards close and never let on what he was calculating in his mind. *Steele.*

Mauser let his finger tap the trigger slightly and softly. The trigger moved the smallest fraction beneath his finger as if it wanted it so bad but didn't dare. "I could take you now, brother. Send you home where you belong," he whispered. *Not yet, though. Someday we will see who has the better shot.*

He tracked Steele in his sights. His former friend limped through the town with a crutch wedged under one armpit and the other arm dangling in a sling. "Got banged up now, didn't we?" he said to himself. "What happened to you?"

A voice whispered beside him. "Sir, is that him? Do you see him?" The helmeted soldier laid prone next to Mauser staring at him, holding his binoculars in one hand.

"Shut up, Private. No one asked you."

Private Vaughn blinked russet-colored eyes. "Sir, we are to report back immediately if we find our target."

Mauser pulled his eye away from his scope. Private Vaughn's Adam's apple moved up and down as he gulped.

"What are you going to do? Call an airstrike? Give me a minute, Vaughn. Trying to figure out what he's up to."

Mauser placed his eye back to his scope, feeling an odd sense of elation as he watched the people below without their knowledge. He was playing a grim reaper and he could take any of their lives at any moment. With a small press of his finger, their souls would disappear from earth, never having known that their lives were in jeopardy of being snuffed out.

A woman with short black hair talked to Steele. She reached out and touched him. Her hand lingered. *Got ourselves a new friend I see. Where's Gwen?*

He scanned building to building looking for the long blonde-haired Gwen. He settled on one blonde woman, but she looked too old. He rubbed his eyes. Even with the magnification of his optic, it still wasn't clear. *Where is that crazy girl?*

He shifted his optic back to Steele. Now, he spoke with a fat biker. *Made some new friends?* He wanted to smile at his old friend, wondering what he was saying. He wondered if Steele was acting all serious like everything was business as usual. He shook the emotion away and remembered why he was there. The sight left a bitter taste in his mouth.

"Sir, what should we report?"

Mauser pulled his head back. "Jesus, Vaughn. Fucking settle down. We're running a reconnaissance op, not running home to tattle to daddy."

A group of six bikers rolled their motorcycles toward the edge of town. Mauser tracked them. *What better report than from the cat's mouth itself?*

Mauser tapped Vaughn and they both crawled, elbow over elbow, until they had sufficient tree cover. He stood up and slung his M24 then picked up his Special Operations Forces Combat Assault Rifle 17, also known as a SCAR-H or SCAR heavy, that shot 7.62x51mm NATO rounds. He brushed himself off.

The six soldiers of his squad stood about in a wooded clearing. His men wore helmets and the brown, green, and gray camouflage of the Army Combat Uniforms. Specialist Brown's ACU jacket was unbuttoned, revealing a surprising gut. He held his M4 carbine casually across his shoulders. Corporal Jarvis was over six feet tall and fiddled with a necklace of rotting, graying fingers around his neck. Claimed it was some sort of good luck charm, but all Mauser got from it was the putrid stink of decomposing flesh.

Two Humvees sat parked nearby on a two-lane track that had taken them up onto the tiny hill and provided them a small vantage over Pentwater. The Humvee doors were open, his men leaning outside. Private First Class Campos sat in one turret. His jaw worked as he chewed the same piece of gum he'd had for weeks. Private Low stood in the other turret, his head tilted downward and his chin on his chest. He appeared to be napping with his M2 .50 caliber machine gun pointing toward the sky.

Red-haired Sergeant Yates leaned against a Humvee, his M4 carbine resting on the ground. His massive forearms crossed his chest.

A single low moan drifted up through the trees behind the Humvees. Yates peered over his shoulder in its direction. Neither concern nor excitement registered on his face.

Mauser's gunmetal-colored eyes darted to the movement in the trees. The others glanced casually around them. Jarvis grabbed his M16A4 and Campos trained his .50 cal in its direction.

"Sounds like one," Yates grunted.

"I got eyes on," Campos called down. "It's by itself."

"What we got?" Low said from the other turret.

Mauser gave him a nasty glare. "Infected, you lazy sack."

"I got it," Yates said. He sliced the pie off the Humvee, taking an angle that would maximize his eyes on target while minimizing his exposure to enemy gunfire. Mauser wasn't sure of its usefulness against the dead, but it never hurt to keep your tactics sharp. The lone infected emerged from the trees.

When it walked, its right shoulder dipped lower in stride with its mangled gait. Its head bent to one side and a skeletal mouth hung open. Pieces of gray skin were peeled off its face and replaced with black rotting flesh, and its hair was mostly gone with only stringy clumps remaining. Inky blood oozed through its t-shirt and soiled sweater, a line of bullet holes draped raggedly across its chest.

"No guns, Sergeant," Mauser said. Yates gave him a glance over his shoulder.

"Pussy. You think we couldn't take that rabble down there with just this squad?"

"Sack up, boss," Brown laughed at Mauser. "You got no faith in us?"

Mauser smirked. "If I didn't think Jackson would lock us up, I'd charge down the hill right now and end this."

The infected raised a tattered sleeve of its sweater, a bony hand saluting the soldiers.

"True," Yates said. He released his straight bladed Ka-Bar from its MOLLE sheath on his vest. "Come on over, baby," he cooed. He waved, extended his hand, and goaded the infected on. "Let daddy release you from your misery." The infected dragged closer and Yates struck quick like a viper, jabbing a black steel tongue inches into the top of the infected's skull. The dead hung for a moment, suspended by his blade. With immense strength, Yates twisted his torso, whipping the dead body to the side, removing it from his blade.

"Low, look alive up there," Sergeant Yates called up at the soldier in the turret. He bent down next to the body, still yelling at the other soldier. "At least face outward or something. Where there's one, there's always more."

"Yes, sir," Low said, the tone of timid irritation in his voice. Low turned his stubbly chin and faced the rear of the squad.

"Is that our boy down there?" Yates asked, standing up.

Mauser looked back down in the direction of the town. "That's them all right."

Sergeant Yates smiled beneath his reddish beard and pulled his carbine back in front of his body.

Mauser turned to Vaughn. "Get Jackson on the line. Tell him we got a hit on the target. Saddle up, boys. We're about to make some new friends."

A wicked grin crossed Jarvis's lips and he gave Brown a fist pound.

"You heard the man. Get ready for a fight," Sergeant Yates said. He marched back to the lead Humvee.

"Let's see what Steele's friends are up to," Mauser said. He tossed his sniper rifle to Brown. He caught it and placed it in the lead Humvee. Mauser pointed down the road. "We'll meet there."

***

An hour later they rolled into Forward Operating Base (FOB) Persistence of Colonel Jackson's mixed National Guard force. The tent city was contained inside a barricade of Humvees in an abandoned state park in a forested clearing for camping.

A soldier with the red keystone of Pennsylvania waved them inside the base. A big segment of the soldiers in the base came directly from Colonel Jackson's battalions from his original unit in Pennsylvania. Most were known as the Bloody Anvil Boys for their steadfast courage in World War II.

The remnants of sixteen National Guard units had all joined together under Jackson's command. The tree and stars of Tennessee, the sword and sunburst of New York, and the circle and star of Ohio decorated soldiers' sleeves inside the base. They were the soldiers left behind in the military's hasty retreat west. Now, they had formed their own unit, forged together in the heat of battle and the crucible of survival.

Mauser's Humvee screeched to a halt in front of a large tan tent. He hopped out of the passenger side and slammed the door. He pointed at Jarvis. "Keep them nearby. He'll want to see them." The rows of tents were not uniform, but still held a level of conformity to them.

Mauser nodded to two soldiers standing outside the tent. He opened a flap and ducked inside. What would normally house screens, computers, and monitors, now only held tables with paper maps spread over them.

A short bald man stood on the far end. Other officers stood nearby. Major Ludlow from the Ohio National Guard looked up as Mauser entered. He was more like a fly than an officer with his bug eyes. Captain Ogden of the Tennessee National Guard was a small man with an apparent Napoleon complex and gave Mauser a look like he wanted to fight for dominance. Lieutenant Colonel Davis from the New York National Guard pointed at a map with a long arm, looming over the other officers.

The light shone off the top of Jackson's head. His hands leaned on the table as he studied the map. He wore ACUs, but the jacket was unbuttoned and relaxed. His face was taut and his skin tight like someone had tightened a drawstring on the back of his skull. His lips were thin and would sometimes quiver before he spoke.

"I received your report from sector six. The only sizable town in that area is Pentwater. Do you agree?" Jackson said.

The colonel's voice was steady and he seemed calm today. For that, Mauser was thankful. Anything else and he would need to tread lightly to avoid an outburst from the man. "That's correct, sir."

"Good. And you saw him? *Agent* Steele?"

Mauser shifted on his feet a bit. It was one thing to not be with him, but working against his former best friend and fellow counterterrorism agent still stung on the inside. He got past it by remembering the murders Steele's renegade allies had committed against the military in what seemed like a lifetime ago.

Mauser nodded. "I had positive identification by his facial scar."

"Did you also see that two-faced traitor, Kinnick?" Jackson's thin lips twitched with the mention of his enemy. His mouth stretched across his skeletal head in a wide frown.

"No confirmation on rebel military forces."

"Did you see any military units with Agent Steele?" Ludlow asked. His wide-set eyes almost didn't blink.

"No, sir. Most of his people were dressed in civilian attire. With an oddly large contingent of motorcycle bikers."

"Interesting," Jackson said, frowning. "Why would he abandon the aid of Kinnick and his Special Forces lapdogs?"

"Maybe they abandoned him?" Ogden said from below.

"Maybe." Jackson considered his map once more.

Mauser waited a moment before he spoke again. "Sir, we were able to capture some of his followers."

Jackson looked up and a smile crawled over his skull-like face. "You are a good soldier, Mauser. One of my best. Finding you amid the wreckage of this earth was a rare find."

Mauser nodded again. "Thank you, sir. Not all of their party made it."

Jackson smiled. "Surely, we didn't need all of them." He waved at Mauser. "Bring them in."

He stepped back to the entrance, flipped open the tent flap, and hollered, "Corporal Jarvis, bring them in."

After a moment, Jarvis swatted a bald biker in a long sleeve leather jacket, driving him inside the tent. He was followed by a fat biker with a brown beard and a woman in her fifties with long brown hair. Their hands were tied and bound behind them. Metal snakes were sewn onto their outer garments.

Jackson smiled. "Gentle people of Michigan, welcome." He was a shark that bared his teeth, begging others to believe that he was only an angelfish. "Tell me about Agent Steele."

The bald man's eyebrows narrowed. "Who the fuck is that?" he spat.

The woman's brow furrowed. "We don't know nothing and fuck you, pig." She spit at the colonel. The colonel followed the spit down to the ground as it landed harmlessly on the floor.

Jackson's smile widened. Mauser was sure he was amused now. "Such vigor. Such angst, and for what? We haven't harmed you."

The colonel nodded to Jarvis. The corporal half swung the stock of his M16A4 into the female's face. Her nose cracked as the butt connected. She bent forward in pain.

"Ow! My nose!" she cried. Bent over, she spit blood and teeth onto the floor of the tent.

Jackson bent down close to her face. He put his thick fingers on her head and squeezed her hair in his hand, pulling her closer to his face. She moaned as he forced her face closer to his. Blood dripped out of her mouth, forming a crimson red lipstick atop her lips.

He spoke softly. "Now you can be angry with me." He kept his face close to hers, drinking in her pain.

After a moment, she stood up straight, breathing hard. She spit more blood from her mouth.

Jackson smirked, genuine mirth settling on his face. "I don't have time for your stupid pride." He blinked at Jarvis. He struck the woman in the stomach. She cried out in pain. He slammed the butt of his gun on the back of her shoulders. Her body hit the floor. She struggled onto her shoulders as she tried to get her knees under her.

Jackson smiled and gave Jarvis a deep nod. He kicked her in the spine, sending her body into convulsions of pain.

The fat one frowned, looking from the woman and back to Colonel Jackson, only just comprehending what the military man was asking. "Wait, you talking about the cripple?"

Jackson's eyebrows rose high on his face. He held up a palm to Jarvis, who took a step away from the woman.

Jackson cocked his head to the side. "Cripple? Did Agent Steele sustain injury?"

"Yeah, he's up there. Got a bum leg and a messed up arm. Leads some community of folks."

The woman looked up at the fat biker. "Shut your mouth, Nader. Can't you see that's what he wants?" Her eyes narrowed at the colonel.

"That's interesting information. Isn't it, Major?" Jackson turned toward Ludlow.

The bug-eyed major smiled. "Yes, it is, sir. Strike while the iron's hot."

Nader looked confused. "Why would you want to do that?"

Jackson tsk-tsked the man, walking forward, one boot in front of the other. "Nader. Nader. Nader. I'm not just going to kill him. I'm going to grind his deceitful little life out of him."

Colonel Jackson stopped close to the trio of bikers. He breathed in their scent. Their leather creaked as they leaned away from him.

"This is gonna be a lot of fun." Jackson looked down and fixed Nader's jacket with a pat on the chest.

Jackson licked his thread-like lips and Mauser shuddered. He hated when the colonel got like this. It made him question their mission or lack thereof. *This isn't going to be pretty.*

Jackson removed a pen from his sleeve pocket. "Let's send Agent Steele a little message."

GWEN
Illinois side of the Mississippi River

Her feet squished in the wet mud bank that led down to the dirty water. She stepped gingerly, trying not to lose her balance on the slick slope. The hazel waters of the Mississippi rushed before her, sweeping over rocks and trees alike near the muddy banks. The second longest river in the United States ran almost from top to bottom of the U.S., north to south, basically dividing the nation in two. From where she stood in Illinois, it was over a thousand meters across to the fertile lands of Iowa.

The engines of her vehicles idled behind her, waiting for her to make a decision. Her greenish eyes gazed across the river at a small town. The buildings in the town looked as cold and dreary as the sky above.

Old one- and two-story buildings rose up in a cluster. The architecture was late 19th-century design of red and white bricks. Other buildings had painted wood sidings of red, blue, and green.

Similar buildings peppered towns across the Midwest. Still standing, still in use for the most part, and from a forgotten time of prosperity and growth, a time that had disappeared leaving only its forgotten ruins behind. There was a chance before the outbreak that they could diversify their economies and make a comeback. Now, they were all that was left. These isolated small towns had only a natural barrier a couple thousand miles long to hold off the dead.

A knot of short and stout two-story silver grain bins sat near the edge of town. Farther away, ninety-foot concrete silos stood, tops capped with white domes. *Prevents the condensation from precipitating back onto the silage causing it to spoil,* she thought. During her days as a little girl until the day she had left, her grandfather had always explained the ins and outs of farming to her.

She shaded her eyes out of habit from an almost nonexistent sun. Her other hand instinctually rested on her lower abdomen. Her belly was already beginning to push out but only enough to make her uncomfortable. She couldn't feel the being that grew inside her, but she knew it was there growing. A life that would be utterly defenseless in a world that was brutal, harsh, and short since the outbreak.

Distant figures moved around the town. From her distance, it was hard to tell if they were alive or dead. *Please be alive.* She didn't know if she could stomach the dead here.

A man grunted next to her. "Is this the place?" The tall welder had muscled arms and held his AR-15 like it was a child's popgun. His greasy long hair lay draped over his shoulders like he belonged in the Middle Ages.

She looked up at the man. The town made her want to smile and cry at the same time. "Yes, it is. This is Hacklebarney." Her childhood home. Home to roughly a thousand people, give or take. The last census was 2010, but she was pretty sure it'd be lower now. With the deaths of the elderly and the departure of the young, it was only a matter of time before it was filled with only ghosts and memories if that time wasn't already upon them.

"Looks like a good place," Gregor said, his voice low.

"It used to be. Not sure now," she said, turning back to the convoy. "I'll be glad to get a roof over my head." She gestured with her head. "Come on."

A dozen vehicles sat waiting: a long yellow bus, a few pickups, two conversion vans, and some cars. Scared but hopeful eyes peered through glass windows in her direction. She opened the passenger side door of a green van and slipped onto the seat. Gregor lumbered around to the driver's side.

A woman leaned forward from the back seat onto the center console between the driver and passenger seats. "Is this it?" Harriet said. She kept an arm wrapped around a young boy and girl.

Sitting awkwardly next to her on the edge of the bench seat was Hank, one of the Little Sable Point volunteers sent by Steele to protect the convoy of the elderly and young people escaping the lakeshore community. His .30-06 hunting rifle was wedged barrel down into the doorframe of the sliding door.

Gwen turned around and faced them. More heads poked out of two more bench seats. A young mother, Joey and her daughter Pattie, elderly gray-headed Ben and May Clemens. Dr. Thatcher petted his nervous Pomeranian with a smile. She ignored the little blond boy sitting in the back next to the window. He stared outside as if he were bored. *He's not real, or is he?*

"This is it." She smiled. The facial movement felt foreign to her as if her muscles had to strain to keep that position, but it was genuine. The passengers let out sighs of relief. "Iowa is just across the river, and grandpa's farm is about ten miles outside of town."

Tears filled May's eyes and Ben squeezed her tight. Harriet shook the shoulders of Freddy and stroked Char's brown hair. The almost teenage girl stared out the window, not showing any emotion. Harriet's eyes looked pained as she watched her and Gwen gave her an understanding look. Char had been adopted by Harriet. Both Char's parents were dead. Her mother had died during the outbreak, and her father had been slain at the Battle of Little Sable Point. She was an orphan of the apocalypse.

"We will be safe soon," Gwen confirmed loudly, making sure Char could hear her. The girl would need so much love and patience to come out of her silence.

Gwen turned back, facing the river again. "Take us home, Gregor."

"Yes, ma'am," he said. He shifted the van into drive and they rolled forward down the road. It had been over six years since Gwen had been back to her hometown. It had been a lifetime in her mind. With each day a struggle to survive, it may as well have been forever. She watched the town as they drove closer. It seemed untouched by the tentacles of the war and the infected. No burnt-out buildings. No bullet holes covering the walls. No bodies in the streets. No tent cities where the leftover refugees fled while everyone else killed one another. Only a small town in the heartland of a dying nation.

Gregor turned the wheel and the convoy entered a two-lane bridge. Rusted steel girders rose up and encircled the bridge, crisscrossing to create a stable platform. Gregor pointed a big finger and took his foot off the accelerator, letting the van slow down on its own.

Two eight-wheeled combines sat side by side in the center of the bridge, blocking both lanes of traffic. One was green and one was blue.

"Infected," Gregor growled.

"Keep driving. We'll take care of them when we get close," Gwen commanded. She turned and spoke over her shoulder. "Hank, get ready." She slipped her Glock 43 9mm out of its holster and set the black handgun on her knee. She rested her hand on it as they grew closer to the blockage on the bridge. Her finger nervously tapped the slide.

Gregor let the van roll to a stop in front of the hulking farming equipment. Gray-skinned infected turned in their direction. Dead white eyes longed for them. She exhaled forcefully.

"Let's move," she shouted. Her hand ripped the door handle and her foot kicked the door. It flew open. Standing partially behind the open door as concealment, she lined up her three-dot sights on the nearest infected.

The infected let out a low moan from a partially open mouth as it reached for her with its bony fingers. She silenced it with a hot round from her Glock. The shell casing clinked onto the bridge. Hank's rifle boomed behind her followed by Gregor's AR-15.

She focused on the ones that were close, letting the other men take out the infected farther away. She had learned early on that trying a headshot with a handgun on a moving target from a distance of more than seven yards was a challenge for her. She notched another headshot from about five yards away.

The last of the infected vanquished, she stared up at the massive vehicles. "Come on," she called at the others, stepping over the recently slain infected. She kicked at the giant tire. Her foot bounced harmlessly off the side.

"There's no way we can move these things on our own," Gregor said. He looked up at the driving compartment, almost in awe of the giant machinery.

"Well, somebody had to put these damn things here," she said. She wedged herself up onto the side of the bridge. She used a rusted steel girder to steady herself atop the beam. Ignoring the water flowing at a good speed below her, she looked past the combines toward the town. Nobody was there.

She clambered up onto a giant combine tire and took a short leap from the tire to the driver's compartment. Wrapping her fingers around the door handle, she clicked a round button. The door popped open.

She hopped into the driver's seat. The cushion was hard foam with a short back. Monitors, a wheel, buttons lined the inside. Glancing around, she smiled and placed her hands on the steering wheel like she was a little kid on the farm again.

"Been awhile since I've gotten behind the wheel of one of these." She scratched her head. Her grandpa's had been a much older version. Not riddled with so much technology. It was a relic repaired and passed down from generation to generation. The family farm was never large enough or lucrative enough to purchase new equipment.

Farming had changed drastically since the old man's time. Farms had grown bigger and the small farmer had been all but plowed under by corporate farming techniques and their financial backing by big business.

She felt around the ignition and then looked up at the visor. A worn picture of a family was stuck in the flap. She tugged on the visor and keys dangled from it, attached to the strap.

"Whataya know," she shouted down at Gregor. She leaned out and jangled the keys at him. The tall welder smiled and laughed.

"Sometimes you get lucky," he shouted back.

"Or you make it yourself," she said to herself. She stuck the key in and twisted it, bringing the combine to life. "Let's get you in reverse." She bent forward, checking her mirror. She squinted when the mirror brought into focus a man.

A country voice spooked her as he shouted. "Now, I know you weren't thinking of moving this expensive piece of equipment without permission, were you, girl?"

Gwen turned over her shoulder and found herself face-to-face with the round barrel of a shotgun.

The voice was slow and sure with a ring of authority. "Keeping your hands where I can see them, how 'bout you move nice and slow out of that compartment and go join your heavy-metal boyfriend down there."

Bit by bit, Gwen lifted her hands off the steering wheel. Baby steps brought her to the edge of the combine.

The voice drove her along. "Go on, now, nice and easy get back down there." The man gestured with his shotgun toward the ground. Gwen did as instructed, stepping and then jumping down to the ground.

With her hands in the air, she turned around and looked up. Armed men in overalls, flannels, and trucker hats aimed guns at them from atop giant combine wheels and around the drivers' compartments.

A man in his late fifties with a graying brown mustache that could rival Tom Selleck's, pointed a shotgun at them with one hand. A gold star was prominently featured on his breast overtop a khaki tan shirt and brown pants. A long revolver hung on his hip along with a pair of steel handcuffs.

His words burst through his impressive mustache. "Just go on now. Turn those cars around and get on out of here. We don't got room for ya, so don't ask. That's an official order from the sheriff in these parts."

Gwen eyed Gregor from the corner of her eye and looked at the cars behind her. The scared faces of the people depending on her stared out from the vehicles. *I didn't come all the way here to be sent away like a scolded child.*

"We won't," Gwen shouted.

The sheriff's mustache twitched under his long nose. "Miss. We don't want to hurt anyone, but the bridge is closed. Hacklebarney is off-limits to the public."

"We're coming across. I got family in these parts, Sheriff," she said up at him. She was surprised at the little rural Iowan twang that had crept into her words.

The sheriff brought the shotgun stock to his shoulder.

"If you did, you don't anymore. I won't ask again. Get." He glanced at his men. "Red and B.B. Get those guns up. What the hell kind of posse are ya?" The farmers hesitantly raised hunting rifles to their shoulders.

"Wait," Gwen shook her head and squinted. *I can't remember his name.* "I'm from here," she shouted.

The sheriff pushed his brown cowboy hat back up on his brow. His gun lowered a bit.

"Ha. I've heard a thing or two in my day, but nothing like that. And who might you be, missy?"

"I'm Gwen Reynolds. John and Lydia's granddaughter."

The sheriff's eyes narrowed as he rubbed his mustache. "Gwen? Nah, that can't be you." The sheriff lowered his gun a bit and leaned forward, trying to get a better look at her.

"Yes, sir, it is."

A big grin spread on his face. "Well, I'll be damned. Let me get a look at ya'." The sheriff helped himself down onto the road. He threw his shotgun on his shoulder and ambled over to Gwen. She let her hands fall to her sides. He walked within a few feet of her and looked down his long nose at her.

"Gwen Reynolds?" he said inquisitively. He reached out and lifted up her chin. She let herself be inspected by the bushy sideburn-clad lawman. "You remember me?"

"No, sir."

"Name's Sheriff Donnellson. You must've been about fifteen or sixteen last time I saw you. Lucky for you, you took after Lydia's side and not that dog John." He looked past her at the line of cars. His face turned to concern.

"These your people?"

"Yes, Sheriff Donnellson. I am responsible for them. All of them."

Sheriff Donnellson nodded. "Town's been under a strict curfew since the sick people started coming in, but I think Mayor Dobson will make an exception for you." He smiled at her. "People said for a long time that it would take an act of God to bring you back to Hacklebarney. Just didn't think it would be an act like this. Jake will be glad to see you."

Gwen squeezed her eyes closed and a surge of panic raced into her stomach. Jake Bullis. The mention of her former high school sweetheart made her cringe on the inside. The terms she had left on had been less than optimal for either party.

"Are my grandparents still here?"

His brow furrowed. "Well, of course. Where else would they be?"

Gwen sighed, relief washing over her. Her family was here. Her childhood town was still here and she was home. She closed her eyes for a moment.

"Thank god," she whispered to herself.

The sheriff turned around and yelled at his compatriots. "Red, you and B.B. get those combines off the bridge. Gwen Reynolds has come back."

"Hiya, Gwen," B.B. said. The wrinkled gray-haired farmer gave her a wave and a smile. "Thought that was you. Couldn't have been sure though. Eyes just ain't what they used to be."

Red grinned at her and moved his dirty ball cap up farther on his forehead. The seventy-year-old had the build of an old-time boxer with a large rounded jaw. "John's gonna be mighty pleased to have you back. He's been worried sick. Lydia's been at the church every day praying for your safe return."

"I'm glad to be back," she shouted up at him.

The two old farmers turned on their combines, and one at a time, reversed them the other way on the bridge. They rumbled away, exhaust pipes pumping dark smoke into the air.

Gwen walked back and sat in the van. The sheriff waved them forward, shotgun wedged into the crook of his elbow.

Gregor stared at her. "Gwen, you all right?" His eyes darted from her to the sheriff.

She sat in a daze, the whims of a small town crashing back onto her. She had ended up right back where she started, facing the very place she had fled.

"Of course," she said after a moment. She sighed. "Let's get over the bridge before they change their mind." She gave Gregor a short smile. Her stomach turned over. An uneasiness enveloped her where she should have been filled with joy at her homecoming. *Why do I feel so out of place?*

KINNICK
Peterson Air Force Base, Colorado

Kinnick's arm was asleep. He took his finger and brushed her long blonde hair off her shoulders. He gently rolled the naked woman off his arm by pushing with one hand and pulling his trapped hand free. She mumbled something and snuggled back into her white pillow.

He rolled over to the side and sat up, his legs hanging off the edge of the bed. He shook his arm out to overcome the pins and needles inside and ran a hand over his head. The room was dark. The on-base lodging for military personnel had all the makings of a hotel room: a couch, TV, dressers, and crappy outdated carpet. The soundproof windows did enough to block out the air traffic of Peterson Air Force Base, but a faint rumbling could always be heard.

Grabbing his boxers from the floor, he pulled them up to his waist. They felt loose like they could fall back down at any moment.

A swift knock rapped on the door. He looked at it for a moment, trying to remember why someone would be there so early in the morning. He walked quickly to the door, scratching the back of his head. When he reached the door, he cracked it open a few inches and peered out. "What?" he whispered, his voice hoarse from a fitful night's sleep.

A private with wide eyes stared back. He blinked with surprise at the colonel's short answer and gulped. "Colonel Kinnick?"

"Yeah, what do you want?"

"Sir, General Daugherty is requesting your presence back at the operations center."

Kinnick yawned and half-covered his mouth. "I'll be over."

The private looked down at his feet. "Sir, he said to hurry." He gulped. "The general, sir."

"Tell him I'll be over soon. Thank you, Private."

"Bu-"

Turning away, he closed the door in the private's face.

A voice came from the bed. "What do they want?"

Captain Gallagher sat up in the bed, using the white sheets to cover herself. Her hair fell about her shoulders, ruffled and disheveled from sleep and the night before.

Kinnick shook his head. "I dunno." He sighed. "I can't imagine it's good, knowing the general."

"He's not a bad leader, Michael. He's gotten us this far." Her eyes darted at him to see if he approved of what she had said. She knew he hated the general for not providing adequate assistance holding the passes of Colorado against the dead, leading to the nuclear holocaust of the western part of the United States.

Kinnick sighed. "Don't get me started on the man."

She gave him a sly smirk. "Not anything like you." She crawled to the edge of the bed, moving like a cat burglar. Her bare feet touched the carpet and she swept up the sheet taking care to wrap it around her shoulders. She walked over to Kinnick, bedsheets dragging behind her like a cape. Her mouth formed a mischievous grin and she cupped his cheeks. Her lips pushed onto his and she kissed him deeply. The sheet fell away from her.

"He can wait," Kinnick whispered.

"But I can't," she said.

***

Colonel Kinnick entered Peterson Air Force Base's NORAD Operations Center. The operations center was primarily enclosed on a large open floor with a multitude of multi-screen workstations for both civilians and airmen working there.

The far wall held large projection televisions displaying maps of the airspace and video of ground operations. The televisions that normally held news reporting now showed a short list of operating airfields.

A concerned Major Thomas stood waiting. His eyes were worried behind his black-rimmed glasses. He immediately walked toward Kinnick.

Major Thomas's words were rushed. Kinnick found it slightly amusing that the Special Forces major could get flustered over a retired Air Force colonel who had failed to stop the vice president from nuking the western seaboard. "Sir, we've been waiting."

"For what?" Kinnick said nonchalantly.

"For you, sir." The major's eyes bounced toward the war room doors. "General Daugherty is furious."

"What's he going to do, demote me?"

The major's eyes darted around the operations center. "Also, Captain Gallagher is late."

Tongues always loved to wag about the office's new romance. Kinnick had dealt with that much of his entire career. Gossip was a mainstay of any military installation. He supposed he was immune from that kind of scrutiny now. He wasn't in the armed forces anymore. In fact, the only place he had been beholden to was wiped off the map a few months ago. Since the Under Secretary of State for Management Garlon had somehow found himself in the Golden Triangle safe zone, it was no longer necessary for Kinnick to fill a useless diplomatic seat now that there weren't any other nations to negotiate with.

Kinnick wasn't surprised that Garlon had managed to make it to Colorado first. Garlon could talk himself off of death row and had walked away from numerous scandals unscathed. He had settled into his new role as a Secretary of State with ease.

Thomas led Kinnick through the cubicles for the war room. The war room was a SCIF attached to the operations center. A red light was on above the door, meaning that the sensitive compartmentalized information briefing had already begun.

Kinnick glanced at Thomas. "Looks like they started without me."

"Yes, sir, but he's waiting for you to disclose a new operation."

"Me?" Kinnick said. He gave the major an unbelieving look. "That guy wants nothing to do with me." Kinnick stopped at the war room door. The light illuminated Kinnick and Thomas in a red glow. All that it meant to Kinnick was that when he entered the room, everyone would have to stop what they were doing, ensure classified information was not exposed, and then let him in. His hand hovered over the flat gray door handle. He glanced at the major.

"Because he wants you to lead it," Thomas whispered.

Kinnick digested his words for a moment and stayed his hand. "Lead it?"

"Yes, sir. The vice president has been very clear and the general is onboard."

Kinnick could feel his gut tightening in a knot. He had fought so hard for countless lives only to have them stripped away in a matter of minutes. He didn't count the soldiers in with them. Those were more personal. The whole thing had left him embittered to any direction leadership wanted to force on the remainders of the nation. "Brady? Why? So they can nuke the next place I go?"

"I'm not sure, sir."

The light clicked off above Kinnick.

"I used to think that I was smart to get out, but I guess I never realized that you can never really leave." Kinnick shoved his hand down on the door handle hard and ducked inside. He closed the door and the red light flicked back on.

He turned, facing the room. In the center was a long oval wooden table. Tall black leather chairs sat around the table filled with military officers. On one end, General Daugherty sat on the right of Vice President Brady. General Monroe sat on Brady's left. Monroe gave Kinnick a friendly nod. Monroe was the only commanding officer that Kinnick felt gave a damn about the nation and the people within.

General Daugherty's eyes narrowed behind his glasses.

"Nice of you to join us," Daugherty breathed. He glanced down at his paperwork, not trying to disguise his irritation with Kinnick.

The vice president sighed next to him as if he was bored, his hands folded around a glass of scotch in front of him. He wasn't even pretending to care about his current appearance. Kinnick was sure the man hadn't shaved in weeks. A patchy beard covered his face and dark circles hung beneath his eyes.

Brady glared. "We've been waiting on you, Colonel."

Kinnick thumbed through the paperwork in front of him. "I was preoccupied."

"Next time, don't be." The look on Brady's face told Kinnick that it was his only and final warning.

Kinnick picked up a stack of papers in front of him. In a block across the top, it read *Top Secret* and below that *Special Authorization Required*. He turned the cover sheet over. His eyes skimmed down the page. *Operation Homefront.*

"Go ahead, General," Brady said with a lazy wave of his hand. He brought his other hand to his lips and took a slurping sip of his scotch.

Daugherty nodded and stood. "Please refer to the briefing in front of you for details while I explain the current situation." He stood and clicked a button on his remote and a Powerpoint presentation illuminated the far wall. "As we all know, the nuclear strikes against the West-Coast cities were a success." He hovered a red dot laser pointer west of the Rockies. "We have minimized the threat from the west." The laser's red dot shifted to the East Coast. "The larger threat still marches from the east. Infected numbering in the millions trickles this way. We are observing a general trend from the East Coast. As the living are annihilated and survivors are driven west, the infected are following. It has been confirmed from numerous sources." He clicked and a new slide appeared.

"Our response will take place in the form of a comprehensive large-scale operation with the smallest number of U.S. Combat Forces possible." A blue background slide appeared. Across the top read *Operation Homefront* in white lettering. The logo was of two hands shaking, one in military uniform and the other in plain clothes with an American flag in the background. Underneath the hands, it read *United We Stand Together.*

"Operation Homefront will be the mobilization and training of all civilians that live along the Mississippi River. They will provide a viable force to combat the enemy and give us the time we need for mass development and distribution of the Primus Necrovirus vaccine."

"You mean they are the buffer force you need," Kinnick said. Officers around the table turned their eyes on him.

Daugherty glared at him behind his glasses. "They are pivotal to the survival of the nation and this government. Providing them essential training and support will greatly enhance both *their* and our opportunity to survive." He hammered the Powerpoint clicker with his thumb.

The slide changed over to a green map of the United States. A thick blue line ran from the center of Minnesota all the way down to New Orleans, effectively cutting the United States into two pieces, east and west. He circled it with his laser pointer.

"The Mississippi runs over two thousand miles. Any sizable towns will be garrisoned by Green Beret units. They will be responsible to train the civilians and defend key segments of the river.

Daugherty clicked and a new slide popped up. It read Southern Mississippi AOR.

"Colonel Canton will take south of St. Louis to the Gulf."

A gray-haired Colonel Canton nodded in his seat. His face permanently looked like he had just eaten a lemon.

"Where do we expect the main body of the infected to strike?" Kinnick asked. He stared at the map, awaiting a response. *Another suicide mission.*

"All of our latest reporting indicates that Iowa and Missouri will carry the brunt of the enemy force. Iowa's proximity to Chicago as well as the northern East Coast roadways and geographical features will take the dead straight into there. Missouri with it's long Mississippi River border will take the brunt of the southern masses."

The general clicked to the next slide. The slide read Northern Mississippi AOR. Kinnick's name was on the slide. "Colonel Kinnick will lead five ODAs from Carson to La Crescent, Minnesota. It's on the western side of the Mississippi across from La Crosse. We will drop you in via helicopter. There you will link up with Marine Corps Lieutenant Colonel Eldridge. He has been instructed to provide an appropriate number of small riverine craft for transportation and support down the Mississippi."

Kinnick held up a halting hand. "Wait. You expect me to lead this operation? Need I remind you I am *retired* Air Force. I'm not sure I am the best person to lead this operation." This was far beyond his skill set. *I have no special operations experience. All I've done is lead a failed stopgap measure in the mountains and lost a bunch of good soldiers.*

The vice president folded his hands loosely in front of his chest. "I requested you myself for this operation. Your grit impressed me in the Battle of the Passes."

A slight smile curled on General Daugherty's lips. "I concurred with the vice president's assessment. I couldn't think of a better man for the job. In accordance with DOD 1352.01, you are now recalled to active duty. Paperwork has already been processed."

Daugherty took a step next to the table and slid a piece of paper across to Kinnick. Kinnick picked it up. In block lettering, it read *Active Duty Report* near the top and *DD 220* in a box at the bottom. Daugherty's signature was scrawled in a box above. Kinnick exhaled from his nose.

I'm sure you couldn't think of a better man to send out on the front lines to get eaten alive by the dead. "I am assuming that there are plenty of Special Forces officers that would love an opportunity to take this command."

Daugherty smiled as he spoke. "There were, and we told them all no."

Kinnick let the paper in his hands fall to rest on the table. "Why me?"

Brady smiled and it was just twisted enough to convince Kinnick he might have lost his mind. He pointed with his glass still in his hand. "Because I'm convinced no one else can do the job."

STEELE
Pentwater, Michigan

The woman's voice sounded distant in his mind. "Steele, wake up." It echoed over and over as it faded to the recesses of his psyche. The words danced around a man in black holding a lighter near his face. The flames danced across his dream vision. The words repeated themselves over and over. Steele cracked his eyes open. The man and the flames disappeared in a cloud of smoke.

The shadowy outline of a woman's head in the doorway of a dark room took his place. He knew her voice. It had a hint of roughness around the edges. Her slender, slightly curved frame slipped all the way into the room and her outline hovered before his eyes. The grogginess of sleep slowly retreated.

"Tess," he groaned. His friend and partner from Little Sable Point was extremely comfortable with little to no personal boundaries. So much that she was the only one who wouldn't knock before coming into his room. He had the underlying suspicion that she somehow had taken claim over him even though his heart was promised to another. He closed his eyes again, wanting to drift back to sleep.

"What is it?" he whispered.

Outside his window, it was still black in the depths of night. His good hand felt clumsily around a desk next to his single bed. His fingers locked around his sidearm, a black military-issued Beretta M9A1. He used the front sight to scratch his forehead and pressed harder on the itchy sides of his head's scar tissue.

Tess's voice was soft despite her normal bad girl attitude. "Seven Sisters came back with some bodies."

He opened his eyes fully and was rewarded by her slightly curved slender frame. "Whose were they?"

"Iron Drakes."

Steele sat up, swinging his legs onto the floor and feeling his Thor's hammer slide on its chain between his pectorals. A reminder of his comrade Jarl's sacrifice. His right arm hung in a browning dirty sling, useless. He flexed his fingers and closed them hard. His fist was weak and unformed.

He glanced up at her. "Infected?"

"You should probably see this for yourself."

He felt around for his pants. "You know I don't like surprises."

She shook her head. Her short-cropped hair stayed in place, slicked back across her skull. She smiled at him, giving a quick peek down at his boxers.

He ignored her wandering eyes. His mind felt fuzzy like he needed a hot cup of coffee before he dealt with whatever disaster was coming their way. Even with the pastor and the Chosen captive, his sleep was spotty at best knowing Jackson was on the loose. He adjusted his boxers, uncomfortable under her gaze.

"What?"

She kept smiling. "Nice boxers, nerd."

He looked down at his underwear. They were decorated with yellow cartoon dogs with badges.

A defensive smile treaded his lips. "Deputy Bucky is a hero," he said to her. "Buckyville would be in chaos without his tenacious crime fighting."

She smirked. "Whatever you say, Mr. Tough Guy."

Awkwardly, he pulled up his ACU pants with his good hand. While he recovered in the fire station, Gwen had cleaned them and then patched the holes where the pellets had shredded the fabric. He cinched his belt tight around his hard stomach. *I'm gonna need a new belt soon or some new holes in this one.*

He gingerly threw a shirt over his body and as gently as possible eased his damaged arm through the armhole. The bandages tugged on his healing skin and he grimaced in pain. *Damn that stings.* He wrapped his sling back around his shoulders and holstered his firearm on his left-hand side, a move that was not familiar to him.

As quietly as he could, he thumped down the fire station hallway with his crutch that whined and squeaked with every step. The rooms in the fire station dormitory were filled with the remaining members of Little Sable Point that hadn't gone with Gwen.

They were his volunteers. Their numbers had grown since the Battle of Little Sable Point, every single person that had fought in the battle joining his all-volunteer force. Others that had fled in the face of the pastor's wrath had found their way back, joining Sable's ranks once again.

The few who had survived the battle had a bit of swagger to them. He didn't know why because they were thrashed and beaten, but they had held out long enough to throw one solid haymaker for the win. That was something to be proud of.

He took the winding metal steps one by one, holding onto the handrail to steady his hopping down the spiral stairs. At the bottom was the fire station garage, empty save for supplies and now a gathering of people.

Men and women wearing all manner of riding leather along with Thunder stood below. Tess followed Steele settling nearby, her arms folded over her shoulder harness that held her black M1911. Ahmed shouldered a baseball bat, standing to the side of the group. *Kevin must be passed out upstairs.*

Steele crutched forward, leaning heavily on his single crutch, and as the men and women recognized him, one by one, they parted.

Three sheet-covered mounds lay in the center. Steele hobbled forward, getting a closer look at them. A man hovered nearby, his hand covering his mouth. His gray-streaked black beard folded out from underneath his hand. Silver metal serpents sat coiled over a field of yellow on his motorcycle club patch. Steele gave him a wary look.

"These your people?" Steele asked.

The man's eyes glanced up at Steele. His hard and angry gaze bounced from Steele's arm to his leg.

"They're mine. Iron Drakes Forever," he grunted.

"Where'd we find them?" Steele asked.

"About a mile south of here. A couple of the Seven Sisters ran across them laid out in a line on the road. Wasn't no accident."

Steele had never doubted it was from the very beginning.

"We have no feud with the Sisters, so there is no reason for them to lie. Frank Rogers, president of the Iron Drakes."

"Mark Steele," he said with a nod. "May I, Frank?" He gestured down at the bodies. Frank waved a hand at him. "They won't mind now."

Steele bent awkwardly down, trying to not flex the muscles in his thigh for fear of ripping open all his small pellet wounds. Ahmed came forward, touching Steele's shoulder. "I got it, man." Steele stood back up and Ahmed pulled back the sheet covering the bodies.

People gasped around him. Steele sucked in a deep breath. The two men and the woman were eyeless. Their flesh, desecrated by slicing stab wounds covering their faces, showed how desperately the victims had struggled to keep their eyesight.

"Lift the sheet up higher," Steele said. Ahmed gave him a worried glance and Steele nodded. "Go on." Ahmed pulled the bloodied sheet up higher. Their bodies were covered in bullet hole exit wounds in the front. Steele stopped counting on the fat biker at about thirty. *Torture and execution. Reminds me of ISIS savages.*

Steele looked at the throng of bikers and Sable Pointers. "Any idea who did this?"

Frank gave him an unapologetic look. "Well, between you and me, we ain't got no love lost with the Grave Guards. But we been on terms since this whole thing started. Don't make sense that they would make a move on us now."

The dangers of acquiring the support of a bunch of rival motorcycle clubs was that they all had a past with one another, good and bad, mostly bad.

"I think this is for you." Frank reached behind his back hip and Steele's heart jumped. His good hand went to his holster.

"Now hold on a second." Frank held out his free hand and took a piece of folded paper out of his back pocket. He leaned over the bodies and handed it to Steele.

"They nailed it to Nader's chest." Frank eyed the paper with malice and looked back at Steele. "Take it."

Steele gulped. Flecks of blood stained the paper and it was crinkled and torn along the edges. He took the paper from Frank. He held it for a moment, feeling the animosity that seeped from its lines. Steele gave Frank a serious glance and flipped the piece of paper over then shook it out to open it all the way up.

Steele held it up in the dim light. The writing was hard and crisp with sharp lines that appeared to have been pushed into the paper. Blood had soaked through the top of the paper where the nails had stuck through both paper and flesh alike. Steele read:

> *Agent Steele,*
> *We see you, but you can't see us. We know you are injured and weak.*

Steele looked at the faces around him. The room started to spin. *Do enemies hide in my midst?* The people looked at him, clueless. He turned and glanced at Tess. Her dark eyes told him nothing. He looked into the spotlighted outside. Darkness blanketed the building, having sent the light into retreat, ready to acquire any space relinquished by its foe. He continued on:

> *Your actions against my command are about to come to a swift and final conclusion. Let this be a warning to that filth that rides with you. We are coming. We will not be deterred until justice is served in blood for what you and the traitor Kinnick have done. We are the legion that remains.*
>
> *Colonel Jackson*
> *Legion Commander*

Steele folded the paper and shoved it in his pocket.

"Who's Colonel Jackson?" Frank asked. His hands had turned into fists and fell to his sides.

Ahmed's face paled at the mention of Jackson.

"Ahmed, double the volunteers." He looked at Thunder. "Make sure someone is on the remote roadside charges, and snipers are up in those buildings. Pull some trucks up and block the road to the south."

Tess stepped up, "I'll run and get Scott's team into the condo firing positions and Margie's team to the water tower."

Steele stared out into the night. *They may be watching us even now. They must be watching us.* Cool sweat beaded on his skin.

"I'll grab Larry and his team and get on the blockade," Ahmed said. He took off running. Steele nodded, an uneasiness settling in his gut causing his stomach to turn and his face to twist. *What will be enough? How can we defeat these madmen?*

Thunder coughed into the crux of his arm. "I'll rouse the Red Stripes. See if we can get some extra guns in place."

Steele nodded. "Thank you." The exhaustion of being on the brink of an unwinnable war crushed down upon him. Thunder's Santa-like face mirrored Steele's worn-out feeling. "Be careful, Thunder."

"Ha," Thunder barked. He lumbered out, tightening his red bandana around his head.

Frank walked around the bodies planting himself in front of Steele. "My people are dead. Who is Colonel Jackson?"

Steele shook his head slightly. "An enemy from our past."

GWEN
Reynolds Farm, IA

The van bumped and lurched along a Level-B dirt road, a minimally maintained road of the county. Tears filled her eyes and a lump formed at the base of her throat when she saw her grandfather's silos in the distance, one about ninety feet high and a shorter one about sixty feet high next to it. As they grew closer, her emotions conquered her self-control.

A dingy white farmhouse with a wraparound porch and faded black shutters grew larger until Gregor brought the van to a stop in front.

A thinning white-haired man sat in a rocker, a shotgun laid across his lap. He wore overalls and a white button-down shirt underneath. Two Labrador Retrievers lay in the yard, one yellow and one black. When the van rolled to a stop, the dogs stood up and started barking.

Gwen wiped tears from the corners of her eyes and snapped the door handle, opening the door. She slid off the seat and her feet crunched on the gravel driveway.

The man stood up, holding his shotgun in front of him at his hip. His remaining hair was combed to the side and his eyes squinted as he tried to see better.

Gwen took a hesitant step closer. She whispered. "Pa?"

The old man shouted, raising a fist. "I don't know what you want, but we don't got any. So be off with ya." He took a few steps closer staying on the safety of his porch, brandishing his shotgun in their direction. The dogs continued to howl. Ruff-ruff-ruff. An old woman came to the screen door behind him.

"Who is it, John?" she asked. "Oh my, so many people," she said, startled. A hand raised to cover her chest.

The old man scolded her over his shoulder. "Get back inside, Lydia." He shooed her with his hand not holding the gun. "And lock the door," he yelled back at her. The old woman nodded and closed the door. Her face appeared in a window a moment later, watching.

Gwen squatted down on her haunches. She pursed her lips and dropped her voice low, "Dutch." The yellow dog's ears twitched and shifted, familiar with the sound. "Rocky, come," she grunted. She pointed down at the ground in front of her. "Come." The labs barked a few more times, but their tails wagged fiercely back and forth. They sprinted for her and swarmed her, rubbing their bodies around her in excitement. Rocky's rear end sent her onto the ground and the dogs proceeded to lick her to death. She sunk her hands into their fur, hugging the animals hard. They smelled like barn and crown vetch and dirty farm dog. They triggered her brain with the faint scent of home.

The man walked out into his yard. He squinted hard. Gwen nudged the dogs off of her. "All right, you fearsome guard dogs, get off of me." She stood upright, dusting herself off. Rocky let out a bark in response as he trotted back to see his master.

She smiled at the old man as recognition came across his face.

"Gwen?" he cried.

"Yes, Pa," she said, her voice cracking. She met him halfway and wrapped her arms around her grandfather. His body seemed smaller and more frail than the last time she'd seen him. They held one another for a moment in silence. Gwen sniffed back her tears.

"We thought with the outbreak in Washington that you were—." His voice stopped and he squeezed his arms tighter around her. The door banged open on the porch and a six-year-old girl ran down the steps.

"Gwenna, Gwenna," she yelled, her ponytail bobbing as she ran. Gwen bent low and scooped her up. The little girl hugged Gwen around her neck.

"I missed you, little Haley," she said into her ear.

"I missed you, Gwenna."

Gwen held the child away from her.

"You've grown so tall," she said, inspecting the child.

"Mommy says we don't have to go to school no more!" There was little remorse in the girl's voice.

Gwen set her down and smiled at her. "More time to play."

The little blonde girl kicked at the ground. "I get bored and all Pa wants to do is play checkers. My iPad don't work and neither does my phone."

Gwen brushed her messed up hair. "Go play in the dirt. You're a kid. You should be outside, but tonight you and me will play a game. How 'bout that?" A rural twang had crept up in her voice, her tongue reminding her she was home.

"Sweet," Haley shouted. She threw her fists in the air. "Wahoo! Finally, somebody to play with."

"Rocky and Dutch prolly want to play fetch."

Haley ran off and chased the dogs. The dogs barked around her as they ran.

Her grandfather grinned. "Come on, Gwen. Gram will want to see you."

Someone coughed behind her. She turned. Her people from Little Sable Point stood outside their vehicles, with tired looks and long faces, watching her expectantly.

She grabbed her grandfather's sleeve. He turned around. "Pa, I brought these people. They need our help."

Her grandfather gave the people behind her a suspicious look. His bushy eyebrows pressed together in concentration. "They look like they seen better days."

"Much better days. We need a place to stay."

He leaned closer to her. "Gwen. There are over a hundred people out here. What are we supposed to do with them? Our house ain't that big." He eyed the people warily. "Some of them look a bit rough."

"Pa, they need us."

The old man's brow wrinkled. "I don't like it," he said, his voice gruff.

"Pa," she said scolding him.

"Just like when you were a kid. Always bringing in the strays. Just for the night now. Then they can leave."

She rose her eyebrows in a threat. "Pa."

"Jiminy Crickets, Gwen. All right, a few nights." He gestured over to a hand water pump. "Never thought we would need the old hand pump again, but here we are. Plenty of fresh water for these folks. I'll see what we can do for food."

"And how about a place to stay?" she said.

He scratched his almost bald head behind his ear. "Barn will have to do." He pointed over to a worn large red barn. Weeds grew tall around its edges. A few shingles were missing from the roof here and there.

"Gregor, let's start getting things set up. Will you give me a few minutes inside?"

Gregor nodded and turned back to the people. "Let's get our shelters set up in the barn." The swarm of refugees trudged across the tall browning grass with bags, backpacks, and blankets.

"I'll throw some more hay down for them in a few minutes," Pa said.

"Thank you, Pa."

He shook his head with a grin. "You've been getting what you want since you were a little girl."

She placed an arm around him and leaned her head on his shoulder as they walked to the porch. A younger woman waited for them there, her back against a porch pillar. Her hair was wavy where Gwen's was straight, but both were the same darker blonde color. She was a bit heavier than Gwen and they shared the same mood-dependent green eyes. Her arms were folded beneath her breasts as if she had been waiting on Gwen all day. One of her hands held a cigarette.

"We were worried sick about you," she said with a half-smile. She put a cigarette to her lips and took a drag. "You couldn't have called?"

Gwen narrowed her eyes. "With what?"

"Well, I don't know. Something." She gestured at Haley with her head. "That girl over there has been asking about you every day for two months, and what was I supposed to tell her? Her aunt was murdered?" Her voice shrank. "Her aunt was eaten alive?"

"I'm sorry, Becky. There wasn't a way."

Becky took another drag off her cigarette, letting the smoke come out her nose. She reached for Gwen and they embraced. "But I'm glad you made it back."

"Me too," Gwen whispered.

Her sister smelled like smoke and a faint hint of lavender. She must have grown lazy about trying to cover up the smell of her smoky clothes a long time ago, yet a small effort still remained.

"Have you heard from Mom or Dad?"

Becky nodded. "Dad got stuck up near Sioux Falls. We haven't heard from Mom." Their parents had been divorced since Gwen was six and they had to move two towns apart. A giant custody battle took place, coming down to a dramatic court decision where the girls chose to live with their grandparents rather than either of their parents. The Reynolds' family farm was the girls' place of refuge in the turmoil of divorce.

"Where's your boyfriend?" Becky asked.

Gwen forcibly exhaled. "We'll talk about it later."

Becky raised her eyebrows. "Terrific."

"Ohhh, Gwen," came an old woman's voice. Her grandmother wore an apron and clasped her hands in front of her with tears in her eyes. "This is just wonderful. I knew you would come back to us."

Gwen hugged the old woman. "Gram, I missed you." Her grandmother held Gwen away from her, looking her up and down.

"You look skinny," her grandmother admonished her. She wagged a finger in Gwen's face. "I won't have my granddaughter starving. I have a nice chicken broccoli casserole in the oven for dinner."

Gwen's mouth instantly started watering. She couldn't remember the last time she had eaten anything real and definitely no comfort food since the outbreak.

"We need to get some food in you," her grandmother said. The old woman gave her a wink. Gwen's eyes darted from person to person in a panic. *There's no way that woman knows by just looking at me. I am not even really showing yet.*

"Is there anything we can feed these people? They're hungry too."

Her grandfather gave a worried look. "There sure are a lot of 'em."

She glanced over her shoulder at the refugees taking shelter in the barn. "They're hungry."

Her grandmother looked out at all the people and she gave a quick nod. "I'll throw a few more on, but it's gonna be a minute."

Pa narrowed his eyes. "Where'd you get 'em?"

"They're mostly from Michigan."

Gram gave her husband a scowl, saving a smile for Gwen. "Don't you worry about Pa. He'd gripe if he had a ham under each arm." Gram ushered her inside. "Don't want you coming down with something."

"Haley, come on in," Becky yelled from the porch. She pushed her cigarette butt into a rusty bucket filled with sand.

They walked inside the foyer. Thick coats hung on pegs and muddy boots had their place on the floor. The delicious smell of casserole overwhelmed the musty old smell that their house usually had.

Gram led them into the dining room and she pulled out a chair. "Now, you take a seat, dear. Let's get some food in you."

"What about the others?"

"They're just gonna have to wait a minute while it heats up."

Gwen found herself seated at their dark wood dining room table. Old pictures of a young John and Lydia decorated the walls, along with their parents and other relatives in black and white photographs. Iowa State Fair photos. Weddings. And the obligatory high school senior photos of Becky and Gwen with the traditional shots: one standing with a basketball, one standing in a field, and one with a regular white backdrop and fancy clothes.

Her Gram emerged from her kitchen domain and set a steaming plate of food in front of her.

Gwen gripped her fork like a starving prisoner. Chairs creaked as they all sat down. Gwen continued to keep a white-knuckled grip on her fork as she held off from digging in like a maniac. Her Gram smiled at her from across the table.

"Well, go on John. Say grace," she said. "Can't you see Gwen's starving?"

Her grandfather bowed his head, and a few pieces of his hair drooped off the top. "Lord, thank you for all your blessings you have given us, for this food you have provided, and for the safety of our loved ones. Amen."

As soon as *Amen* was out of his mouth, Gwen shoved her fork into the chicken and broccoli. Scooping the food high on her fork, she shoveled the food inside her mouth. One after another, heaping forkfuls of food delighted her taste buds, but she ignored that and shoved more in.

In a few minutes, Gram was inspecting her plate from across the table. "Want some more, honey?"

Gwen could only smile.

"You were always such a good eater growing up."

Gwen nodded. "Please."

Her grandmother stood and moved back into the kitchen. What her grandmother really meant was that she had been pudgy as a child and her grandmother's cooking was partially to blame. Even when you said "no" to another helping, it was piled onto your plate regardless. Another mound of food was set in front of her. She shoveled that down, barely stopping to breathe, and when she was done, her stomach felt and looked as if she were further along in her pregnancy than she was.

Her grandfather leaned his elbows on the table. "How bad is it out there?"

Gwen adjusted herself in her seat, too full to be comfortable and feeling the need to lie down. "Bad. The East Coast has been overrun by the infected." She turned to Haley. "Haley, sweetie, how about you set up a game in the other room?" Gwen raised her eyebrows, nodding her head encouraging the girl to leave.

Haley's little face looked sad. "Why can't I stay with you guys?"

Becky's voice grew stern. "The adults have to do some grown-up talking. Go to the other room."

Standing up, Haley pouted and her blonde hair flung all around her.

Gwen held out her hands and Haley put hers inside of Gwen's. "I'll join you in a few minutes to play sweetheart. Promise."

A smile spread across the young girl's face. "Okay," Haley chimed and ran off.

Gwen watched her go, an ache of relief in her heart that her niece was safe. Everyone had always told her that it would be different with her own children but she couldn't imagine loving any child more than the way she loved that girl. She turned back to her grandparents and Becky.

"The infection is real. It turns people into wild monsters. Cannibals."

"That's nonsense, honey. That's just the news trying to scare you," Gram said.

"Let the girl speak, Lydia," Pa growled.

Gram humphed and got up, busying herself by clearing plates.

"Pa, it's real." She let her voice drop in case little ears were sneaking a listen. "I've seen them *kill* people. I've *killed* them. They can't be stopped. Only killed." She had also killed a victimized woman and an American soldier, but she left those parts out of her rendition.

Her grandfather sucked the side of his cheek. "I saw it on the news before the power went out. Just couldn't believe it. They said old man Waverly had something exotic like. They tried to take him to county lockup, but he ended up in Iowa City for observation."

"Governor closed schools pretty quick," Becky chimed in. "It's all well and good until it's time to pay the bills and you don't have any money to buy groceries." She looked down at her food.

Gram brought in a pot of coffee and set cups in front of each person.

Pa nodded as if it were settled. "Might not be pretty, but this farm seen this family and our parents before us through a lot worse storms than this."

Gwen hesitated but still took a sip of her coffee.

"Not by feeding an extra hundred mouths out in the barn," Becky said, baiting Gwen.

Gwen set her coffee down. "Those people need our help. It's more than just the infected out there. Law and order has disintegrated. Civil society doesn't exist."

Her grandfather sucked his cheek again. "Nonsense. Sheriff and the mayor have things under control 'round here."

Gwen tilted her head. "Pa, people are killing each other for food. A man shot Mark and took me prisoner. We escaped to Michigan, only to get wrapped up in a battle against some cult."

Becky's eyes went wide. "Is Mark?" she started.

"No, he's alive." *That mule of a man better be alive because I sure as hell ain't raisin' this baby without him. There's that small town Iowa farm girl coming through again.*

"Where is that friend of yours?" Pa interrupted.

"In Michigan with the rest of our group."

"There's more of ya'?" he said. He frowned, perturbed at the thought of more people requiring his assistance.

"Many more. Mark sent us ahead to make sure we were safe from Colonel Jackson's troops."

"Who is Colonel Jackson? And why is he after you?" Pa asked.

"It's a long story, but things have gone really bad."

Pa folded his arms over his chest. "What have you gotten yourselves mixed up in, Gwenna?" He shook his head. "I never understood what your obsession was with the city. All these things you talk about are flat-out crazy. You never should have left home, Gwen. The only thing that comes from outside Iowa is trouble."

Gram took a seat back at the table. She took a small sip of her coffee. A little smirk snuck on her face like she held a secret. "You know who I saw the other day?"

Jesus Christ, Gwen thought. "No, I don't." *Yes, I do, of course I do.*

Gram's neck wavered back and forth in excitement. "I saw Jake Bullis. Asked about you." She sipped more of her coffee, holding the cup with two hands.

"I'm sorry, but what does that have to do with me?"

Her grandmother shrugged. "Just thought maybe you two would want to catch up."

Gwen gave her the best smile she could muster. "We shall see."

"Jake's family have a lot of cattle. If this is as bad as you say it is, you would do well to treat that boy with some respect. He could be feeding us all winter," her grandfather said.

"Gwenna," Haley shouted from the other room. "Come and play."

"Just a minute, sweetheart." She switched gears back to Mark and the others. Anything to not talk about Jake. "Pa, whether you like it or not, Mark is coming this way with a lot of people."

Her grandfather huffed. "Well, it ain't me you got to convince, but I'll tell you one thing. We got enough on our plates with all the folks already here." He pointed a finger out the window. "What happens when they eat us out of house and home? Will you just move on again? 'Cause I ain't leaving." Her grandfather looked away from the table, agitated.

"Of course not," Gwen mumbled.

"You need to think about what you are asking this family to do."

"They're not useless mouths. They can help you bring in the harvest and build shelters. I've brought a few that can fight too."

Her grandfather's eyes narrowed. "Fight?"

His look pulled on her heartstrings. "Pa, we need people who can fight, whether it's against the living or the dead."

He cocked his head away, disapproval settling on his face. "We ain't fighting nobody."

They sat quietly for a moment, each enamored in their own conflicting thoughts.

She reached out and took his weathered, wrinkled hands in hers. "I'm asking you to save these people's lives. Give them a chance."

Pa nodded his head as if he had thought long enough about it and released her hands.

"I'll take you to town in the morning and get you a meeting with the mayor. Nothing happens without his approval."

Gwen drank a bit of her coffee. "Perfect." She turned to her grandmother. "Can I help you with that food?"

Lydia stood shaking her head. "Of course not. Give me another ten minutes here and we'll take it out to them."

A knocking at the door turned all their heads.

"I'll get it," Gwen said, pushing her chair backward. "It's prolly Gregor checking in on me." She smiled at Gram and walked back into the foyer.

"Gwenna," Haley whined from the other room.

Gwen wrapped her hand around the doorknob while looking at the other room. "Just a minute, babe," she said. She swung open the door. A man leaned on the doorframe. He was over six feet tall and his face was smooth and handsome. His brown hair was partially brushed to the side to make way for his protruding brow bone and deep set dark eyes. A fine plaid shirt was tucked into his Carhartt pants kept in place by a large silver belt buckle. His lips formed a wide smile when he saw her.

His deep voice had a slower rural cadence to it. "Well, Miss Gwen Reynolds." His smiled widened. "I can't believe it's you. It's still Reynolds, ain't it?"

She tried to give a pleasant smile, and she brushed her hair out of her face in a fluster. "Hi, Jake," she said and sighed. "It is still Reynolds." Her eyes met his after a moment spent trying to avoid him.

"That's good to hear. Sheriff told me you came in today, so I thought I would stop by and say hello for old times' sake."

She crossed her arms over her stomach, holding it. "That was very sweet of you."

His mouth settled into a smirk. "You know what they say about Iowans. We're nice. Speaking of, how's saving the planet out in Washington?"

His tone and look irritated her. "Jake, do you realize what's happening out there? So many people have died, and you're acting like nothing ever happened."

He shoved his hands into his pockets. "Well, it ain't too bad out here. Seen a few of them. Sheriff's puttin' 'em down like rabid dogs with a slug to the head. News said the world was ending before the power went out, but we ain't so bad. It's got many a folk saying we must be in God's country to be so lucky."

"Sure seems like it," she muttered.

She felt little hands pushing on her hips to get by her.

"Uncle Jake," Haley screamed. She jumped into his arms, and he hoisted her up easily into his arms.

"And how's my favorite niece?"

Haley wrapped her arms around him. "Bored. Nobody will play with me."

Gwen gave Haley an unimpressed look. "I said I would come and play in a minute."

Jake gave a knowing smile at Gwen. "I'll tell you what. How about you stop by the farm tomorrow and we can feed the bottle calves? But only if your Aunt brings you by."

"Yeahhhh," Haley exclaimed. Her eyes lit up at Gwen. "Can we please?"

Gwen rolled her eyes. "After I get done talking to the mayor, but only if we have time, can we stop by Jake's farm."

Jake set her down. "Now, go run along, little girl."

He gave her a smirk. "I'll see you tomorrow, Miss Gwen."

"Goodnight, Jake." She put a hand on the door, closing it save for about a foot.

His boots clomped down the porch as he marched back out to this pickup truck. She watched his lean body walk away. He was every bit of muscle from working the farm from the time he could walk. *What am I doing?*

"Old habits die hard," Becky said from behind her.

Gwen closed the door quickly and gave her a dirty look.

Becky smirked. "Just saying."

Gwen gave her a nasty stare. "All right, Haley, let's play."

KINNICK
Peterson Air Force Base, CO

The female Air Force captain looked like an adult child ready to throw a tantrum. Her lower lip pushed out a hair.

"Why are they sending you?" Gallagher asked softly.

Sarcasm dripped from his voice. "The VP hand-picked his finest." He was far from a great warrior or superior commander. He could fight, but he wasn't the best man to shore up a collapsing nation by organizing and training the civilian population along the Mississippi River in order to hold the front against the infected. He was a nuisance and had overstepped his station attempting to prevent the use of nuclear weapons on the West Coast. Now, he found himself going to the other front line. He was better left out of sight or dead than to continue showing up at Peterson. *I should have left the government a long time ago. Then I could have died with everyone else out East.* He wouldn't have been in the Golden Triangle if he wasn't tied to the government. He would have been stranded in Washington and perished with the millions of others stuck in the district as it collapsed. *Like your wife and kids.* He pushed that thought far away and deep into his guts.

Her blue eyes clouded at the injustice. "You aren't even Army. You're Air Force."

He nodded, "I know sweetheart, but it doesn't matter." He tossed multiple uniforms into his pack. *Nothing matters to them. Just get the job done and be quiet.* "I'm retired. Well, was retired. I shouldn't even be alive. Yet here we are."

She crossed her arms. "What does this mean for us?"

There's an us? He turned to her, trying not to wear the reality of the situation on his face. Her friendly, almost doe-like eyes were scared and sad at the same time. "Kate, you're a good woman." He reached up and ran his hand gently down her cheek. Her skin was soft beneath his fingertips. "Do whatever you have to do to survive. I won't lie to you and tell you I'm coming back. I feel like I've been too lucky as it is."

She shook her head no. They had only been shacking up for a few weeks. She had latched onto him because he provided her some sort of emotional support. He latched onto her because everything else he had was gone, and she was a pleasure to pass the time with as they waited for the end.

"I don't want that," she whispered.

He avoided her eyes. He didn't want to hurt her, but that was the world they lived in. "You stay safe."

She tilted her head in pain and then looked away as her eyes watered.

He gently put a finger on the side of her chin turning her face back to him. He leaned in and locked lips with her, kissing her for all his worth. *Probably the last time I'll do that with a woman.* Her mouth felt warm and welcoming, all her emotion building into a single kiss. He let their lips disconnect. He hesitated for a moment, his face lingering near hers. He pulled away. Her eyes were closed and her mouth still open.

He took a step away from her and looked her up and down one more time. Even in her Air Force hoodie and sweats, she was a lustful reminder of what he was going to miss for what were mankind's final days on earth. *Her figure is to die for and those hips and those lips. Damn, I am a dumbass.*

"I'm getting too old for this," he said to her, but it was more for him.

He hoisted his pack up onto his shoulder and snatched up his M4 carbine that rested propped up in the corner of the room. He opened the door and left without another word. Some of the best things were better left unsaid and far behind.

***

When he walked onto the airfield, a soldier with a thick brown beard and a black eyepatch met him. A SCAR-H was slung downward on his chest. A nice optic lined the top of his weapon. His battle belt was lined with multiple magazines for his sidearm. His chest was covered with magazines for his rifle. A ball of chew stuck out of the lower left side of his lip. Next to him stood a half-Asian soldier, his face expressionless. He carried a short-barreled M4A1 carbine. His kit was lighter than that of his comrade, but he was no less deadly. The wind whipped and fluttered his longer black hair.

Kinnick smiled at the two men. "You two look happy to see me."

Master Sergeant Hunter's single eye darted in the direction of his comrade. He spit on the ground and the brown juice splatted the pavement. "I will speak on behalf of Hawk and I. We're both about as happy as a possum with a sweet potato to see you." Hawk's eyes gave a half-blink in agreement with Hunter's words.

The Green Beret winked his one eye and dropped his voice. "Thanks for getting us off this base. We were starting to get bored waiting for Turmelle."

"That's," Hawk chimed in with a baritone voice. He paused.

Hunter turned in his direction, his jaw dropping a bit.

"Correct," Hawk finished. His mouth set back in a thin line. His contribution to the conversation was complete.

Kinnick nodded at his two Special Forces soldiers. "Sins and skins, gentleman."

Hunter spit again. "Sins and skins, Colonel."

"Let's get everyone organized," Kinnick said. He gestured at a cluster of eight UH-60 Black Hawks. "This us?"

"Yes, sir. We got a solid crew." They walked toward the gray-green Black Hawks. The helicopters' rotors rested tilting downward.

"I've worked with at least half of the men in the past."

"That's good. Once we get in the field, we won't be seeing them much."

"That's just the way we like it."

A cluster of rugged-looking men lounged near the helicopters. Their natural face armor consisted of long beards that gave them the appearance of a biker gang. All of their gear was unorthodox and modified, none of it standard-issued. They eyed Kinnick and the remnants of the "Skins" ODA 51. They knew when to listen and stood gathered around Kinnick, awaiting instruction. Hands rested atop gear, others had their fingers wrapped through loops on their vests.

"Gentleman. We have a long road ahead of us. You will be tested and tried in the field without a doubt. Good part about it is you don't have to take any language lessons for this op. At least depending on how far south you go." This garnered a few chuckles. "It's up to us to get the American public involved in the fight and to hold back the undead. This is your mission and I expect you to complete it."

The five Operational Detachment Alphas of Green Berets, roughly sixty men total, nodded.

"I'm sure you were expecting one of your own to lead you. Don't be offended by my presence. The Air Force sent their best field operator to lead you." More of the Green Berets smiled at this. They knew he had only a fraction of their field experience. *Can I imagine sitting them at the controls of a C-130 and saying 'fly'? No. Laughable.*

"Yet times are tough. If you'll show me to the nearest golf course, I'll be on my way."

The men outright laughed now. They smiled, showing teeth through bushy beards.

"In all seriousness, don't expect much relief out there." Smiles faded away from the younger men's faces. They knew what to expect. "Whatever you've experienced, expect less. Your nation expects you to do more with nothing. There is no telling when you will get any support in the field." He took a deep breath before he continued. "You don't need a reminder, but I'm going to do it anyway. The indigenous people out there are Americans. They're your neighbors. They're scared and need our help to weather the coming storm. Let's get them in the fight. Good luck, gentlemen."

A short man with wavy black hair and captain's bars on his chest stepped in front alongside Kinnick. "You heard the colonel. We will be linking up with a portion of the 4th Battalion, 2nd Marines in La Crescent where we will be acquiring our SURC rides. Be ready in five mikes to hit the skies. Hooah."

"Hooah," the Green Berets responded.

"Captain. A word," Kinnick said waving at the man.

Captain Boucher was a small man. He had a sharp chin and a glint in his eyes that said he'd seen enough violence.

"You know that we will have no support out there."

Boucher smiled. "Shouldn't be a problem. We've been all over the world. This is our backyard. I even got a few boys from along the river."

"That's good. You'll be on an island. Whatever advantages you have, use them."

"I read you loud and clear, sir."

Kinnick checked his watch. "Let's try and link up every Sunday at 1800, central time. I know comms are extremely limited, but let's try to keep everybody connected. We are going to be a long thin line."

"Yes, sir."

Kinnick hadn't noticed the Air Force lieutenant colonel that had joined them. The man walked up to Kinnick and stopped. "Colonel Kinnick?" the man asked.

Kinnick frowned. "Yes, Colonel."

"I have a message from General Daugherty, sir." He stuck out his hand and a white envelope quivered in his palm.

"Love letter?" Hunter said, pushing down the chew in his mouth with his tongue.

Kinnick gave him a glare. "Not likely." He ripped open the envelope by running a finger down the seam. He removed a thin white piece of paper and unfolded it.

It was a short message, but its words were clear. He read the paper once and then again. He glared up at Boucher and Hunter.

"Sir?" Boucher said. His eyebrows narrowed together.

"'Dear John' letter?" Hunter said.

Kinnick crumpled up the letter and threw it on the ground. "That man is a bastard. A fucking bastard."

Hunter bent down and picked up the piece of paper and his single eye scanned the page.

"Must be a sick joke?"

Kinnick's lips twisted. "He doesn't joke. This is the same man who

47

launched nukes on our very own nation."

"Sir, I'm confused?" Boucher said, eyeing each man in turn.

Hunter handed it to the captain.

The captain read it quickly.

Boucher frowned. "I'm not sure how to take this, sir? Is he asking us to kill Americans?"

Kinnick stared out, watching the soldiers load the helicopters. "Per Executive Order 17766, all communities are to enlist in the defense of the quarantine territories or be destroyed as enemies of the United States of America."

STEELE
Pentwater, MI

A fire crackled before him. Shadow-flames danced across hanging beards, glinted along shiny bald heads, lit up braided goatees and long-haired faces alike. Men shouted and hollered at one another. Crushed beer cans lay on the ground. A bottle of whiskey was passed from man to man.

On Steele's left sat Thunder. He was a big-bellied man with a red bandana holding his long hair in place. A gray beard fell down to his chest. A grin split his lips as he laughed at a joke. He glanced at Steele from the corner of his eye.

"What's the matter?" His bulbous nose was even rounder from the jab that Steele had given him after the Battle of Little Sable Point. "Drink this." Thunder handed him a bottle of whiskey.

Steele held the bottle in his good hand for a moment. "You know," he said before he took a long swig, feeling it burn down his throat and into his gut. Steele passed the bottle Tess, her hair slicked back on the top of her head, and she took a gulp and passed the harsh alcohol along.

Thunder spoke from the corner of his mouth. "I know how this is going to go if we put it to a vote."

So do I. Steele scratched beneath his bandaged arm nestled inside a sling. His skin itched horribly where the bullet had entered his bicep and blown out the back of his tricep. The healing wound always felt on the verge of overheating even in the cold.

He crunched numb fingers into a half-fist, feeling the pain of not using his arm in days. He nodded. "Less mouths to feed means more for us, but we need their support now. Jackson is close."

Thunder nodded. "Yeah, and you don't ask an enemy to watch your back."

"Can we trust them?" Steele said, nodding to the bikers, "to watch our backs?"

Thunder looked over, hurt on his creased features. "Last I recall, the pastor and his altar boys were dumping gasoline on you, ready to burn you alive. Not the other way around."

"I haven't forgotten." *I could have been a pile of ashes blowing in the wind.* "We need the Chosen if we're going to stand a chance. You know this."

Thunder grunted in response, neither acknowledging nor denying Steele's words.

Steele watched the rough bikers. "We owe these men and women, but I need them in some sort of line. I need them to be dependable."

"Then give them a reason to be loyal. They came, didn't they? And they've stayed since the battle."

Steele watched a biker with an eight of spades tattooed on his head tip the bottle of whiskey back. He started chugging. "For the food that we promised them, food that is rapidly disappearing."

The fire bounced on Thunder's features. "Then let's find them the food."

"But that doesn't solve my problem with them." Steele stole a glance at the Pentwater High School gymnasium. It loomed across the street from the fire station the group sat in front of. The gym was a tall, long brick building the shape of a rectangle. Steele could see the faint forms of armed men sitting outside the doors. Inside the gym were over two hundred of their enemies. *How do we turn our enemy into our ally?*

The Chosen people. A faction of religious zealots that had come to destroy Little Sable Point and enslave its people in the name of God. Their elderly leader, known only as the pastor, had been captured as well. Steele's forces had held on until the last moment, allowing Thunder to spring a trap, and it had caught their overzealous enemy off guard. Steele had lost plenty of people in the battle and had taken a wound that he might never recover from. He worked his fingers open and closed.

Now, he must decide their fate, given the biker gangs didn't administer their own form of apocalyptic justice.

Two of the biker leaders were not laughing and hollering. They stared at one another, eyes never lifting from the other. A fight was in the early stages, brewing up beneath the surface.

The young biker with the eight of spades on his jacket and head stood up tossing the empty bottle of whiskey. He pointed at an ancient biker with a trimmed white beard and a gears patch on his riding leathers. His hair was pulled back into a braided ponytail.

Veins popped in the young biker's tattooed neck. "Fuck you, War Child. That shipment of food was ours."

The old motorcycle club president looked like he was going to laugh but instead lunged from his seat. He led with his right hand and threw an uppercut into the younger man's chin with a smack. They started lashing out at one another with fists. The others watched the fight with dull interest.

Steele's mouth flattened even harder. This group of men and women were as unruly as they were hard. Steele watched them fire fists at one another, flexing his damaged hand the entire time.

Thunder spoke as they watched. "The young one with the eight of spades is Gat, and the Rip Van Winkle looking cat is War Child."

"Isn't he a bit old to be called War Child?"

"He wasn't when he started running guns for the cartels." Steele nodded. He readjusted himself in his seat, leaning his weight on his uninjured leg trying to take the pressure of the pellet-ridden one.

Gat was getting the best of War Child until War Child pulled a long dagger from his boot. Guns were pointed in their direction. War Child stood back, holding the dagger in the air and huffed out a wheezy breath. Steele ran his off-hand over the handle of his handgun resting on his hip, but he left it in its home.

The two men's chests heaved. If they had allowed the rest of the bikers to attend the meeting, it would have been an all-out war between the two clubs.

That was precisely why Steele had heeded Thunder's advice and only called the leaders.

"That's enough," Thunder said. The biker club leaders holstered their weapons and the two took a seat on either side of the fire. Thunder sat back down.

"I didn't call this meeting so we could kill each other," Thunder said. The leaders of the gangs turned his way. A large black man looked like he had just noticed Steele for the first time. The lone woman of the group, older with flaming red hair, regarded him like he was going to be her next pool boy.

Next to her sat a man with a long black, braided goatee that reached the center of his chest. He smirked, black wolves dancing on his vest. "Why exactly did you call us here?"

"I called this meeting on behalf of Sable Point's Captain Steele. It was his plan that won the battle, so let's hear what he has to say."

I'm not a captain.

"You mean Tiny Tim?" shouted the large African-American man. He had matching crisscrossed hammers on his vest and arms. Steele gave him a hard glance. The thick man wasn't phased by Steele's gaze. He ground his teeth as the wounds in his leg painfully rubbed against his chair.

"No, I mean Captain Steele," Thunder said.

Steele leaned forward in his chair and placed a hand on Thunder's arm. "I got this, Thunder." He looked out on the presidents of the clubs. "I am Mark Steele." His arm felt like it was on fire in its sling. He wanted to run a hand over the scar along his scalp but held it in check. "We were lucky at Little Sable Point. I'm indebted to you for your help."

"We did it for Thunder," War Child said. "Not some little hippie commune by the lake."

"When do we get what you promised?" shouted Macleod, his goatee wiggling like a black snake hanging off his chin as he spoke.

Steele grimaced. Thunder had promised the bikers free reign on a food supply that wasn't nearly enough for all the people. *Our supplies will be gone in a week. Even faster if we have to keep feeding the Chosen. I don't know how long we can keep up the facade of unlimited food stores.* He was sure that this wasn't lost among the clubs either.

"You'll get your food. Don't forget we defeated a common enemy."

"An enemy we chose to fight," Macleod spat.

"Why we even keeping them around?" shouted the big African-American motorcycle club president. "They're just eatin' our rations."

"Jefferson's right," croaked the flaming-haired woman. Her skin was tan with the texture of a well-worn leather. Wrinkles surrounded her mouth and eyes from years of smoking and too much exposure from the sun.

Steele raised his functioning arm. "Because there's a greater enemy that bears down on us."

Gat spit in the fire, his tattoos reaching for the top of his skull. "The fucking infected. Screw you. We can handle those fucks." He drew a serrated blade and pretended to lick it then flung it into the ground. The hilt of his knife quivered.

"Don't patronize me. We all know about the infected. Give me my share and my boys are gone," War Child said. A chorus of agreement went up from the biker chiefs. Steele's loose confederation of free motorcycle clubs was about to disintegrate, most likely ending with a bullet in his chest.

"No, not yet."

The bikers quieted down and Steele could feel Thunder tensing at his side.

Macleod laughed and he threw a thumb at Steele. "This guy serious?"

"I'm dead fucking serious. Five days ago, we spotted a military convoy. They've gone rogue, but their guns are real enough." He glanced at Ahmed and Kevin. They nodded in turn.

The bikers looked around as if it were a joke.

War Child laughed. "Who's to say we don't turn you over to them?"

Jefferson smiled at War Child's words, his white teeth contrasting against his dark skin. "We could watch them grind you up real slow. Ain't that right, Red Clare?"

The lone female leader laughed uproariously at the thought of Steele being ground up into pieces. "He's too pretty for that."

Steele ignored them. "They don't give two shits about you. Not these men. If they let you live long enough, you'll be mere slaves beholden to their every whim. I'll make you first in line with me. We'll all be treated as equals." All their eyes were upon him.

"We already be our own bosses."

"Our colors bend for no man."

"I'm not asking you to forsake your colors or take mine. I'm asking you to ride together like you did against the Chosen. Apart, you will ride free and the dead will take you piece by piece, man by man, woman by woman, until you're all gone. Together, we stand a chance."

Frank nodded from across the firepit. He'd been quiet tonight and he'd listened hard when Steele spoke. He knuckled a fist inside his other hand as if he planned on hitting somebody. His brown eyes were vengeful. When he started speaking, the other men and women grew silent. "I want revenge for what they done. Nader, Harry, and Sam didn't deserve that kind of death. I'll stand with anyone who wants to take the fight to them. I know you all would do the same for your clubs."

The bikers murmured amongst themselves. Mean, untrusting eyes looked at Steele and considered Thunder. Thunder had good standing with the club presidents, and Steele was sure if he wasn't by his side that the biker chiefs would have left by now. At the worst, one of them would have tried to send him six feet under.

Thunder leaned over. "All this 'Don't Tread on Me' is good kid, but some of them don't care about that. They want a guarantee. They want something they can see and touch."

Steele nodded. "You won't starve again, but I need your support. I need your guns with me."

The War Child's voice sounded like crackling paper. "We can scavenge on our own. Been doing it long enough now."

"You won't need to scavenge. Food will be readily available where I lead you, and there will be fewer infected too."

Gat sneered. "Bullshit."

"If you follow me and we fight together," he paused and gave Gat an extra glance, "I will take you to a place where there is food aplenty."

"Oh yeah, where's that?" Gat said. The biker licked his lips, his tattooed face drawn tight over his skull.

"Sounds like heaven," Jefferson joked, looking out at the other bikers. The men and women chuckled.

Steele made sure to hold their attention with his gaze. "No. It's Iowa."

The bikers looked at one another.

Red Clare's voice rasped when she spoke as if it yearned for a cigarette. "Is this a joke?"

Steele flexed his hand. "I want to leave tomorrow."

Macleod eyed his fellow biker leaders. "This fucking cripple wants us to ride to Iowa where he promises a safe supply of food forever? Never heard nothing more stupid."

Steele loosened his tomahawk on his hip.

Macleod gave him a nasty curl of his lip and stood up, making himself more dominant. "And then he wants us to fight the U.S. military along the way?"

Steele's hawk flew from his hand. It did a quick half-rotation and stuck in the ground between Macleod's legs.

Alarmed faces bounced from chief to chief. Macleod's eyes squinted fiercely, only anger emanating from them. *Don't do it*, Steele thought. *My left-hand draw is slower than it should be, but I won't hesitate.* Steele locked eyes with the man. Steele's off-hand fell onto the handle of his Beretta M9A1 9mm pistol at his hip.

Macleod's smile faded on his black-goateed face and his arm slowly dipped to his side.

Steele's firearm was out of his holster. It felt slow, but it was fast enough. He lined up his sights on Macleod, and Macleod's hand still inched its way to the handle of his gun. Steele kept the sights lined up on his center mass.

"Any more questions?" He let his eyes bounce around the biker chieftains. "You can hold me to my word." The fire snapped and the men watched each other in silence. Most watched to see if Macleod would try to off him anyway.

Macleod's eyes didn't blink as if he were trying to drink in every inch of Steele's person, making him disappear into his very own abyss. Steele let him stand in defiance.

Next to Macleod, War Child erupted in laughter. The old biker wheezed in his laughing fit, slapping his knee. The other bikers picked up the laughter with him.

War Child finished laughing and wiped the spittle from his mouth. "I'll go to see what he does next." His wrinkles creased and he shook his head in disbelief. "If he lies, we'll kill him when we get there and take the Iowans' food anyway." He wheezed a laugh at the thought.

Steele grimaced at the man's words. *I could be bringing greater danger than Jackson to the Iowans.* He pushed the thought away. *Anything is better than Jackson.*

Macleod grinned and pulled the tomahawk from the earth and raised his eyebrows. He flipped the hawk around a few times, judging the weapon. "Sounds like a ride in the park." He tossed the hawk back to Steele. Steele snagged it out of the air. "You're an ugly bastard, but me and the Wolf Riders are in."

"If there's no food, I'll break him up into little pieces," Jefferson said.

"What the fuck," Gat smirked. He lit up a cig and spoke from the side of his mouth. "We'll ride with Rolling Thunder until something better pops up, but what about them?" Gat pointed at the gymnasium.

Steele stared at the dark building. "Tomorrow they make a choice. They join or they die."

THE PASTOR
Pentwater, MI

There were no lights on in the dark gymnasium. The only light crept in from the cracks beneath the emergency doors now chained shut. The heat from over two hundred men made the basketball court stuffy, and the air felt stale and used up like his followers.

His men lay and sat all over the shiny court. They were the remnants of God's great army, bloodied, tired, and broken. A righteous army who had victory snatched from their grasp by the devilish cunning of their opponent.

Men coughed and the injured moaned in the dark.

The pastor sat with his back slumped and his legs crossed beneath him on the polished wooden floor. His legs hurt. His back hurt. His entire body ached like he had the flu, but the ache came from not some ailment of his body, but from the depths of his soul. *Why did you abandon us in the heat of battle, O Lord? Did we not follow your word? Did we not do your bidding?*

The pastor opened his eyes. He clasped his leathery, knobbed hands together in front of his body. Even his fingers hurt as he interlocked them one with another. *Everything hurts worse in defeat. Something will come. It is all in his plan.*

His disciples sat in a tight group around him. Bruised and bloodied, they had survived the battle. His second-hand man, Peter, sat with his hands under his chin, staring at the pastor with intensity. His blond curls dangled down his forehead, some matted to his head with sweat, the others still holding a bit of springiness in them.

Greasy long-haired Luke sat beside him. He leaned backward, his thin arms holding him up. He was a cruel man. Not by chance either. The pastor had sensed his natural violence from the very beginning. Next to him sat blond comb-over Matthew, who looked more like a boy than a former banker. He definitely did not have the face of the slayer of hundreds marked by the beast. Others were there, all brothers in Christ. Thad, Thomas, and Anthony. Only his most trusted followers.

"Let us bow our heads and pray for Brothers Gabe and Andy, true martyrs in our fight against the unbelievers. May the lights of their souls never be extinguished in the eyes of the Lord. Amen."

A quiet chorus of amens acknowledged him. He let them sit in silence for a moment to reflect on their fallen brothers of God.

Anthony's hook-nose flared and he broke the silence, clearly done with his reflection. "What are we going to do? My family is at Temple."

"God will show us the way. He has not forgotten us," the pastor said. *Hear us, O Lord. Do not forget your people.*

"How can you be sure?" Anthony said. He leaned forward, his bird-like neck stretching, and spoke quietly. "They slaughtered us out there."

"Even defeats are a part of his plan. Perhaps he is punishing us for our lack of self-control and discipline? Even God's people are capable of such sins."

"We must escape," Anthony hissed. He looked at the others. "There's only a few at the door. If we jump them, they won't be able to catch us all if we run."

Peter frowned. "No. There are hundreds of Gentiles outside. We will be gunned down."

The pastor lifted his chin. "Peter's right. If escape was in our plan, God would show us a better way than that."

Anthony glanced at the door. "But my family."

"Those that escaped will provide for them. That is our way."

Anthony frowned, his face pained. "But those things out there. On top of those animals that have us trapped here."

"That is enough, Brother Anthony. There will be no more talk of escape until God has shown us the way."

"But-"

"Enough." The pastor breathed hard through his nose. "I find your lack of faith disturbing."

Anthony bowed his head and Luke sneered in his direction. *Young men are rash. Old men are patient. It should be the other way around.*

"Forgive me, Father," Anthony said in deference.

The pastor held up a hand. "Do not ask my forgiveness for only the Lord can wash away your sins." He lowered his hand and bowed his head. "Now, let us pray for the safety of our families at Temple. May they find comfort in God's grace. Amen."

His men responded with another chorus of amens.

"When Christ was on the mount, the devil tried to win him-"

He was interrupted by a formidable dark-bearded man in a forest green jacket and camouflage pants. He bent low next to the pastor and whispered. "Pastor, please come. We need you."

The pastor's eyes questioned his follower. "Brother Robert?"

The man's eyes were filled with grief. "Yes, Father."

"We are in the middle of our prayers. Why do you interrupt us?"

Brother Robert's eyes darted back and forth from his disciples to the pastor.

"I apologize, Father, but one of our brothers is ready to move to the next phase."

The pastor nodded. "I understand. Tell him to hold on. I will be over soon."

Brother Robert gave him a weak smile, stood, and left.

"Peter, you may come with me. The rest of you may continue your prayers," the pastor said. His joints popped and creaked, as he stood tall. He had shrunk over the past few years and the weight of the end times seemed to make him even smaller. Even so, he was still taller than most. It gave him a more domineering yet fatherly look. He pushed on his lower back, hoping that it would straighten itself out.

"Come," was all he said to Peter.

They walked around his men lying on the basketball courts. They weren't cold but many huddled together. It must have been for the peace that being near a brother brings when being held at another's mercy. A few of them cried as he passed. *The devil has wormed his way into their souls and robbed them of their ferocity.* He said a silent prayer. *Fear not, brothers, for our battle with evil is not done.*

His walk ended at a man covered in a blanket. The man's skin was almost yellow in the darkness, and sweat beaded atop his forehead. Brother Robert knelt on one side of the man. A bald man knelt on the other side. He wiped the injured man's head with a rag.

The pastor eased himself down until his leg gave out and his knee banged onto the floor painfully. *My age is catching me.*

"Brother Adam." The bald man bowed his head. He raised it again and his mouth twitched as he blinked.

"Can no more be done?" the pastor said softly.

Brother Adam shook his head. "I can't do anything for him. They patched him up with bandages, but I think the wound is infected." As if to explain himself, he hurried to continue. "I was only a nursing assistant. All I can do is make him comfortable without help." He rolled back the blanket and peeled a bandage on the man's stomach.

The smell hit the pastor's nose and he tweaked his head to the side. Brother Robert covered his face with his sleeve.

"Oh, god," Robert said.

The pastor stared at the grotesque wound for a moment. "I see. Cover him." Brother Adam replaced the bandages and pulled the blanket up over the man.

"What's your name, son?" the pastor asked softly.

The man's eyes fluttered open. His voice was weak. "Edgar." He reached a hand out for the pastor and he took it. Edgar's palms were damp and his skin clammy.

"May God be with you, Edgar. Though you walk in the shadow of death, you shall not fear because he is near," he whispered.

Edgar's eyelids dipped lower.

The pastor bowed his head. "God, take this man's soul into your custody.

He has lived his life in your name. He has fought in your name, and he is coming to you a martyr for your cause. Forgive him for his sins for his work on Earth was just and true. Amen."

When the pastor lifted his head again, Edgar's soul had left him. Brother Adam ran a hand over the dead man's eyes, forever closing them. The pastor gently placed Brother Edgar's hand across his chest and set the other on top.

Peter helped the pastor upright by his arm.

"Put him with the others," the pastor commanded. A pile of dead lined the corner of the room. Every night bikers would come in and collect them. Another of his flock had gone on to heaven, his battle in creating God's kingdom at an inglorious end. Brothers Adam and Robert picked up the dead man by his arms and legs and carried him away.

Peter watched them leave. "We've lost so many."

"They've gone to a better place. God calls us home when he wants, Peter. Do not despair. Our time is coming."

"I will pray for them, Father." Peter lowered his eyes. Men coughed in the background.

We need your help now more than ever. "That's good, my son, and I must rest. Walk with me to the bleachers."

They walked together to the bleachers and the pastor sat. Peter left him alone to his own thoughts.

He clasped his hands in front of his body and rested his elbows on his knees, holding his hands to his head. *Show us the way. I thought I knew the way and you let us be crushed by the vile unbelievers. Give us revenge on them. Let us feed our holy fires with their corrupted souls. Grant us the chance for a glorious death in your name, Father.*

The rattle of chains banged on the emergency door and echoed throughout the gymnasium. They clanged against the metal doors, announcing to all the arrival of their captors. The pastor made the sign of the cross, his hand touching his forehead, his belly, his left breast, and then his right. He stood along with his men. Murmurs cut through his followers. He hoped Anthony wasn't desperate enough to try something stupid and get himself killed.

The doors burst open and light exploded upon the distraught people. His men covered their eyes and shaded them from the sunlight.

Men covered with leather and tattoos, holding all manner of weapons crowded inside. They were the jagged salt of the earth. His men backed away, fearing violence at their hands, but the pastor walked through the crowds toward them. He stopped in front of their captors.

A man limped inside, his arm in a sling, a tomahawk in his hand, and a wicked scar running atop his shaded skull. *He has come to martyr me in front of my men.* He smiled. *I will soon stand by Christ's side.*

Steele marched forward and stopped in front of the pastor. He looked up at him, his beard making his face longer than it should be, the hair wild and disarranged.

"Pastor, come with me."

His men moaned in despair and shouted in the back. The pastor raised his hands in the air.

"Chosen, do not fear for God is still with you."

Steele waved his tomahawk at him and limped out of the gym.

The pastor followed and the bikers encircled him. The sunlight touched his skin, and even in the cold, it warmed him. *Yes, Lord, you will set me free this day.* His smile grew larger and larger as he walked, and he turned his face upward to the sky.

KINNICK
La Crescent, Minnesota

Kinnick pulled back the flap of the woodland green command tent. He stepped inside not knowing what to expect. A short woman with black-hair stood at the far end of the tent, wearing the woodland Marine Corps Combat Utility Uniform. Her hair hung only to the neck of her collar, and her hands were clasped behind the small of her back.

Two Marine captains stood up. The taller one that looked like an Olympic wrestler turned toward the short female. His voice was meant for a caveman and sounded like grunts. "Ma'am, we have guests."

Hunter and Boucher followed behind Kinnick coming into the tent. The woman turned to face them. Her face, stern but not unfriendly, gave one the impression she would give you an order and then clap you on the back for a job well done. An oak leaf rested on the center of her chest. She looked up at Kinnick with mocha-colored eyes.

"Colonel, we've been expecting you." She lifted a hand, fingers tightly pressed together, and pointed at a chair. "Please. Come in."

Kinnick stepped forward. "Major?"

Her mouth never left its flat line. "Major Alvarado, sir."

Kinnick moved closer to the table and stopped. "I was expecting Lieutenant Colonel Eldridge." It was not lost on him that the last time he went looking for a colonel, he ended up a hostage. She took his silence as if he had asked a question.

"He was killed in action sixteen days ago."

"How?"

Her jaw clenched as if anger simmered under the surface of her taut face. "Leading a combat patrol into La Crosse. He was separated from his unit and pinned onto the river. Tried to swim for it and didn't make it. Cold water. Gear. Perhaps he was bitten before he went in, but he did not reach Barron Island."

Kinnick looked into her brown eyes. *Or he was fragged by his men. Why was the light colonel leading patrols?* "That's unfortunate. I'm sorry for your unit's loss." He gave her a short nod.

"So are we." Her eyes glinted and her mouth stayed flat.

Two more men entered the tent, a taller than average master gunnery sergeant and a youthful looking lieutenant.

"Marines," Alvarado said.

Kinnick acknowledged the two Marines and moved next to the table. "Your outpost looks like it's in good shape. A good perimeter."

"Yes, sir. We've found this place defensible. I'm not sure it was by initial design, but it has been adequate so far."

Kinnick peered down at the map on the table. "I didn't expect La Crescent to be so small. About five thousand civilians here?"

"Only about two thousand civilians now. Most of our success has been based on keeping the civilian population isolated from La Crosse on the other side of the river and not letting the Zulus cluster with regular mobile patrols." She pointed at a map on the table. "We were fortunate to be training overland at Fort McCoy when this started. We've done a hell of a lot better than Camp Lejeune. They rushed us to La Crosse and sent us some small watercraft to work with."

"The SURCs?"

"Yes, sir. Small unit riverine craft. They were a game changer. After a few weeks of almost constant fighting, we found that Barron Island was a much better setup for our outpost than the city streets. One entry and exit by land. Easy access to water with the SURCs as deadly transportation."

Kinnick gave her an approving nod. "A Marine's dream." He was impressed by her adaptable leadership.

Her face was somber. "I wouldn't call this a dream."

"A battlefield is chaos. Those that control their own and their enemies will emerge victorious."

She didn't miss a beat. "Napoleon, sir."

"That's correct, Major."

She looked back up at him as if she didn't want to ask the question. "So what can Outpost Barron do for you gentlemen?"

Kinnick nodded to his short Cajun Special Forces captain. "Captain."

"During our briefing, leadership told us you had a contingent of small watercraft. How many are operational?" Captain Boucher asked.

She nodded. "We have eighteen operational SURCs. Each has a Ma Duece, a minigun, and is manned by a pilot and an additional crewman. The Marines on this outpost are all well-versed in small craft tactics."

Kinnick looked at Captain Boucher.

Boucher smiled and nodded. "More than enough space for us. Hell, we only have five ODAs."

"I hate to do it, but we are going to need to split those teams in half," Kinnick said.

Boucher nodded. "We did it all the time in Afghanistan."

Kinnick could tell by the look on Boucher's face that he wasn't thrilled about splitting his units, but they were self-sustaining and able to operate off the grid for a long period of time. *They are self-reliant, but they will need support and they will get none.*

For Special Forces units, their primary mission was to train and lead unconventional warfare forces or irregular guerrilla forces behind enemy lines. They played the game of war well, far from home and with little support. They had other primary missions—counterterrorism, special reconnaissance, and direct action—but mobilizing and building up indigenous forces was their specialty. They would ensure that the American civilians would keep up the fight until conventional forces could be mobilized. Kinnick was sure their journey would not end there, but they would be forced to fight the entirety of the conflict, perhaps indefinitely, but this was their wheelhouse, and he had no doubt they would perform to the highest standard.

Major Alvarado stared at Kinnick expectantly. Her dark eyes transfixed him. "How many SURCs do you need?"

"I'd say at least ten."

She glanced at Heath. "That will cripple my unit's combat effectiveness." Her tone was not one of a junior officer but of an equal that was not pleased. He entertained her questions because he knew he asking a lot. Their situation was dire as was hers, but he needed her cooperation.

Kinnick stared down at the map. He let his index finger hover along the long blue line splitting the green on either side. "We will be dropping units along the west bank of the Mississippi River to train the civilians to fight. It will be a massive effort by only a few men." He looked at Boucher. "Albeit, very capable men." He thought he saw a flicker of her eye narrow when he mentioned "men." There were no women in the Special Forces ODAs, so he wasn't making a jab at her, but he surmised that being told of the differences between men and women was something she had been subject to her entire career.

"What civilians?" she asked.

Kinnick looked up at her. "All of them."

Her brow furrowed. "With only five ODAs?" She paused, waiting a second for him to explain. "Not much of an operation."

Kinnick grimaced. "It is all we were given."

"We don't have many Marines here." Her eyes lowered as she thought. "Only three partial companies." Alvarado's eyes darted back up at Kinnick and his men. She clasped her hands behind her back. Her back was erect and unbent as if a spine of steel kept her upright. "I will send a company with you under Captain Heath."

Captain Heath smiled down at them. The massive Marine's ears stuck out the sides of his head like short stumpy wings.

It was Kinnick's turn to smile. "We would be in debt to you."

She held up a crisp firm hand and twisted her head to the side. "You owe no debt. We fight for the same thing."

The Marines and soldiers stood silent for a moment contemplating the dire position their beloved nation was in. Their nation had been battered and broken and would never look the same, yet here they stood defending it to their last breath.

"Mind you, Colonel. It's not a full company. We started this situation with four companies of Marines. I'm down to about two and a half. You'll get about seventy more Marines. Pieces of three platoons, meaning only two rifle squads per platoon. They should operate fine independently broken down into squads."

Kinnick looked at Boucher. "Let's leave three ODAs split and two intact." He eyed the small woman. "We will have the six rifle squads man the other craft." He glanced over at Alvarado. "This will not leave you undermanned?"

"Sir, no base manned by a Marine is undermanned."

"You will be the end of the line."

"We'll hold."

"No doubt in my mind, Major."

Her lips barely curved upward in what Kinnick thought was an all-out smile of satisfaction.

Alvarado gestured toward her map. "Here, Colonel."

Kinnick moved closer to the table and leaned over, inspecting the map.

"We're here," Alvarado said, pointing at a circled La Crosse and La Crescent on the map.

Kinnick ran his finger down the map. "We are going to hit any town that has an access point across the river. If there's people still alive, we're gonna drop a unit. Starting here." He tapped his finger on the map. "Lansing, Iowa. Then we will move to the next town McGregor. We'll continue down the river south. Once we get moving on the river, Captain Boucher will advance with a few units to St. Louis to see what is salvageable there. That might be more of a containment operation."

Captain Boucher nodded, staring at the map with an M4A1 strapped to his chest in a downward safe position. "We will set up outside of St. Louis. Portage des Sioux looks isolated enough."

"Use your best judgment, but that will work, Captain."

"What about south of St. Louis?" Alvarado asked.

"That area falls on Special Forces Colonel Canton. His responsibility is to hold southern Missouri to Louisiana."

She nodded. "Understood."

Kinnick looked at his fellow officers. Stubbly checked and wavy-haired Boucher, the ox of a man Heath, and the short steel-rod of a woman Alvarado.

"Operation Homefront is about Americans. Let's give them hope." They all nodded in affirmation, mentally preparing for the long road ahead.

Alvarado lifted her chin. "I'd like to show you the SURCs."

"That would be appreciated, Major." He lifted a hand toward the tent opening. "Lead the way."

They followed Major Alvarado and Captain Heath out of the command tent.

The outpost had been setup in an RV resort and marina on an island in the Mississippi River between Minnesota and Wisconsin.

Kinnick followed Alvarado through the outpost. Woodland green tents were placed in a neat linear fashion, their spacing from one another uniform. A giant warehouse was enveloped in the outpost along with a brown-sided grocery store.

"We took out the bridge and moved to sorties with the SURCs," Alvarado said as she walked. She pointed over the tents toward La Crosse. Short skyscrapers sat across the river and a blue-wired suspension bridge dipped into the river wires dangling from the collapse. "Interstate 14 runs from La Crosse, Wisconsin to La Crescent, Minnesota and cuts through the island here, but we're much closer to Minnesota. This island is made up of only thin strips of land. It's covered with little canals. If the water raises in the river too much, we will flood out." Water sat between the RV resort and Interstate 14 like a moat.

They walked down to a small marina. A few white motorboats and pontoons rested in their slips. A host of houseboats bobbed along the docks that had men and women standing on them. Alvarado gave a crisp wave and they waved back.

"They were here when we set up our outpost." She paused, waiting for Kinnick to reprimand her for keeping the civilians within the facility.

Kinnick gave her a nod. He understood. This was total war. The virus was indiscriminate about who it infected. The dead were nonselective as to who they infected. Civilians were fair game just like anyone. Exposing them to the virus only swelled the dead army's ranks.

"The SURCs are over here." Alvarado pointed to cleared-out slips. They marched down a dirt path to the dock. Once they mounted the dock, their feet rang as they walked along the silver metal.

Dark gray small unit riverine craft were moored in a long row, each one accessible from the dock. They had rigid hulls and Kinnick estimated they were over thirty-eight feet long. A GAU-17/A Minigun was mounted on one side of the bow and the venerable M2 Browning .50 caliber machine gun matching it on the other. Near the center rear of the craft was a covered overhang and the helm.

"We operated these in Iraq for a period of time. Then they gave the program over to the Navy. Since we left Iraq, we're back to using them again. Seems that with the more counterdrug, antiterrorism, humanitarian missions that we incur, the more useful they are. Captain Heath, please enlighten our colonel."

The large Marine captain smiled and swatted the thick collar running around the sides of the boat. His hand bounced and an airy buoyant noise reverberated from the collar. "This small craft can carry a rifle squad or sixteen people over two hundred and fifty nautical miles." He pointed to the back engines. "Twin Yanmar 6LY2A-STP Diesel Engines and Twin Hamilton waterjets HJ292 give this puppy the capability to turn 180 degrees in less than three boat lengths and accelerate to twenty-five knots in less than fifteen seconds."

"Sounds perfect." Kinnick eyed the craft up and down. "Reminds me of the River Patrol Boats of Vietnam." He looked up at the hulking Marine. The Marine gave him a half-grin.

"That's exactly what they came in to replace. Sure there were other small craft between, but this is our version of it. Faster. Longer range. Better armor. This collar around the top." He ran his hand along it. "Solid cell foam. Provides stability, redundant buoyancy, and small-arms ballistic protection. Been known to deflect an RPG." He pointed down at the rigid metal hull. "Has beaching plates too. This was made for us. Oorah, colonel." Captain Heath gave him a wide smile.

Kinnick gave him a grim grin. "Oorah, captain." *I only hope it will be enough.*

STEELE
Pentwater, MI

Steele led the entourage of bikers and the Sable Point volunteers surrounding the pastor. He limped along without his crutch, slowing down the entire group, but he felt that it was necessary for his appearance to be less incapacitated. He ignored the grating of the pellets grinding away under his flesh. The ones that were too deep were left inside him by one of War Child's gang, who had been a corpsman in a previous life. Steele flexed his hand, stretching his fingers and making a fist.

The throng of people walked to the center of Pentwater's main streets, Lake Shore and Main, in view of the fire station. Lounging bikers watched them curiously from buildings and on the street corners, the former occupants of Sable Point sprinkled among them.

Steele turned around and the group widened as if they were afraid of the pastor, giving him plenty of space like a man-eating tiger on a long chain.

The pastor stood before Steele. His black clothes were soiled and his collar blood stained from where Steele had pricked his neck with his axe. He had the look of a weary new-world missionary who had found his first convert after so long in the bush. His face was tired but his eyes held fire like he was on the verge of exhaustion but happy. *What does he have to be happy about?*

The pastor closemouthed grinned at him, looked toward the sun, and shut his eyes.

He kept his eyes closed as he spoke. "You may take your revenge, Mr.

Steele, but it will not soothe your soul and it will not bring back the dead."
He opened his eyes at the end and his gaze was unafraid of what was to come.
"I made peace with death a long time ago."

Steele stared at the man he had spent weeks trying to make peace with,
and all he had gotten was fire and blood. He flexed his fingers again.
*Appeasement never works. They always want more. This lanky old man has caused
me so many problems and taken good people's lives. How many lives have you
taken?* His mind mocked his morals.

"I am not here for revenge, pastor." *But maybe I should plant my hawk into
his skull anyway and be done with the man. Nobody here would care. They all
hate him.*

"Then why have you released me from my prison? Surely you do not
intend to release me after our——." He paused, searching for the word in his
mind. "Conflict."

Steele gripped the head of his tomahawk tightly and pulled it from his
belt, holding it beneath head. *Be fair*, he reminded himself. *To be fair is to
exact justice.* His mind shouted at him while he stared at his enemy. *Remember
the bigger picture. Jackson is coming.*

"I may yet take your head."

The pastor spread his arms. "I give it freely for I am at peace with God.
My soul is already his."

"Fuck you," shouted Gat.

"Don't give us your pious bullshit. You're a murderer, you bastard," Tess
shouted at him. Her hands balled into fists at her sides. "You murdered
Pagan," she screamed. "He only ever wanted to help people and you burned
him alive."

The pastor bowed his head. "If I made a mistake in burning Pagan, then
God will forgive me for my heart was in the right place."

Steele held up his tomahawk in the air. "Enough." He gave Tess a side eye.
She scowled at him in return. His eyes panned over Ahmed, the stocky
Egyptian-American, and Kevin, the lanky high-school teacher, standing side
by side with M4s. *They are with me.* His eyes reached Thunder. Thunder's
eyes were level, giving no indication of his true emotions. *Is he still with me?*

He knew he might lose Tess with this, but what other choice did he have?

"We've had our differences, but now that I have the upper hand, I will show what it means to create *peace*. I will show you what mercy looks like," Steele said. He gave Tess a side glance. She fumed. He ignored her and pushed on.

Steele walked closer to the pastor, his left leg slow on the uptake. The pastor's eyes peered down at him. Steele spun his hawk in his hand. The pastor smiled at him in a truly carefree manner. *Does he have no fear of death?*

Steele got within three feet of him and looked up at the pastor's long-worn face.

"I will make it easier, son," the pastor said. He bent his head low near Steele's. "Send me home," the pastor said softer. The man began murmuring the Lord's Prayer under his breath. The crowd held in silence awaiting his justice.

A swing and this troublesome man is out of the way. Everyone will be happier. He stood, twirling his hawk in his hand, staring at the top of the pastor's thinly haired head.

"You are free."

The pastor raised his head a bit, his eyes peering from beneath his brows. "Pardon me?" he whispered.

"You are free under the following conditions."

The pastor only raised his head and eyebrows at Steele.

"You and your community are to join ours. You will not harm, burn, or condemn anyone not infected to any sort of damnation. In return, your people will be treated as equals and will suffer no abuse at our hands."

The pastor blinked slowly as if he were contemplating which was better, the terms or certain death. His voice came out slowly. "Our approach can be modified. God's will reaches further than the flame sometimes."

"I'm not finished," Steele said. "You and your men will fight with us against the dead and the living."

The pastor's eyes lit up. "You will return my men's weapons?"

"Yes, once they have sworn not to use them against my people." Steele swallowed hard, knowing that this could start another war, but Colonel

Jackson and his legion were close, and he needed the pastor's men if it came to a shootout.

"I will see to it that they do as you ask."

"There are no chances on this. They follow or they die."

The pastor grinned. "We will not have any issues."

Steele eyed the man again, trying to see if he held deceit in his eyes.

"Then you and your men are free." Steele waved Kevin forward. Kevin handed the pastor his carpenter's hammer. The pastor's smile grew wide. He looked up at the heavens and raised the hammer above his head.

"God wills it!" he shouted. No one took up the call. Murmurs of dissent rippled through the bikers and volunteers alike.

"No!" Tess screeched. She marched over to Steele and the pastor. "You can't be serious? This man tried to burn us alive and you're going to free him?"

Steele took in a deep breath. "It's the only way."

"The only way?" She jabbed a finger at the pastor. "This guy is a fucking monster! Kill him. He just brainwashes people. You know it. You've seen it." Her voice dropped to a low hiss. "He murdered your mother."

The pastor sheathed his hammer through his belt. "So much hate in such a small body." He raised a hand in her direction. "I forgive you, my daughter. May God cull your anger and use you for his own good work." He bowed his head in her direction, keeping his hand outstretched. "I forgive you."

"Screw you," she shouted. Her arms wrapped tightly around her chest. "Why are you doing this? This is not what we had agreed on for Sable."

"We are bigger than Sable now."

The pastor stuck his hand out at Steele. "I dare not know why, but God has drawn us together on a single path. It is his will that we partake in this journey together. You have my word in God's name." His hand wavered as he held it outstretched to Steele.

Tears of anger formed around Tess's eyes, but he couldn't go back now. Everything would fall into chaos and disintegrate before their eyes if he did. Steele turned away from her and faced the pastor. He took the pastor's slender hand in his and gripped it tight.

"God has a plan for us. You've let my people go." The pastor let go and turned his back on them and raised his hands to the sky. "God is great."

Steele nodded to Thunder. "Make sure they get food and water. And let's keep them apart from the others until tempers die down."

Thunder waved forward his sergeant-in-arms. "Garrett, grab War Child and his boys. We will need some help with the supplies."

Steele hobbled back to the fire station, a red brick building with two large garages stacked with supplies. He plopped down in a lawn chair, feeling the exhaustion of moving around at his inhibited pace. Tess had followed him and now paced in front of him.

She spread her arms wide as she walked. "You can't do this."

"I just did."

"Take it back. They are our enemy. Keep them locked up. Or we can take them as prisoners with us."

"They would be useless mouths to feed. Now we can use them to scout, scavenge, and hopefully fight."

"Sounds like you're afraid." She gave him an evil eye and continued with sarcasm. "That must be a first."

"I am afraid of a lot of things. If you knew better, you would be afraid too."

"What's so scary about this Colonel Jackson? What is he, a relative of yours? Why can't we handle him like we did the pastor?"

His blue eyes locked with her almost black ones. "The pastor is a madman with an army of followers. Colonel Jackson is a madman with hundreds of trained soldiers. His ranks are filled with veterans of multiple wars, soldiers who've been trained by the best. With my limited knowledge of strategy, I outmaneuvered the pastor, who knew nothing about warfare. But the colonel is just that, a colonel. An O-6. Just beneath a brigadier general. He's read all the books. He's conducted operations. He's led hundreds if not thousands of men in battle. He's survived when other soldiers have been overrun."

She looked at him silently, her eyes still smoldering.

"I haven't done any of that. I set a trap for an unskilled tactician and it almost didn't work."

He rubbed his brow with his good hand and sent his hand over the puckered wound where he had taken a rifle round to the top of his head.

She sat down next to him. "I don't care what he can offer. He murdered Pagan. I will never forgive him." Anger and hate blazed in her eyes.

He knew she meant every word. "I know you won't." He looked over at her. The embers of her eyes were cooling down.

"You're a lot older than when I first met you. One might even call you old with your bum leg and bum arm and bum head."

He grimaced and smiled. "A lot of trouble a few weeks will do to you. Don't remind me." He paused watching the bikers remove some of the boxes of food. "I won't let the idea of Sable be extinguished. Our people are still free." He glanced at her. "Will you promise me not to kill the pastor?"

She gave him a coy look, raising a black eyebrow. An amused look spread over her face as if she had already killed the pastor a hundred times over and he didn't even know about it yet.

"I promise not to kill him," she said softly.

"Thank you. This is important." He leaned his head back and relaxed for a moment. Shouting erupted from the gym, forcing his exhausted head upright. Tess heard it too. Her features hardened like stone, and she stared in the direction of the commotion.

They couldn't make out the words at first but the chant grew louder and louder until the words took shape. "God wills it. God wills it. God wills it," reverberated over the town, rising up to the sky.

Have I unleashed a monster? "Tomorrow, we leave," he whispered.

GWEN
Reynolds Farm, IA

Gwen sat atop her grandfather's old yellow mare, Patsy. The leather of her saddle creaked as the horse walked. She controlled the old horse with her legs and Patsy easily let herself be steered, having many years of experience beneath her.

A cold fall sun sat in the sky, releasing enough sunlight to give them some extra warmth on their journey. Her grandfather rode along beside her. He had insisted on taking the family horses to save fuel. She had made it clear that she could make it to town on her own, but the old man was adamant that he travel with her for safety. Not wanting to hurt his pride, she obliged.

She watched him as he rode. John's back had a deeper hunch than normal in it, but the old man still was a proficient rider. The eighty-five-year-old still had strength in him despite a quadruple bypass two years prior. The hooves of his horse clopped as it moved at a steady pace along the country road.

She half believed he wanted to go with her to show her off to his fellow neighbors. He had always been so proud of her and would always beam when he spoke about her.

"You know Hacklebarney has survived worse." He rested a wrinkled hand on an well-used leather pommel. "My father, Fulton, used to talk about the famine of 1912. Crop went bad three years in a row. No one had food and no one had money to buy any. Then there was the flood of '49. Whole town went under water. Twenty-six people drowned."

Gwen gave him an endearing look. She had heard all these stories before, but she humored him out of love.

"Wasn't that the time you saved Gram from atop the grocery store?"

The old man smiled and nodded. "Yes, it was. She was trapped up top of Archie's. You see, she used to work there when she was right out of high school. Me and Nathaniel canoed right up to the rooftop. She jumped into my arms and—" he stopped when she interrupted.

"The next fall you were married," Gwen finished with a smile.

"That's right," he said. The horses swayed beneath them.

His voice wavered a bit. "Nathaniel left us that next summer." The old man stared out. "Died in Korea."

Her grandfather never talked about his brother much. His death still haunted the old man.

Pa shouted loud and gave a wave. "Hey there, Van." A dirty farmer in the field gave a wave with one hand, the other leading a team of horses by the reins.

Van used a team of horses to pull a wagon of hay. A young man and woman assisted him as he goaded the team along. Shotguns and rifles hung off their backs. The presence of firearms on the farmers struck Gwen as out of place for home where guns usually only came out during hunting season.

Van's hand cupped his mouth and he hollered. "Hiya, John." He shaded his eyes. "Who's that you got there?"

"Gwen's back in town," her grandfather yelled. His face brightened as he said it. He pulled his horse to a stop and Patsy followed suit.

"Gosh darn, that's great to hear. She stayin' this time? You know the city don't have everything."

"God willing and the creek won't rise," Pa yelled.

"Hi, Van." Gwen gave him a friendly wave. She covered her eyes so she could see him better.

"Good to have you back, Gwen. Might be you save me a dance on Friday," Van yelled.

"I'll always save a dance for you, Van," she said and smiled in his direction.

Van went back to work leading his team of horses.

Pa goaded their horses back into a walk with a soft flick of his reins. He stared ahead as he spoke. "We've been lucky the Amish had a good year. Got plenty of draft horses for rent. They be good folk."

"Seems like we're going backwards in time," she said.

The old man smiled as if he remembered his childhood. "The past ain't so bad. Simpler. Harder in some ways. Easier'n others."

They steered their horses onto a better maintained paved roadway. The horses seemed to know the way as their hooves resounded hard off the pavement.

"Not too much farther now," her grandfather said. The old man didn't turn at the rustling in the trees, but Gwen heard it. A tattered figure in hunting camouflage shambled up the ditch and onto the road.

"Pa, look out!" she yelled. He looked at her, startled, not having heard the man prior to her yelling. She drew her compact Glock in one hand. Pa saw the man and steered his horse in his direction.

"That's Dan Macintosh," he said, oblivious to the danger. With a snarl, the infected man made for him. John's horse neighed and tossed its head as it got closer.

"Watch out," Gwen shouted. She pulled her reins hard, putting herself between her grandfather and the infected. Her horse breathed hard and smacked its lips, nervous.

The infected man swiped at Gwen's horse and it reared up. She struggled to hang on, using her thighs to squeeze the horse's sides while leaning closer to the horse's neck. When Patsy let her down, Dan grabbed her leg and Gwen stretched out her arm, putting a bullet into the top of his skull with her Glock. His lifeless body dropped onto the road and lay unmoving. Dark-red blood leaked out the exit wound.

She turned her horse in a circle, holding her gun in tight to her chest with the reins in her other hand, scanning for more infected. None in sight, she guided Patsy back toward her shocked grandfather. "Are you okay?" she breathed.

Pa sat on his horse and stared at her in disbelief. His eyes barely blinked.

"Pa," she said louder. She worried the scare may have given him a heart attack.

He shook himself. His lips trembled. "Gwen, you shot Dan Macintosh." His eyes blinked rapidly as he tried to digest what had happened.

She scanned the trees before she holstered her weapon. She grasped for him, resting a hand on his arm. "This is the way it is now. He's infected. They either kill us or we kill them, but only one of us walks away."

"I'm-" Pa shook his head. His mouth clamped closed. "I've never seen you act like that. You rode up and put a bullet in Dan's head."

She gave him a sympathetic look. "Things have changed more than fuel shortages and power outages. It's worse than a famine or a flood. It's violent out there and I won't be a victim." *Not again.* Flashes of Puck's ugly face desecrated her mind.

Her grandfather visibly calmed down. "You've never been a victim, dear. You got Lydia's genes in ya. Forgive me if I'm a little shocked that my granddaughter shot somebody as causal as asking for a glass of water."

She gave his arm an extra squeeze. "No one is more surprised than me. You should have seen Mark during the beginning." The thought of her love brought sadness into her heart and worry into her gut. "He's the reason I made it."

Pa nodded. "He always seemed to treat you nice. Just lives too darn far away." A smile settled on his face. "Me and Gram sure are happy to have you back."

"I am too." She meant it. Being back with her family gave her some hope that things could be okay.

"About another half-mile." He gestured with his hand holding the reins.

Within a ten minutes, they rode into Hacklebarney. It felt as if they had stepped back in time. Horses pulled carts behind them. The only modernity, a pickup rolled down the street with a group of young men in the back. They waved guns in the air as they drove by, giving Gwen stares like they'd never seen a woman. A beer can rattled across the pavement.

Her grandfather shook his head. "Should be helping their fathers get ready for harvest, and instead, they're out burning fuel looking for the crazy ones."

"They think it's a game," she said softly. The infected population was light enough in Iowa that they weren't facing endless hordes of the dead, only the unlucky few that drifted in from cities.

"We're gonna have a hard enough time as it is. We're gonna lose a lot of crops without help," Pa said. They passed small shops with wide windows in late 19th-century-styled two-storied buildings.

Pa nodded to a balding man outside his shop wearing grease-stained clothes. "Morning, Kenny. How's Jenny?"

"She's doin' all right. Better than yesterday. That Gwen?"

"Yes, sir," she said. She grinned down at the hardware store owner.

"By golly. Been a long time."

"Say, you wouldn't have any old kerosene lanterns or anything?" she asked.

The man's eyes rolled upward as he thought. "I'll have to check in back. Been a bit picked over lately. You seen Jake?"

She tried to mask her displeasure with a smile. "Yes, I have." No matter how long she had been gone or how many other boyfriends she had dated, everyone always assumed that she and Jake would be together. The Bullises. Living on a farm with a dozen kids and never leaving. If not now, eventually they would be together, or everyone around town assumed they were still together.

"I'll stop by later," she said. She clicked her tongue and Patsy started back down the street. Her pa said hello to a host of people along his self-imposed parade route. There was Nowlton and Millie Gebert, both in their late thirties, who inherited a family farm north of town. Bill Thornburg, the town dentist. The DeVaults, dairy farmers, waved on the way by as they talked to B.B. Palmer's wife, Annie.

They passed a post office with an American flag hanging out a window. The next building was a single-story with an old police Bronco outside. The truck had rust on its bumpers and wheel wells. A gold sheriff badge hung on the wall of the office and an American flag hung from a silver flagpole in front.

"Whoa, Cline." He tugged the reins a bit and the horse stopped. "I'm gonna meet with Sheriff Donnellson and tell him about Dan Macintosh. Might want to ride up that way and check out the farmstead. He had a wife and two older boys." He pointed. "Mayor's got an office right over in that building yonder. Should be in." He swung a stiff leg off his horse and gingerly stepped down. Stretching his back, he gave her a tired smile.

"Not quite as limber as I used to be."

She gave him a sad smile. "You look good, Pa." Her grandparents' age was always something that worried her. It was a fear that she wouldn't have time for them and then one day they would be gone. They would fade and become only memories of when she was young.

She gently pulled the reins, leading her horse back to the street. Clop-clop, Clop-clop. Each hoof lazily sounded off on the ground. She stopped her horse in front of a brown-brick, two-story building with a well-swept sidewalk. An American flag hung off a pole that stuck off the side of the building. A sign on the door read Mayor Dobson's Office in black and gold lettering.

"Guess this is it," she said to the horse. She gave Patsy a pat on her thick neck.

She swung one leg off her horse and then the other, noticing how sore her inner thighs were from having not ridden in years. She squeezed her legs together. *I'm gonna be hurting tomorrow. Been away too long from the farm.* She wrapped the reins around a light pole that had lost its purpose with no power.

"Now, don't go nowhere, Patsy," she said, patting the horse's white nose. Patsy smacked her lips and nestled at Gwen's hand. Gwen stuck her hand in her pocket and pulled out a white square sugar cube. The horse's lips greedily curled together and tickled her hand as it took the cube.

"There. That should hold you for awhile." Patsy flicked her nose in the air. Gwen gave her a frown. "Geez, Patsy. Later." She playfully swatted at the horse. Patsy tossed her head in return.

Gwen walked over the sidewalk and grabbed the brass door handle, twisting the knob. The door opened to an old staircase. The steps groaned on her way up. At the top was another door. She knocked on it.

"Well, come on in, already," shouted a man.

KINNICK
Northern Mississippi River

Water whipped up from the behind the small unit riverine craft as they plowed down the center of the brownish waters of the Mississippi River. The spray from the river was cold and damp, and the sky was a menacing fall gray. It was as if the heavens were whispering, "Harsh times ahead."

The river ahead was the color of a chocolate milk shake that had been left in the sun too long.

The roar of fourteen pairs of engines sounded off as they moved in tandem down the river. Kinnick had left four of the craft with Major Alvarado to assist in her ongoing operations, not wanting to rob the major of one of her most valuable assets. The SURCs were spread out about sixty yards from one another in a long chain of riverboats. The engines were loud enough where Kinnick couldn't hear the men around him speaking.

Kinnick had taken a partial Marine rifle squad composed of two fire teams and a mean-looking sergeant with a permanent scowl on his face along with the remaining Skins ODA 51. Two Marines stood posted on the bow machine gun and a minigun, but nothing had been remotely close to threatening Kinnick's flotilla of riverboats.

Kinnick stood in the pilothouse paying close attention to the radio so he could issue orders as they moved down the river. "Ride of the Valkyries" played in the back of his mind as they cruised. His flotilla would soon shrink in number as boatloads of his Marines and Special Forces soldiers would peel off to their respective towns and cities along the Mississippi. His men would be on their own organizing and training civilians to do the dirty work that the United States military couldn't undertake on their own. It was a long flank, but it was home field, the homeland, the motherland, their land.

The pilot, Coffey, was an average-looking corporal with a mustache, who loved to stick out his tongue as he focused on safely navigating the craft down the river. Kinnick left the corporal to his work of dodging trees, bodies, and rocks alike, and walked for the bow of the ship with the Marines. He used the starboard side of the SURC to steady himself as he stepped toward the bow. He took a seat near the helm next to the senior enlisted Marine in charge of the rifle squad. The Marines were all sizes and races, clean-shaven, and tough-looking. They were multi-ethnic and multi-sized clones of one another and that was the point, to decrease individualism and increase group cohesion. It was never us and them with the Marines, only us.

"Sergeant," Kinnick said.

"Sergeant Volk, sir." The Marine's face bordered on a sneer, and by the looks of him, Kinnick assumed that was his natural state. "Corporal Washington and Lance Corporal Boone are my fire team leaders." A thick African-American showed Kinnick some teeth and his counterpart looked like he came straight from the backwoods. The thin white man dipped his helmeted head toward Kinnick.

Boone shouted over the motors in a thick Tennessean accent. "Colonel."

"Then there's Hanger, Duncan, Gore under Washington and Whitehead, Ramos, Tran under Boone."

The Marines nodded, waved, and smiled at Kinnick.

Kinnick shouted. "You boys look ready."

Volk looked at him, mouth tight. "We are. We were wondering where our first stop is?"

"We're headed to Lansing, Iowa. It's about forty miles from here. When we stop there, Captain Boucher and six of the SURCs will head further south of our AOR near St. Louis. I'm going to stay with Captain Heath for the first phase and then move down to St. Louis and reconnect with Boucher. We're going to be isolated, but this is where our nation will make or break itself."

He nodded out at the land. "On these riverbanks."

"I see, sir." Volk shook his head in almost disgust. He snorted, looking down at the ground.

Kinnick cocked his head. "Is that a problem, Sergeant?"

"No, sir. We are always down for a fight. Permission to speak freely, sir?"

"Granted."

"Is this really going to make a difference? I mean, there's only a few hundred men and you are talking about defending a river that runs a couple thousand miles."

Kinnick stared at him coldly. "We don't have a choice. Our hope rests on the backs of these brave people. If we cannot get them to hold this river, then we will fall. Whatever remains of our nation will be overrun, extinguished like the rest of the world."

Volk's mouth tightened up more like he was going to spit. "Yes, sir. We're it? I mean. No one else is out there. In the world?"

For a moment, Kinnick watched the trees along the river disappear behind them. Their leaves were mostly gone, and now, they looked naked and dead as if they were preparing to join the infected dead.

He brought his focus back on the sergeant. "As far as I know, we are the only nation left and Operation Homefront is our effort to mobilize the remainders of America into a fighting force."

"Mad Isabel always is getting us into a scrap." His brownish-yellow eyes were hard.

"Old girl always puts out," laughed Hanger.

Washington shook his head and grunted. "She be crazy."

Boone grinned. "Madder than a raccoon on crack."

Volk yelled at the Marines. "You hear that Marines? We're it. We are all that's left on earth. This fight is not just for America. It's for humanity. We lose here and we disappear like a group of virgins on prom night. Except for Whitehead. He's still jerking off in the corner."

Whitehead shook his head. "I ain't a virgin," he whined. A chorus of laughter and Oorahs echoed from the Marines. Then they proceeded to ream Whitehead for his lack of sexual experience.

"I swear, there was a girl from back home. We did stuff."

"Bah, haha," Ramos chimed in. "You wouldn't know a chocha if it fell on your dick."

Kinnick ignored the berating of their comrade. He spoke softer to the sergeant. "I have a question for you, Volk."

Volk clenched his jaw, thinking he was going to get reprimanded for the way his men spoke about their commanding officer. "Yes, sir."

"Why do the men call Major Alvarado 'Mad Isabel?'"

The watercraft skipped over the currents, causing the men to readjust their grips on weapons.

Volk's brow crossed before he answered as if he were angry to have to speak. "She's meaner than dirt, sir. Got a lot of feistiness in her like the little Latina she is. Ain't that right, Ramos?"

"She spicy," he said with a smirk.

Volk turned back to Kinnick. "Tough as shit on us. Fair, but all discipline. Asks a lot from us and gives her all for us. Pulled a lot of us out of some shit near McCoy, fought like a Marine possessed, and expects us to do the same. There's a reason we haven't lost a Marine in sixteen days."

"Let's keep it that way, Sergeant."

"Oorah, sir."

The land skimmed by as they sped downriver, everything along the shore dead or dying. Two hours later, their engines slowed to a low rumble. On the Iowa side of the Mississippi, nice waterfront homes lined the shore. A thick beamed bridge the color of a blueish-gray sky grew larger in the distance. Kinnick's flotilla of SURCs drifted closer, easily passing beneath the large bridge connecting Iowa and Wisconsin. A road ran away to the Wisconsin side through a series of tiny swampy tree-covered islands.

On the Iowa side, a small town appeared on the banks of the Mississippi. It was covered in historic red brick, two-story buildings. Eaves were painted green, blue, and black. A few of the buildings were painted white, cream, or gray. The main street ran straight into the river with a boat landing. Small wooden and metal docks lined the shore. Kinnick pointed Coffey where he wanted him to maneuver the craft. "Make for there." Coffey turned the wheel for the shore.

No more than a thousand people could have resided there. Nothing moved. The town seemed still. An abandoned town filled with only the ghosts of the past. The only things that moved were Kinnick and his men.

A few of the buildings near the center were blackened and burnt. Kinnick scooped up his radio. "Captain Boucher, take Madison One and Two, Franklin Two and Three and Jefferson One and Three and continue down the river. Let me know of any issues coming up." Kinnick was giving the captain most of the ODAs under his command, the best soldiers for training the civilians, but he thought it better to keep the captain tied together with the other Special Forces soldiers.

Boucher's voice had a Cajun twang to it. "Copy," echoed from the radio.

"Good luck, Captain." He looked back at the other boats closing in from down the flotilla column.

"Don't you worry 'bout us, sir. We'll get them civvies all trained and ready for a scrap."

"Thank you, Captain. Our rally point is Hannibal, Missouri."

"We'll see you at Portage des Sioux."

Six pairs of SURC engines kicked back up from a low idle and they motored away through the water.

Kinnick set the radio down and stared at the dead town. The clouds above were thick enough that he thought it might rain, adding a high level of misery to the mostly open-decked watercraft.

Master Sergeant Hunter leaned over the side of the boat and pointed. "Look at those things."

Gray bloated bodies floated in the river. Fish nibbled at their heads and bodies.

"Fatter than a hog in heat," Hunter said.

Sergeant Hawkins stared, unmoving. He pointed at the small town.

Kinnick barely could make out the residual figure that ran between the buildings.

Kinnick rubbed his eyes. "Thought this was a ghost town. Looks like we got somebody to talk to. Take us in." He waved at Coffey.

"Aye, aye, Colonel." Coffey turned the boat hard and oriented them to the shore.

Master Sergeant Hunter shouted. "You heard the colonel. Get ready to get hot."

Kinnick picked up his microphone. "Hamilton Two and Adams One. Move in with us." For this operation, he thought he'd bring it back to the beginning. All his boats were named after Founding Fathers. His SURCs would be known as the Founding Defenders.

Coffey took Hamilton One right alongside a riverside dock. It was made of warped faded gray wood. Neon-green water mold grew up along the supporting legs in the water.

Hamilton Two and Adams One slid along docks farther down river. Marines stormed the ashore. "Get moving," Volk shouted. Marines clambered onto the dock of a riverside restaurant.

Hunter launched himself onto the dock like a gymnast and offered a hand to Kinnick. Kinnick took it and the soldier yanked him onto the dock.

"Washington." Volk pointed the African-American corporal toward the building. Marines ran beneath a large porch overhang. "Boone." Volk pointed at another building split by a boat landing. The gangly lance corporal and three more Marines ran that way, and with a glance back at Kinnick, Volk followed. Kinnick hefted his M4 and followed Washington's men, who scrutinized the inside of a dark restaurant that was filled with empty tables. They all took cover against the windowed wall in a single-file line.

Master Sergeant Hunter jogged down the line and did a quick check around the corner. He pointed out at the other fire team. He presented his fingers. Three. Two. One. Both fire teams burst onto the sidewalks of the main street. Guns were pointed in varying directions but never at one another. The streets were empty of traffic and people alike. Abandoned cars had collected a brown dust that coated them from lack of use.

The Marines and Green Berets hustled down the street searching for the person they'd seen.

"Nobody's here," Hunter whispered.

"Somebody's here and they're hiding," Kinnick whispered back.

An American flag fluttered above a shop. It whipped back and forth, cracking and snapping in the wind that threatened rain. Signs swung in the turbulent air and softly creaked as rusted hinges were worked. Small studios, businesses, eateries, and a bank lined the main town block. They moved quickly down the street. *We could be too late. What if every town was just like this? Abandoned or dead. There will be no one left to fight.*

The Marines' combat boots padded down the street. Kinnick looked behind him. The other SURCs' soldiers and Marines spread out to side streets. His men tested door handles down the other side of the street.

A door groaned and Kinnick turned. He scrutinized a blue door cracked open only an inch. He could see nothing but darkness inside. He touched Hunter's arm and gestured. The door closed. Kinnick, Hunter, and Hawkins stacked on the door with Washington's fire team. They waited a moment as the men collected themselves to make entry.

A second later, Washington put a big boot to the left of the door handle. The doorjamb splintered and the door swung open. The Marines charged inside. Kinnick was the last one in and button-hooked to the left. People cried out in terror.

A tall man stood behind the counter and pointed a shotgun at them. He took turns aiming the gun at one Marine and then another. People crowded near his back, cowering.

Washington's voice roared at the man. His stance was compact for such a big man and his voice aggressive. "Drop the gun." He repeated himself again and again.

"Hold," Kinnick shouted. He let his gun swing down to his side.

The thick-mustached man frowned. Glasses sat atop his nose. He gestured with his shotgun a tiny bit. "Get on out of here. You got no right busting in here." A little girl looked out from behind him." He swatted at her with his off-hand. "You're in so much trouble, young lady."

Kinnick took a step forward, holding out a helping hand. "Sir. We are here to help."

"Prove it. The last batch of you robbed us blind."

Kinnick held up his hands showing him that he was unarmed.

"I am Colonel Kinnick of the United States Air Force. What is your name, sir?"

Behind him, he could hear Hunter snort a laugh about the air force comment.

"I'm Brian Watson," he said with a little nod.

"Mr. Watson, we are here to help. We don't want to rob you or harm your family. We are here to make sure they survive."

Brian dropped his gun a fraction. "How's you suppose that?"

Kinnick kept his hand held in the man's direction. "We're going to train you to fight."

"To fight?"

"To fight against the dead."

"How do I know you're telling the truth?"

Kinnick peered over his shoulder at Hunter and nodded. Hunter ducked out of the building.

"Give me a minute, Brian."

After a minute, Hunter came back inside holding a large box. He brought it forward and set it down in front of Brian.

"Go ahead, Brian. Take a look."

Brian's brow furrowed, but he bent down slow as if his back hurt and picked up a brownish tan package. He held it up, inspecting it. His eyebrows rose. "MRE?"

Kinnick held his hand up. "It stands for Meal Ready to Eat. There's five hundred there and we have more. We want to make sure your folks are taken care of."

The tall man gulped but nodded his head gravely. "I trust ya. You got a better look than the last bastards. Thank you." He lowered his shotgun all the way to the ground. The tension faded from the room.

"It's all right now," Brian shouted behind him.

People flooded out from the room that he blocked with his life. Men, women, and children came out to look at the Marines and Green Berets. A little girl and boy, who were clearly siblings, walked up to Kinnick. They both had bleach blond hair and blue eyes.

"I wanna be a soldier one day just like you," the girl squeaked.

Kinnick bent down.

"You will. What's your name?"

"Monroe."

Kinnick reached out a hand and ruffled her hair.

"And yours?" Kinnick asked the boy.

The boy stood silent.

Kinnick smiled at the boy. "Would you like to be a soldier?"

The boy nodded his head slowly.

The little girl stared at her brother and back to Kinnick. "His name's Alfie. He's the quiet one."

"Alfie the soldier."

Monroe gave him a tough look. "I'm the big sister. I look out for him."

Kinnick chuckled and gave her a smile. "Well, you keep looking out for him. You both need each other. Remember that. Always look out for one another. When you're ready, I expect you to join one of our units."

Her eyes drifted back and to the left as she thought. "I'm only seven now, but when I'm eight, I think I'll be ready."

"And we'll be waiting." Kinnick stood back up.

The little girl seemed satisfied with his response. "Bye, mister," she squeaked. She took Alfie's hand and they ran off together.

Kinnick stood. The people hugged and shook hands with the Marines. Master Sergeant Hunter picked up a child. "Thank you" and "God bless" and "Our prayers are answered," could be heard over and over from the people.

A white-haired woman wrapped her arms around Hawkins. "We knew you'd come." She reached a hand up and squeezed his cheek between her fingers. Hawkins blinked fast. His stoic face almost showed a sliver of emotion.

"Such a handsome lad too," the old woman said.

Hawkins looked at Kinnick, his eyes wide. Hunter barked a laugh and shifted the child in his arms.

"Are you a pirate?" the child in his arms peeped. Hunter laughed.

Hunter did his best pirate voice. "Of course me am, laddie."

The tall, mustached leader stepped in front of Kinnick. His shotgun hung loosely in his fingers and was casually pointed to the ground like he was walking through a forest to hunt quail. Two tall young mustache-lacking men stood behind him, clearly his sons.

"Now, Colonel, how can we help you?"

Kinnick looked up at him. "Can you fight?"

Brian looked back at his sons. "Yes, sir. We can fight. We ain't got no formal training, but we can learn."

"That's all I ask."

STEELE
Pentwater, MI

Gunfire penetrated his dreams, echoing across his semiconscious plane of existence. He awoke in sweat-soaked sheets. His damaged arm ached. It held a permanent itch in and around the wound and felt claustrophobic underneath the bandages.

He inhaled deeply. Touching the bed next to him, he was reminded she wasn't there. He crumpled a handful of sheets with his functioning hand. The emptiness of the room gnawed at him. The vacancy on the other side of his bed made him ache even more. He embraced the void of her absence and exhaled loudly. *She is safe.*

Sitting up, he let his feet fall to the floor. The floor was cold beneath his rough soles. He brought his good hand to his forehead, running his fingers through the hair that still remained on his skull.

A faint sound touched his ears. His eyes darted to the black M4 that leaned on his bed nearby. His tomahawk rested on his bedside next to his black M9A1 Beretta sidearm. Still, he was drawn to the window.

Shirtless, he limped over to the windowsill, resting his hand on the wooden frame. The darkness of the early morning sat waiting outside, begrudgingly giving up its stranglehold on the land. On the west side of the fire station sat a marina leading out to a small lake. The town stretched along Pentwater Lake connected by a channel to the "Big Lake" or Lake Michigan. Steele's window faced south of the station. Southeast sat a forested hill. It was more of a slight elevation compared to its lower surroundings.

He could make out shadows near the edge of town standing next to motorcycles. Portable floodlights poured light down the road that ran along the lakeshore. Two hunched-over forms stood exposed on the water tower, huddled together in the chill of the night. *At least they're still upright.*

Smoldering fires sat outside a small office building across from the fire station. It had been annexed by the Chosen after he'd set them free. He could make out the armed brothers and sisters standing outside.

Earlier in the day and under the watchful eye of the Red Stripes and the Iron Drakes, the former Chosen prisoners had been escorted back to Temple Energy to collect their families and the remainders of their armed forces. By the time they had all trickled back into Pentwater, the Chosen numbers almost doubled Steele's united motorcycle gangs and Sable Point members. He watched the building warily, debating in his mind if he had made a mistake. *The pastor will be true to his word. The problem is his words are those of a psychopathic egotistical demigod.*

Time would tell if he made a mistake, or a bullet in the back, but he knew deep down it didn't matter because Jackson's forces threatened them operating somewhere unknown in the countryside. He would keep the pastor close. It was the enemy out of sight that concerned him.

The dusky outside was turning a lighter gray as morning took over. Highly trained and hostile American soldiers were operating nearby. They knew only one code and that was loyalty to the unit. As far as they were concerned, the government had turned their back on them. Left them for dead. Now they wanted his head on a platter because he had defied them with Kinnick and the remnants of loyal American soldiers.

He let his head fall to his chest, not realizing he was holding his breath. By the end of the morning, his people would put some distance between themselves and Jackson's men, hoping to disappear into the wooded north of Michigan.

The faint tinkle of glass hitting the floor jarred him. A hole appeared in the glass next to his head. Steele considered it almost casually, wondering if someone had thrown a rock through his window. The window spiderwebbed along the edges of the hole. His heart leapt in his chest as realization flashed in his mind, and he threw himself on the floor. He grunted as pain seared through his damaged arm, sucking the wind from his chest. A round shattered the rest of the glass and struck the wall above him sending plaster into the air.

"Shit." He crawled over, using his single arm, and pushed over his pack in front of him. The door to his room kicked inward. He stared at a booted foot.

"Jesus," Tess exclaimed. A shot embedded itself into the door. She flinched, bending down into a low squat. She scooped up his pack and M4 quick and slung them over her shoulder. "Where the hell?"

"Dunno. Keep moving," Steele grunted as he snatched up his handgun and tomahawk, his muscles not wanting to participate in such a quick, laborious movement. Tess helped him through the doorway and into the hall. People scrambled down the dimly lit hall, guns in hands.

Margie emerged from her dorm and hopped up and down as she forced on her pants. Getting both her legs inside, she ran for him. "Scott's crew is reporting large numbers of soldiers on the south end of Lake Shore Drive near the condo tower."

"Tell them not to give up their position unless the soldiers advance. Give the rest of Sable time to round up."

The perpetually worried woman in her late 50s nodded vigorously and ran down the corridor. Tess wrapped an arm around his torso and helped him down the hall. As they hobbled down the metal steps, the fire station garage erupted in chaos.

Motorcycles zipped by. Men loaded trucks. Single gunshots rang out but not the sound of automatic fire. *Perhaps it is a scouting party, or a lone sniper sent to terrorize us.*

"Tess, please help Margie." She eyed him for a second and nodded, tossing him his M4. He caught it and held it by its pistol grip handle. *Not going to be much use.*

Thunder jogged up, chest heaving beneath his club colors. "I sent War Child and the War Machines to the north end, and the Wolf Riders northeast. If they've encircled us, we're done."

"We'll be pinned on the water," Steele breathed. He looked over Thunder's shoulder to the outside.

"We should have left sooner."

"We should have left as soon as we saw his forces." Steele looked out over at the Chosen's office building. The pastor stood outside, watching him as if he thought Steele's men had turned on him. He quickly nodded to Steele and waved his men out of the building. His followers surged out into the street with supplies and gear.

Steele turned back to Thunder. "Get everyone loaded up. We have to leave as fast as we can."

"I got it," Thunder grumbled. "Garrett, let's get the boys mounted and ready to ride," he shouted.

The big sergeant-in-arms nodded his head and shouted, "Let's mount up."

Steele eyed the trees. *How many enemy soldiers do you hold?*

A small red pickup truck rolled up and brakes slammed it into a halt. Tess was behind the wheel. She ran a hand over her slicked back black hair. "Get in," she said.

Steele used the truck as a brace to reach the other side then opened the door and plopped in.

They stopped as Peter stepped out into the road, gun in his hand. Steele gripped the M4 in his good arm prepared to use it. Peter ran around to Steele's side of the truck.

He stuck his sandy curly-haired head inside and Steele was only thankful it wasn't his AK-47 rifle.

"We're almost all loaded up. We have a few older folk who might need some more time."

"They have five minutes and we roll out." The ground erupted near Peter. He ducked his head low and looked over his shoulder at the trees.

"Hurry," Steele said. Peter nodded and ran toward the building housing the Chosen.

Tess gassed it, making the tires squeal, and she handed him binoculars. "You're going to need these."

Steele held them for a moment. She sped to the edge of the town and slammed on the brakes. "There." She pointed through the windshield up at a wooded hill.

The enemy sat there like a line of mounted knights. The .50 caliber machine guns were their lances that greedily itched to reach out and touch you. An armored wall of tan Humvees lined the road, blocking the way south. Soldiers peered down M2 .50 caliber machine gun barrels. They sighted him with M240 machine guns and Mk 19s with 40mm grenades strung together in belted boxes.

A man stood atop of one of the Humvees. His head was uncovered and it was clear with the shine from the top of his skull that he was bald. He held a long bolt-action sniper rifle in one hand. Steele snagged up the binoculars and pressed them to his eyes. He leaned closer to the windshield, but he already knew the answer.

A skeletal head laughed with the men next to him, and he brought the rifle up to his shoulder. He took aim. Boom. Fire erupted from his gun. A biker collapsed onto the ground down the street and didn't move.

The bald soldier roared with laughter and one of his men handed him an AT4, an 84mm, single-shot, guideless, anti-tank weapon. Cheap, low recoil, almost dummy proof, and effective against both light armor and structures.

Steele pulled his eyes away from the binoculars and glanced at Tess. "Scott's team is in the condos," he said it more to himself. He had given the order for them to hold their position.

Tess peered up at the condo tower on the edge of the marina.

"They are."

A projectile screeched with a smoky tail across the sky and a room inside the tower exploded outward into a fiery inferno.

"Shit," Tess cursed. She threw the car in reverse and spun the truck's wheels. She ripped it back into drive and jerked the steering wheel.

"Scott's team," Steele said, looking back at the tower. Black smoke billowed out of the building.

Tess gunned it down the street. Steele dug his M4 into the floor to keep himself steady.

She spoke fast and worried. "We don't have time to worry about them."

Steele glanced behind them, looking through the dirty glass of the truck's rear cabin. The Humvees slowly rolled down the hill toward the town.

"They're coming," he said.

The pickup passed a side street. Humvees rolled down the residential street. She sped up, passing another side street. Tan vehicles rumbled along that road toward the main drag, slowly squeezing Steele's forces between the lake and north. Tess stopped the truck near the fire station. A host of Red Stripes ran boxes of food to trucks.

"They're rolling in from all over," Steele said.

Thunder looked back at the hill. "I saw 'em. Fucking cowards been taking potshots at us. We had a couple causalities. The Chosen are loaded up and on the road. We're the last."

Steele nodded to the big biker, placing his M4 on the window frame. "We run."

GWEN
Hacklebarney, IA

Gwen walked up the steps to the second story of the building. She knocked on a black door at the top.

"Come on in," a voice called out.

She opened the door to the mayor's office and stepped inside. A slightly chubby man in a white button-down shirt with a red tie sat behind an old wooden executive desk. Old green carpet ran all the way through the office. Dark stains covered the floor. Gwen assumed it was a combination of spilt coffee along with mud and dirt from the surrounding farms that had been deposited over countless mayoral terms. A tall bookshelf stood on the far wall, and framed pictures lined the other.

She took a step inside. "Hi, Mayor Dobson," she said. He had been a car salesman in Dubuque before moving to Hacklebarney. His hair was receding but combed over the top of his head. His cheeks were borderline pudgy from being outside his prime.

He looked up from what he was reading and smiled. "Gwen Reynolds. Sheriff said you might be stopping by soon. Been too long since I last laid eyes on you." His eyes made a quick dart to her chest and back to her face. Her breasts had grown painfully larger in the last few weeks despite her limited diet as her body prepared itself for the arrival of her baby.

He waved a hand in front of him. "How 'bout you take a seat?"

She did as she was asked and pushed a green velvet chair closer to his desk.

He held out a small glass bowl filled with white candies. "Mint?"

She shook her head. "No, thank you."

He set the bowl down and leaned back in his brown executive-style chair that squealed with every up and down.

He shook his head in disbelief and smirked. "I bet John about had a heart attack when you showed up." He continued shaking his head. "He must be thrilled to have you back." His chair continued to bounce up and down.

She folded her hands in front of her body. "He is very happy to have me back." He sat back up quickly and interrupted her before she could continue as if he had a whole list of meetings lined up for the day.

"So what can I do you for today?"

"I came to speak with you about refugees."

He smiled, but somehow, she wasn't sure it was genuine. "Sheriff Donnellson did the right thing by letting you over that bridge. We are happy to have your people." He looked to the side before he continued. "Of course, your grandfather's farm will bear the brunt of that burden."

She pursed her lips. "They're good people. They can contribute in many ways."

"I'm sure they can. On *his* farm."

"What if I was to tell you a much bigger group of people are headed your way?"

The mayor blinked a few times and continued to smile. "How many people are we talking about, Gwen?"

"About a thousand."

He rolled his eyes and whistled as his chair bounced back away from his desk. His eyes and tone grew disapproving. "I know you aren't about to ask me to let in more people than this town has in it? That is out of the question." His chair bounced back toward his desk and he leaned in. "Do you know how hard things are going to get this winter? Let alone the extra hundred that your grandfather has taken in? The stress that puts on the sheriff to keep things orderly is plenty enough." He shook his head at her suggestion. "Ya know, I'm going to say this because most people in this town are too nice, but you got a lot of nerve coming in here and placing that burden on all of us. What if we can't feed them? Or they get sick? Then I'm responsible for their abuse, even their deaths." His eyes widened. "What if they get us sick? Think about the people here."

She leaned forward. His eyes darted down away from her face again quick. "I don't think you understand. This is more than being without power or cars. Millions of people have been killed or infected. At some point, they will end up here. You have to let them across the river or they'll be killed."

He furrowed his brow at her. "Gwen, I don't have to do anything. We have gone way above and beyond our responsibility to other communities. There's no telling what kinds of people you bring in here. You are asking me to put my constituents and the great people of Hacklebarney at risk. And for what? What do we have to gain?" He waved his hands to the sides.

"So you can save people's lives and they can help us defend Hacklebarney against the dead. Not only are there infected, but there are criminals and military units fighting. One unit is after these people."

The mayor snorted and his soft belly jiggled a bit. "The United States military is after you?"

Gwen shook her head quick. "No, not the military. A rogue unit. Defectors."

Mayor Dobson smiled in disbelief. "You want me to give asylum to people who are on the run from the military? Defectors or not, those are American fighting men and women. They deserve our gratitude for sticking their necks out for us." He crowded forward, inching across his desk.

His voice dropped down low. "What you're proposing is treasonous. Your grandfather would be embarrassed if he heard the words coming out of your mouth. He's a veteran for Christ's sake."

"Then let them pass through. My people will go somewhere else," she pleaded.

"Listen to yourself. My people. Gwen, if I remember correctly your people are here." He pointed back and out his window. "Whatever is across that river are just freeloaders. They're using you. I don't mind helping people in need, but listen to what you are saying. Standing against our military, that's madness. Feed and clothe thousands of people, madness. We are barely a thousand ourselves!" he exclaimed, getting worked up. His face was beginning to turn red.

She felt the heat rise to her cheeks too. "Let me tell you what's madness. A United States Army colonel hunted others and myself for helping a doctor discover Patient Zero in Michigan. Do you know what that is, a patient zero?"

"No." He leaned back away from her and his chair creaked.

"That is the first person to contract the disease. Our scientists needed him to come up with some kind of cure. And that man hunted us for it. Killed us for not obeying him. Maybe he wanted it for himself, but it doesn't matter because it's all insane. Don't you tell me about madness. Madness is standing by while that man butchers the innocent," she growled.

The mayor folded his hands in front of him as he went into politician mode. "I understand your passion, Gwen. Even if what you say is true, you would be putting every man, woman, and child here in Hacklebarney at great risk and I will not allow it. I'll have the sheriff and his posse stop anyone that tries."

She tried to reach him at an even more personal level. "My boyfriend is leading that group. He will be trapped over there if we don't help him."

His smile turned flat. "That, *my dear,* is not my problem." He licked his fingers and thumbed through some papers, averting his eyes. "Thanks for stopping by today." His eyes glanced up from his papers as if he expected her to vanish before him. "Tell your grandpa I said hello."

Gwen's mouth hung open. This bastard was going to end the conversation like this.

"I'm-" She sat flustered. "I will." She stopped. "Thank you, Mayor," she forced out.

"The pleasure was all mine," he oozed. His eyes crept down again toward her chest.

She stood abruptly and stormed for the door. Her hand closed around the doorknob.

"Oh, and Gwen." She stopped opening the door and turned around.

"Don't go off doing anything brash. I have no problem sending your people back across the river to wherever they came from."

"Don't you worry about me." She made sure to slam the door on her way out.

She pounded down the steps and made for her horse. Patsy eyed her with big brown eyes, still standing in the same spot. The horse picked her foot up and let it stomp on the ground sensing her irritation. Gwen unwrapped her reins.

"I know. He's an asshat," she whispered to the horse. She patted Patsy as she walked around her. She looked up toward his office as she mounted atop Patsy. Mayor Dobson stood at the window watching her. She snorted up at him and he smiled down at her, hands in his pockets.

Gwen pulled Patsy's reins away and they walked down the street. Her grandfather rode up on his horse. He gave her a concerned look when he got close enough to see her face, wrinkled lines creasing his weathered face.

"What's happened?"

"That man is an asshole." She kept her horse walking and her grandfather turned his horse around and followed her.

"No need for such language," he scolded.

Gwen gave him a death stare. "I'm a grown woman, grandpa. I can say what I like."

"Just cause you can, doesn't mean you should." He closed his mouth and nodded. "Sometimes us old folks forget that you kids are all grown up."

She laughed a bit. "That man is a selfish ignorant fool, is what he is."

Her grandfather chuckled. "He is a fool."

They rode in silence for a moment, only the sound of their horses' hooves connecting with the road echoing.

"He won't help, Mark. There will be hundreds of people that need our help."

She could see him tense at the mention of more refugees. "The mayor is a fool, but remember, we can't take everyone. Our town is small. Things will be difficult with the extra mouths to feed as it is." His eyes were grave.

"They will die if we don't help them. Between the crazies and the military, they will be cut down."

John's mouth twitched a bit. "I know, sweetheart. We will find a way. Have faith."

Gwen couldn't help but tear up at the old man who had loved her more than a father could.

"I love you, Pa."

"Love you too, sweetheart."

KINNICK
Northern Mississippi River

There were over three hundred people hiding in Lansing, Iowa. Kinnick left Hamilton Two, manned by a detachment of Marines under a ruddy chain-smoking sergeant, to collect people from the surrounding area and train them to fight.

Within an hour, Kinnick took his remaining seven watercraft and traveled south on the river. If Kinnick could make it to one more town before nightfall, he would consider the first phase of the operation a success.

The onboard radio buzzed on the Hamilton One. "Captain Boucher to Colonel Kinnick." The radio clicked off.

Kinnick picked up his microphone and spoke into it. "This is Kinnick."

"Sir, we've reached Harpers Ferry, Iowa, sir, and we've got a bit of a problem."

"I understand Harpers Ferry is the next town on our tour."

"Clarifying, sir. These are commonplace names."

Kinnick shook his head. "Copy, Captain. What's wrong with Harpers Ferry?"

"Well, we have a lock and there ain't nobody home."

"What do you mean?"

"A dam and lock, but no one is manning the control station on the Illinois side. We cleared the station out, but we caused quite a commotion out there. I expect that there will be more infected drawn in by the time you get there.

104

I want you to be well-briefed on what you're sailing into. Then there's the bad part."

"Bad part?" Kinnick clicked off his microphone and looked out over the water.

Captain Boucher clicked back on. "You're going to have to hope that the generator's got enough juice in her for one more go around town, or you are literally up shit creek."

Kinnick rubbed his brow. "Thank you, Captain. Carry on."

"My pleasure cruise has already passed Marquette."

"Be safe."

"You as well."

Kinnick waved Hunter up off the ground. The master sergeant lifted himself up using the side of the boat. "In the next hour or so, we are going to run into a dam."

Hunter's eyebrow lowered. "Prolly get out of the way of that."

Kinnick gave him a short smile.

"Boucher got his boats through, but they had to go real hot. We're going to have to be fast and quiet or risk getting overrun. Take Hawk and Boone's fire team and get that lock open."

Hunter rolled the wad of tobacco in his mouth to the other side and squeezed with his lip. "Well, hot damn. Can't wait." Hunter turned back to Hawk over his shoulder. "You hear that, Hawk? We get to open the locks for the boss."

Hawk gave a slight nod of his head.

Hunter turned back to Kinnick and spit over the side of the boat. "He's ready."

***

After about an hour cruising down the river, a concrete dam rose up out of the water. Large thick arches were spaced evenly and stuck up even higher than the wall running over the river. Next to those were smaller concrete arches.

The Marine on the .50 caliber machine gun turned back and shouted.

"Looks like they got both roller and Tainter gates on their dam."

Boone rolled his eyes, staying seated. "Here we go with the college boy."

"What's that mean, Marine?" Kinnick said.

"Don't get him started," Hanger shouted.

"He knows more shit about shit that don't mean shit," Washington said.

Kinnick ignored the Marines. "Go on, Gore."

Gore looked like the teenager next door. Hairless face. He had an almost goofy look with boyish freckles, except he had a ballistic helmet and manned a .50 caliber machine gun. He twisted in the turret so he could see Kinnick. "Grew up north of here in Hastings, Minnesota, on the banks of the Mississippi. We had one like it, but we only had Tainter gates."

"What does that mean for us?"

Gore released a single hand off his machine gun. "I'd avoid 'em if you don't want to get destroyed by the current. Tainter gates are floodgates that are shaped like a pie slice with the round end facing upstream. It forces only a little bit of water through the dam at a time, preventing bank erosion downstream." Gore held up his hands linked together in a round shape. "You see, the cool part is the water bears on the convex of the upstream-."

Volk swatted at the Marine. "Shut up and get on the fifty. We ain't paying you to talk about your cervix."

Gore looked abashed and took his place back on his .50 caliber machine gun. He pointed. "Far bank, that white building's where the lock controls should be."

Kinnick pointed to the eastern bank. "Take us over."

Coffey motored the boat to the eastern shore.

Haggard forms followed them down the riverbanks toward the lock. More infected wandered toward the control station and down the riverside road from the surrounding forests. A group of them clustered around the white station, sitting on the edge of the dam. They were going to have to clear them out to operate the lock.

Kinnick looked at Hunter. He was already sizing up his next war challenge.

A concrete pier wall formed a side of the lock and already had infected crawling all over it. They could have been men and women fishing until they started to reach over the metal railings for the SURC.

"Hit 'em with the mini," Kinnick ordered. Volk nodded and yelled, "Duncan, fire away."

The minigun blared out, sounding like a high-speed bumblebee buzzing bullets. Bodies disintegrated before them. Bullet holes appeared in the building behind them almost like military magic. After each iteration of rounds, the gunner would check his targets and the minigun would come to a rotary stop, rattling. A red river of blood ran down from the concrete pier mixing into the brown water.

Coffey stuck his tongue out in concentration as he maneuvered the SURC close to the concrete sides of the lock. Hunter and Hawk jumped up and heaved themselves onto the platform followed by Boone and his fire team. Gunfire sounded off. Then muffled gunfire as they entered the building. It was followed by relative silence. Only the faint moans of the coming dead filling the air.

The SURCs clustered into the lock one after another, packing the space without drifting too close for fear of damaging their vessels. Captain Heath stared at the pier with his carbine to his shoulder. His gun banged and the dead along the pier toppled over and into the water.

Motors idled as they waited for Boone's fire team to take over the controls. "Keep your distance from one another," Kinnick said into the radio. The SURCs coasted apart inside the confines of the walled lock, constantly idling. More guns pinged from the SURCs as the Marines and Green Berets took potshots at the dead along the pier.

Coffey looked cautiously at Kinnick. "Shouldn't we be careful about drawing them in?"

Kinnick eyed Heath's boat then looked at the boat next to his led by a lean sharp-nosed First Sergeant DeCicco. DeCicco's men laughed and their guns boomed like they were on a drunken duck hunt.

Kinnick held the radio to his lips. "Boone, how're those controls coming?" A moment later, Boone came out of the door of the building and gave a thumbs-up.

The large metal lock gate began to close inch by inch behind the SURCs, and the upstream river disappeared from view. It was like a prison cell door locking shut. The direction Kinnick's men were traveling downstream meant that the elevation was decreasing with every lock. The lock would have to drop to the water level of the next part of the Mississippi River before they could continue on their journey.

The water in the lock started to dip as if someone had pulled the plug on a giant river drain, but only a fraction. Inch by inch the water disappeared below them.

Kinnick shouted over at Gore who was facing the railings with his .50 caliber machine gun turret. "Gore, how long do these things take?"

The Marine kept his eyes on the railings rising higher and higher above the SURC. "Depends on how low the lock itself needs to go to step down to the next water level. I'd say about ten to twenty minutes."

The lock walls seemingly grew larger and larger as the SURCs sank deeper and deeper. Hunter's voice crackled through the radio. "Sir, we are getting some serious pressure at the front of the building. Door's gonna give."

Kinnick picked up his microphone, pressing it near his lips. "Hunter, you gotta hold until we're through." Kinnick glanced over at Franklin One. Its .50 caliber machine gun was trained toward the lock walls. Six feet became twelve feet and it was harder and harder to have any idea on what was happening above them.

The muted gunfire picked up in the building, sounding like a string of firecrackers going off. Duncan swiveled his minigun and pointed it upward. The other SURCs had lost their targets and now stood silent, watching the overhang above. Eyes darted back and forth looking for their comrades. Water lapped the craft and the lock alike.

His men could feel it. Kinnick felt it deep in his gut. It was about to go bad. Kinnick followed his instinct and slowly set the radio mic back onto the receiver and picked up his M4, pointing it at the platform above. He gave himself a wide stance so as to not fall over as Coffey idled the Hamilton One in tiny circles.

Kinnick scanned the railing. *Come on, gotta get this open.* Only more gunfire kicked off. It sound ricocheted from wall to wall inside the lock as they waited.

Volk squeezed his radio, scowling. "Boone, what's your sitch?"

Volk moved his head back as a screech blared through his radio. The screech hung inside the lock trapped. "They're all over."

"Get that lock open," Kinnick said, looking up at the platform. "Or we'll be trapped inside."

A face with charred skin on one side and dead gray on the other leaned over the railing. Its pale white eyes didn't register a thing, only seeing more flesh for infection. Its ugly mouth dropped open and a low moan emanated forth. A carbine pinged and its head bounced back on its neck. The dead slumped over the railing and free-fell into the water that mushroomed upon impact. Water sprayed the air and the body faded as it disappeared from the surface.

More ugly faces peered over the edge at them. They snarled and growled, hands extended with malice.

"Fire!" Kinnick screamed. His voice was immediately drowned out by the heavy du-du-du of .50 cals and the zipping roar of the miniguns. Gore twisted his turret back along the pier, and Duncan let the minigun go in bursts. The dead were obliterated off the edge. Faces were smeared by large caliber bullets, leaving little to nothing where once infected stood.

Kinnick ducked and covered as an arm fell onto the Hamilton One. With a smack, the remainders of the body crunched into the SURC deck.

The infected lifted itself up with one remaining arm. Kinnick took the butt of his carbine and crashed it into the thing's head. Its head bounced off the deck and its curdled-milk eyes stared back up at Kinnick. It reached again unrelenting and clawed for Kinnick, letting out a moan. Kinnick repeated the strike again and again until the butt of his carbine met sloppy mush and the hard deck.

He looked up in time to see an intact dead crash from above onto the turret gunner of Jefferson Two. Marines scrambled to help their fallen brother. When the turret gunner rose up again, he had found new brothers in the infected. He bear-hugged another Marine, tackling him onto the deck.

Adams One tried to reverse to get away from the wall and its engine penetrated the hull of Franklin Four.

Marines went into the water. It was difficult to distinguish the Marines trying to swim versus the dead floundering nearby. The lock was an enclosed pool filling with more infected by the moment.

Kinnick gave another glance up at the ledge. The dead were toppling over in droves as his men reloaded their machine guns. Marines shouted as Franklin Four started to slip beneath the surface of the water. The remaining Marines that hadn't been thrown overboard were bailing water in an attempt to stay afloat. Infected and Marines alike gripped onto the gunwales trying to get aboard. The small craft sank rapidly, and the Marines onboard quickly joined their comrades in the frigid river water.

The Green Berets onboard Madison Three were collecting the Marines that hadn't been pulled beneath the depths of the water by the dead.

The deep earsplitting groan of metal on metal resounded out like a river titan coming to life. A fissure cracked the lower gate. The fissure became a rift, revealing open Mississippi water ahead.

"Go, go, go!" Kinnick screamed into the radio. Engines roared and the other SURCs gunned it for the next section of the river.

"Coffey, keep us moving." Coffey spun the boat in a small circle. *Come on, Hunter.* Only the ugly faces of the dead leered over the railings. Gore swirled his turret back in the direction of the lock. His .50 cal blared a loud repetitious "du" for each round shot. Body parts were flung off the lock.

"Colonel. We got men running down the pier."

Kinnick's eyes scanned along the lock and the pier leading away from it. Camouflaged shapes sprinted over the concrete. Kinnick could barely make out the one in the back, twisting his body around to blast his gun into the pursuing dead. "Coffey, there they are!"

Coffey's tongue split his lips and went into the corner of his mouth. "I see 'em, Colonel." Kinnick had to grab onto the side of the boat as Coffey shifted his hand on the throttle, ramming it forward. The SURC picked up speed and leveled out atop the water. The motor hummed behind them.

Gore's machine gun continued to throw rounds as he let loose into the dead chasing Hunter and Boone's men. Coffey took the craft right to the edge of the pier. Boone's wild-eyed face stared over the railing.

"'Bout fucking time! We been runnin' our asses off!"

His fire team crawled down the pier wall and hopped into the SURC. "Keep that fifty on them," Kinnick said. He pointed back toward the lock. Gore turned his turret. Hawkins hopped down.

"We must move. More come."

Kinnick heard a thud next to him as Hunter landed on the SURC deck.

Hunter grimaced as he stood up, dusting his knees off. He pushed the chew down into his lip as if it were helping with any pain he might have had from the leap. Coffey threw the boat into forward and it skipped away from the pier.

Kinnick eyed the tough soldier. "You okay?"

"I'll be good." Hunter straightened his back and rolled his shoulders.

"Why'd you jump?"

Hunter squinted his single eye and a slow grin snuck underneath his whiskers. "Looked closer from up there."

STEELE
Outskirts of Beulah, MI

The convoy neared the edges of Beulah, a small lake town north of Pentwater on the west coast of Michigan. Most of the homes had been built in the early '50s and '60s along the main drag and the few side streets branching off. Homes dotted the edges of the eight-mile long inland lake.

Tess glanced over at Steele from the driver's seat. "We've been going for over two hours." They hadn't spoken a word the entire journey. "Jackson isn't that close. Thunder hasn't reported anything from the south and neither has War Child in the north or Macleod in the east."

Steele ignored her, studying his map. *Too many options and none of them good. How do we get out of this?*

"Yo, Bearded Man, we need a plan. We can't keep running without a place to go."

He continued in silence. He ignored the phantoms of his newest fallen comrades, Scott's team, and focused on a way out of this mess.

"What's wrong with you?" she hissed over the steering wheel, anger rising in her voice. "You're supposed to be in charge."

"Enough, Tess," he growled. "I'm trying to figure it out. Give me a minute to think."

"'Bout fucking time, I was wondering if you had a stroke." She gave him a snarky smile.

He gave her a warning glance, his brows furrowed together. *Women: the driving force behind any action.*

Steele stuck his hand out the window, waved the convoy down, and called them all to a halt. His convoy had gone hard and fast into the morning light. A disorganized mass of cars, trucks, buses, motorcycles, and over a thousand scared people fleeing north.

Steele brought his radio to his lips. "Thunder, we are bringing it to a halt outside Beulah. Let us know if you catch any wind from Jackson."

The radio scratched with white noise. "We're about five miles behind you. We'll pull over and see if he sends any recon our way. Last we seen of anybody was Ludington."

Steele switched to the group channel by turning a knob on his radio. "I need all the group leaders to form up on me."

Steele opened the door and stepped out of the truck. He shook out an atlas of Michigan. The state was shaped like a giant left-handed mitten with the thumb on the east side of the state. His group was up near where the pinky finger would be. He set the map on the hood of the pickup and waited for his followers.

Steele waited, hearing nothing except the low hum of the engines around him until individual motorcycles weaved through the convoy. The bikers revved their choppers as they cut around vehicles. Red Clare and War Child rode in from the north together and Gat cruised up from the east with Macleod and Jefferson while Vigo and Frank rolled in separately from the south.

Kevin and Ahmed walked down the cars, carbines in hands. Margie joined them, hunting rifle in hand followed by another Sable Pointer, Tony, a well over six-foot-tall IT programmer with an AR-15.

The pastor rolled up in a newer dark blue Jeep Wrangler. Peter drove him and Luke sat in the back with an AK-47 clutched in his hands. It wasn't lost on Steele that a short time ago these men were going to burn him alive. They hopped out of the doorless vehicle.

The biker presidents cut their engines and kicked their stands. Jefferson stood, arms across his broad frame. Red Clare stood next to him, lit up, and placed a cigarette between her smoke-wrinkled lips. War Child held up a cigarette of his own, and she let him light up off the tip of hers. Vigo massaged his mustache that hung all the way off his chin, and Frank looked like a badger with his black-and-gray streaked beard.

The only club leader not there was Thunder, Steele's leading translator and attache for the unruly group, who manned the rearguard.

The pastor looked expectantly down his nose at Steele, a fresh set of all black garb clothing him. He almost glowed with exuberance.

I have to take advantage of our strengths. "Colonel Jackson has superior firepower and enough men to run us over in a force on force conventional battle. I have no doubt he would love for us to turn and fight."

"We wouldn't stand a chance," War Child said, sounding like two pieces of sandpaper rubbing together. "Unless you got some missing air support I haven't seen yet."

"Wish I did," Steele said flatly.

Steele looked at the old-time biker. "You saw no sign of the military north of here?"

The leathery old biker folded his arms across his chest with a groan from his riding leathers and blew smoke out his mouth. "No sign of them as far north as Empire. Wouldn't expect them to spring a trap this far north when one further south would have done just fine."

Steele nodded. "True. I'm not sure why he hadn't encircled us earlier, but his neglect is our advantage." He tapped a finger east of their position on the map.

"Macleod, any signs of them to the east?"

"Nah, we went all the way out to Copemish and cut up northwest from there. Saw no signs of anybody."

"Good."

"What's the plan, kid? Upper Peninsula and lose them in the woods?" said Frank. He ran a hand over his beard as he thought.

Steele exhaled. "I thought about it, but if the bridge is closed, that leaves us trapped on the water with nowhere to go."

Jefferson slammed a black finger on the map. "We are about fifteen miles from being penned in now." The man was right. If they continued to follow the coast, they would end up on the Leelanau Peninsula, a slender peninsula jutting out of the northwest of Michigan about thirty miles into Lake Michigan. After Jackson caught up to them, they would be pinned and slaughtered on the rocky private beaches of million-dollar lake homes.

"You're right," Steele said.

"What the fuck are we doing then?" Gat said, his tattooed neck veins bulging. "My boys ain't sticking around to get our asses kicked."

War Child smirked beneath his white beard. "What are you scared of? Some punk-ass National Guardsmen?"

Gat's face twisted in anger. He swung an arm back and the other club presidents stepped in the way. "We ain't scared of nothin'." He spit and calmed a fraction. "But I ain't getting killed for nothin' neither." He pulled down hard on his leather coat.

The pastor looked perturbed by the man's outburst. "So much anger, my child."

Gat looked at the pastor with a crazy eye. "Shut the fuck up, you crazy old bat, or you'll get what's coming to you."

Peter put his broad shoulders between the pastor and Gat. "You watch your tongue, you *freak*."

Gat sneered. "Ah, the little altar boy sticking up for his master." Gat's head bobbled back and forth as he mocked, "You gonna get another spanking if you don't watch your mouth."

Peter kept his composure and looked at the pastor for permission to fight the biker. The pastor's chin rose even higher and he placed a comforting long-fingered hand onto Peter's shoulder.

"There's no need for violence against one another when other enemies are so close." The pastor nodded at Steele, making him slightly uncomfortable. *Since when did this guy get so friendly?*

"Back to the issue at hand," Steele said, peering back down at the map, but it was too late.

The men and women broke into side conversations. Steele stood watching them.

"He makes a good point. We need a plan. I'm with Frank. Plenty of places to hide in the Upper Peninsula," said Vigo, Grave Guard patch on his left breast, president patch just below it. He lit a cigarette hanging from the corner of his mouth. "I even know of a few myself."

"We should go south," Jefferson argued. "They won't expect it."

"I want to kill the bastards for what they've done to my club," Frank grumbled. "I want a fight."

Tess pounded her M1911 on top of the hood of her truck. "Everybody shut up. Let Steele speak for Christ's sake." She finished with a glare at the pastor as if to dare him to call her out on her usage of the Lord's name in vain. The men and women begrudgingly closed their mouths and all stared back at Steele.

"We have to play to our strengths. We don't have many, but we'll be in a better spot if we can make it to Iowa. We don't have the numbers, and even if we did, I wouldn't be thrilled to take on the entirety of Jackson's forces. So until we have a better situation, we're going to evade and avoid. Let me show you."

Steele pointed at the map at Beulah. "All of your clubs are mobile and perfect for running interference for the main group that is slower and bogged down with food and excess people. Right now, Jackson thinks we're running scared north, so we're going to do the opposite."

"How would we accomplish such a task?" the pastor said. "You said yourself we cannot win in a stand-alone fight."

"I don't believe we can. At least right now." Steele traced a roadway on the map. "Vigo, you're going to be vital to this plan. You're going to head east and then north for the Upper Peninsula by the most direct route. I want Jackson to believe you are us. We will outfit a bunch of trucks and semis for you to drive. We want you to lead them across the bridge if you can."

Vigo nodded. "What if the bridge is closed?"

"I know a spot where there should be a boat you can commandeer. If things get too dicey, abandon the trucks and flee into Mackinaw City. Either way, you're going to have a long ride." Steele outlined a route through the Upper Peninsula. He looked up at the man. "You'll have to cut down through Wisconsin to get back to Iowa. We're headed here." He unfolded the map and made it bigger and pointed to a tiny square in the southeastern corner of Iowa. "Hacklebarney, Iowa."

Vigo nodded his acceptance, fingers twisting his mustache near the side of his mouth. "All right."

"I'll need the Geminis to head east. The same idea applies. Turn south around the town of Mio, and we can link back up near the border, here." He pointed at a tiny square on the map all the way south near the Indiana/Michigan border. "Burr Oak."

The powerfully muscled biker nodded. "It'll be good to ride hard again."

"Gat and the Eighters, I need you to head northeast. Curl around the top of the state, and somewhere around Rogers City, go south and link up with the Geminis. Then you will need to make double-time to rejoin us before we leave Michigan."

"Not a problem. But what about our bikes?"

"You can put them in the back of the empty trucks if things get sticky, roll them out, and hightail it out of there."

Gat nodded his acceptance. "Aight."

"Good. The rest of us are going to curl back away from the lakeshore toward the middle of the state and head south. They are expecting us to run north, so we go south." He eyed them to make sure they understood the plan. "The War Machines and the Red Stripes will be scouting out front of our main convoy. Wolf Riders will take our right western flank as we move south. Margie, make sure that teams of volunteers are ready to run interference on any masses of infected or Jackson's forces we come across. We've been lucky that not many people live this far north."

War Child took a drag off his cigarette before he spoke. "Are you sure we should be splitting our forces?" At his age, he had to be a veteran of some forgotten war.

"I want our enemy to think we are everywhere and nowhere. In a concentrated engagement, we lose. So let's make him spread out and follow us in every direction. Hopefully, it will be enough to let the main group break free."

War Child only gave him a slight nod. "Could work," he grunted.

Steele turned toward the pastor. "Please have your men ready. We may need them to fight a retreating action."

The pastor dipped his head. "God's people are always ready to crusade on his behalf."

Steele's radio crackled. Thunder's voice came through. "We got a scouting unit coming up the road."

Steele ground his teeth, making his jaw hurt. "We need more time. See if you can draw them off or kill enough of them to make them think they are facing the entire convoy."

Thunder's voice was muted through the radio as if he spoke while holding it away from his face. "Copy. We'll try and give them the runaround."

"We gotta move people," Steele called out. "We have a short clock."

"You heard the man!" Tess shouted. "Let's get those trucks divided up between the clubs."

The bikers mounted their motorcycles and rumbled off to their respective clubs. The pastor nodded to Steele before he sped away in his Jeep.

"It was a good idea splitting up some of the rival gangs," she said.

"I thought so too, but what if War Child is right? Maybe I should be concentrating my forces instead of spreading them out. I know the general principles of war, but I'm not a practitioner."

Steele folded his map and peered south.

"Well, you're about to be a practitioner, so let's hope you read the right books because it's too late to change now," she said.

"I know."

The faint taps of gunfire rumbled in the distance as if Jackson himself knocked on their door.

GWEN
Bullis Family Farm, IA

Gwen walked her horse down a dirt driveway. New red metal-sided barns stood ahead, along with a beautiful renovated blue farmhouse with a freshly painted white porch ringing around it.

Haley held onto Gwen's stomach as they rode. "I see 'em," Haley squealed into Gwen's back.

Cattle tramped around an unraveling hay bale behind a thick, gated fence. Jake walked over to another bale of hay. He cut the twine off and a drove of cattle attacked the food.

"Easy now, Trixie," Jake laughed. He shoved a cow out of his way. He exited the enclosure and waved at Gwen with a work-gloved hand and a deep smile. He wiped his brow and walked for them. She waved at him, her heart fluttering inside her chest for a moment. *Why am I nervous?*

When he got close, she pulled her horse to a halt and he patted Patsy's flank.

"Whoa, Patsy," he said, rubbing the horse's thick shoulder.

He looked up at her through his five o'clock shadow. "I was wondering when you'd show." He looked the same as when she had dated him. Bigger and older now, his face more filled in, but still handsome with a farmer's strength.

"Had to run into town and talk to the mayor," she said.

"That old sleazeball." He scratched Patsy's nose.

"He hasn't changed."

His water-blue eyes met hers. "Some things don't." His eyes lingered in hers, the sparkle promising her a farmer's wife's life. A life she had almost had. A life she had turned away from.

"I wanna feed the calf," Haley hollered from Gwen's side.

"All right, little girl." Jake reached for Haley and she leapt into his arms. He brought her gently down to the ground. "You're gettin' heavy." He ruffled her hair. "Gram's been feeding you well."

"I eat what I want," she said in a high-pitched voice.

Jake patted her and pointed. "She's in the barn over there. I'll grab you a bottle real quick."

He offered to take Gwen's reins, and she handed them to him. He walked her horse over to a water trough. He wrapped the reins loosely on a post nearby. Gwen threw a leg over the horse and stepped down onto the ground. She gave Patsy a pat on the hindquarters.

"Uncle Jake, hold my hand," Haley said. He took his glove off and grabbed Haley's, heading for the barn and leaving Gwen behind. Jake pushed hard on the barn doors, rolling them open one at a time.

They walked inside. It smelled like dry hay and cattle. Jake walked over and picked up a bottle. "She's over in that stall," he said loudly.

Haley sprinted over to the stall and looked between the rails. "She's so little," she shouted, looking up at Gwen with the wonderment of seeing another creature that was young and little like her.

"She is," Gwen said. She smiled at the small calf. It couldn't have weighed more than sixty pounds. The calf lifted its head that seemed too big for its body and let out a weak high-pitched moo.

Jake leaned on the stall gate. "Yeah, the mother had a hard time. It was after all the craziness started." He bent low next to Haley, handing her the large bottle. "Here you go, kid. Now remember it's a baby, so you gotta be nice to it. You promise?"

Haley's head bobbed up and down. "I promise."

"Good," he said. He unlatched the gate and Haley ran in. Gwen followed them. Jake knelt down next to the calf and petted the top of its head. "Shh.

It's okay, girl." He waved Gwen over.

It had been so long since she had been around farm animals and their young. The calf reminded her of the tiny human life that she had inside of her.

"Go ahead, Hale," he said. Haley reached out and patted the calf. She held the bottle in one hand while petting with the other.

"Good girl," the little girl repeated. She put the bottle nipple near the calf. It stretched its neck to latch on.

"She's doing it," Haley hollered. Eyes wide, the calf sucked with all its might.

"Yes, she is," Gwen said, laughing. Jake laughed too and gave Gwen an extra smile. "She's a good eater. Just like someone else I know."

Gwen pretended to be offended. "Stop."

"Girl, I remember when you used to house those grinders at the state fair. Don't tell me you forgot already."

She laughed and then narrowed her eyes. "Who said I couldn't still?"

"Haven't seen it done in awhile," he said with a smirk.

"Doesn't mean it hasn't been done."

He put his gloves in his back pocket. "It's good to have you back home." His eyes seemed to twinkle at the thought and the reality alike.

She didn't lie. Being home felt right. "It's good to be back."

He licked his lips. "You know, I never had a chance-" he started.

Gwen held up a hand. "Jake, please."

She could see Haley eyeing them. "Can we walk outside?"

He nodded. "Sure."

"Haley, Uncle Jake and I are going to go take a walk. Do you remember what I said about the sick people?"

Haley rolled her eyes. "Gosh, like every ten seconds you talk about it. Don't let them close, run away, and tell an adult."

"That's right. It's very important. We'll be just outside."

Gwen and Jake walked outside, striding along the cattle enclosure. She crossed her arms over her body to hold in her butterflies and to keep warm.

"I never got a chance to plead my case," he started. His words always came out slow like he had all the time in the world for conversation. "I felt blindsided by the whole thing. It was like one day you just up and left for the city."

She kept her eyes downcast. "Jake, it wasn't about you. It was about something I had to do for myself. I needed to leave."

"And now you're back," he said with a small smile and a shy glance.

"Not by choice. You realize that the world is collapsing? People are eating each other alive. The government has broken."

He gave her a cocky smile. "No better time to be in Iowa then."

She was not humored. "I shot Dan Macintosh in the head on the way to town," she said quickly.

His face darkened. "Now, Gwen. I don't like the way you're talking."

"Ask my grandfather. It's true. Things will never be the same." *In the world or between us?*

He looked down at his feet. "I know, Gwen. I don't understand all of it, but I know it's bad. I seen 'em down by the river. I helped the sheriff take away some of the bodies, but it doesn't mean everything is different. People have to keep living, and there are still some good parts of life ahead."

She stopped and took his hands in hers. She felt the tears growing in the corners of her eyes. "Jake, I'm seeing somebody else. You know this. He's out there somewhere." She let her eyes drift out over the fields. *Or rotting in the dirt with the rest of my friends.*

"But he ain't here. And he ain't us," Jake said, jutting his rounded chin out.

The cattle mooed as they rummaged into their food.

"I know he isn't, but he's coming."

"I'm hearing what you're saying. Just remember that the way I feel won't change. There's just no one like you, Gwen."

She shook her head. "I'm not that farmer's daughter you fell in love with anymore." She let her eyes float away from him. "I'm not sure what I am." *Aside from pregnant.*

He cupped her chin and reached up, wiping away a tear from her eye. His hand smelled like dirt. "Sure you are. You're exactly that girl I fell in love with only a little older." He smiled. "And a little skinnier." His hand fell to her hip in exactly the right spot. "And a little more sure of herself." His face leaned close. "But still the same." Their lips connected and for a moment, she fell back in time.

KINNICK
Mississippi River

The island town stuck out of the Mississippi River as if it were built on a barge near the center. It seemed that any manner of flooding would take the island down beneath the water like a Midwestern Atlantis. A white water tower with a red roof gave the impression that the townsfolk had built a rocket in an attempt to flee to outer space.

Coffey took the throttle down and cut the SURC to an idle while the men aboard stared at the town. A cool breeze buffeted the SURC. They were the only boat on the river now. All the others had continued down the Mississippi River to the next villages and towns to build the defensive front.

Kinnick pulled out his map. GPS was a mess. All they ever got was a "connecting error" every time they tried to use it. At this point, they left the device off. His eyes scrolled south from Dubuque. They had overnighted in the middle of the river, anchored while the men slept. A sliver of green stuck out on the map centered in the river. Kinnick turned the map sideways and held it closer to his face. In tiny black lettering, his eyes could barely make out the name Warden written on the map.

"Should be Warden," Kinnick said, looking out at the island.

Coffey peered in the same direction. "Decent-sized town."

"Good vantages. Good control of the river. Easy control of access. This would make a formidable bastion. Now we only have to figure out if anybody's home."

Kinnick gave a short nod and Coffey instinctually maneuvered the SURC in the direction of the island without Kinnick asking him to do so.

A metal railroad bridge rose in the distance. The steel girders formed arching triangles and were rusted reddish-brown. A section of the bridge was swung out, separating a portion of the track from the rail. It appeared as if it had been moved for a barge to pass, but the operator had forgotten to move the track back in place.

"Either they're smart for separating the railroad to Illinois or they've already been overrun." Kinnick glanced at Coffey. The young Marine's gaunt face was taut like a bowstring and his mouth flat as if he had prepared to be punched in the face.

"Let's find out, Marine." Kinnick tried to keep his fears of finding the island infected deep below his surface.

"Oorah, sir." The SURC throttled up and toward the island. White water whipped up along the hull of the craft as it sped for the island.

As they got closer, Kinnick pointed, "Let's aim for the wooden dock there near the edge of the island. Volk, prepare your squad for contact."

Volk stood and shouted at the men with a nasty grin on his face. "You heard the colonel. Lock and load, Marines."

The Marines checked their M4s and M16s. They lifted magazines from their carriers, inspecting to make sure they were topped off with bullets and replaced them back inside their vests. Charging handles were inched backward to ensure rounds were chambered. Gore swung the machine gun toward the town and Duncan followed suit with his minigun.

"A little more time for Lucinda to get some love," Washington said. He held his M4 carbine upward and kissed the barrel.

"Why you call her Lucinda?" Boone drawled over to Washington.

"That's my grandma's name." The thick African-American man smiled, licking his lips, staring at his gun with affection.

Boone grinned with a confused look on his face. "Why in the hell would you name your gun after your grandma?"

Washington narrowed his eyes. "She's the best woman I've ever met, just like this fine piece of kick ass." He looked over a Boone. "She would whoop the whole lot of ya up and down the street with just a look."

"Must be one big mama," Hanger joked.

Washington gave him a glare. "Watch yourself, fool."

Boone smiled. "You gotta picture?"

Washington unfastened his shirt pocket. "Right here." He gave the photograph a loving look and spun it toward the group of helmeted Marines. A big round woman was centered in the photograph and could have been Washington's twin with a wig.

Volk gave him a smile. "What's she bench?"

"A hell of a lot more than you, Sergeant."

They roared in laughter.

Volk stood and looked over at the island. "You ugly sons o' bitches look absolutely badass. Get ready."

The Marines quieted down. Hunter and Hawkins were already standing crouched down, ready to jump ashore.

Hamilton One drew in closer to the island. Waterfront houses built in the '60s and '70s lined the shore.

Coffey let them glide within ten yards of a small private white sand beach.

Sergeant Volk pointed. "Drop the hatch." Two Marines popped open a hatch linked to the front of the boat. It flipped open and steps dropped down, getting them close to the shallow water where the Marines could jump the rest of the way.

The Marines and the two Green Berets splashed ashore followed by Kinnick. Kinnick's boots submerged in the water and its chill made him shiver.

No one complained as they marched onto the lifeless beach. His men turned quiet as they checked for threats, living or dead.

They walked past single-story homes with wide windows facing the water. Some were rundown or worn with age, and others had a newer look with better-kept lawns. The crew crept from the beach, guns in an aggressive low-ready, passing beach houses for the sidewalk adjacent to a two-lane street.

The sidewalks were different in front of every home as if each household was responsible for their own upkeep. A few of the slabs were chipped and cracked while others had fresh, newly cemented ones.

Kinnick's men moved cautiously down the street, passing houses with only dark windows. Other windows had been boarded up with random pieces of wood. Guns skipped from doorways to windows as they stalked by. Every man held the tension as if they expected to be attacked at any moment.

They reached a four-way stop intersection. A gas station sat on one side. Cars were parked in its four-spot lot. A small single family home was situated on the other side of the street. A brown wood-sided two-story restaurant was located on the other corner. The neon sign was dead in front. The lifeless letters made up the name Sheldon's Lucky Number Seven. Kinnick could feel the weight in the air as if somebody was close. His eyes bounced over the windows and doorways of the houses.

"I don't like it," Hunter whispered. He kept his eye moving like an automated turret.

"No infected," Kinnick breathed. The wind picked up and a mini sand cloud spiraled over the street and was blown away. The street was in bad need of a repair and sweep.

Hunter spit chew onto the ground. "We need to keep moving."

A voice boomed out down the street between the structures. "Come no closer." Guns pressed hard against shoulders. A few of the Marines took a knee to make themselves smaller targets. Others stood, training their guns on the different buildings, fearing an ambush.

A man stood on the wooden balcony of the restaurant. He wore a tucked in plaid shirt and a cowboy necktie with faded blue jeans. His hair was gray but encroaching on white. He leaned on the balcony handrail as if he were a king overlooking his domain. "Tell your men to lower their weapons. We don't want no trouble." His voice was strong and had an honest tone to it.

People appeared from the shadows of buildings and from windows. They were all armed with every manner of firearm. They held wood-stocked AK-47s, pump-action shotguns, AR-15s with optics, and scoped bolt-action hunting rifles.

"We got tangos on the left," said Duncan, his M249 SAW finding a target but staying silent.

"Same right," said Boone.

Hunter transitioned from window to window. Hawkins's gun was trained on the man on the balcony. Kinnick raised a hand. *If we walk out alive, there won't be many of us left. Only the dead and the recently dead, and who will stand up to the infected when they come streaming across the bridge and into America's heartland? No one, because we killed each other in the streets over nothing.*

Kinnick's gaze jumped from man to man to woman of the village. Almost all were white and wore every manner of clothes. Jeans, camouflage, hoodies, and tan work jackets. Most were dirty with untrusting eyes. "Lower your weapons," he commanded his men.

"Sir?" Volk said over the stock of his M4 carbine.

"Lower your weapons," Kinnick said louder.

The Marines bitterly obeyed and Kinnick thought they hesitated a bit too much.

Kinnick took a step forward and spoke loudly. "We didn't come here to fight." His words were for the man on the balcony, but they also served as a reminder to his men. *Remember that. These are Americans. We're here to protect them.*

The man on the balcony nodded. "That's good. We've seen a bit too much violence these days." The old man walked down the wooden balcony stairs. They complained as he stepped his way down. He strode the ground with friendly confidence up to Kinnick.

"Gary Sheldon." He stuck out a hand. The wind whipped his graying comb-over. A kind smile spread along his lips.

"Colonel Kinnick, United States Air Force." He would have said retired, but his paperwork said active now. He shook hands with the older man.

"To what do we owe the pleasure, Colonel?"

"Are you the mayor here?"

Gary smiled. "Nope, but I suppose I'm in charge all the same. Owner of Sheldon's Lucky Number Seven." He gave a proud glance back at the two-story restaurant. "Best meatballs this side of the Mississippi. One might say world-famous." He gave Kinnick a wink and a smile, but his smile faded after looking at Kinnick's face for a moment. He gulped uncomfortably. "What is the United States military doing here, Colonel?"

Kinnick nodded. "Can we talk inside?"

"Of course." Gary turned back to the people standing in front of their houses and taking cover in windows. "Everything is fine here." He waved at the people. "No need to worry. The military is here to help. Go on home."

Kinnick and his men followed Gary across the street.

Gary held open a storm door and twisted the door handle to his restaurant.

"Volk. Put Gore and Whitehead up on the balcony. No surprises."

"Yes, sir." Volk pointed at Gore and Whitehead and gestured upward. The two Marines trotted off. Their boots thumped up the wooden steps.

"Come on in, fellas. Take a load off." Gary held the white storm door open for the soldiers and Marines.

The restaurant was filled with four-person white-topped dining room tables. Black chairs sat around each one. A long counter ran along the far end and one could see into the back kitchen that lay dormant. The dining room was dark.

"Forgive me, Colonel, but we don't have anything but candles."

"Not a problem, Gary."

The old man bent down and lit a few. An older gray-haired woman came down the steps from what appeared to be living quarters above the restaurant and into the dining room. She looked nervous and rubbed a blue handkerchief between her hands in apprehension.

"Martha, this is Colonel Kinnick and his men. Can you put on a pot of coffee for them?"

She nodded. "Of course, dear." With a timid glance at Kinnick, she went into the kitchen.

Gary turned and smiled at Kinnick. His teeth were stained yellow from a lifetime of drinking coffee or chewing tobacco or both. "Power's off. I got propane rigged up to the stoves, but I don't suspect it will last the winter. Then, I'm not sure what we'll do."

Gary pulled out a chair and sat down. "Please," he said, offering a seat to Kinnick with his free hand. Kinnick followed suit, pulling a chair out and taking a seat. Hunter took a seat at the table next to Kinnick and Gary.

The Marines clustered at a few tables, removing helmets and gear that made it uncomfortable to sit down.

Gary folded his hands out in front of him, resting them on the table. "Colonel, what's been happening out there? We haven't heard a thing in over a month. TVs don't work. We get a bit of radio chatter, but it seems that nobody knows a thing and not knowing makes people's imaginations grow wild."

Kinnick met his eyes. "I'm glad to see everyone here safe, but I can't say much of my news is good." He paused. "But I hope to change that."

"It's a blessing to see you and your men, but I expected more men."

Kinnick tightened his lips. "Unfortunately, these are all the men we have. Over time, we should be reinforced." *Will they? I must keep their hope alive. If hope dies, then we die with it.*

Gary's eyebrows bunched together in consternation. "That's good to hear. Those things come from across the river. Terrifies the little ones, and I'll admit, it scares me too."

Kinnick took a deep breath. "Scares me too, Gary." *If you only had an idea of the hell that was coming.* He didn't say what he thought though for fear of destroying any fragile hope the man might have. "We're here to do more than help. My men and I are going to train you how to fight against these things."

Gary gave a half-smile. "What do you mean *train?*"

"We've been sent by the United States government based in Colorado Springs to assist in training civilians along the Mississippi River to fight the infected."

Gary's eyes narrowed and his brow scrunched. "Government in Colorado Springs? What about the government in D.C.?"

Martha set down cups of coffee in front of Kinnick and Hunter. Kinnick nodded his thanks.

"Thank you, ma'am," Hunter said, picking up the brew and sipping it. "Damn," he said under his breath as he burnt his tongue.

Kinnick blew on his before taking a sip of the hot coffee, letting it warm him up.

"I hate to be the harbinger of bad news, but Washington is gone. It was overrun by the infected in the early days." Kinnick watched Gary for signs of mental fatigue at the news.

Gary looked down at his hands. His eyes held sadness. "Worse than we thought. With all the violence and unrest, I suppose it was bound to be true." He sipped his coffee, his thoughts running away with him.

"All is not lost, Gary. The United States government is secure in Colorado Springs. It's a stronghold. We're still in the fight. Although there are a lot less of us now." Kinnick had left out the part about the nuclear holocaust engulfing the west coast.

Gary's eyes blinked as he came back from his daydream, and he glanced down at his coffee. "Warden's done fine without any government help so far."

"That will change. Masses of infected march this way, and that's why I'm here. I've been sent with hundreds of soldiers and Marines to help train communities just like Warden to fight against the dead."

"We would be grateful for the help, but I don't think we're really those kind of people. We're a beach community. We've got a few vets. Mostly they sit down at the Legion, tellin' stories."

Hunter chimed in with a smile. "Anyone can be taught. Training is my wheelhouse. I've trained goat herders in Afghanistan how to operate and ambush hardened Taliban fighters. If that can be done, and I assure you it is no easy feat, then I can teach your people here how to fight."

"We aren't soldiers."

Hunter smiled through his beard. "We aren't going to make you soldiers. We're going to make you fighters. We're going to instruct you in speed, surprise, and aggression at the highest level."

Gary nodded and looked a bit nervous. "We'll do our best." He savored his coffee. "Most people should come out."

"I'm sure they all can be brought in with some encouragement."

Gary looked down at his hands. "We can hope." They sat in silence for a moment.

A gunshot sounded from outside. It's boom repeating as the sound spread out like an earthquake. Hunter's chair banged onto the floor and he was out of his seat in a fraction of a second. Volk flipped a table, and Boone and Hanger hit the floor.

Kinnick was slow to reach for his gun, but his fumbling hands wrapped around the carbine and he moved it in slow motion to his shoulder. The Marines scanned out the window, trying to get an angle on the shooter while staying near cover and concealment.

"Where's it coming from?" shouted Ramos. The small Hispanic Marine crouched behind the wall, peering out the side of the window with his M249 SAW pointed out.

"I got movement by the water tower," Hunter said.

Then the screaming started. "Ahhh!" Someone wailed outside. Whitehead's voice intensified with urgency. "Help. Help."

Kinnick moved to the wide-stretch of window spanning the restaurant's front wall. Hunter crouched lining up his sights through the window. "Fuck. I can't see him." He turned his head. "Boone and Ramos, you and me, on three lay down cover fire toward that building by the water tower. Hawk, get up those stairs to that balcony and get that boy down here faster than green grass through a goose."

Hawk nodded, crouching near the door. Hunter gave him a smirk and shouted. "Move!" He shoved the door open and bolted outside followed by Boone and Ramos. The crack and ting of carbines and the bang of Hunter's SCAR dominated their ears. Hawk was through the door and up the stairs in a second.

Gunfire rippled through the street and Hawk came barreling down the stairs with Gore across his shoulders in a fireman's carry. Whitehead aimed his gun outward toward the small town. Hawk and Whitehead ran through the door. He laid the man on two dining room tables and began stripping his gear from his torso.

"Hunter, you're clear," Kinnick shouted.

The Marines and Hunter ducked back through the door. The Marines cautiously built barriers out of tables and chairs, covering the windows.

Hawk slipped scissors up Gore's shirt, cutting it off.

"Argh," Gore grunted in response. He coughed and cried, one after the other. "Please."

"Hold there," Hawk said calmly to Ramos.

"Oh, what the fuck, man," Ramos cursed. The white gauze turned red around the edges as blood seeped through.

Kinnick stood up and moved to where Whitehead stood panting.

"What happened?"

Whitehead shook his head tersely, still struggling to catch his breath. "I dunno. We was standing there smoking a cig, a second later, Gore is laying on the ground screamin'." Kinnick pushed past him.

Kinnick pointed his gun at Gary. "Who did this?"

The blood drained from Gary's face and he paled a lighter shade of white. "Please." Martha covered her face with her hands.

Kinnick took a step closer and pointed outside. "Gary, who did this?"

Gary glimpsed outside nervously. "I don't know."

STEELE
Burr Oak, MI

The small southern Michigan village was about ten miles from the Indiana border. The village had been completely overrun. Shattered windows. Broken-in doors, hinges bent and destroyed. The remains of over eight hundred souls were scattered about or outright missing. Gunshots cracked the air for twenty minutes as Steele's convoy made quick work of any infected stragglers that remained. The time between shots slowly trickled down to a few then none.

Tess parked Red Rhonda next to an old general store filled with antiques and other miscellaneous items. The sign read Bonnie's. Ahmed emerged from the front door with Larry and Nathan.

"It's clear," Ahmed said.

"Thanks, bud." Steele popped the door handle and gingerly stepped out onto the ground.

"Stinks like shit on the main floor, but upstairs is okay." Ahmed had found a way to cut his fuzzy-haired head since Pentwater but had left his impressive jet-black beard making him look like a foreign relation to Steele.

Steele took a few steps. His limp was getting better, but he still felt the pellets grinding away inside the tissue of his leg. The swarthy Egyptian-American man gave him a pained smile.

"Need some help?"

Steele gave him a brusque wave. "No. I got it."

Ahmed nodded his head and walked back toward the pickup bed. "I'll grab your gear."

Steele walked inside the two-story building. He ducked his head into the crux of his elbow as he stepped over the infected remains of the dead. On the far back wall, steps led upward. He hobbled for the stairs.

When he reached the upper floor, family photos surrounded him. The store owners must have lived above their store. Three small rooms and a common area with a kitchen were furnished in high 60's decor.

Steele made a beeline for a mangy-looking brown couch and set his M4 to one side. He used the armrest to lower himself down and exhaled. His bad arm ached, stiff with lack of movement. It begged to be stretched and flexed, his muscles needing both healing and exercise.

Ahmed's form emerged from the stairwell lugging two backpacks and he tossed Steele's bag nearby.

"I'll get my team up on one of those silos."

Steele looked at his friend. "Better yet. How about you get one of the pastor's teams up there? You and Margie can go check out that market for food."

"Not a problem." Ahmed turned to leave.

"Thank you," Steele said after him.

Steele propped his leg up and leaned back on the couch. The couch had sunken in butt-filled divots from years of use yet seemed to cushion him enough to be comfortable. *Not bad.* Within moments, he found himself in an exhausted sleep. He was blessed with no dreams of the pastor or the ghosts of the fallen. He awoke to knocking.

"He's sleeping. Come back later," Tess said.

When did she get here? He pushed himself forward on the couch and wiped the drool from his beard.

"The pastor wants to talk to him now," the voice said. The voice's tone was highly irritated.

"Then the answer is definitely no."

"He will take this as an insult," the voice said angrily.

If Jackson didn't string him up for a traitor, the incessant bickering of his divided people would certainly kill him.

Steele was actually surprised at how long Tess had debated the man. He lifted his voice up. "Tess, let the pastor in. I'll talk to him."

Tess glanced back at him and then at the interrupter in the hall. "You woke him up," she said with enough venom to kill a grown man.

"It's fine," Steele said, running a hand through his hair. "Let him in."

Curly haired and broad Peter entered the room followed by the tall pastor.

Steele flexed his hand on his injured arm. Peter planted himself in the room and averted his eyes to the side. The man was still afraid of Steele even in his current battered state. The pastor glided in with his hands behind him and took a seat on a faded maroon recliner, looking uncomfortable at the thought of kicking back and relaxing.

He stared at Steele for a moment before he spoke. "Mr. Steele, we must speak about our current disposition."

Steele gave him a fake smile.

"What is that, Pastor?"

"Like the Jews fleeing the Pharaoh, we must continue to make our escape or be caught in the Red Sea with our harassers." The pastor folded his hands in front of him. "I will speak frankly. The jeopardy of a few far outweighs the jeopardy of the whole. Our safety is assured when we move."

Just like Sable Point.

Steele's voice was steady. "I promised those men we would wait two days."

"The collective is far more important than the single man. Their sacrifice was for the better of all of us."

And drastically unbalancing the numbers between the Chosen and everyone else.

Steele kept his eyes hard. "If these men know I will leave them for the infected at the drop of hat, why will they stick their neck out for me? Why would they fight with us?"

"Those men fight for a better chance at survival. They knew the risks when they rode south against my men. They knew the risks when they rode north away from Jackson's men. If Jackson catches us here, he could envelop us like the Philistines did the Israelites at the Battle of Eben-Ezer, where the Israelites lost the Ark of the Covenant."

"I understand that, Pastor. I'm willing to risk that." *He's right. We should continue to run. Every minute we wait, Jackson gets closer.*

The pastor lifted his chin and let it fall slowly as if he were considering not agreeing. "I will pray for our salvation." The pastor stood, lengthening his tall frame. He towered over the crippled, sitting Steele.

"I hope to reconvene on the matter in the morning."

"We will talk then."

The pastor bowed his head slightly. Peter gave Steele a dark stare, and when Steele returned the look, Peter turned away like a whipped dog. The men left the room, creaking down the stairs.

Gunshots echoed outside the building. Steele grabbed his M4, leaning over the couch to get a look at the outside. His men shot the dead that wandered onto the main street of the town.

Tess appeared alongside him, angling herself to get a better look. "There are so many more the further south we go." Forms fell in the street, blackish blood leaking from their bodies.

"I expected as much. We are driving from the jaws of one enemy into the teeth of another."

A rap on the door drew their attention away from the sporadic gunfire on the street. "Come in," Steele called. Kevin's head poked in the door.

"Thought we could pass some time the old-fashioned way while we wait for the motorcycle clubs." He showed them a bottle of the Madam Scarlet Grey's Whiskey. "Grant's favorite."

Steele smiled for the first time that he could remember. "Ahh, the good stuff."

"The best rye," Kevin said excitedly. He sat down in a chair at a half kitchen table lined up on the wall. He inspected the former occupants' shelves, removing drink glasses. "These will do." He blew in one and dust puffed up in a small cloud.

Steele couldn't help but smile at the man. Kevin always knew how to lighten the mood. He set the glasses on an old kitchen table and poured the mahogany liquid into them.

Kevin picked up a glass and held it close to his face, sniffing the alcohol. "I know Ms. Tess will take a glass."

"That she will," Tess said.

Kevin cupped the glasses together, pouring the whiskey into each of them. He handed the partially filled glasses to his patrons.

Steele swirled the booze around in his glass, letting it coat the sides. Kevin slurped some of his down.

"Something on your mind, big fella?"

Steele continued to swirl. "Ha. I got a lot of things on my mind."

"Care to lighten your load?"

Steele gulped down some of the brown-gold whiskey. "Pastor wants us to hit the road and leave the Eighters and Geminis behind. The rest of the bikers are at each other's throats and are tied to us by a single thread." He took another sip, eyeing Kevin. "They may desert us before they fight for us." He rested the glass on the arm of the couch. "It's clear we can't trust the pastor, and with our forces spread out, he's running the majority in this camp." He flexed his hand, making a weak fist.

Kevin whistled and slurped some more whiskey from his glass. "Sounds like a right old mess."

"And he's worried about Gwen," Tess chimed in.

Steele gave Tess a glare. "Thanks for reminding me." He held his glass up sarcastically. "Good times." He downed a fraction of his drink.

"Mmmm, before I forget." Kevin held up a hand. He produced a worn brown book with yellowing pages. When he opened it, the spine of the book rasped with the effort.

"What's that? Another history book?"

An intoxicated smile stretched on Kevin's lips. "You betcha. A good one too." He held it closer to his eyes and read the spine and tapped it with his finger. "The Life of General Daniel Morgan. Looks to be an original too," he said excitedly. He turned the book in Steele's direction. The brown cover was beautifully embossed with twisted foliage surrounding four smooth rectangles brought together in the center with a shield-covered American bald eagle.

"Revolutionary War?" Steele asked, the name ringing a bell in the back of his mind.

"None other. Won some pretty important battles for us with some of the more innovative tactics of his day. You should take a read. Maybe you'll learn something useful." He leaned over and handed the book to Steele. The book had a decent weight to it. He flipped through the musty pages with care not to damage any. He held it up at Kevin. "Thanks. When I get a free minute, I'll take a look." He stuffed the book into his pack and he weighed the pros and cons of the extra weight.

"Just my two cents, but you should wait for the bikers. It could be the pastor's way of putting a wedge between you and the clubs." Kevin took a sip of his whiskey. "Not to mention the loss in manpower."

Tess lounged on the couch as if it were her pad. "Fuck the Chosen. Let 'em leave. We don't need them."

"As much as I'd rather them not be here, they have agreed to fight against Jackson. And I want these people close, not roaming around the corner waiting to sucker-punch us."

Tess's eyes narrowed. "I don't trust them."

Steele threw the rest of his drink back. "That makes two of us."

"Another?" Kevin said, raising the bottle in the air.

"Why not? Definitely making my arm feel better."

Kevin stood up and poured Steele another drink. His hand shook while he poured.

"You all right?"

Kevin gave him a quick smile, his eyes drooping. "Nothing that another glass can't fix."

Steele nodded. His friend's drinking was on the last rung of his concerns. Whatever got the man through to the next day, even if it was copious amounts of alcohol that made him wake up in the morning. They could have that conversation later. Nearby gunfire suppressed empathy for his friend. He snagged up his carbine by the pistol grip and spun over onto his knees. He sank into the deformed cushions and peered out the window below.

Filthy gore-stained hands beat the doors of the brick building across from him. People stared from above. Steele waved to them and showed them his carbine. Tess leaned over and shoved the window up, and Steele laid his carbine over the couch and the barrel out the window.

With one hand, he zeroed in on the infected. *Same as always big fella. Nice and easy on the trigger. Don't think, just let the trigger come back.* Crack. The downward angled shot entered the back of the skull like something had tapped really hard on its head. The bullet sprayed the infected's chin onto the doorframe. It collapsed onto the door smearing brain matter as gravity pulled it down the front of the door.

"Nice shot," Tess said.

"Not bad for the old worthless left hand of mine." He turned back to Kevin. "Feels good to get behind the trigger."

"I bet," Kevin said, nervously taking a sip of his drink.

Steele lined up his red dot on the other infected, his confidence growing. *At least this forces me to practice with my off-hand.* Crack. The other dropped. Steele looked up at the people across the way. He didn't recognize them, probably Chosen, but they gave him a thumbs-up.

Motorcycles zipped down the street. They only slowed to avoid the bodies in the streets. Steele's heart leapt for a moment thinking they were the Eighters or Geminis, but these riders had black wolves as their club colors. Macleod's club. They rounded the street engines roaring.

"They came back in a hurry," Tess said.

"They did." Steele snagged up his radio. "Macleod, what's your status?" He waited a moment before he repeated himself. "Macleod, status?"

"Ah, me and my boys are getting elevated. We got a pretty thick group of them coming up from the southeast."

"How many is that?"

"Five hundred or so. Hard to tell, they all kinda look the same and were packed together."

"Copy."

Macleod was silent, but he could see the man riding hard down the street.

Steele turned to Kevin. "I need you to spread the word down the street. We aren't all connected with comms and I don't want anyone caught off guard. I'll make sure all the biker chiefs and the pastor knows. Tess, can you get Margie and her team up here with me?"

Kevin belched.

Tess gave him a disgusted look and ran down the steps.

"Sure thingy," Kevin slurred. He stood with a waver and steadied himself on a chair for a moment before he made for the stairs.

Steele watched as Kevin stumbled onto the street. He pounded on a door. "The infected are coming," he yelled up at the people inside. He tottered for a moment like a child learning to walk for the first time and wobbled for the next building.

Heads poked out the windows of the two- and three-story buildings making up the main street. Heads were replaced with guns propped on windowsills.

"Commanders, this is Steele. We have a large group of infected coming our way. Get your people elevated and ready for an attack."

"We'll get them moving," Peter sounded off.

Others answered back in acknowledgment of a threat. Steele held the radio near his mouth for a moment.

Someone knocked on his open door. Margie stood there as if she waited for permission to enter his room. Her eyebrows always made her look worried, but her eyes had changed and now held a certain fierceness, like a mother bear getting ready to defend her cubs.

"Come in. Come in." He waved her inside.

"Sorry, Captain. Ms. Tess said to come up, but we didn't want to bother you." The mother almost looked embarrassed.

Steele gave her an irritated glance. "I'm not a captain. Get your crew set up. Are Trent and Larry up with their teams?" He had split his volunteers into small fire teams with a senior volunteer as their lead.

"Yes, Captain. Trent and Larry's teams are up," she said. She looked over at her volunteers. "Boys. Rick, Tony, and Harvey." Three Sable Pointers followed her inside. Rick and Tony had AR-15s, and Harvey had an old Remington Model 700 bolt-action rifle. They were all adult men in their late thirties, early forties. The men over ten years his senior nodded in respect to Steele as they entered.

"Captain," they said as they passed him. Steele wanted to bang his head against a wall, but some battles just weren't worth fighting.

"Volunteers," Steele said with a nod. *Why fight them on something that gives them hope? It gives them an identity. Units need an identity.* The men opened windows and pointed their guns onto the street, directed by Margie.

Steele pointed with this good hand. "They're going to be coming from that direction."

"That's perfect," Margie said with a smile. "Me and my boys can handle it." She took the closest position, resting her rifle barrel on the wooden frame of the window. She sighted her rifle.

Rick had brown curly hair and smiled. He whispered as if he worried the enemy would hear him. "She's the best shot."

Steele smirked. "I know she is. Lucky to have her."

Rick put his AR-15 up to his shoulder resting his stubbly cheek against the stock. "We agree."

They waited. Fifteen minutes later, Kevin stomped up the steps. "I saw them. They're here," he heaved. "You're lucky you got a bum leg or I would have made you do the run." He sat in a chair and poured himself another drink. He mumbled something into his drink. "You owe me a few at this point."

"I wish I could," Steele said.

Margie's hunting rifle cracked as a round exploded from its barrel. She pulled the bolt-action back and placed another brass-cased round in the chamber, sliding the bolt back in place.

"Get ready, boys." She zeroed in again. Boom. "'Cause here they come."

GWEN
Reynolds Farm, IA

Her grandmother, wielding a spoon like a dangerous weapon, gave her a disapproving look. Her grandfather sat at the parlor card table next to her and smirked trying to avoid eye contact with either woman.

Gwen placed her hands overtop her hips. "I'm *not* going."

"Oh, Gwen. Don't be such a stick in the mud. It'll be fun," Gram said.

Gwen's adamant tone turned to an irritated, endearing one. "Gram, there are people dying out there, and you want me to go to a town dance. Do you realize how insensitive that sounds?"

Gram's brow lined with wrinkles. "Nonsense. Who said you can't have fun during the tough times?" She raised her eyebrows in a declaration. "Me and Pa are going."

Pa looked up from his checkerboard and gave a short nod. His hand drifted to the board and he eyed little Haley. He picked a red piece up and set it back down. Gwen's phantom blond boy sat next to her grandfather, his hands beneath his cherubic chin while watching him play. It gave her anxiety knowing he wasn't real yet was still a part of her world.

Pa shook his head. "No, that won't do." He picked up another and set it back down. "Nope."

"Come on, Grandpa," Haley whined. The little girl squirmed as she waited, unable to see her phantom cousin sitting nearby.

Will she live long enough to know him? Will I? She steadied herself, trying not to be overcome with emotion.

He held up a red checker at Haley. "You must have patience, my dear." He clicked it over the board. Click. Click. "King me."

"Oh, come on," Haley said, exacerbated. She picked up a red piece and put it on her great-grandfather's. Haley picked up a black piece and jumped it once, twice, three times over her opponents.

"That's a triple bouncer," Haley exclaimed. She wiggled her head back and forth in a celebratory manner.

"What a fool." Pa smacked his forehead in mock disbelief. "No matter what I do, you're always two steps ahead, my dear."

"That's cause I'm smart and you're bad at this." She stuck her tongue out at him.

"Put that tongue back in your mouth or I'll snatch it," he half-threatened. He raised a hand in the air, pinching his thumb together with his index finger like a crab. "Just like your nose." The older man moved quick for his age. He brought his hand up to her face and squeezed her nose, pretending to snatch it away all of a sudden.

He held his hand up with his thumb wedged between his index and middle fingers. "See?"

Haley brought her hand to her face, feeling to make sure her nose was still there. "Nuh-uh, grandpa. I still got mine."

He opened his mouth and threw the invisible nose in. "Gone forever." He twisted his hand in front of his mouth as if he were locking it up tight.

Gwen laughed. Becky leaned over the table. "Well, I'm going to the dance. There's bound to be at least one man worth a damn in these parts."

Gram didn't look very pleased. "You're a mother, Becky. Language."

Becky rolled her eyes. "Maybe some of your friends want to go, Gwen." Her grandma nodded with encouragement.

Gwen gave her a glare. "Oh, my God. Fine. I'll ask them." She let the screened storm door swing closed behind her as she walked outside to the barn. Gregor had circled the vehicles around the barn to provide them with some sort of perimeter in case of an attack from the dead. She had felt guilty staying inside the house when her people had been stuck outside, but they insisted, considering her pregnancy. A tidbit of information that her family didn't know yet and a conversation she was actively avoiding.

Hank sat on a chair outside the barn. "Hi, Hank," she said on the way in. "Everything going all right?"

Hank managed a half-smile. "Slept better on the ground in a barn than I have in months in a camper. Just feels safer, ya know?"

"Yeah, I do. Remember, the infected are still around here. I killed one a few days ago."

The man gave her a half-smile that faded away in the realization he could never fully relax again. "I know."

She walked inside. Families had outfitted the stalls normally used for animals with blankets and tarps to give themselves extra privacy. The Clemens had even hung up a little sign that read their name on it.

People waved at her and made small talk with one another.

"Hiya, Gwen," Freddy said. The small boy ran up to Gwen and gave her a big hug.

"Hi, Freddy. You give such good hugs." She squeezed him tight.

Harriet stood near a stall gate and watched the boy, sadly smiling. "He's always been a lover." Gwen patted the boy's back and Freddy ran off.

"That's the happiest I've seen him since this all happened, and look," Harriet gestured with her chin over her shoulder. Char sat in a corner of the stall reading a book. "Your grandfather gave it to her."

Gwen couldn't help but smile. "What is it?"

"*Grapes of Wrath*," Harriet said, turning her head to watch the girl. "Not the most uplifting of stories, but I think she can find some commonality with her current situation."

"Say, what do you think?" Gwen paused, contemplating for a moment that she was even considering suggesting they all go to a dance.

Harriet's eyes turned questioning. "Yes?"

"Sorry. It's hard for me to think that this is a good idea, but there's a dance in town tonight. There'll be a band and everyone gets together."

Gwen read Harriet's brown eyes, looking for some indication that she was either an idiot for suggesting such a thing or a genius for finding something for them to do.

"Yes, Gwen." Harriet nodded. "Yes," she looked back at Char. "That's a great idea, music." Harriet sighed and she put a hand over her chest as tears filled her eyes. "Music. Instead of crying and moaning. That is a fantastic idea."

Gwen laughed. "I. Wow." She gave a sigh. "For a moment, I thought you were going to jump all over me for being insensitive, but you're right. We could use a distraction from all the chaos. And I haven't heard the sweet strum of a banjo-" She stopped herself. Images of Puck and the moonshiners back in West Virginia flashed through her mind. Puck's huge hands. Ashley's laugh. Casey's mean sneer. Lucia's dirty face. Gwen felt like she couldn't breathe. Lucia's lifeless face stared at her in her daydream. She couldn't inhale as the images stole the precious oxygen from her lungs.

"Are you okay?" Harriet asked, reaching out for her.

Gwen breathed hard as she came back to, feeling like she had run a sprint. "I'm sorry." Gwen shook her head. "A dance will be nice," she said slowly. Gwen gave Harriet a weak smile and walked to the middle of the barn. She had to shake the horrible memories from her mind.

"Hey, everybody, listen up." She waited until she had everyone's attention. "Hacklebarney has a tradition where every third Friday they have a town dance. Everyone is welcome. Might be a good way to get to know some of the Hacklebarney folks. Harriet and I will take anyone interested into town. If you decide to come, don't forget a weapon."

An hour later as the sun dipped in the gray sky, Gwen went back outside from her grandparent's house, dressed in an old red dress of hers from high school. A little snug on the hips and belly, but everyone would probably think she had just put on a few pounds since leaving Hacklebarney.

A crowd of people greeted her. She gave them a friendly smile. "It's good to see that everyone wants to go." She looked over at Gregor. "You want to fire up the bus and cram everybody in?"

"Sure thing," he said. The diesel engine fired up and her people crammed inside.

Twenty-five minutes later, they sat in front of a brick American Legion building. The windows were blacked out and two glass doors were propped open. A flagpole stood out front with the Stars and Stripes.

Lantern and candlelight poured outside the American Legion doors. She could hear the fast fiddle work of what had to be Jerry Jessup and the accompanying banjo of Nowlton Gebert. She turned to her group. They sat crowded in the seats and stared as if they had never heard music before. Tears appeared in a few people's eyes.

"Well, we can't dance in here, so let's get off this bus," she shouted. Everyone filed off the bus. They crowded the front door of the American Legion building looking in, hesitant to be the first ones into a dance they weren't invited too. They parted for Gwen and she stood in the doorway.

The music had a fast beat. B.B. Palmer jigged with his wife, Annie. Next to them, Kenny twirled Jenny Hamlin like he was trying to spin the dress right off her. The fiddle slowed down when the band finally saw her standing in the doorway. She took a bold step inside and the music stopped. The Iowans gawked at the Michigander refugees like they were ghosts. Gwen supposed they may be ghosts of a world that had passed.

Jake waved at her from across the room. "Gwen," he exclaimed. He walked up to her. "I'm so glad you made it."

She avoided eye contact, feeling awkward about their entire situation. "Ah, me too." Anxiety stirred inside her. The Michiganders cautiously walked inside and huddled near one another.

Jake caught her vibe and waved at the Michiganders. "Come on in, folks." He ushered them closer. He wrapped an arm around May Clemens, putting a hand out for the old woman's hand.

He turned to Ben with a gracious nod. "May I?"

Ben nodded his head vigorously. "You may, young man."

May gushed, holding a hand to her cheek. "Oh, I'm so flattered. You big schmooze, you."

Jake led her by the hand onto the dance floor. The band watched the newcomers.

"Well, come on, Jerry. That fiddle ain't gonna play itself," Jake shouted. "How about 'Amarillo by Morning'?"

Jerry grinned beneath his mustache. "You got it, Jake." He wedged his fiddle under his chin. Bringing his other hand with the bow up, he sawed into the strings with a flick of his wrist.

The rest of the band started in on the song with muted tones without speakers to magnify their sound.

Emboldened, Gwen's people mixed in with the Iowans. Red Newbold pulled at Gregor's hair.

"Damn boy, look at all that hair," he exclaimed.

Gregor stood silent for a moment regarding the old farmer. "You got any beer?"

"You betcha. Whatya fancy?"

Gregor thought for a moment. "You got PBR?"

Red nodded. "My kind of lad. Of course, we do. Come with me." The two went off in search of beer.

Millie Gebert came up to Harriet. "How old is she?" Millie asked Harriet. "She is so precious."

"She's twelve." And a little softer she said, "I'm kind of a surrogate for her parents."

Millie nodded. "These are hard times, but God will see us through. You know my Roland is twelve. I think they would make good friends."

Harriet smiled. "Of course. Char, why don't you come over here?"

Char reluctantly placed herself next to Harriet. She folded her arms across her chest and avoided the eyes of the older women like a prisoner looking to escape.

"Roland, get over here," Millie shouted.

A boy with red hair and freckles walked over with his head low. Any interaction with the opposite sex was the most awkward and terrifying experience he could imagine.

"Roland, tell Ms. Char she looks pretty," Millie commanded down at him.

"You look pretty," he peeped out. His eyes drifted toward the floor, embarrassed by the forced communication.

Char cracked a tiny smile. "Thanks," she whispered.

"You should ask her to dance," Millie said down at Roland.

Roland stood dumbfounded. He shuffled his feet. "I. Um." His mom nudged him closer. "You wanna dance?"

Char nodded shyly, and he took her by the hand. The two young people hustled onto the dance floor. Jake spun by with a beaming May Clemens. His eyes searched for Gwen, and when he found her, he gave her a wide smile.

Gwen watched the people as they swirled and swayed to the music. People danced in the night as if the world wasn't ending around them. Maybe for the Iowans, it hadn't really hit home, or maybe they were just carrying on with what they knew best.

Even the Michiganders seemed to be forgetting their problems. Hank danced with widower Bonita Perkins. Gregor drank beers with Red and his buddies. Kenny Hamlin twirled Joey around in circles and she smiled for the first time since Gwen had known her.

The music took a distinctly slower beat and the dim lights finally felt appropriate for the tune.

Jerry's voice washed over the crowd. "Ah folks, we're gonna slow it down now for some belly rubbin' music. Find yourself somebody to hold on to and don't let go." He tucked the fiddle back under his chin and began a slow tune.

Couples rejoined with one another. Jake made his appearance in front of Gwen. She knew this would happen sooner or later, but dreaded it nonetheless. He offered her a hand. "My lady, may I have this dance?"

She gave him an irritated look.

"Come on, for old times' sake." He looked nervously over his shoulder. "If you don't, Mrs. Wilkins is going to, and I can't handle her bad breath. So think of it as saving me from a fate worse than death." His eyes pleaded. "Please?"

She rolled her eyes and smiled. She placed her hand in his and he gently pulled her onto the dance floor.

His hand was warm holding hers, and his other hand drifted to her lower back. "You're even beautiful when you're upset," he said. She twisted her face away, not looking at him. He took her hand and spun her in a circle. She let herself be led around the dance floor by his hand that was dangerously low on her back.

"Come on, Gwen. Why do you look so downtrodden? I can't be that terrible of a dancer," he said.

She looked over his shoulder at the other dancers. "You know it's not you."

"Then what's got your goat?"

She gave him her best you-should-know face. "You're kidding me, right?"

He spun her again. Her dress picked up. She couldn't help but give up a tiny smile. "There it is," he said with a grin.

"Dancing with me isn't going to change what's happening outside."

He smirked. "But it sure helps." He dipped her low toward the floor and scooped her back up.

"Jake, I'm serious. Don't you get it?" She grew angry, her brow creasing.

He tilted his head back. "Sure. I do."

She put a hand on his chest and pushed him away. "No, you don't. You can't pretend this away."

She spun and looked at all the people. "You hear me." Jerry's fiddle emitted a few more notes and then the music died down. Everyone stared at her.

"Death marches this way and all you people can do is have a town dance? You have no clue what's coming, but I'm here to tell you." She turned in a circle and marched up on the stage.

Her voice boomed. "I'll tell you what's coming, Hacklebarney. Hundreds of thousands of the infected dead march their way across the land toward here. They consume everything in their path like a swarm of locusts. They leave nothing alive in their wake." She pointed at B.B. "They will bite you and tear you to pieces alive if they get the chance, and all you'll be able to do is watch yourself be ripped apart." She slapped her forehead as if she almost forgot. "Oh, and the men that come this way are even worse. They're led by a madman who will stop at nothing until he exacts some kind of vengeance upon us."

A child in the crowd started to cry. Millie looked angry. "Gwen, you're scaring the kids."

"That's good. They should be scared. You know why? Because it's the truth. Death is coming this way, and we don't have time to pretend it's not real."

Gwen stormed off the stage. Jake tried to reach for her and she blew past him. She went outside, breathing rapidly in sharp movements. Her breath misted in the cold night air. She put her hands on her hips for a moment then crossed her arms over her chest. The Mississippi River burbled as it flowed, lapping the mud banks as it passed by.

She felt warmth as a coat and arm were draped around her shoulders. The jacket protected her from the nipping night air. Jake squeezed her shoulders as he pulled her in tight, his bicep pushing her into his chest.

"That party sure died," he said.

She swatted him with her hand on his chest.

"These people don't understand. Those people from Michigan have only seen the tip of the iceberg. Jake, if you would have seen them pouring over that wall in Pittsburgh or those fences in Virginia. No one could stop them. There's just too many. And that's not to mention the threat of Colonel Jackson's army. U.S. Army, Jake, and they are hunting us."

She let herself fall onto his chest as if he were Mark, but he wasn't. It still made her feel safe and took her back to simpler times.

"I'll help ya." He looked over his shoulder back at the hall. "Even if they don't, you can count on me."

She looked up at him, straight into his eyes. "Truly?"

"You have my word and a man is only as good as his word."

He leaned down to kiss her again and she turned her head away, simultaneously putting a hand on her small rounded belly. He kissed the top of her head.

"Thank you," she whispered. Soft tears filled her eyes as she stared out at the black river.

GAT
Northern Michigan

Gat swerved his black-metal Victory Gunner around a rotting brown carcass in the road. Torch veered his Harley Davidson Street Glide the other way, avoiding the remains. They rejoined in the middle of the road behind a white 15' box truck, one that was probably used to deliver newspapers before the outbreak. Torch glanced back over his shoulder. His long red goatee blew in the wind, floating to the side of his neck.

"They're still behind us," Torch shouted.

Gat chanced a look back. The tan Humvee followed about forty yards behind the convoy. The bastards had followed them for almost ten miles, hanging back and pointing the .50 caliber machine gun but not firing.

The box trucks were slow, and no matter how much Gat pushed them, they couldn't put any distance between them and the single Humvee. Soon he would have to do something, but he had to dismantle the .50 cal or it would literally annihilate his club in seconds.

He gripped harder on his left handlebar and lifted his gloved right hand off the other side. He felt on his hip for his holstered Glock 18 9mm automatic pistol. He cross drew the pistol and pointed it over his shoulder. He used his legs to keep his 600-pound motorcycle upright. He bent close to the engine and flipped his Glock to the side, his arm outstretched behind him.

Bang. Bang. Bang. The handgun recoiled as he shot and shell casings disappeared in the direction of the ground, eaten up by the road.

He nodded at Torch.

"Tea-bag the fuckers."

Torch gave him an evil smile. He shifted his motorcycle and sped up the side of the convoy. A moment later, Siren and Goat drifted off to the side and turned down a forested side road with Torch.

The trees were naked, only a few dying leaves still clinging to their branches.

Gat watched them ride away. He looked back to see what the soldiers in the Humvee were going to do now. The gunner in the turret turned toward his bikers speeding away.

"Fuckers," Gat growled. Without looking, he twisted his arm back and fired off another six rounds. He didn't care where they hit. Killing wasn't the point, but if he caught one or two of them, he wouldn't have been upset.

"Over here," he shouted behind him. He needed the soldiers to follow him so his other men could get behind the Humvee and take it out. The Humvee continued to trail the biker gang. The turret swirled back in Gat's direction.

"Fucking retards," he said to himself.

He turned his bike a bit to the side and it shifted to the left. He edged the throttle and raced up alongside one of the trucks.

The trucks held only the motorcycles of the Eighters driving them, not the piles of food and ammunition like they had been designed to convey. They were similar to the convoys led by the Geminis and the Grave Guards fleeing east and north of Eighters.

Gat took his motorcycle near the door of the truck. Spook looked down through an open window at him. He was ugly with a fat nose and a scraggily brown and white beard running off his chin.

Gat gestured with his chin and yelled, "Turn this thing sideways when you reach the bend in the road. Make a run for the trees. Those Army boys are gonna prolly start shooting once we stop."

Spook grinned. His mouth was filled with brown teeth. "You got it," he shouted over the sounds of the road.

Gat moved his motorcycle up to the center of his gang. Forty-six bikers made up the Eighters. The playing card eight of spades was emblazoned on their leathers as the gang's colors.

He pulled up alongside his enforcer, Bodey, and gave him a nasty look. "We kill them at the turn ahead."

Bodey had a burn scar running down the center of his forehead down and along his nose, giving him a pink and red top-heavy T down the center of his face. It was a permanent warning from the Hell Hounds to stay off their turf. A Hell Hound hadn't been seen in Michigan since the Eighters went to war with them three years back. Gat had organized their extermination. He'd had their clubhouses burnt down. Their shipments of guns intercepted. Members shot in their homes and in the streets. No mercy was asked and no quarter given. Once the Eighters went to war, it was either Gat and his club or death for them all.

His club got ready to take the bend in the road. The Humvee behind them slowed down leaving them more distance. Gat zipped to the front. He nodded to his Road Captain, Sphinx. The grizzled man nodded back in return. He was a true "Yooper," hailing from the Upper Peninsula of Michigan and knew Northern Michigan well. Not the first time they were in a tight spot and it wouldn't be their last. That man knew all the roads and had adjusted their route when the military had picked up the chase.

Gat had expected the military to catch up eventually. That was the plan. Now it was time to scrub the bastards off the planet's surface. He adjusted himself as he bent to the side to act as a counterbalance to the motorcycle. He blinked. A boxy vehicle filled his eyes. Not more than one hundred yards away sat a Humvee sideways across the road. In a fraction of a second, smoke bursts pushed from the end of the turret gunner's .50 caliber machine gun.

"Fu—," Gat shouted. He threw himself to the side and the bike crashed on top of him, but he didn't stop. When you put your bike down, there were over a hundred and one ways that one could be ripped apart. There was road rash, the removal of the upper layer of skin that came from sliding at high speeds across the pavement. There was any kind of head and neck trauma that came from banging one's skull off the concrete. The mangling of limbs resulting from high impacts with the ground. Then there was sliding into trees, walls, guardrails, and other vehicles. Gat had laid his bike down a few times in his day and that's what made riding leathers essential. It blocked the elements—wind, rain, sun, and bugs—but more importantly, gave the rider a chance to slide on the pavement without needing a skin transplant.

Gat's body hit the ground hard and the bike continued to rocket forward ahead of him. He covered his head with his arms trying to keep his head from acting like a brake. It would only take a couple of seconds for the pavement to rub away the skin of the skull to the white bone underneath. He instinctually picked his feet and legs up. The sliding of his leathers buffeted his ears but was overpowered by the fast-paced booming du-du-du-du of the M2 .50 caliber machine gun. His body drifted to the side of the road and cement turned into gravel. In a fraction of a second, he was slammed into a dead-leaf filled ditch.

He flipped himself over onto his belly, adrenaline driving every muscle in his body. If he had busted anything, he wouldn't know it for the next few seconds. His formed a nasty snarl as member after member of the club were putting down their bikes. A few had driven into the ditches and crashed before being thrown over handlebars. As they impacted the trees, their bodies and limbs mangled and splintered with sickening thuds only overpowered by the machine gun fire.

Gat watched, the event frozen in slow motion, as another motorcycle glided over the pavement in his direction. He rolled to his right over and over, and the beautiful Harley flew past him, bending itself around a pine tree. Gat pushed himself to his knees and stood up. He squeezed his eyes together tightly for a moment, his mind still disoriented from the crash. *Did I fucking crack my skull?*

The Humvee held its ground in the middle of the two-lane road. The .50 cal was obliterating his club with deadly efficiency, scattering his gang across the pavement and into the trees. A new member, Junior, tried to stand up and the .50 popped his shaved head clean off his neck. Davey crawled over Granados trying to reach the forest. The machine gun twisted him sideways into the air as if a fire hose filled with bullets drove him down the pavement.

Gat reached to either side of his waist and released his dual Glocks from their holsters at his hips. Each one held an extended magazine of thirty-three hollow point rounds. They would melt onto armor, but into exposed flesh, he was guaranteed extra damage to his victim. He canted his handguns at forty-five-degree angles for slightly easier aiming when dual wielding. He let his thumb ride up near the rear of the side of the handguns to full-auto. He limped out of the ditch, pointing the guns at the Humvee.

Gat aimed low, knowing that his rounds would ride up as their velocity drove the barrel upward. A camouflaged soldier knelt next to the Humvee, taking three-round burst shots at the fallen bikers.

"Hey, you fucking cucks. Over here," Gat shouted.

The soldier looked his way, surprise lighting up on his face. Gat let his left handgun buzz in his hand. He wasn't counting, but the force of so many rounds so fast took the soldier to the ground. Gat let his right handgun ride up the windshield of the Humvee into the soldier on the turret. He let his right Glock go empty on the soldier. He chucked his piece to the ground and it clattered on the pavement. He limped his way past the first soldier who was a bloody steaming mess.

The soldier laid on the ground, eyes as wide as he could make them. He sucked air in through his nose.

As Gat got closer to the Humvee, he stood next to the gasping soldier, stretching his neck to see inside. Without a glance, Gat's left Glock buzzed and he sent a few rounds into the lying soldier's head. The quick succession of bullets stopped the man from breathing, denting his face with entry wounds. Red blood, white bone, and pink brain splattered the pavement.

Gat walked by the passenger window. He let his Glock spray into the window, bursting it inward and finishing the driver who slumped over an empty windowpane. He clicked the magazine release on his weapon, letting it drop to the ground. He dug a long, full thirty-three round magazine from inside his jacket and inserted it into the magazine well. He pointed the weapon back inside the Humvee.

Dead eyes stared back at him from the turret gunner who had crumpled down onto his knees inside the Humvee, his arms still suspended on the turret above. He limped around to the other rear side of the Humvee. The stock of an M4 lashed out. Gat dodged to the right and brought his arm up at same time. The soldier swung his M4 wide like a baseball bat, clubbing Gat's gun from his hand.

"You fucking twat," Gat screamed. His hand seized in pain, trying to absorb the trauma. He backhanded the soldier in the face, sending him crashing into the back of the Humvee. The soldier dropped his empty weapon. Gat reached down to his boot and drew a long blade from his ankle. He took a swipe at the soldier, driving him away from his weapon. The soldier rolled off the back of the Humvee and made a quick run for the rear driver's side door. Gat chased him. The soldier threw open a tan door and dug around in the back of the Humvee.

"Face me like a man," Gat taunted him.

The soldier started to turn around, but Gat already had him. He grabbed the soldier's chin and cupped it with the bony part of his wrist. The soldier's skin was rough and unshaven beneath the skin of his arm. The soldier cried out and squirmed. Gat wrenched him by his neck and drove the tip of his blade into his right kidney. Once. Twice. Three. Four times his blade pierced the soldier's ACUs penetrating his flesh in rapid succession. The soldier screamed in unimaginable pain and spasmed in Gat's vice-like grip. Gat kept shanking the soldier until he stopped squirming and went limp in his grasp.

Gat shoved him facedown into the backseat of the Humvee. The body slid down onto the floor. Hot blood ran down his hand. Gat flicked his wrist. He looked back at the remainders of his motorcycle club. Pieces of his members lay discarded on the ground. Their motorcycles were scrap metal, almost unrecognizable as having once been highly functioning machines. The men were a mix of blood, leather, and flesh, scattered everywhere as if a bomb had exploded in the middle of them.

"Well fuuuuuck you guys," he cursed. He looked back over his soldier lying on the floor of the Humvee. The soldier's arm moved an inch off the floorboards. Gat cocked his head to the side. "Gotta little juice left in ya, huh?" He turned around and marched back.

He got within a few inches of the soldier's face. "You stupid fucks," he screamed, dry saliva flying from his mouth. He drove his knife into the soldier's front torso over and over. "You think this is a fucking game?" His blade sunk into his belly. "Cause I ain't playing." He jabbed again, ramming the blade into his chest. He raged on the soldier long after he'd expired, his body transformed into an unrecognizable slab of chopped stew meat. Gat bent close to his face, hacking spit from the back of his throat. "You dirty."

He heard its wheels crunch slowly over the metal of the bikes adding insult to their desecration. The shocks absorbed the weight as it drove over the bodies of his club. A Humvee rolled up from the other direction.

He took a step away from the dead soldier and faced them. The tan Humvee braked only ten yards away. Gat could clearly see the faces of the driver and passengers and the all too deadly .50 caliber machine gun sighted in on him. The barrel pointed down on an easy target to destroy.

A staff sergeant stepped out of the passenger side. He had a dark mustache that was turning into a full beard.

He shouted. "Where's the rest of the convoy?"

Gat gave him a wicked sneer. "Come over here and I'll show you."

The staff sergeant waited a moment, looking down at his feet before he spoke. "Is Steele here?"

"Yeah. He's back over there."

The staff sergeant looked over his shoulder and back at the bodies. His eyes glanced at the woods and then back at Gat.

Gat started to walk toward them. His riding boots clicked off the ground and he spread his arms wide. "Why don't you little fuck boys put down your guns and see if you can take me out the old fashion way?" He waved his knife at them. "Come on. What are ya? Chicken."

"Stop where you are," the staff sergeant yelled. His gun bounded up to his shoulder and his shoulders hunched as he made his form tighter and compact.

Gat took another step forward and licked his teeth. "What? 'Fraid I'll bite?" Gat sneered. *One more step and I'll be close enough to charge the fuckers.*

He felt the fire bite him before he heard the roar of the machine gun, but not enough for his brain to register there was a difference. The ground grew closer and he knew something was terribly wrong. He tried to gather his feet beneath him, but only bloody shredded stumps moved in the air.

"Oh fuck," he screamed. He looked down. White bone and jagged destroyed flesh remained above his knees. He could see his leather boots nearby. After a second, he realized the rest of his legs were still inside them.

The staff sergeant walked his way and stopped, staring down at him. "Consider that our warning shot."

"You fucking blew off my legs," Gat snarled.

The staff sergeant's lip curled. "Be thankful I didn't have them aim a bit higher. Could have lost your third leg."

The soldier squatted down on his heels. "Was Steele here?"

The pain morphed into an unbearable searing sensation. Nerve endings screamed to be reconnected inside his legs. Gat could feel his heartbeat pumping blood out of his body with every thump in his chest. He stared down at his stumps and laughed like a madman.

The staff sergeant snapped his fingers. "Hey. Hey. I'm up here. You don't have much time before you bleed out, but I'll get you some morphine so you won't feel it when those infected get here." His dark eyes looked distantly down the road.

Gat ground his shaved head into the pavement. Upside down, he peered farther down the road. A hazy form stood in the distance. He looked back at the soldier. "Fuck me and fuck you."

The staff sergeant nodded and stood upright. He clicked his tongue. "If it were me, I'd hope to bleed out before they got here." He glanced down the road again and back at Gat. "But I ain't you." He stared off into the distance. "Don't worry about the whole Steele thing. We were only sent out to make sure no stragglers got away. Jackson didn't bite on whatever this little mission was."

"Go fuck yourself," Gat spit. His mouth finally had moisture in the form of frothy metallic blood.

"Already did this morning." The staff sergeant walked away.

Gat pushed his chin up to watch the man close the door. The Humvee rolled forward. He could hear the soldiers faintly talking to one another as they checked the dead behind him. Gat felt a certain detachment as if his body didn't belong to him. His body grew cold as if winter had set in only on him.

He struggled to get his belt off then wrapped the looped belt over his thigh. He grunted as he cinched it as tight as it would go, but he knew it wouldn't matter. He lay there breathing hard, trying not to die. He heard the Humvee engine rumble away then the faint moans of the infected who had come for their share.

STEELE
Burr Oak, MI

Bodies of the infected dead lay strewn over the small town's sidewalks and the paved streets. They had been gunned down from the safety of windows and rooftops as they marched into the town. The infected had moaned in defiance as bullets exploded their skulls into thick pieces. Steele's forces had performed with violent expediency that only apocalyptic experience could provide them.

Steele's upstairs room was filled with smoke from the gunfire. Harvey and Tony shook hands in success near the windows.

Margie looked up from her handiwork below with a glint of satisfaction in her eyes. "Good shooting, boys." She stood up, slinging her hunting rifle over her shoulder. She was well into her fifties and did not look like a soldier, but she was one. "Let's go meet up with Bessie at the truck. We'll get those mags refilled and some more rounds."

Steele nodded to the men.

"Captain," they each said as the volunteers filed out of the room.

Steele stopped Margie. "Your team shot well. You are a natural leader."

She looked a bit abashed, and her eyes drifted to the side. "I only did what you and Thunder taught us to do."

"You do it well. Be careful out there. Could be stragglers."

Her eyes met his again and she gave a small smile. "We'll take care of them." Faint gunshots still rang out from other parts of town.

Steele nodded to her. "Carry on, volunteer."

She bowed her head and disappeared down the steps.

"How about a victory shot?" Kevin said. He held up the bottle of Madam Scarlet Grey's. The remaining liquid sloshed inside the bottle. Steele shook his head no.

"I think I've had enough for one day."

Kevin shrugged his shoulders. "Suit yourself." He tipped the bottle back and poured the liquor into his glass. He gave Steele a drunken smile as he imbibed the alcohol.

"My leg needs a stretch." *I also need a new arm.*

"I'll be here," Kevin said. Steele left his M4 on the couch.

"You want some company?" Tess asked. Her arms were spread wide on the cushion backs of the couch. She was as comfortable as she could be in somebody else's house.

"No, I'm fine." She watched him with dark eyes as he walked lamely away.

Steele limped through the room for the stairs. He hobbled down some steps, using the railing as a crutch to make his descent a little easier. When he reached the bottom, he padded through the general store. Bodies had been shoved away from the door by Margie and her team.

Vacant white eyes stared up at him. The poor tortured soulless leaked their dead insides into murky pools on the street. Red guts had been split and splashed onto the pavement. Pieces of bone, muscle, and flesh muddied the ground like a split bucket of slop. He gave them a wide berth.

The town only had a single main street with a few buildings. Every subsequent street had fewer buildings and more houses. A grain elevator rose up from behind the small town businesses. He walked unevenly down the street until a hand reaching from a pile of the dead stopped him.

The infected man's cheeks were gaunt as if he had starved for months before turning. Its hair was stuck to its skull. Part of its scalp was ripped away exposing white skull bone. Bodies pinned it to the ground, its legs broken and disfigured beneath them.

It moaned at Steele in a low guttural call of the wild. Its struggle was fierce and sad. It had all the pieces of humanity within it except life and awareness. Dirty fingernails clawed the body in front of it. It raked the dead body repetitively, trying to extract itself from its flesh and bone prison.

Steele let his left hand fall onto his sidearm. The motion was foreign to this hand. Most of his training had consisted of transitioning to the off-hand only if his dominant hand was injured in a fight. It was a temporary survival measure to ensure victory, but now he was asking his off-hand to do all the work. He would have to teach himself how to reload with a single hand and charge the weapon as well as work on drawing the gun out of the holster. Thunder would have to switch the magazine release to the other side of the weapon so he wouldn't have to use his index finger to release a mag.

He drew his sidearm. The weight felt off in his hand. His left hand was like a younger brother always mimicking the elder brother to his right, who did everything with confidence. His middle and ring fingers gripped the scratchy taped handle hard. He let his pinky finger wrap loosely around the handle. His index finger fell awkwardly on the trigger. The tip of his thumb arched off the gun but simultaneously squeezed the frame. His sight picture was flat across the front and rear of the weapon.

Steele and the infected stared at each other for a moment. The infected snarled at him, their eyes never leaving each other. The slide cycled backward and the gun recoiled up toward the sky much more than he would have liked. *My grip will be more important without a supporting hand.* He wouldn't notice it too much from seven yards out, but the farther back he got from seven, the harder it was going to be for him to shoot accurately with only one hand. *I guess I should be thankful most gunfights happen within five yards.* He turned the gun on its side, looking at it. *I'm going to have to work on this if I want to gain any sort of speed out of the holster.* He put the gun back near his holster, finding the edge of its hard plastic with the barrel of his weapon. The metal rubbing as it settled into place. His weapon secured, he looked up.

A cluster of twenty men moved down the street at a slow pace. As Steele grew closer he recognized them as Chosen men with axes, bats, clubs, knives, and batons as they walked among the fallen infected bodies. They swung their weapons violently downward, executing any of the infected yet moving. Peter led them with a mini-sledgehammer in his hands. The sandy-haired man eyed Steele with mistrust.

"How was it?" Steele called out.

"No problem," Peter shouted. Other men stopped to look at Steele, hatred in their eyes. Anger. Steele was the direct result of the deaths of so many of their friends and family. A few swung weapons back and forth. A man slammed his cudgel, a short stick with a knotted end, into the skull of an infected. It made a sickening *thwack*. He glanced up at Steele with a mean gaze on his mustached face.

They plowed their way through the bodies in his direction, crushing skulls as they navigated the carnage.

Steele stopped as they got closer. The men drifted in around Steele. At first it was three men, then a few more walked up casual and confident. Steele backed away touching the brick building behind him. It took another moment, but more gathered around him in a semicircle, Peter at their head.

The hairs on Steele's neck stood up. A gang of men with weapons.

A few laughed under their breath. The man with the cudgel tapped it in his hand, blood dripping from its rounded edge. A Chosen man in plaid laid a wood axe across his shoulders. He looked like he wanted to spit on Steele then split him in half with the axe. The others pushed in a bit closer.

Peter stood the closest. He was brave when surrounded by his men. He never would have been so brazen with Steele alone. His grip was white-knuckled on his sledge like he was trying to strangle it.

"You know, you really have to be careful out here," Peter said. "With that limp and ugly scar on your face, you might be mistaken for one of the dead."

If Steele was a patrol officer, he would already be calling 10-33, officer in need of assistance, retracing his steps in a swift backpedal for his cruiser. *Can't outrun them.*

"Well, lucky for me, we are having a conversation."

A long greasy black-haired Chosen smiled at Steele. His teeth were browning with scum.

"I only see one thing that needs to be purified here." He licked his lips as if the thought made him salivate.

The man in plaid spit on the ground. "He looks like the devil himself."

"He's the asshole that caused this mess," added the man with the cudgel.

"That's debatable," Steele said, giving the man an unafraid glance.

The energy from the group started to turn violent. Peter fed on the energy gaining confidence by the second. The group inched forward. Steele's hand was on his gun, but how many shots could he get off before one of them took a club to his head? *Three?* They didn't care. They only wanted revenge.

Take the initiative. "I'm gonna play you guys straight. If this goes down like you want it to, at least three of you are gonna die. Now, I'm using my left hand and I'm a bit out of practice, but I won't miss. Not this close."

"He lies," the long-haired one hissed, his lips quivering.

"That's right, Luke. Close your ears to the serpent's tongue," Peter commanded.

Steele kept his eyes moving from threat to threat. "I'm not lying, Luke." Steele couldn't step back any farther.

Luke smiled as he waved a knife from side to side.

Steele looked right at him. "I'll be sure to put the first round through your gut." Steele shifted his eyes to the man with the axe next to him. "Then I'm going to put two into your chest. I'd do one, but you're a big boy, and I want you to know you're out of this fight. You'll die in about a minute." Steele's eyes moved to the man next to him. This man was losing confidence with every second. "And you will probably take one through the jaw. I'll ride the recoil up into your face. Really depends on if I want to save an extra round for Peter." Steele's eyes drifted back to Peter. Peter's throat moved up and down as he gulped.

"Peter, you remember our time together, right? Tell your friends I don't lie."

Tension hung over them and Steele counted down in his head. *It's gonna kick off on my terms. Five, Four...*

His radio popped, crackled, and blared. The men stopped staring at Steele. A few glanced at his radio on his belt. He'd have to move his hand off his gun and to the radio.

"Steele, this is War Child." War Child was scouting north, arguably the most important direction for Steele to keep informed about. Their last contact with Jackson's Legion was south of Grand Rapids and north of their current position.

"Steele, War Child. Do you copy?" War Child's voice grated on the other end of the line.

Steele took his hand off his gun and slowly put it on the radio. It was one or the other. His eyes never left Peter. If they came for him now, he would most likely only get off one shot before they took him, but Steele made sure Peter knew it would be him that took that bullet. He brought the radio to his lips. "Steele here," he said low into the mic.

"We're coming in hot. We got some of Jackson's scouts following us hard. Boys are definitely itching for a fight. They may be after something I picked up for us."

"What'd you pick up?" He brought the mic away from his face a moment. The Chosen hadn't jumped him yet. They listened intently to his conversation. *Run or fight?*

"Found an almost full fuel tanker at a rural gas station. Gas looks good, not too dark. Should keep us going for a while."

"Excellent. Lead them into the town. We'll set up a little surprise for them, but protect that cargo."

The Chosen men watched him with less volatility, but anger still simmered under the surface.

Steele hooked the radio back onto his belt, feeling better now that his hand was back on his sidearm. "Jackson's scouts are coming in fast. Do you want to do this now?"

For a few seconds, Steele thought he would be living his last. The Chosen stared defiant, contemplating his demise.

"Or can we put a hurting on them instead? I need men on top of every main street building." Steele's heart rate sped up in his chest.

The Chosen stood silent for a moment before Peter spoke. "You heard the man. Luke, let's get them resupplied and in position."

Luke gave Steele a nasty stare that turned into a devilish smile as if he would enjoy sticking every inch of his knife in Steele's flesh.

"Brother Peter's orders. Let's prepare a welcome for the Roman scum." Luke and the Chosen men jogged off. Peter stood for a moment. Steele thought he might say something.

"Remember, Jackson is the enemy," Steele said to him. He didn't wait for Peter to respond. He turned around and limped away from them, an easy target to be clubbed down from behind but no strike came. People darted back into buildings and scrambled back into firing positions.

Steele walked haltingly inside the antique store, sidestepping the bodies and going up the stairs. When he reached the top of the stairs, he was exhausted. He tottered for the couch. Tess turned and looked at him from behind.

"Wondering about you. Saw you making friends down the street."

"If that was making friends, I'd hate to see what making enemies looks like. On that note, we're about to make a few new friends." He picked up his M4 in one hand and draped the sling around his shoulders.

"Jackson?" she asked.

"Who else?"

Tess's eyes darted back out onto the street.

"Get to the roof for this one. Better against somebody that shoots back."

Tess and Steele climbed more steps to the roof of the store. The roof was flat and sealed with black tar. Brick walls rose up, encircling the entirety of the two-story building. Steele limped over to the wall and rested his M4 on it. Tess followed his lead and joined him. Kevin wobbled up and set his M4 against the wall.

Tess gave him a questioning look. "You sure you can shoot straight?"

"Wouldn't be able to without the stuff." Kevin hiccuped and wiped his mouth.

Steele peered out. Heads poked up from the building across the road from them. As far as he could see, his people were lining the buildings of the small town.

Footsteps pounded up the stairs and Margie with her team ran in. They took their place along the roof edge, and their weapons clinked on the red brick. Margie whispered something up to Tony and he squeezed her arm.

They sat in quiet anticipation, each contemplating what they were about to do to the soldiers coming their way.

Steele could hear the motorcycle engines before he saw them. The War

Machines slowed down when they hit the village limits and began navigating the bodies layering the streets. A semi drove behind them along with a fuel trailer hitched to the back.

War Child's voice came through the radio. "Thanks for the heads-up. You get in a fight recently?"

"We had a large pack come through."

"I can see that." The old biker was in front, off-roading his bike over a body. The fuel-truck barreled over the dead, unfettered from the bodies.

"There they are," Tess whispered. She held a set of binoculars to her eyes. The leafless trees allowed them even more visibility from the rooftop. About eight blocks away, a convoy of Humvees followed the bikers in hot pursuit. Dead leaves blew up in the air as they sped through them.

Steele put his radio near his lips. "Commanders. Don't open fire until they reach the center of town. Watch the crossfire. I don't want any blue on blue out there, but I want them in too deep so they can't escape. War Child, get that tanker out of harm's way."

Affirmatives echoed over the radios. People nodded on rooftops and windows. The message went down the line from building to building.

The tan military vehicles rolled past the first buildings. The men on the turrets were fixated on the last of the War Machines turning the corner. The front Humvee turret barked in the direction of the bikers. The bikers in the back ducked low and cut the corner on the opposite edge of the main street.

Steele set his M4 carbine on the wall using the roof ledge to rest his weapon. He squatted painfully down for cover. *We need cover. These devils fight back.*

The soldier in the lead Humvee's turret slapped the top of the truck as they drove excited to get in the fight. The Humvees slowed as they ran over the bodies in the streets. The man in the lead turret glanced upward. His eyes widened when he saw Steele and all the guns aiming down on him. He swung his M2 .50 caliber turret up. It didn't matter. Steele had been tracking him the whole way. He decided that this one would be the first to die.

Steele's bullet blew through the man's cheek and exploded the man's neck into the top of the Humvee. The whole right side of the soldier's neck disappeared, turning into red mush. The soldier's arm still held onto the gun as his body collapsed into the turret.

Hundreds of bullets destroyed the first Humvee, and the turret gunners on the second and third Humvees were killed outright. The driver in the rear Humvee of the recon unit had quick reflexes, and in a single second, he had thrown his Humvee in reverse and was racing backward down the street.

The gunner on his .50 cal machine gun sprayed windows and rooftops. In the chaos, another soldier appeared in the second Humvee turret and unleashed hot lead into the building across from Steele. In a flash of deadly violence, those people were gone. The bullets turned breathing, living people into red mist, totally destroyed by the large caliber rounds.

"Everybody on that gunner," Steele screamed. They concentrated their fire on him and he took cover as the driver navigated backward.

Near the edge of the village, the Humvees set up in a V with their vehicles. Soldiers hopped out and took cover behind doors. The gunners unloaded into the nearest buildings, driving people into cover. The gun battle blazed away from Steele's building, but he knew what they were doing.

In a stationary battle, his forces would lose. Surprise was his only actionable tool. That and mobility.

"They're keeping us occupied until Jackson's main force can get here." He lifted the radio to his lips. "Building by building get everyone into the trucks. We're getting out of here."

He turned down his line. "Margie, I need you to reinforce the pizzeria and the church down the road. No risks. Just keep them wasting ammo. I don't want anyone getting hurt."

Margie nodded, her eyes wide. Americans had been conditioned from a young age to respect and admire America's fighting men and women for not only their prowess but also their bravery. Now, he was asking them to go toe-to-toe with the military, numbers the only discernible advantage in the fight.

"They may be trained by the best in the world, but these men are not those honorable men and women who still fight for this country."

Margie frowned and nodded at the same time. "I know."

"I'll go with you," Tess said. She met Steele's eyes for a moment.

He nodded. Tess was one of his staunchest allies and one of his only friends. Losing her would be detrimental to his position, on top of losing a close friend. "Okay, keep it safe."

They filed off the rooftop, staying low as they moved. Steele listened to the rattle of the .50 caliber machine guns versus the small caliber weapons popping off in retaliation. His people's gunfire sounded weak and insignificant in the face of their foe, a child's complaints versus their parents' commands.

He brought the radio back up. "We're leaving. Retreat southwest."

KINNICK
Warden, IA

Private Gore groaned in the corner of the restaurant. Duncan and Ramos pointed M249 SAW light machine guns out the storefront windows. People sprinted across the street outside. It wasn't clear if they were running from the Marines inside or the snipers outside. Either way they ran in an attempt to not get hit by gunfire.

Gary sat in a chair, wringing his hands in front of his body. Hunter grabbed Gary by the collar and fear plastered his face. Hunter hoisted him out of his seat. "You set this up, you treacherous ferret?"

Martha sat in a chair at the table and held her face in her hands, sobbing. Gary stammered. "I. I. No, we didn't."

Hunter got his single eye close to Gary. "It doesn't look like it."

"I swear. We didn't. I don't know who would do such a thing. We're honest good folks. We wouldn't hurt American fighting men."

Hunter stretched his lip with his tongue in frustration as if it were searching for a wad of chewing tobacco. "Well, somebody did."

"Enough, Hunter," Kinnick said. He paced, trying to figure out his next move.

Hunter released Gary and the old man fell back in his chair. Martha sobbed and Gary wrapped a comforting arm around her. "It's okay," he whispered to her.

Gore moaned out. "Hawk, can you make him more comfortable?" Kinnick said in his direction.

Hawkins walked back over to the injured Marine and checked his bandages.

"The bleeding's stopped," Hunter said. He looked over his shoulder at Hawkins. "Hawk is good at what he does, but he isn't a doctor and we aren't in a hospital. Gore needs a doctor."

Kinnick looked at Hawkins's back. The man's movements were calculated and precise as he worked on the wounded Marine.

Sergeant Volk approached them, his steps sharp and volatile. His face was extra bitter. "With all due respect sir, what are our orders? The shooter is still out there. They could be organizing an attack on us as we speak. Let's kill the cuck."

"I know that, Sergeant."

The man's face said he was all but too eager to enact vengeance on anyone he saw fit. "We have to find the people that did this. We'll make them pay."

"Enough, Sergeant," Hunter said. His one eye conveyed extreme violence in Volk's direction. "Show some respect for the colonel."

"Yes, sir." Volk went and took a seat near the impromptu barricade. He leaned close to Whitehead, speaking in hushed tones.

"Gore needs a doctor," Hunter repeated.

"Then we'll get him one." Kinnick turned toward Gary. "Do you have a doctor in town? Or a clinic?"

Gary's eyes worried. "Course we do. Dr. Yentz is just down the street."

"Get him."

Gary looked confused and gulped. "Okay, we will." He wiped some thinning hair across the top of his scalp and gestured at Martha to stand up. He grasped her hand in his. "Come on, honey."

Kinnick gave Hunter a short nod. Hunter put a hand on Gary's shoulder. Gary flinched. "She's gonna have to stay here."

Gary's lip stiffened and he brow furrowed. "What do you mean? She's my wife."

"And she's going to stay here with us until you get back. It's safer this way."

Gary looked at Martha and she bit by bit took a seat back at the table folding her hands in her lap.

"Hurry up, Gary," Kinnick said sternly. He didn't like keeping the woman as collateral, but he saw no choice. If the man loved his wife, then he wouldn't get into any foul play.

Gary bent down and kissed his wife. She hugged onto him for a moment. "I will be back with Dr. Yentz." Gary moved with surprising agility for a man his age and exited the building. He quickly disappeared down the street.

Kinnick turned toward the Marines. "Volk, get Hanger and Tran over to the SURC. There should be a harbor around the other end of the island. Go check that out for any signs of people or anything that doesn't look right. I don't want our crew left defenseless while we figure this shit out." He turned toward Martha. "Is there a way out the back?"

Martha nodded, her chin quivering in fear.

"We aren't going to hurt you, Martha, but we need your help to stop these people."

She blinked rapidly. "Of course you won't. Why would you?"

He reached for her and she winced, cupping her hands in one another. She stared down at her hands.

"We won't," Kinnick repeated.

She nodded her head slightly, staring out into nothing. "You shouldn't be here."

Hanger and Tran passed by them, trooping through the kitchen to slip out the back.

Kinnick turned back to her. "We're here to help."

"Not everyone wants you here," she said, staring at her hands.

"Who doesn't?"

She sat silent her eyes distant.

"Who doesn't?" he repeated. He watched her for a moment before deciding she wasn't all there.

Within twenty minutes, Gary returned with Dr. Yentz, a middle-aged man with gray hair and thick glasses. His eyes were wide beneath them as if he were stuck in a constant state of surprise. He looked at Hunter and the Marines and blinked, taking in their rugged fierceness.

"Where's the boy?" the doctor asked. He held a brown leather medical bag in one hand.

Volk led him to where Gore lay on the table. Gary walked quickly back to Martha and hugged her. Kinnick ignored them and approached Hunter, still watching the doctor with an untrusting eye.

Kinnick brought his voice low. "We need to get these people in line and on board, or we must leave."

Hunter's one eye glanced at Kinnick from the side. "Copy, sir, but what about Executive Order 17766?"

Kinnick sighed and looked at the wall. Pictures of people drinking, eating, and celebrating dotted one side of the restaurant. *Surely the whole community didn't deserve to be burnt down for the actions of a few. Unless they were all in on it.* He eyed the back of Dr. Yentz again. *He could be killing the boy now.* "I cannot give that order without more evidence and it better be damn clear."

Hunter turned his way. "Sir, it's damn clear they don't want us here."

Kinnick shook his head. "I'm not leaving here until we have a definitive answer. This is a good strong location. This could be a key link in our chain of defensive outposts."

Hunter sighed. "Just to have them shoot us in the backs when we get done teaching them how to shoot. I've seen it happen before."

"Our mission is to mobilize these people. They're scared and somebody is making them scared. If we can free them of whatever devil plagues them, then we will win them over."

Hunter smirked. "Win over their hearts and minds, Colonel? Maybe you should kiss a few babies while you're at it."

"Hell, I'll babysit their kids if it brings them on board."

"With all due respect, Colonel, shouldn't they already be on our side?"

"They should, but they are mistrustful and with good cause. When they needed help more than ever, we were too busy arguing over the political ramifications to take the necessary actions to defeat the virus. Now, we have to play make up. We have to win them back. It's a hostile homefield crowd."

"I think I'd rather be playing at a friendly away game."

"Me too, Master Sergeant."

Kinnick walked near the table where Dr. Yentz hovered over Gore, his back bent.

After a moment, he looked at Kinnick from the side with very wide eyes magnified by his thick glasses.

"What's it looking like?"

Dr. Yentz blinked big deer-like eyes. "Your medic did an exceptional job, but without taking him across the river to the hospital, I can't be certain what his fate might be." Yentz let his voice drop low. "He probably needs surgery, but I can't tell without actual testing. I'm afraid he's suffering from internal bleeding that I'm not equipped to stop in the long term."

Kinnick rubbed his brow. "Is the hospital operational?"

"Went dark over a month ago."

The young Marine's face was pale, his soft fuzzy mustache barely visible. His chest rose slowly and fell as if he only slept.

Yentz looked disappointed. "His fate is in God's hands now."

Kinnick nodded. "Thank you. Do you know who did this?" Kinnick threw it out there. *What could it hurt to ask the man if he knew of anyone?*

"I can't believe anyone would do this. Sure, we have our fair share of local idiots, but they're harmless." He paused and spoke lower. "But I wouldn't put it past them neither. There's been a lot of talk 'bout where y'all been. To see you show up now may have rubbed people the wrong way. Aren't you supposed to be helping us, not asking for help?"

"No one can do this on their own. We need each other or this won't be much of a fight at all." Kinnick met his eyes. "Do you understand? If we could do it on our own, we would have already done so."

"It's that bad?"

"Worse."

They stared at one another for a moment. Kinnick debated whether or not to tell the doctor about the nuclear holocaust engulfing the west coast. He figured that wouldn't help the trust between them and held his tongue.

"You may go, doctor."

Yentz's eyes lit up. "Really?"

"We aren't in the business of taking hostages. We're here to help."

"Thank you, Colonel. I will check back tonight to make sure he's comfortable."

The doctor took his medical bag and wandered toward the front entrance.

Volk pointed. "Where's he going?" He watched the man quickly open and close the door, leaving the blinds on the door quivering. The doctor retreated down the sidewalk at a brisk pace.

"I let him go." Kinnick was calm. He knew he was playing the long game with these people. He needed to take one hundred perfect steps for every mistake he made with them. That's how trust was built, one good step at a time where he made the right and sensitive decision with the people's well-being in mind. Then they would see him and his men like they were supposed to, as protectors and liberators and not as occupiers and invaders. He didn't think it would be fast, but he believed it was possible with enough calculated persistence.

"What if he's one of them, telling everyone about our defenses?"

"He's not."

Volk's eyes scrunched up. "But how do we know? Shit, he could have been the one pulling the trigger."

"I can tell, Sergeant. He's not our suspect." *He's not telling the whole truth though. He was hiding something, but he's not the shooter.*

Volk shook his head in disagreement. Kinnick thought he heard the sergeant say "bullshit" under his breath.

Kinnick turned to the side, looking over his shoulder. "Gary. Come here."

Gary stood up and hesitantly walked to Kinnick like a timid dog that needed more convincing. "Yes, sir?"

"Can you get everyone together? I mean everyone in Warden."

Gary looked scared. "I...I can try."

"Call them all together."

Gary looked at Kinnick.

"Now," Kinnick commanded.

Gary stepped through the Marines and walked up the stairs to the balcony. Kinnick followed him. Hunter grabbed his sleeve.

"Colonel, what are you doing? There's a sniper still out there."

"We have to trust each other. No one is going to buy in if I stand next to him with a gun to his head or hide inside with a gun to his wife's."

Hunter shook his head in disappointment. "Sir. I don't think that's a good idea. In fact, I don't think it's a good idea for us to even stand here. Kitchen is better."

Kinnick patted the soldier on the shoulder. "Sometimes it's better to be brave than smart."

Kinnick followed Gary up the wooden outdoor stairs. He took a step next to Gary. The small island town was laid out before them. Nothing moved, almost as if it were deserted.

"Go ahead," he said to the man.

Gary hesitantly put a megaphone to his lips and his voice boomed. "Warden," he said and his voice magnified. "Warden, come on out. It's safe. They won't shoot."

A minute passed before the first person emerged from their house. They were followed by groups of ones and twos. They trickled into the four-way intersection in front of the restaurant.

They stared up at Kinnick and Gary. Kinnick looked at the crowd, wondering if one or more pointed a gun at him from afar. If the sniper struck him now, he wouldn't know it was coming. Only a zip, pain, and then the echoing of the rifle from afar, or if he got lucky and hit Kinnick in the heart or head, it would just be black out, game over.

"Is that all of them?"

Gary looked out. "Looks like it."

Most of the people had guns and worried looks on their faces. Some looked angry, others generally upset.

Kinnick motioned he wanted the megaphone. Gary placed the megaphone in his hand and took a step back, wary of what Kinnick was about to say or maybe he knew the shooter was zeroing in his rifle on Kinnick at that very moment.

Kinnick cleared his throat and put the megaphone to his lips. "People of Warden. You have a murderer in your midst, and I want him alive."

STEELE
Roseville, IL

He crumpled a plastic bag in his hands. Crumbs lined the bottom, but its caloric contents were gone. He let the bag float to the floor. The chain grocery store's front windows had been shattered at some point and the shelves inside picked clean of anything useful. Animals had gotten everything else.

"You find anything?" he called out at Kevin. The former schoolteacher looked at him overtop the short aisle shelves and grimly shook his head.

"Nothing," Tess shouted from the other side of the store. She kicked a grocery cart with a boot, sending it rolling away. It banged as it struck the wall.

Steele walked down a dark, empty aisle. His damaged leg still hindered his natural gait, but it was manageable. He cut through a checkout lane, its number three sign dead. The gum, candy, razors, lighters, and soda had been cleaned out of the small shelves near the register leaving them empty. It felt wrong to him and out of place for a store. The cash register drawer was busted open. A few dollar bills stuck out. He snagged one and held it up for a second. George Washington's iconic face stared back.

Kevin spoke. "They called him the American Fabius."

Steele held the dollar in his hand for a moment. "What's that mean?"

Kevin hiccuped, clearly already well into his daily allotment of liquor. "Derives from the Roman Quintus Fabius Maximus Verrucosus, well-known for many things, but in our case, he developed the Fabian war strategy closely followed by good old George there."

"What's the Fabian strategy in a nutshell?"

Kevin smiled. "You don't know, do you? You're a follower and don't even know it."

"No, I don't."

Kevin shrugged. "It's a strategy of war where you avoid frontal assaults and pitched battles in favor of attrition and indirection."

It was Steele's turn to smile. "Ha. If you call retreating every chance I get 'indirection' then yes, that's been my plan the entire time."

"Not a bad tactic for the underdogs."

"True." Steele shoved the dollar in his pocket. He never expected to use it. "I just wanted a memento of the old world." Bullets, food, and water were this world's currency.

They exited the store, crunching through broken glass to reach the outside.

His convoy of cars, pickups, semis, and motorcycles stood in a long line looking more like a rural county Fourth of July parade than anything resembling a fighting force. Macleod sat atop his motorcycle, watching Steele with untrusting eyes. His long black goatee draped down his chest.

Steele shook his head at the man. "No food."

Macleod's face twisted in anger, and he spit in disgust. He waved his Wolf Riders forward. He roared his engine, taking off back to the front of the convoy.

The food situation had gone from bad to worse when it was discovered almost half their stores of food inside the semi had expired. Now the convoy was forced to stop and quickly scavenge in towns as they fled before Jackson's forces. Steele chanced a glance back in the direction they had come.

War Child and his War Machines had formed the rearguard and were a few miles away. A good sign, for the time being was that Jackson wasn't right on top of them. Unless he was flanking Steele's bogged down forces while they stopped for supplies. Or perhaps he was enveloping them as they foraged, encircling them with a noose made of men, guns, and Humvees. Frankly, Steele didn't know much about his enemies movements.

Steele walked back to his pickup and Tess ran around to the other side, hopping into the driver's seat and turning the ignition. The engine turned over and then after a struggle started. "That's a girl, Red Rhonda," she said to the truck patting the dash. She steered the pickup back into the convoy.

She stared ahead as she spoke. "We don't have enough food."

Steele gave a hasty knife hand out the window and the convoy rolled to a start. "I know that."

"People need to eat and things are going to get nasty if we don't find anything." She closely followed the truck in front of them, bringing the pickup to about fifteen miles per hour.

He didn't say anything. He didn't have an answer. "Hey, you. What are we going to do?" She continued looking back and forth from the truck to him.

Steele watched the trees, houses, and businesses ease by them. The sky was a muted gray as if the world was suddenly devoid of all color, mirroring their dire predicament. "I don't know. We either starve and go fast or slow down and scavenge for food."

Her voice grew soft as if they could hear her. "What about the clubs? They are in it for the food, and now, we don't have any."

"They'll get what they were promised when we reach Iowa. Right now, nothing matters unless we get there in one piece."

"So you're going to let us starve?"

His face set in a scowl. "Yes, goddammit."

She shook her head. "This is messed up. What kind of leader lets his people starve?"

"One that doesn't want his people shot."

"We need food too," she continued.

Steele threw his hand up. "I knew this wasn't going to be a walk in the park, but I need your support. There are no magic bullets here, just bad and worse options."

Tess shook her head. "You swore to lead and defend these people through the worst times anyone has ever seen." She placed her hand on his arm. "No one said it was going to be easy." She released his arm. "That's why you have me."

"Thank you, Tess, but if we panic, we'll break. I need you to help me keep everyone together."

Bright red brake lights slowed them down, and the convoy came to a rolling halt. Steele ignored it for a minute. He scooped up his radio.

Before he could speak, gunfire sounded far-off from the front of the convoy.

"What's going on up there?" he said into the radio. Static scratched out. He glanced at Tess before he leaned out the window, trying to get a better view. The drawn-out line of vehicles stretched over a mile along a dusty rural road.

"Sounds like it's coming from the pastor's contingent," she said.

"Shit. What the hell are they shooting at? Take me up."

Tess twisted the steering wheel and rolled up the side of the road, cruising past all manner of vehicles.

She slowed near a section of the convoy that was splintering off the road down a residential street. Over fifty men clambered down the center of an unlined bucolic avenue. A blond man with a perfect comb-over waved a wooden flail around his head like he was a knight in medieval times. On the other end, a horde of infected marched their lonely way toward them in opposition.

"Forward, brothers and sisters. Let us cleanse the earth of this wretched curse," he shouted. Tess stopped the pickup behind them.

"Hey!" Steele shouted. He pointed out the window at the blond man. "Hey, you." The blond man turned to face him, fervor in his eyes and a fresh white smile upon his handsome face.

"Yeah, you. What's your name?"

The man walked closer. His khaki pants were somehow clean during the apocalypse. "My brothers call me Matthew."

"And what are you doing?" A volley of gunshots kicked off as the Chosen men moved forward at a slow walk. The bullets struck the infected, knocking some back and others down, but any infected that hadn't been impacted by a headshot rose back up and continued their trudge. "By the time the infected reach this road, we will be long gone."

Matthew laughed too loud and it turned Steele's insides just a touch.

"God has other intentions for us that you do not control. Join us and help purify these tormented souls."

"We don't have time for this."

Matthew gave Steele a small bow. "No man may command me for God moves my feet and directs my hand." He turned his back on Steele and walked back to his line of followers. They walked slowly, firing at will.

Steele shook his head in anger. His hand drifted to his sidearm, but it rested there in anticipation of the battle to come. No good would come from a shootout between him and fifty Chosen, but their blatant disregard for the convoy's safety and waste of ammunition were enough for to make his blood boil.

"Look at them," Tess said. She scrutinized them with fire in her eyes. "They're insane."

Steele clenched his jaw. "And stupid. They are compromising our position."

The long line of Chosen kept up with their intermittent gunfire. Infected tumbled and fell as bullets aimed high bit through their rotting flesh. When the unorganized remaining infected got close, the Chosen men and women changed over to bats, clubs, knives, and spears.

Steele watched the blond man run forward ahead of his followers and swing his wooden flail side to side, the weighted end cracking skulls from its front swing to its backswing.

Steele spied the pastor's navy blue Jeep sitting in the open ahead.

"Take us up there." Steele pointed. Tess rolled the pickup forward, pulling alongside the pastor's open-air Jeep. Peter sat behind the wheel and dirty-haired Luke stood in the back an AK-47 in his hands.

The pastor perched regally in the passenger side, his hands folded in his lap. His black shirt's lines were crisp as if it were freshly dry cleaned and pressed. His long face watched his men destroying the infected with a pleasant fervor. Tess rolled down her window and Steele yelled through it.

"Pastor!"

The pastor's lips twitched in pleasure and a slow smile crawled across the older man's lips. "Mr. Steele." He nodded. "Have you come to watch my people at work?"

Steele twisted his neck to the side as if he were stretching. His lips ground together in a frustrated half grin. "No, Pastor, I did not."

"A pity. Matthew has quite a knack for it."

Matthew whirled his flail over his head and arced it down, smashing an infected woman's skull. Bodies covered the residential street as if they were having a block party and everyone passed out at the same time.

"Pastor, with all due respect, we do not have time to stop and *cleanse* this neighborhood. There's a greater enemy on our trail and I don't want them catching us."

The pastor blinked slowly as if Steele's words annoyed him. "With all due respect, Mr. Steele, there is no greater threat than those marked by the Beast."

Steele weighed him for a moment. "Can we wrap this up? I would hate to have to move the other parts of the convoy forward and leave your men and women exposed."

Cheers went up on the residential street. Steele couldn't make the words out, but he knew "God" and "Victory" were two of them. The Chosen walked among the bodies, whacking anything that still moved with blunt weapons.

The pastor stood up and saluted his men. "Bravo, my good men."

"We don't have time for this."

The pastor finished acknowledging his men and waved Steele away as Matthew approached.

Blood soaked the man's preppy sweater. His khakis were saturated with guts and grime.

"Excellent work, Brother Matthew. You have done a great service to this community. God's Kingdom grows today because of your valiant actions."

Matthew bowed his head in deference.

"Any causalities?"

Matthew smiled. He took the back of his hand and wiped his forehead, smearing blood across it. "None, father."

"A blessed victory. You may bring your expedition to a close for I fear Mr. Steele is very concerned about Colonel Jackson's men catching up to us and I agree. We must be going."

"As you wish, Father. We came across a family down on the end. They are grateful and wish to join us."

"Give them a fair share of our food and water. If they are sick, have Adam or Carter to see them. We care for all our people." He gave Steele a small smile and a sideways glance from the corner of his eyes. Matthew bowed and walked back to his waiting cohorts.

"Great shooting, everyone. We are going to be on the move in five minutes." He held up his hand, fingers spread out. "God has blessed us this day."

Steele crunched his teeth until his jaw ached. The pastor had defied him. He had destroyed a number of infected as well as rescued people and recruited them to his cause all in one move. *I must keep this man closer than kin.*

"If you stop again, we leave you," Steele said at the pastor, not to him. If the pastor wanted another debate, he wasn't going to get it. Steele had stated a fact. Steele would ultimately lose if he had to leave the pastor behind, or lost his people to Jackson, but the point had to be made. He needed the pastor in line.

Steele pointed a knife hand forward. "Let's move out." The window was up before he was finished. Tess rolled the pickup forward.

"I don't like that guy," she muttered. "With his mumbo jumbo, do you hear these people? Father this. Father that. It's like he thinks he's some kind of gift from God."

"I'm pretty sure every time we talk, I sprout a few more gray hairs. I don't like him, but we need him."

Tess snorted. "We don't need those crazies."

"We do," Steele ground out. "I don't like it, but we need him if we are ever going to stand a chance against Jackson. We just need to find a place where we have the advantage, and that place is not here. Remember the plan."

Tess's dark-as-coal eyes darted his way. "If he even looks at us wrong, I'm going to put him down with a nice little .45 caliber bullet."

Steele let his head fall back on his headrest with force. *To think that only a few months ago I wanted to be a team leader.*

He watched the tall oaks and younger maple trees scroll by. "I know you will."

MAUSER
Roseville, IL

Colonel Jackson drew his forces to a halt along a rural road. The Humvees sat idling and turrets swiveled as soldiers scanned, waiting for orders. Farm fields lay fallow, stretching away from the road. Waist-high yellow grass dominated the fields. It gave the gunners on top of the Humvees excellent coverage of their surroundings. It also gave Mauser a minute to relax.

Mauser's two Humvee squad was in the center of the column. He put a foot up on the dash, a SCAR-H pointed downward between his legs. His slid down his seat using the back to lean his head against.

"You think it's Zulus?" Brown said. His hand was looped on the steering wheel. He stretched his neck trying to see what the hold up was over the other Humvees and was still too short to see anything. He shrunk back down.

"Don't matter. We'll go balls deep in some Zulu ass," Jarvis piped up from the back. He leaned forward closer to the front seats, the smell of his rotting fingers wafting forward. Mauser shifted in his seat away from the soldier.

Brown smirked. "Ha, like those chicks last night."

"They was all about it." He nodded. "Mauser, when you coming out with us, man? I'm telling you, these chicks will bang anything. The apocalypse makes them so horny."

Mauser waved a hand at them. "Not my style, man."

"What, you like dudes?"

"No, but I don't like to troll the civilians and get sloppy seconds from one of you heathens."

Brown gave him a side eye. "'Fraid of bein' Eskimo brothers?"

"I ain't afraid of nothing except what Jarvis has got."

Jarvis smirked. "Can't catch what you already got."

Mauser wrinkled his nose. "Come on, man, what did I tell you about those fingers? They fucking stink."

"Good. Luck. Charm. The infected don't like it."

Mauser peered over his shoulder. "They fucking stink like Bigfoot's dick."

"I got Bigfoot's dick, sir, right here." Jarvis grabbed his crotch over his pants and pulled on it.

Mauser shook his head. "Jesus Christ, what's wrong with you guys?"

"Nothin," Jarvis said from the back, defensive. He gazed out the window.

The radio buzzed drawing Mauser's attention.

"Squad Foxtrot, position?"

Mauser reached for the black receiver and picked up the microphone. He held it close to his mouth. "Squad Foxtrot is near the center of the column."

"Move on up. Colonel wants to see you."

***

Colonel Jackson laughed. It was way over the top for the situation and it made Mauser uncomfortable. He gave Mauser a wide-eyed, crazy look.

"What the hell is this kid thinking? What is he? Some sort of martyr?"

Mauser stared out at the bodies laying discarded in the street. They looked like discarded human trash. "Were they attacked?"

Jackson gave him a dirty look. "They're way too far off the beaten track to run into." He shook his head in an exaggerated manner. "No. No. Somebody went out of their way to kill those monsters."

Jackson touched a stubbly chin with his finger. "Kid moves much slower and we're going to catch him in the next ten miles." He held up a map. "Or we'll catch him on the river."

"You don't think he'll split his forces and try to give us the slip again?"

Jackson snorted and shook his head. "Why? Didn't work the first time."

He chuckled. "Sergeant Baxter's squad finished off one group and Lieutenant Rhodes chased the others across the Mackinaw Bridge. If he has half a brain, he will try something else. I know you were his friend and that his betrayal stung us both."

Mauser avoided Jackson's eyes. "It did." *More than you can know.*

"That's what joins us even more than the rest. I gave him a chance and he embraced it with a knife in the backs of my men. He betrayed us both." Jackson stared out at the lifeless bodies. "Do you know why we are a legion?"

Mauser followed the colonel's gaze. "Because of our size."

Jackson smirked, a skeleton grinning. "Partially yes. We have over a thousand fighting men here, but it's more than that. We are a group of men that all share something more than merely being in the same unit. I have men from sixteen different commands within my unit. Do you know why?"

Mauser glanced at him, feeling uneasy that he might come up with the wrong answer. "Survival."

Jackson snorted. "Deeper than that. Steele's group has banded together to survive. We are more than a band or even a war band. All my men here share something that unites us as one unit."

Jackson paused and the two men watched blackbirds circling overhead.

"Do you know what truly unites our legion?

Mauser shook his head no.

Jackson grabbed the back of Mauser's neck in what was supposed to feel like a fatherly grasp, but it came across as awkward like he was going to hold him under water until he stopped moving. Mauser's muscles stiffened in his neck and upper back.

Jackson leaned closer to Mauser and hissed, "Betrayal by our government." He released Mauser after a long pause and gestured at his column. "Every single man here was left to die. Every man abandoned for dead. That's not what this nation was founded on." He pointed in the direction of Steele's forces.

"That man sided with the government. He betrayed us again and again. He cannot be allowed to survive. We must crush his forces and teach them the lesson that traitors will not be allowed to live. We are the remaining."

"Why don't we speed up and catch them then?"

Jackson's smile grew wide enough to show all his teeth.

"I could have had him at Burr Oak. If we push on ahead, we could take him before nightfall. But why haven't I?"

"I'm not sure why, sir."

"Because it's about the chase, not just the outcome. A boxer doesn't get into the ring and knock his opponent out with a single punch. He dances, he jabs, he blocks, he lets his opponent think he's winning and then something changes. He continues to pummel his opponent with precise and evaluated strikes. Then his opponent begins to fear because he thought he was getting the upper hand, but he wasn't. He begins to realize that he is outmatched. His adversary is technically sound and he's going to lose."

Jackson sucked in air through his nostrils and they whistled. "After another round of this, he knows he will lose, but maybe he can make it a bit longer. The bell dings. He is in survival mode now, thinking just don't get knocked out, just make it to the next round. He's most vulnerable then. He's thinking only about surviving and not about winning. He's only thinking about his next move, not the next ten steps it will take to get him there. Survival will only take you so far. That's when the final blow will be struck. Only after I've taken every shred of dignity from the boy."

Jackson nodded his own words moving him. "In the end, it's not a boxing match, but a fight for a man's soul. That is what we must take. His soul. The only way to defeat a traitor is to take their souls. If we don't take their souls, then the traitorous seed will continue to grow in others and we will fight them forever." He pinched his fingers together in front of him. "We must grind that seed until only dust remains."

Mauser gulped, swallowing Jackson's words like a charred steak. He nodded in acknowledgment. "He's a different man than he used to be."

Jackson clapped his back. "But you aren't, Mauser. You and me are the same. We know what's right and we do it. We don't run away because we don't like our orders. We complete the mission and move on to the next one. We are men of purpose. Steele is only a boy. He doesn't know his right from his left. His people are a rabble, a collection of hooligans better suited for a riot than a war."

Mauser nodded and his words came out hollow. "I made a choice that was logical. This command is the only thing keeping all these people alive. It gives people hope."

"That's why we're here. We're all that's left in the field. It's our duty to survive. The lines have been drawn in the sand, and it's up to us to do the right thing."

"Yes, sir."

Jackson brought his binoculars to his eyes. "We are only in round two. My forces will continue to eat away at him. He will know what's it's like to have no hope. That is when his throat will be crushed beneath my boot. I will be there when his eyes dim and his soul is mine."

Mauser peered at the ground. He disagreed vehemently with Steele, but it was still a hard pill to swallow that they were going to kill him. Some of those old feelings still lingered on the outside of Mauser's subconscious. He pushed them away. There was no room for feeling here. Only the power to survive and Steele had shown time and time again that he couldn't embrace that power, so he would fall before those that had an intimate understanding of this new world.

"You are released back to your squad," Jackson said.

"Yes, sir."

Mauser turned and walked back to his waiting Humvee. The column stretched down the road. All colors and creeds of soldiers waited for orders, all bound together by Jackson's command. Men that had followed him from the early days of the Pittsburgh quarantine to the Battle of Steel City and to the retreat from Youngstown Airfield. He only recognized a few of their faces, but most held that look that men have when they fight a war with no end.

His Humvee idled in park while Brown had the door open. He dug a tan spoon into a tan plastic package and spooned some of its contents into his mouth with a slurp.

"What's the big guy have to say?"

Mauser's deadpan expression gave nothing away. "We're still on track to hit the enemy force along the river."

STEELE
Eastern Banks of the Mississippi River, IL

Hulking farm equipment layered the two-lane rusted brown bridge. One blue combine and one green combine had been parked side by side, blocking the bridge over the muddy waters of the Mississippi River.

Steele's convoy was strung out on the banks along the Illinois side of the river. The occupants in the long trail of vehicles were stalled, waiting for their next move. Steele stood outside Tess's red pickup parked right on the edge of the river.

He watched the town, flanked by some of the motorcycle club chiefs and Ahmed. They had finally reached their place of refuge only to find it isolated from the rest of the country and barricaded off from the rest of the world. Probably one of the only reasons the small Iowa town still had living people in it. He flexed his damaged hand. He could make a light fist now. *It may take forever, but I will make this arm work again.*

"There ain't no way we can move those," Frank said. His vest had a metallic coiled-snake patch on it. The black and gray-haired biker crossed his muscled arms across an equally thick chest. "Over yonder's the town we're supposed to find all this food at?"

Steele took his binoculars out and held them up to his eyes. Short rural town buildings rose up across the river. Brown, white, brick, and wood buildings gave off a down-home feeling. It gave off the vibe you could leave your keys in your car and your doors unlocked at night and never have a worry in the world.

It was the kind of place where everybody knew too much about Bill's extramarital affair with Cindy and that Roger got a speeding ticket on Thursday. Or Melissa got on the front page of the paper because she grew the biggest pumpkin in the county, but her methods were under speculation because Mr. Franklin's pumpkins won every year and his pumpkin had mysteriously caved and died before the pumpkins were officially judged.

Through the binoculars, Steele watched a few men walking with guns in their hands. A dead traffic light hung on one end of the street. Sandbags lined the streets like they were expecting a flood, but Steele knew it for fortifications. *So they aren't all dead.* He turned to the other side of town, reading the sign. In swirled curving letters it read: *"Hacklebarney: If it ain't heaven, it's close."*

"This is it. This is where Gwen is supposed to be," Steele said. *If she made it.*

"I wonder what the pastor thinks of Hacklebarney's motto?" Ahmed said. He gave a glance back over his shoulder where the pastor sat in his dark blue Jeep Wrangler.

"He's probably jealous he didn't come up with it," Steele let the binoculars drop down.

"Doesn't look like they take too kindly to strangers," Thunder said. The big biker gestured at the farm equipment blocking the bridge. "Those are some big rigs."

"They are a cautious lot, but Iowans are nice," Steele said with a smirk. Gwen had always prided herself on the friendliness of people from Iowa, something she took to heart. She always loved to tell the story about when she had slid off the road one Christmas Eve in Hacklebarney and at least a half a dozen people stopped to help her. It was their way.

"This is exactly the response I expected from them. Hunker down and close off from the real world. Wait it out." It was really just an extreme version of what they do in times of normalcy. Keep to themselves. Steele pulled on his beard, unsnarling it as he thought. *Except Gwen was supposed to prime the pump and get them on board before we arrived.*

Frank skimmed the opposing shore with his eyes. "I guess I can't blame 'em. If you got something worth fighting for, you better be prepared to fight for it." He pointed to a dock. "There's some boats over there."

Fishing boats, rowboats, and pontoons were beached along the shore. They had been dragged up onto the banks as if they hadn't originated there but had been haphazardly collected.

"Me and a couple of the boys can swim over and acquire a few," Frank said.

"You got a wetsuit? That water is freezing cold, and I don't want to spook them by showing up in the night armed to the teeth. They're probably already scared."

Thunder's brow wrinkled beneath his red bandana. "What are you thinking? This is the only bridge for about thirty miles. Long way around."

"I don't want to go around. I want them to open up and let us through." *Then I'm going to blow the bridge so Jackson can't get across.* He hadn't vocalized this part of the plan yet, but if he could close off most of Iowa from both Jackson and the dead, he would do it. Even if it was only to buy time.

"What about Gwen?" Ahmed asked. The swarthy man had his M4 on his back and held his bat with one hand. He gently let the bat swing back and forth as if it helped him think. "You think she can get them to open up?"

Men in overalls and ball caps stood on the other bank now. *They know we're here.* They held what appeared to be shotguns in the crook of their arms as if they were prepping for a deer hunt. It was possible that they were going hunting. Iowa was deer country, arguably some of the best white-tailed deer hunting in the nation. Steele's stomach grumbled in complaint.

"The plan was for her to get us access, but it doesn't look like it worked." *She has to be there.*

"Steele," a voice said loudly behind him. There was malice laced with anger in the way his name was uttered. His group turned around. Macleod stood there with a portion of his motorcycle gang. Yellow-eyed black wolves were their club colors. Macleod stood in a wide stance and his eyes were wild like those of a drunk man itching for a fight. His long black goatee hung at chest level.

"*Where's* the food? You promised that if we got you here there would be food and plenty of it."

Steele flexed his hand on his damaged arm. *You knew this was coming.*

"Macleod, you'll get your food after we get across."

Macleod licked his lips. "We want our food now." Steele locked eyes with the man and broke contact as he counted the Wolf Riders at Macleod's back. Twelve bikers to our four. *Would Frank even fight?* Either way, bad odds for coming out in one piece let alone alive.

"I don't have your cut here. We have to get across to that town."

Macleod took a step forward, his boot digging into the earth. "I'm not sure you understand. I want it now."

"I'm not sure you understand. It's across the river." *Do I draw down on him?* None of the Wolf Riders had guns out, but they had handguns shoved in their pants. They also had knives and bats with them.

Steele squeezed his right hand shut. It was still worthless in a fight. *You aren't as fast with your left hand.* He let his left index finger dangle on the side of the gun. The rough grip brushed the very tip of his fingers.

Macleod's men shifted on their feet. Tension hung around them like a bad stench that one knew would get worse by the minute. Macleod's cheek twitched below his eye.

First round's for you.

A female voice with some swagger broke their stare down. "Hey, boys." Tess sauntered up. Her gun wasn't out, but her hand wasn't far from it. Margie was behind her, her hunting rifle pointed downward with Tony hovering close to her trying to look brave behind his thick black glasses.

"Mr. Steele, what did I tell you about having parties without me?"

Steele's eyes glanced her way. "Never to do it."

The other volunteers followed them. Bald Larry and curly-headed Rick had AR-15s. Long-haired Tom, whose hair hung past his fur-collared blue denim jacket, held a Heckler and Koch SP5K, the civilian version of the MP5 except it was shorter, lighter, and semi-automatic, meaning it only could shoot one round every time the trigger was pulled.

Reinforcements. Steele gave her a smirk.

"Clever boy." She drew herself up near him, her Sable Point volunteers clustering around them.

"We were discussing how we're going to cross that bridge."

Macleod's black goatee shook a bit with his head. "And payment."

"And payment," Steele repeated. He let his eyes narrow a fraction at the man.

"But that's settled," Thunder added. "It's already been agreed upon."

"We can wait a little longer before we make any hasty decisions," Frank added with a glare at Macleod.

Macleod pointed at Steele. "Payment, Steele. Remember, I won't wait forever." He waved his followers away and they left. "Come on."

Tess put a playful shoulder into Steele. "You guys playing nice?"

Steele raised his eyebrows. "Macleod has an itchy finger for payment."

"He won't move on you while I'm here," Thunder barked in an attempt to whisper.

Frank watched the retreating bikers over his shoulder. "I never liked the Wolf Riders much." He turned to Steele. "But let's not forget what we're doing here and that's finding a way over that bridge."

Tess unslung a backpack from her shoulder, digging around inside. "Thought this might help," she grunted. She pulled out a black portable CB radio, setting it alongside the pack. "Don't ask what I had to do to get all these batteries."

Steele smiled. "Lips are sealed."

"I told you I was your girl," she said with a smile. She pressed on the power button and twisted a volume knob. Static flared up. The channel knob clicked as she twisted it left and right. "Hello?" she said with every click. "Hello, anybody there?" She was met with static again and again. She glanced up at him, her dark eyes worried.

"Keep trying."

"Come on you rednecks, pick up," Tess said. She rotated the knob in a circle. "Hello?" Click. "Hello?"

"Yellow," barked through the speaker.

Tess's lips curved as she spoke. "Hi there, sugar. This is Tess of the Sable Point volunteers. We're over on the other side of the river."

The man's voice was wholesome and rich. "Not sugar, darling. Sheriff

Donnellson here. We seen ya. We knew you's was coming."

Tess and Steele exchanged a glance.

"They knew," Tess said excitedly.

Steele couldn't help but grin. "Gwen."

Tess gave a sly smirk, looking down at the microphone. "Did anyone ever tell you you sound like a young Marlon Brando?" Her voice oozed into the microphone with enough sultry tones to make a man blush.

A deep laugh vibrated through the speaker. "You sure know how to make an old feller smile."

"So can we talk about moving those tractors? I'd like to see if you're handsome like Brando too." Tess gave Steele a big grin and he returned it. Ever the flirt, Tess had a way with men that Steele could never explain. He flexed his damaged hand. It was nice to be on the receiving end of some good news. It seemed that everything of late was only bad. He stole a look behind him at his drawn-out haphazard convoy. *We may squeak by yet.*

"Well, darling, there's two things. One, been a married man for almost forty years, so all's you can do is look. Two, those be combines not tractors and they ain't movin'."

Tess's smile turned upside down and she wiped a hand over her short, slicked back hair. "Sheriff Brando, what do you mean? You said you knew we were coming."

"Yes, I did. A big part of why we closed down that bridge. We don't want anything to do with the likes of you people. Don't take it personally. You seem nice enough but we took drastic measures to ensure outsiders can't access our town, and we aren't about to open it up because some girl on a radio asks us all pretty like."

Thunder let out a whistle.

"*Damn!*" Steele mouthed to Tess. He shook his head and motioned for the radio. She handed it over to him.

"My turn."

"Be my guest. Old fart doesn't know what he's doing."

Steele gave her a sympathetic grin. "No, he doesn't." He brought the microphone to his lips. "Sheriff, this is Counterterrorism Division Agent Steele."

The radio went silent for a few seconds. "Agent Steele. Hmm. Never heard of no Division. Probably some sort of government pork spending, no doubt."

"I assure you we're real, Sheriff. I got the badge and scars to prove it."

"Can't say I've ever had to deal with your agency before. Had some ATF agents through here about eighteen years ago. Buncha tenderfoots." The microphone clicked off.

Steele snorted a laugh. "None too friendly toward my buddies."

Thunder's face was unchanged. "I don't like 'em much either."

Steele offered him the microphone. "Do you want to talk to him?"

Thunder grunted. "No."

Steele clicked the side of his microphone. "The Division mostly works overseas." He held the microphone near his hip while he waited for a response.

"I wouldn't know much about that, but I'll give you the benefit of the doubt and assume you are a fellow man of the law."

Steele nodded to his fellow companions. He built a fragile rapport with the man on the brotherhood of law enforcement. "Yes, sir." He paused. "Some of my people should already be there."

The sheriff's voice sounded unbelieving that this outsider could know somebody in his small town. "And who might that be, Agent Steele?"

"Over a week ago, I sent almost a hundred people with my girlfriend, Gwen Reynolds. Are they there?"

He was met with radio silence. Steele waited a moment and then rushed. "Sheriff, how copy?"

The sheriff's voice was dour. "I'm here, son."

Steele's brow narrowed.

"They came through."

Steele exhaled and Tess smiled. Thunder grinned too beneath his beard. He clapped Steele's back with a slap.

"We're with them. How about you let us across too?"

He was met with more silence as if the man was thinking on the other end.

"I'm sorry, son. We can't take ya."

Steele's mouth tightened. "Sheriff, you took my people. Why not the rest of us?"

The radio crackled. "You understand that I have a responsibility to the great people of Hacklebarney. They elected me to serve and protect them. Now, I've done a pretty good job so far. We've only lost a few folks to the sickness. But to let in your band of vagabonds, gangs, and other unsavory types would just not be in our best interest."

Steele pounded the microphone off the front of his forehead. *This hometown hero.* His heart raced. *I'm definitely going to have a heart attack by the time I'm thirty-five.*

Steele composed himself, seething on the inside, and spoke into the mic. "Why did you take our other people in then?"

The sheriff sounded offended on the other side of the line. "For God's sake, man, they were women and children. Why would you ever send them so lightly guarded baffles me and makes me question how much you actually care for your people."

"We have more women and children over here," Steele growled.

The sheriff's voice grew stern. "Now, this is no reason to get angry. The decision has already been made. Your group cannot come across and that's final." His voice softened. "You'll have to find somewhere else to go, but I assure you Miss Gwen is safe and sound where she belongs and everyone is accounted for."

Steele twisted his head to the side, swallowing his anger. "Sheriff, you are going to have to let us across."

"By God I do. We will defend this town to the last man. And don't think for a second we won't."

Steele met Tess's eyes and he barked. "The nerve of these people. They're as stubborn as mules."

"And to think I called him Brando." Tess shook her head in disappointment.

Steele brought the microphone up to his lips and muttered, "I have no doubt you would, but we're coming across."

"Son, I wish I could help you. I really do. But it's just not gonna happen. My advice is that you roll on back down the road and take refuge somewhere else. Sooner or later, the government is going to take care of this. We just have to wait for those Washington bureaucrats to get their act together."

"There is no government," Steele said louder into the microphone.

"Now son, don't you get frisky with me. I'll thump ya real good. There sure as hell is a government and it's American. I won't entertain any other such bull hockey. I bid you a good day."

Steele ground his teeth. "And I bid you good day, sir."

TESS
Steele's Camp, IL

Tess walked along a country dirt road. Recent tire tracks from the convoy had churned up the loose dirt leaving clumps of earth in its place. The sky hovered close to the ground above her, a gray and white lining of her earthly ceiling.

Steele's convoy had set up camp in a unplowed field along the river only a few hundred yards from the entrance ramp to the bridge that led across to Hacklebarney.

Tents of every color speckled the field like it was hosting a weekend music festival. Trucks and motorcycles were parked haphazardly. Bonfires roared in the biker camps, and smaller fires were interspersed in the other camps. The group was split by their respective factions, avoiding the chance of intermingling with one another. Mistrust of the others had created divisions in the entire group's cohesion. She guessed that was a product of fighting one another in their recent history. The widest divide was between the Chosen and everyone else.

On the other side of the dirt road sat spaced out pickups. People stood sentry in truck beds against the living and dead alike.

The wind picked up and a chill swirled around her. She hugged her drab green coat tightly and she wished she was near one of the fires. She shoved her hands in her pockets and kept onward.

A group of bikers with Wolf Rider patches on their vests stood around a ten-foot-wide campfire. They took swigs off a brown bottle and laughed uproariously at one of their number dancing. Heavy metal played through a rigged up speaker. The biker bobbed his head back and forth every now and again throwing a fist in the air. *Clowns.*

Their unwanted stares zeroed in on her as she grew near as if they could smell a woman by herself. A Wolf Rider with a black beard and a bandana around his head nudged a short, fat, and apparently chinless man with his elbow.

She pulled her coat tighter around her. Her M1911 hung heavy in its holster right beneath her armpit. The weight was distributed over her shoulders by her leather harness. In the very beginning, she had lifted it off a thick-mustached detective near Grand Rapids.

The black-bearded Wolf Rider took a step closer to the road and cupped his mouth.

"Hey. Where you headed, sweet stuff?" His voice had an unpleasant rasp to it like he belonged on a street corner selling drugs. "Will you look at that, Pork. I'd split that in two." He grinned and several of his teeth were missing.

"Bet you that's real nice," Pork added. He huffed as he laughed.

She didn't even contemplate not responding to the vulgar bikers. She turned around as she continued to walk backward and gave them a broad view of her middle finger.

"Well, fuck you too, bitch," he hollered at her, grabbing his riding leather-covered crotch.

"Keep searching, sweetheart. Maybe you'll find something down there." She spun around, continuing to walk away.

The biker spit in her direction. Pork raised the spot where his chin should be, more like a layer of fat. They started following her down the road at a jog.

Tess stopped, hearing them coming. Her hand leapt inside her coat. She felt the heat from inside her armpit as her fingers wrapped around the warm grip of her M1911, a nice .45 caliber handgun that packed a punch. She drew the weapon and turned around, keeping it held behind her back. *Ass clowns.*

The black-bearded man got close enough. His name patch read Roody on his black vest. He gave her the creepiest of smiles. "We only want to talk for a minute, for a second. Why are you out by yourself?"

This dimwit thinks I'm only a girl.

He reached for her and she dodged him, throwing her shoulder back.

Her cheeks rose as she spoke with a mischievous smile. "I'm not the kind of girl you're looking for."

Pork licked his lips. The tiny ears on his round face, his beady eyes, and a pushed-up nose made him resemble even more of a pig close-up. He breathed heavy, and Tess wasn't sure if it was the jogging or the prospect of being close to a woman. "We like all sorts of girls," he breathed out.

Roody glanced back over his shoulder at the fire. "Yeah, why don't you come back to our fire?" He gestured with his hand back at the fire. "We can talk for a bit. We got some weed and pills maybe even some X. We got something that will help you loosen up, babe."

She took a step back and rolled her eyes at them. "You two little peckers can run along." She shooed them with a flick of her wrist. Her other hand still tucked behind her. "If you want it so bad, how about you play with each other? The fat one's got some cushion."

Roody's mouth snarled. "Now, you listen to me." He pointed at her from above. "I was being nice before, but if you want to play rough, then rough is what you'll get." One of his heavy paws swooped down, trying to grab her. She dodged, backtracking, and whipped her handgun out from behind her back. She took a step closer to him.

Roody's eyes went wide.

She cocked the hammer of the gun for emphasis. "I told you. I'm not the girl you're looking for." She used the gun to gesture at Pork. She spoke slow and condescending to ensure they understood. "Now, you and Mr. Piggy can leave. You feel me?"

Roody took a step back and Pork looked like he was trying not to shit himself. The smell coming from his area made Tess wonder if he had already released his bowels.

"Don't be hasty. We meant no harm," Roody spit out.

She rolled her eyes again. "Right. Get out of here." The men turned their backs and retreated to their campfire with frequent turnarounds to make sure they weren't going to take a shot in the back.

"And tell Porky Pie to check his pants." She shook her head in disgust and holstered her M1911. She snapped the button on the leather retention strap, securing her firearm in the harness.

"Fucking juvenile delinquents," she said to herself. She stuffed her hands in her pockets and continued along her own way. She passed more biker gangs and a few Sable Pointers, but she wasn't interested in them.

Her little stroll was to check up on an old friend. About four hundred yards from the Sable Point volunteers' camp began the Chosen camp. Steele had purposely stuck the Sable Pointers between the bikers and the Chosen. It was risky for many reasons. First, the two factions had recently been at war. Second, if any of the gangs decided they wanted revenge on the Chosen or vice versa, Sable Point volunteers were stuck in the middle of hostile groups.

There was a stark difference among those in the Chosen camp. Their campsites were spaced closer together and the people seemed, oddly enough, happy as if they enjoyed one another's company.

Children ran about the camps playing their hearts out. Men and women stood guard over the others in pairs. A man shook another man's hand and gave him a plastic bag of canned food. Everything was just swell and dandy in the pastor's camp. It made her mood sour like milk left curdling in the sun for two weeks.

She followed the road, strolling, trying to appear nonchalant as she searched. Stepping into a ditch and then into the fallow field, she nodded to a man and woman. The man held a machete and the woman a shotgun.

"Peace be on you, Brother and Sister." *I know it's some bullshit like that.*

The man scrutinized her for a moment. "Don't I know you?"

Her eyes kicked upward. "Can't say we've met. I'm looking for somebody to pray with. Thought I'd see if your people could help."

The man nodded enthusiastically. "You are most welcome, Sister?"

"Sister Theresa." *Ah, Jesus. May as well have called myself Mother Theresa.*

The woman piped up. "Brother Peter is leading a group in prayer over there." She pointed behind her into the thick of their camp.

"Better head on over. Don't want to miss it," Tess said. She lightened her eyes and gave her best heartwarming "I just baked you these cookies" smile. *Definitely not going to see that drone, Peter.*

"Peace be unto you," the man said.

The woman smiled and Tess smiled back, trying to seem happy and content like one of their own brainwashed people.

"Peace be onto the highest." She clamped her mouth shut. *Too much? I never fucking know with these people and their secret passwords.*

Both sentries nodded and she walked past them. She spit on the ground to get the kiss-ass taste from her mouth. "Who are you?" She chided herself quietly.

She cut through a weed-ridden trail that had been beaten down with hundreds of feet. People at the campsites smiled at her. Others sat around fires and shared all manners of food and drink.

She peered from face to face, seeking the tall man among the throngs of people. Most of their faces were unknown to her. Every now and again she would see a familiar face but not the one she searched for.

She stopped and stood on her tiptoes, trying to find a better view from around the camp. An older woman stirred a black kettle over a fire with a long wooden spoon. The aroma wafted into the air, tickling her stomach with hunger pains. *Beef stew?* She contemplated joining up just for a piping hot bowl of the stuff. *How do they have so much food?*

The old woman squinted up at her and Tess expected her to tell her off for staring. Her gray hair was held in a tight bun on the back of her head.

"Are you hungry, child?"

Tess felt herself nodding.

The old woman waved to her with a free hand. "Come here and warm yourself. The chill will make you sick." The old woman continued to stir the stew in a circular motion. She glanced up at Tess and gave her a sad smile. "Not my best, but we make do with what we have."

Tess took a seat cross-legged at the fire. Three small children and a teenage boy sat around smiling as they ate. A young woman probably in her twenties stared out across the field as if she expected someone.

"It's good," the teenager said. His mouth was full as he spoke. He had the beginnings of a weak blond mustache, the kind he definitely would have been made to shave if they still lived in a normal world.

"Danny, mind your manners," the old woman chided.

"Not as good as at home," one of the little girls said, picking at hers with a spoon. She had curly blonde hair and looked to be about six-years-old.

The old woman gave her a disapproving look and dug her spoon into the pot and ladled it into a tin cup. She tried to hand it to the young woman, but she wouldn't lift her arms to take the food. Her eyes were blank as if nothing resided inside her. Her brown hair was unkempt and strewn about her shoulders and her lips were barely parted as if she had something small to say.

The old woman set the stew down next to her. "I'll feed you later," she muttered to herself.

She gave Tess a tin cup of the red stew. "Thank you," Tess murmured into her steaming tin.

"He will provide all we need, honey," the old woman said with a sad smile. "Now, all of you eat up." She shook the spoon at the children. "Especially you, Georgia. I won't have you complaining later that you're hungry when there's food to eat."

Georgia nodded her little curly-haired head and poked at her stew.

The heat from the stew permeated through the small blue metal cup and warmed Tess's hands. She sat for a moment, taking in the delicious smell of the savory broth. "Where'd you get beef stew?"

The old woman smiled faintly. She leaned over and whispered to Tess. "The Lord provides, but it's mostly squirrel. Don't tell the wee ones. I don't want them refusing to eat."

The old woman clanked her spoon on the side of the pot as she stirred the stew. Tess shrugged. She didn't really care what the meat was. *Tasted enough like chicken, or was it beef?* It didn't matter. It tasted decadent.

The elder woman spoke while she stirred. "The pastor sends out men every time we stop to scavenge for food and hunt. It's not a lot, but we ain't starving. Prayer and food is enough for us to keep going." She gave Tess a toothy smile.

She gestured with her head at the young brunette. "Her husband was killed during the outbreak. She found a nice young lad in the camp later. The pastor blessed the marriage. He is always encouraging the young to join in the replenishing of the earth. It is God's will." She stopped stirring for a moment as she thought back. "It was a wonderful day amongst all this misery." The thought seemed to turn to ash in her mouth and her lips twisted in disgust. "He was killed in that battle with those filthy heathens on the lake."

Tess took a bite of her hot stew. The broth burnt her tongue. She immediately scratched her tongue on the back of her teeth trying to mitigate the burning sensation.

The old woman carried on. "If it were up to me, I'd as soon as see them all burn for their many indiscretions, but the pastor says we follow the scarred one now. So we do. Even the Israelites were forced to follow the Egyptians for a period when they had been enslaved." She peered back down at her stew, stirring and stirring round and round.

"They can't all be bad people," Tess said.

"Anyone who doesn't believe is bad." The old woman nodded her fierce affirmation. She gestured out to the farmland. "Those things out there are evil and they don't believe. There isn't any other way to see it."

Tess slurped up some of her stew. "This is delicious. I can't tell you the last time I had such fantastic *beef* stew." Tess set her cup down. "Say, you haven't seen our glorious leader, the pastor, have you?"

The old woman smiled. "Of course, my dear. He stays near the red barn at the end of camp. Him and his disciples."

"His disciples?" *Jesus, he thinks he's Christ.*

"You don't know them?"

Tess shook her head. "Of course I do. There's that handsome blond one."

The old woman gave her a broad knowing grin. "Matthew. He's a catch that one. Handsome and brave. Or are you asking about Peter? He's our rock, such a pious man and strong." She raised her eyebrows in dismay. "I know you can't be referring to Luke. Are you?"

"No," Tess said softly.

"He's a different one. Holy and loyal."

"Are they always with the pastor?"

"No, of course not. They are constantly working to preserve us and defend us from the wicked, just like the pastor instructs." The old woman shook her head in wonderment. "As pious as Jesus, that one."

Tess nodded. "He sure is." She averted her eyes and picked up the brown stew. It had cooled quickly in the fall air. She tilted her head back and poured the stew in her mouth. "I have a prayer meeting to go to. Thank you for the food." Tess stood.

"My dear, you are always welcome here," the old woman said with a wide smile.

"Go with God," Tess said, biting her burnt tongue.

"May he always be on your side," the old woman said. Tess waved at the little children. The teenager blushed. "Bye, Danny," she said, pursing her lips. The boy looked away, ashamed of his hormonal teenager tendencies.

Tess weaved through the campsites, keeping the barn on the edge of the field in her sights.

Near the end of their camp sat a simple weathered barn. The color was so faded that one could barely tell that it was once a vibrant red. Time, wind, and rain had stripped it down to a dull chipped gray. The timber was warped, and in some places, outright missing. If it rained, it wouldn't provide much shelter. It would only get in the way as the water ran along the wood until it dripped inside. The barn doors were closed and two men stood out front. One held an AR-15 and the other held a wood-stocked AK-47. They both held their guns loose in the bend of their elbows.

A towering old oak tree stood, withered branches extended outward. Tess continued to walk and took cover behind the tree.

"They say we're going to have to fight our way across," said one guard. He wore a full hunting woodland camouflage suit.

The other one wore a navy ballistic vest. "Shit, I'd rather swim it."

The hunter shook his head. "I'll tell you one thing. I'd rather fight these backwater yokels than go toe-to-toe with the soldiers."

"No shit. We won't stand a chance when we're pinned on the river and old Scarface won't keep us moving." He wiped a hand through his greasy hair.

"What a moron. I'm telling you, I had a shot on him at the battle on the lakeshore."

The man in the ballistic vest turned toward the other guard. "No way. Why didn't you take it? This shit would have been over and we could have stayed put at the Temple. Now we're stuck out here in the middle of nowhere."

The hunter tilted his head to the side. "He ducked."

"How'd you know it was him?"

"What other guy's got a huge scar on his head?"

"True. True."

These men still want us dead. Even the old woman disdains us. I knew they couldn't be trusted, but the key lies with their leader.

Having heard enough of the guards' bravado, Tess followed a dirt path around the barn. She weaved between a pickup and a bus.

She crept to the back of the barn and listened. Men's voices leaked out from the cracks of loose graying boards. She thought she heard the pastor's voice, but she couldn't be sure. She pushed her face near a crack in the boards.

Dark forms moved on the other side. *Damn, can't see anything.*

Long grass had grown up along the edge of the barn, and she crept along until she came across a wooden ladder lying sideways on the ground. Her eyes drifted upward to an opening to the hayloft. The door was open and swung loose against the barn wall.

As quietly as she could, she lifted the ladder upright and leaned it against the hayloft opening. She climbed rung over rung up the ladder. At the top, she sidestepped onto the barn loft. She crouched down for balance and peered through cracks in the wood below.

She couldn't miss him. He was like a black-clad specter in his preaching garb, white collar at his neck. He wasn't alone.

Roughly twenty men stood in the middle of the dark barn. No lights illuminated them, and the gray sky above provided only a dim glow from outside. She listened hard, turning an ear in their direction.

"Christ is the only one who can save you from this hell," the pastor's voice said. He stood in the front of the barn, holding a small book in his hands.

"You there in the hat. What's your name?"

"Young," the man said.

"That's a fine name. I am old and you are young," the pastor said. He gave a rich laugh and so did the people in attendance.

"Young, you are part of a pretty tight outfit, aren't you?"

"Yeah. The War Machines are a tough club. They would fight for me and die for the club."

Tess inched her way across the boards, hoping none would give her away.

"Of course they would. They're your guys, but if you're so tight with them, why are you here? What do you seek?"

Tess peered through the cracks in the wood. The man crossed his arms and his body language was that of a man with severe indigestion.

"I dunno. All this death and destruction got me thinking."

"May God show you the way, Mr. Young," the pastor's voice was grave. "I wish I had a hundred lives to give. No, a thousand lives to give for my people. And you know why, Mr. Young?"

"I guess not."

"Because I know that when I die, the angels will come down to earth and carry me on their wings to heaven. I don't think it. I know it. And knowing that gives me strength. More strength than a hundred armed men. More strength than the army. More strength than your gang."

The pastor's voice grew quiet. "What happens to you when you die, Mr. Young?"

"I...I don't know. Go to heaven, I guess."

Tess stared hard, trying to recognize the people as her eyes adjusted to the weak light. At least half of the ones in the audience wore biker vests. She saw the skull and gears of the War Machines, the seven ghost women of the Seven Sisters, and a skull with the crimson streaks of the Red Stripes, along with a short curly-haired man. *Rick. That idiot. Why is he here?*

The pastor continued. "That's why you're here. That's why all of you are here." The pastor paced on the wood floors, his cowboy boots echoing along the creaking boards. "Some of you are seeking a community. Some of you are seeking salvation. Some of you only want to feel like things are back to normal." The pastor stopped pacing. He stood erect. "I can give you this if you can give him your souls. He asks for so little but gives so much." The pastor's hands spread wide.

This guy is recruiting more zealots right underneath our very noses. Just wait until Steele hears this. He will put a stop to this preaching. And if he doesn't, I will.

"I only ask this. Drop to your knees now and swear to him that you will uphold his holy laws. Swear to destroy those who bear the Mark. You need not join us openly but go and watch the others. Be silent among them, but celebrate our joy with us for we are the many. Kneel," he commanded.

The old wooden floor groaned as feet turned into knees. The pastor gestured to a man who kept standing. "You need not be afraid, Brother. Kneel and all your fear will be taken away."

The man hesitated but knelt. "May you look down upon your people and bless them for these are your Chosen people. These people will build your Kingdom. Give them your strength to stand up to the unbelievers and those marked by Satan." The pastor bowed his head.

"Rise as his champions. Go and do his bidding." The wood moaned and the newest Chosen rose upright.

The pastor hugged a woman and shook a man's hand. "There will be food over by my tent. Please come and celebrate."

Tess shook her head, watching the suckers with their false sense of security. The traitors to the others. *Come on, Rick. You were one of us. Damn, he's no better than the dead. Steals our people and makes them his own.*

KINNICK
Warden, IA

"Who took the shot?" Kinnick repeated through the megaphone.

He regarded the desperate faces below. The people stared at one another in confusion. An unshaven man in a tank top covered with a blue windbreaker spoke up. "Ain't nobody here took no shots. We be honest folk." He finished with a nod.

Kinnick looked downward for a moment, collecting himself. "There is a nineteen-year-old Marine dying on a table inside. Somebody must know something or seen something that can help me bring the perpetrator to justice."

A light murmur rumbled through them, almost like a faint wind of voices, but no one spoke loud enough for him to press further.

Kinnick shook his head. "I didn't want to do this, but for everyone's safety, we are putting Warden under strict curfew. Anyone out after dark, living or dead, is considered an immediate threat and will be shot on sight."

Faces snarled and anger rippled through them. Voices grumbled.

"We don't need you!" shouted a woman with a fist in the air.

"You can't do that," the man in the windbreaker said.

Kinnick stared down the man. "I can and I will." He let the megaphone down for a moment, watching them. He would not budge on this. "We're here to help, but until this criminal is brought to justice, we will occupy and enforce martial law over this island."

People waved him off. Kinnick handed the megaphone back to Gary.

Gary held the megaphone to his lips and his other hand in the air. "Now, everything's going to be all right." He patted the air with his free hand as he spoke. "If anyone knows anything about the shooter, please come to me or the colonel before dark. Anytime after that and we will need to wait until morning."

The people wandered away. They melted between houses and back to their docked boats. Kinnick and Gary watched the people drift away. Gary leaned on the wooden railing, looking down at the street. He glanced up at Kinnick. The wrinkles around his tired eyes were deep but filled with more worry than anything else.

"Colonel, we are a simple people. Some folk may not take kindly to strangers, but we ain't violent. Worst I seen them do is fistfight at Jack's Lookout."

Kinnick sucked in air through his nose. "We didn't come here to fight you. We came here to help stiffen up any resistance that Warden and the other towns have to offer." Kinnick glanced down. "But somebody shot my Marine and I will see justice done. We don't have room for detractors. Our nation is on the edge of defeat. I implore you." He stopped and pled with the man with his eyes. "No, I beg you to help me bring this man to justice so we can prepare for the real fight."

Kinnick peered out across the Mississippi River. A dim sun covered by opaque clouds was close to setting behind them, leaving almost no color on the water. A larger town could be seen farther north on the Illinois side of the river. A bridge and long road stretched through swampy islands, connecting Warden to Garfield. "The dead are coming. We don't have time to fight amongst ourselves."

Gary gulped and nodded gravely. "I wish I could help you, Colonel, but I don't know who did it." He squinted out over the dark brown water. "We haven't had too many of them cross the river. With your help, I'm sure we can weather the storm."

Kinnick pointed out over the horizon. "Tens of thousands if not more will end up here." Kinnick didn't know the truth of his words. He only knew it was going to be bad, and even with his help, these people would most likely be annihilated by infected tooth and nail. "You must be ready or you will be overrun."

Gary blew air out, puffing his cheeks. "Woo. That's not a pretty picture you're paintin'." He gave Kinnick a quick genuine smile and placed a hand on his shoulder. "Come on, Colonel. Martha will fix us up something nice."

Kinnick followed his host back down the stairs and inside the restaurant. Washington and Duncan were posted on the windows.

Hunter looked up, holding a radio in one hand. "Hamilton One has circled the island twice now. Seen a few people moving around, but nothing out of the ordinary."

"Tell them I want a patrol around the island once an hour after dark. Vary their routes. Between runs, I want them sitting right off the dock. If we need any heavy firepower in the night, I want them ready to go."

Hunter nodded his head, gripped his radio in one hand, and relayed the message. He turned to Volk.

The Marine sergeant puffed up, making himself look bigger and ready to rumble.

"Volk, split your men into twos. You only patrol in eyeshot of Hamilton One. After forty-five minutes, come back here, and after a few patrols, rotate with the next team."

"Yes, sir." He glanced at Whitehead. "Boone and Ramos, you two drew the short straw. You got first patrol."

"Ah shit, Sergeant," Boone said.

Ramos lifted his chin. "Esto es una mierda."

Boone frowned. "English, por favor."

Ramos scooped up his helmet. "Come on, you redneck pendejo."

Boone's brow crossed. "You know I can't understand you when you talk like that."

Ramos slapped Boone on the shoulder. "That's the point. Come on."

"I would appreciate if you worked on your communication skills in English."

The two Marines donned their helmets and walked outside while Boone still complained at Ramos.

Kinnick sat down at a square dining table and ran a hand through his hair, feeling the grease of not having washed it since being inside the Golden Triangle. A few minutes passed and Hunter joined him. The two men sat in silence.

It darkened outside the restaurant as the sun began to disappear, its fight to stay in the sky finally lost. Martha brought out a candle and set it on Kinnick's table.

Smells of cooking food tickled the men's noses, and Kinnick could hear the faint clank of pots and pans.

Hunter gestured with his eyebrow at the kitchen and Kinnick shook his head no. They had to trust their hosts with a fraction of faith or this experiment would never get off the ground.

"What you think they're making?" Hunter said softly.

Kinnick stifled a laugh. "I don't think it matters, does it?"

Hunter nodded as he eyed the kitchen. "Suppose not, but Martha has a look to her like she can make some serious food."

"We can only hope."

The candle flickered and the wick crackled. The Marines not on watch or patrol snoozed, helmets slid over their eyes, packs used as pillows. Hawkins sat near Gore, his eyes closed, but seemingly ready to jump in the fight or to save the man's life at a moment's notice.

Shadows emerged from the kitchen and they turned into Martha and Gary. They carried big serving dishes of food. Gary set one down and Martha followed with two more dishes of food.

Kinnick's mouth instantly began to salivate. The aroma was a combination of ripe tomato and fresh garlic all combined together in a rich marinara sauce. A deep bowl of yellow spaghetti pasta was smothered in chunky red sauce and thick brown meatballs sat on top like robust craggy boulders. Steam lifted off a whole loaf of bread cut down into thick slices. The couple set a stack of plates, forks, and knives on the table.

Gary gave Kinnick a sorry smile. "Bread's the frozen kind and a bit old, but we kept the freezer going as long as we could."

Martha averted her eyes, inspecting the floor. Her hands were clasped in front of her and she nervously rubbed them together. "Not my best. We canned all the meat we could when the power went out."

Kinnick dipped his chin in thanks. "You have my thanks, Martha. This looks wonderful." He turned toward Volk's dozing form. "Sergeant. Wake up."

Volk shot up with a scowl on his face and his gun in hand. He stared at the Marines that were supposed to be standing watch near the front of the restaurant.

Hunter was already at the table filling up his plate. "I knew Martha was a good cook." He gazed over at her. "Martha, my dear, if Gary hadn't married you, I sure as hell would." He shoved a whole piece of garlic bread in his mouth and spoke with his mouth full. "Hawk, I got you, bud." He chewed loudly. Crumbs from the bread dropped into his beard. He dug a spoon and fork into the pasta and pulled it up high into the air. Thin strands of spaghetti struggled to hang onto his utensils and plopped on the plate. Volk stood behind him with a softer scowl than normal.

"We'll rotate Duncan off the barricade, next." He spoke loudly over his shoulder at the other Marines. "Leave some for them or you're on barricade duty all night."

Washington snatched up a plate. "Ramos and Boone are gonna be so pissed," he laughed. He smiled, thinking about his fellow Marines missing out.

"Oh, man, home cooking!" exclaimed Whitehead. He rubbed his forehead with the back of his sleeve, his other hand holding his plate to his chest while he waited for a chance to get food.

Kinnick waited for all his men to rotate through the line before he ate. It took all of his fortitude to resist the food, but he'd served with fighting men long enough to know a leader always eats last. The food seemed to lift their spirits despite the darkness that hung over the group with Gore's still, haggardly breathing body in the corner. Martha and Gary sat quietly, eating at a separate table.

Kinnick filled his plate and sat down next to Hunter. He spun his fork around in the pasta, collecting a wad of the starchy goodness on the edge of his fork. He hooked a chunk of meatball on the end and shoved it into his mouth. It hit his tastebuds and he couldn't help but moan with a bit of gluttonous pleasure. He picked up his garlic bread and used it as a backstop to soak up the extra marinara sauce and give the pasta the extra support it needed to successfully transport the food to his mouth. Hunter looked up at him, nodding in enjoyment. Red sauce and bread crumbs nestled into his beard as if they were trying to hide.

"Best chow since I can remember. What do you think, Hawk?"

The quiet man gave a thumbs-up from next to Gore. His head neared his plate as he slurped up the strands of spaghetti.

"Do you want us on patrol tonight?"

Kinnick wiped his mouth. "Yes. I want everybody close and radios up."

Hunter nodded. "I'll make sure they know." Hunter put his fork down and snatched up his radio. He walked away from the tables while he talked to Volk and the Marines.

Kinnick leaned back in his chair, his belly swollen with a carb-heavy meal. He forced himself up and went over to Gary and Martha. They both gave each other a quick glance when Kinnick walked up to their table.

Gary's voice came out like a seasoned-saloon owner in the Wild West. "How can I help you, Colonel?"

"My men and I would like to bed down here tonight in the restaurant. That is, unless you have any issue hosting us?"

Gary wiped his mouth with a napkin. "Not at all, Colonel. Be a pleasure." He glanced at Martha. "Can you bring them some extra blankets?"

Martha nodded timidly, stood, and left the table.

Gary grabbed their dishes and stood up. The old man's eyes were tired. "I'm sorry for your man. If there was something I could do, I would do it."

Kinnick weighed the other man's words for a moment. *Truth? Fiction? Half-truths?* "Thank you, Gary. We'll get to the bottom of this. I promise you."

Gary nodded his understanding and took away the dishes. Kinnick watched the man's boxy frame disappear into the kitchen. *Can we even begin to trust these people? They are Americans, but somebody on this island shot one of my men.*

215

Martha came from the upstairs apartment, her arms filled with old blankets. Kinnick helped her by taking some. He took the first one over to Hawk. Hawkins laid it over Gore and tucked it in around the Marine, trying to make him comfortable.

"Thank you, ma'am," Volk said. His scowl had almost disappeared from his face. The Marines all said their thanks. "Duncan and Washington got first watch."

"Hawk and I can take the second watch," Hunter said. Hawk nodded his agreement. "We'll let the colonel get his beauty sleep." The Marines gave a chuckle, not sure if they should laugh at the informal joke made at Kinnick's expense.

"Me and Whitehead take the third patrol," Volk said.

Kinnick nodded. "Just let me know if anything is going on."

Hunter gave him a wink. "I'll wake you up if there's a fire."

Kinnick shook his head. "Thank you, Master Sergeant."

Kinnick bedded down using a musty but soft blanket as a pillow. He settled in and fell asleep in a matter of minutes, falling deep and hard into the realm of dreams.

The next morning, Kinnick cracked his eyes, feeling refreshed and invigorated by his restful night's sleep. He could hear whispering, and little tentacles of sunlight crept through the barricade of tables lined over the windows. He thought he could hear birds chirping followed by explosions of gunshots, shattering the peace of the rising eastern sun.

TESS
Steele's Camp, IL

The sun rose in the East, assaulting the horizon with fiery gold. Tess sat up in the back of the truck bed. She stretched her arms over her head. Fires smoldered, gray smoke drifting from the dead cinder. A few people moved here and there, stoking the fires back to life. Sentries stood along the edges near trucks. Tiny embers moved from mouths to their sides as they smoked. Guns were slung on their shoulders.

She hopped down from the back of Red Rhonda, wishing she was able to bring her camper instead of the small Ranger pickup. She slept in the open air with a pile of blankets around her like she was in a nest, only her head poking out.

Steele always slept nearby, but not too close, as the man was extra careful about confusing the situation. He treated it as if they were two friends on a campout, always placing himself on the other side of the fire. Sometimes she considered backing out on her deal with Gwen and jumping the man's bones, even if it only got her a few minutes of mindless pleasure. Anything to break the hold of their lifeless world. Holding back wasn't in her nature, but not rocking the boat kept her at arm's length from the man.

He was gone now, a pile of blankets in his place. Her heart felt heavy as she remembered the last man to share a piece of her heart: Darren Pagan. He had been burned alive by the pastor and his disgusting followers. It was something she would never forgive nor forget.

She wrapped an old patchwork quilt around her shoulders and walked through the Sable Point volunteers' camp. Someone coughed hoarsely in the early chill of morning. Another snored from a few tents over. She smelled the faint arousing fragrance of coffee brewing, but no food, no salty bacon, no creamy eggs. Steele had cut their rations so low that they would be without food in just two days. *That's when people will get ugly and that's when mistakes will be made.*

A beaten path led her through a thin set of maples, oaks and elms dotting the riverbank. At first, his form was faint. As she walked closer, the shadowed figure grew more into focus and a man emerged ahead of her.

His arm hung slightly bent at his side. His left arm moved fast as he worked his weapon handling skills. She stood back, watching him as he practiced. She leaned against a wide-leafed maple tree. Its remaining leaves were reddish-brown ready to fall at any moment.

He started with one hand in slightly above his belly button, his hand extended out like he was in the early stages of trying to keep someone away. His gun sat nestled in the front of his body in an appendix carry holster in such a fashion that she wondered how comfortable he was that he wouldn't shoot himself in his privates. In fact, she wasn't comfortable with the gun's placement on his body at all.

He drove his hand down on the handle, his thick belt keeping the gun almost in place. Tucking his elbow tight to his body, he would rip the gun free in a fluid motion. The gun would rise up mere inches from his abdominals, and when it was level with the center of his chest, he would drive the weapon out away from his body. His arm extended, he would squeeze the trigger with his index finger until the gun would go with an audible click. Each time it would click instead of boom as he dry-fired his weapon. He did all this with his left hand while his right hand hung bent with his thumb lopped onto the front of his pants. He would holster his weapon and begin anew every few seconds. Click. Holster. Wait. Draw. Click.

He then pulled out a magazine and started to practice loading with one hand. Resting the gun in its holster, he would shove a magazine into the magazine well, pull the gun from the holster, and rack it downward off his belt. Then he would raise it up to his eye level, aiming.

After a few minutes of watching him, she spoke. "It's fun to watch you work."

He looked fiercely in her direction, gun in hand. "Jesus, Tess." He shook his head. "Not a smart idea to sneak up on a guy working his gun."

"You can say that again." She strode down the small embankment.

He holstered up and ran a hand over his head scar. "How'd you sleep?"

"Not too bad considering I was in the back of an old pickup."

"I'm assuming it wasn't the first time."

She lifted her eyebrows. "And I assure you, it won't be the last."

He smiled and flexed his right hand.

She inspected it with her eyes. "Does it hurt?"

He gave her a pained look. "Always. Over time you just become accustomed to the pain." He scrutinized his damaged limb, willing it to work as he concentrated. "I feel naked with only one hand and downright useless. My left hand is slower than dirt and clumsier than a clown on skates." He shook his head. "Not fast enough."

"It will come around." She glimpsed through the trees in an effort to make sure no one else was nearby. She took a step closer, not trusting that the trees that might have eyes and ears hidden among them.

She tightened her blanket around her, trying to stave off the coolness of the morning. "I took a walk through the pastor's camp the other day."

His smile faded. "Please tell me you didn't do anything."

"Who? Little old me? Never." She fluttered her eyelashes at him. *I'd have killed him given a chance.*

"You thinking about joining up? You would be his greatest conversion yet."

"No, but I did see something that I thought you should know."

His thick blond beard with hints of brown moved in the wind. His eyes were a beaten steel blue. "And?"

"Your tall friend, the pastor, has been holding small conversion parties in that barn on the far side of the fields."

"Conversion parties?"

She wrapped the blanket tighter around her body. *Jesus, it's cold.* "Yes. He was recruiting new members to his church club."

"So? If they want to join, who cares? They're with us now."

Tess frowned. "I care."

"He's welcome to do what he wants as long as he upholds his side of the bargain." Steele turned away from her and did a quick draw of his gun, pointing it downrange. "It's about economy of motion. That's why I wear the appendix holster. The gun starts out almost entirely centered with the core of your body. I don't have to bend my arm back to draw like you would if it was on your hip or even worse, along your back. Can't do a backflip with a gun tucked on the backside, but up front you can."

She smirked. "You gonna do a backflip?"

"Ha. No. All you have to do is draw up, point forward and aim in."

"Thank you for the lesson, but what about the pastor?"

He put the gun back, looking down. "What about him?"

She took a step closer. "Steele, he had bikers in there." She peeped over her shoulder. Wind ruffled the few remaining dead leaves still clinging to the trees. "I also saw one of ours."

Steele gave her a sidelong glance. "I don't want to know." He shook his head no at her.

"Why?"

"Because. It's not my job to police our people and their beliefs."

Her words came out hurried. "You could have spies close to you. People that report back to the pastor or worse."

He raised an eyebrow. His left eyebrow always rose higher than the right one because of the scar tissue running along his scalp. It was as if the eyebrow had to lift more than its partner to reach upward. "Worse?"

Her voice quieted. "You could have an assassin in your midst and not even know it."

He stared at the ground, weighing her words.

He met her eyes. "That's possible." His words sounded distant and foreign as if it were a faraway idea for him.

"You aren't going to do anything?" she exclaimed.

"Nope." He drew his gun out again and the hammer sprung forward with a click.

"You're an idiot."

He snorted and turned to her, gesturing, his arm wide. "No, I'm just trying to hold this together. What do you want me to do? Execute the Chosen member? Call out the pastor? What does that get us?"

She narrowed her eyes. "One less psychopath and eliminates a threat among us."

"I will not move on this information and that's final. If they move first, I will deal with them, but so far, the pastor has upheld his word. I will not breach his trust and give him a reason to."

She shook her head in disgust. "You're going to get killed by one of these bastards and leave us here under their control." *This guy is a pig-headed imbecile.*

"That's a possibility."

"Can you hear yourself? Why aren't you doing anything? The threat is there." She leaned closer to him and spoke at a whisper. "If you don't do something, I have no problem silencing this prick." Her eyes stared into his for a moment. She wanted to make sure he knew she meant it. She would kill the pastor and leave the Chosen leaderless. If a new person stepped into the fold, she would do the same to them.

His eyes grew angry like a blue tempest and his voice grew mean. "Goddamnit, Tess. You will not." He brought himself under control and he whispered in harsh tones, "He's our ally. Unless he makes an open declaration of hostile intent, we don't do anything. Our peace is fragile."

She pointed a finger at him. "You will regret not taking action now."

"Then so be it." He pointed at her. "But I forbid you from doing so."

"Fine." She agreed but her word was a lie.

She spun and walked back through the trees, her blanket flying up behind her as she walked.

"Stupid man, doesn't know what's best for him. If he's too scared to see the truth, then I'll do it for him."

GWEN
Reynolds Farm, IA

Two more days had passed since the town dance debacle. She had isolated herself inside her grandparents' farmhouse from everyone, including the Sable Pointers. Jake had even come calling one night, and she yelled at her grandfather to make him leave from her upstairs bedroom. At breakfast the next morning, she sat swirling little puffs of eggs on her plate.

As long as she could remember, her grandparents had kept a hen house that produced eggs on a regular basis. They were fresh and brown, but they were only eggs and she could only eat eggs for so many days in a row before the sight of them made her sick to her stomach. She choked them down anyway. Baby Steele needed all the nutrients she could supply him with, and if she had to eat one thing every day, eggs were far from the worst thing she could fuel her growing baby with.

Her grandfather looked at her and smiled. It was that same happy smile that she had seen so many times when she had been with him.

"You love Gram's eggs, don't ya?"

She smiled back, faking it. "Love 'em."

"You hear that, Gram? She loves your eggs."

Gram cackled a laugh. "I'll go get you some more. They won't keep for long, so we gotta eat 'em."

"No Gram. I'm fine. Thank you."

Gram pretended like she couldn't hear Gwen and left the dining room for the kitchen. She came back into the small dining room with a black metal skillet. She scraped the last of the dried eggs onto Gwen's plate and gave her a smile.

"You were always such a good eater."

Code for I was a chubster when I was little. That was part of her reason for being so focused on fitness as an adult.

"Never could find a leftover in the house when Gwen came to visit," Pa added happily.

"She would even eat off my plate," Becky chimed in with a smile. If anyone knew what bothered you the most, it would be a sibling, and if Becky had the opportunity to highlight one of Gwen's insecurities, she took it.

Gwen gave her a fake smile.

Her grandfather put his hands beneath his chin and leaned on the table. He cleared his throat. "I meant to tell you last night, but you weren't receiving guests."

"What's that, Pa?"

He shifted uncomfortably in his chair. "Well, you see Gwen. I debated whether or not to tell you at all."

"Paaaa?" she said with a disapproving stretch of his name.

"Jake brought some disturbing news."

She cocked her head to the side, brow furrowing. "What's that?"

Pa stared at his hands first, collecting himself. "He said a large group of folks was trying to cross the bridge. Sheriff said it was Steele. Now, I don't know if I believe him." Gwen cut him off and flew out of her chair.

"Pa. That's Mark! I told you he was coming this way. He needs our help."

Pa lifted a hand in the air in an effort to defend himself. "Now hold on, those people could be dangerous."

She ran from the house, the door banging behind her. She sprinted for the barn. Gregor sat outside the barn door and eyed her as she ran out.

"What's going on?"

She marched into the barn and grabbed a thick saddle, carrying it back outside. Patsy tossed her head in the coral. Gwen tromped over and draped it over Patsy's back. She tightened the cinch around Patsy's stomach, making sure the horse hadn't held its breath while she was tightening it.

"Gwen, wait," her grandfather called from the porch. Gregor leaned on the fence.

"You okay, Ms. Gwen?"

She looked up for a second, fixing a twisted strap. "Steele's here."

Gregor smiled. "Great."

"Those imbeciles in town aren't letting him across."

"Isn't there another way around?"

"Not for about thirty miles, and I'm sure Jackson's on his tail."

"Damn," Gregor said. He scratched his head.

She jumped on the horse and locked her feet quickly in the stirrups.

"Gwen, don't overreact," her grandfather said, walking as quickly as he could through the yard. "I was only trying to protect you."

"From what?" she screamed at him. Patsy seemed to sense Gwen's irritation and stomped her front hoof into the earth.

Pa gazed at her from below, worry clouding his face. "I only want what's best for you. It ain't safe with them."

She scowled down at him. "You don't get to decide what is best for me." Her tone was harsh, but she wasn't a child, even if she was his grandchild. She pointed out at the river. "I love that man over there." She pulled on Patsy's head hard to the side. The horse neighed in response and she trotted for town. She could hear them shouting after her, but she ignored them. Her hair flowed behind her as she rode, and she tried to keep from riding the old horse too hard. She kept her at a canter, and soon the buildings on the edge of town came into view.

Gwen patted Patsy's sides. "Whoa, there, girl. Nice and easy," she said, soothing the horse. Gwen could feel Patsy's sides trembling between her legs from all the hard work. She trotted the horse right up to the sheriff's office. She dismounted and patted Patsy's side as she wrapped the reins around a dead light pole. She walked down to the riverbanks and peered out across the brown waters.

Pickup trucks, buses, motorcycles and all manner of cars lined the banks along the other side. Men stood on edge of the river in biker vests. She thought she saw a man hobbling among them in combat uniform. The wide brown river stretched between, always flowing downstream. *He's made it. He really made it.* She shook her head. *That man should already be in my arms and instead, he's stuck over in Illinois because my hometown can't find the goodness in their nice little hearts to let him over.*

She spun around and marched up to the sheriff's office. She ripped open the glass doors and walked in. Diane, the receptionist, waved at her.

"Good morning, Gwen. How can we help you today?"

Gwen breezed past her.

"Gwen, you can't just go in there. The sheriff's busy." Gwen ignored her and walked right into Sheriff Donnellson's office.

He leaned back in his old reclining leather office chair. His cowboy-booted feet were propped up on his desk. His beer belly sat plump in the middle and a gold-starred brown Stetson hat rested atop his head.

Pictures of the sheriff and local politicians at state fairs and homesteads adorned the walls. He set his feet on the ground and smiled.

"Well, Miss Reynolds, how are you feeling today? Your grandfather told us you weren't feeling well at the dance."

She placed her hands on his desk and leaned across. "Have you talked to them?"

Sheriff Donnellson frowned. "I don't like your tone of voice, young lady." His mustache fluttered a bit beneath his nose.

"Let me repeat myself. Did you speak with the people across the river?"

Sheriff Donnellson's mustache twitched even more with anger. "You can't talk to me like that."

"If you keep avoiding the question, I will punch you in the mouth. I don't care how nice Mrs. Donnellson is. I'm sure she would understand her husband is being a total horse's ass."

"I thought better of you Miss Reynolds. You've sure gone back on your raisin'. But if you must know, I did speak with the people across the river."

"Was it Mark?"

The sheriff cocked his head. "I spoke with a young lady." He smiled. "Kept calling me Brando."

Gwen frowned at him. "Sounds like Tess."

"Don't reckon the lady gave a name." The Sheriff's eyes darted up as he recollected the conversation.

"And a Mark Steele. Was he there?"

The sheriff twisted his mustache as he thought. "Now that I think about it, I did speak with an Agent Steele." He leaned forward.

"You did?" she said excitedly. "What'd he say?"

"I did. Pushy fellow. Very serious." He organized a stack of papers on his desk before he continued. "I know that this whole thing has been tough on you, but the mayor isn't wrong about this. We could hardly afford to take in the people we did, let alone hundreds or even thousands more."

"You're wrong." She turned her back on him. *He's here. He made it.* "He's coming across."

"Now, Gwen, don't you do anything hasty. I got men watching that bridge day and night. There's no way they're coming across."

She ignored him and walked out. She pushed open the glass doors and left him standing and shouting from his desk.

"I'll lock you up if you try and help them. Don't care who your grandfather is," he yelled after her. She unraveled Patsy's reins and glowered at the vehicles parked on the other side. *My people need my help.* Her thoughts surprised her for a moment. *Those are my people, but these are my people too.*

"I'll be watching you," Sheriff Donnellson called from the doorway.

She hauled herself up onto Patsy. "Be my guest," she yelled at him. She gave him the middle finger as she walked her horse away. "How's that for raisin'?"

"Your grandfather will hear about this," he yelled after her, shaking a fist.

***

The moon didn't shine in the night, covered by thick fall clouds. They took a wooded path down the shore of the bubbling Mississippi River. The two horses' hooves squished into the muddy trail, making a sucking sound every time a horse pulled a hoof free. Wet leaves smeared the riders with droplets of water on their way by, and branches slashed at their faces as the horses walked slowly in the dark.

They stopped the horses a little way from the town that was only an outline of buildings in the dark. A candle here or there in a window gave off the only light. Gwen dismounted. The glow from Steele's camp was like that of a sieging army. Muted orange flames from large campfires across the water dotted the riverbank. Gwen's partner in crime joined her.

"Hold this," she said, handing him the book from her grandfather's library.

Jake took it from her. "What are we going to do with this book?" he whispered. His white teeth flashed a confused smile.

"Hold on." She dragged a match along the rough sandpaper-like striking surface of her matchbook. The short match lit and she held it inside her lantern. The wick caught fire and the kerosene lantern let off a mellow yellow glow.

The horses stamped and Jake's handsome face illuminated along with his checkered red-and-black flannel shirt. It hadn't taken much to convince the man to help. He was willing to win Gwen's affection through any number of means.

"Why do we have to do this at night?"

"So no one will see us."

"'Member that time we snuck out on Old man Waverly's fields? You were drunk as a skunk and tried to tip that cow, but fell in the manure instead. You were covered from head to toe in the stuff." He laughed a bit. "Then when the sheriff caught up to us. You told him Rosie ate your necklace and you's was searching for it."

She snorted a laugh. "I do." Young and dumb and in love. She touched his arm and pointed away from the horses toward the town. "Keep watch. Nobody can know we are doing this."

"No problem." He turned around and faced the town, taking a knee. He held a hunting shotgun across his worn work jeans.

He spoke quietly. "Like coyote huntin' 'cept without the spotlight."

"You keep running that mouth and someone will spotlight us." She flipped open the book and set it on the ground. Thumbing through the pages, she stopped on one. "Perfect."

Holding the lantern, she said quietly to herself. "Now, let's get their attention." She took out an old sack and placed it over the lantern for a moment then flashed the light with three quick flicks of her wrist. She waited a moment and did it three times, slower. She waited another moment and did three quick flashes again. She watched Steele's camp. *Come on, guys.*

She repeated the process again and again. When she stopped for the third time, a flashlight flicked on and off from their camp. She smiled. In Morse code, she signaled G-W-E-N, and the person on the other side signaled two long flashes. She ran her finger down the page. *M. Mark*, she thought. Her excitement grew butterflies that fluttered in her stomach. He was there, and even if they spoke mere fractions of words, it gave her hope.

She flashed out her message to the other side and waited for acknowledgment. Three long flashes came back along with a long, short, long beam of a flashlight. "O-K," she whispered. She waited a moment before she continued. Something moved in the night. A twig breaking turned into feet trampling through the forest undergrowth.

"Jake," she half-shouted.

"We got some company," he said back. He walked toward the approaching people, gun held on his shoulders.

Flashlights beamed back and forth in the woods and shouts of men tracking went up. The searching lights stopped on Jake, and Gwen dove for the riverbank, sliding down near the water. She covered the lantern with her sack.

"Jake?" the sheriff's voice said. She peered over the edge of the embankment. A group of men surrounded Jake. She recognized Red, Dory, and Colton, along with a few others. "Well, Jesus, man. We thought you were one of them trying to sneak across. What're you doing out here?"

Jake gave him a smirk. "Just bought these horses from John Reynolds and I'm taking them back to the farm."

The sheriff shined his light along the horses. "Only two? Hope you didn't pay much 'cause those beasts look pretty sorry."

Jake glanced at the horses. "We're running out of fuel, Sheriff. Soon it will be all we got to farm."

Gwen peeked out from the bank.

"And you needed them tonight?" The sheriff pushed the hat up on his head and scratched his thin head of hair.

Jake grinned. "You know me, Hugh. I'm always trying to jump on a good deal. The Reynolds are hurting with all those mouths to feed."

Gwen ducked back down. The water lapped her ankles. The sack heated up in her hands. She started quickly flashing the lantern across the river.

Flashlights beamed her way, illuminating the dirt embankment above her head. "What's that?" Sheriff Donnellson said. Gwen continued spelling in Morse code. Long-long-short. G. Short-short. I. Short-short-short-long. V.

"You ain't never seen a glowing catfish, Hugh?"

Red's voice piped up. "I lived here my whole life and ain't never seen one."

"Me either," Colton agreed.

Footsteps grew closer as they walked toward the river.

Jake interjected. "Sure me and my brothers grabbed them all the time when we was kids."

Short. E. Gwen hurried as fast as she could.

Jake spoke really fast. "But it ain't nothing to see. Did I ever tell you the story about that three-headed calf we had last year?"

The footsteps grew closer her way, sticking in the mud, but she ignored them. Long flash. Long flash. M.

"You sure did," said a voice so close she couldn't believe they didn't hear her. "And what do we have here?" Hands gripped her shoulders forcibly and ripped her out of the muddy shallows. The lantern fell from her hands and sizzled out as river water splashed onto it.

The sheriff's mustached face got closer to hers. "I told you to not be sneaking around trying to help those lowlifes across the river, and here I find you sneaking around trying to help 'em."

His hand slipped down and pulled her firearm from her hip. He tossed it on the ground. He turned back to Jake. "And you, Mr. Bullis, have been lying to me to cover up for your girlfriend who thinks she's above the law?" Sheriff Donnellson gave Jake an angry stare.

"Sheriff, no need to get angry. She wasn't doing no harm," Jake protested.

Red frowned, his thick jaw widening. "She's betrayed her own town. Talking with those criminals across the way."

"I have not," Gwen hissed. "I'm trying to help people in need."

Sheriff Donnellson frowned. "And kill us all in the process." He pulled her closer, lifting her up onto her toes. "What are we going to do with this common criminal?"

Gwen's eyes darted toward Jake.

Jake reached for them. "Sheriff, I'm gonna take her home."

"You touch me, boy, and I'll smack you down." The sheriff turned back to Gwen and a slow smile crept across his face.

"I gonna do something that should have been done a long time ago." The sheriff released her and rolled up his sleeves to his elbows.

"Sheriff!" Jake shouted.

STEELE
Steele's Camp, IL

Steele held his binoculars to his eyes. His zoomed-in optics were black as he scanned the shore across the river. The light flashed again. It waved around frantically and disappeared as if the darkness had stamped it out.

The cloud cover blocked any semblance of the moon, leaving a night with almost no light. No visual assistance from houses, street lamps, or buildings.

Thunder's voice boomed, although he was still trying to be quiet. "I don't know that one." His long hair was topped with a red bandana tucked into the back knot and keeping his hair back.

"Looks like whoever was sending that code was stopped," Steele said. He let the binoculars rest. His heart sank in his chest. It had to have been Gwen or someone acting on her behalf. He glanced over at Kevin. The lanky man was a beanpole in the night. "What was the first message, again?"

Kevin held up a piece of paper near his face using a red light to read. "M-A-Y-O-R. End. W-O-N-T. End. H-E-L-P. End." Kevin read.

"What about the second line?" Steele asked.

"G-I-V-E. End. M. That was the last letter."

"Give what?" Steele glanced at his friend glowing red, his features shadowed like he was in a photography dark room.

Kevin appeared unsure. "Money?"

"You think these people want money? What the hell would they use it for?"

231

Kevin shrugged his shoulders in the dark. "Maybe they don't think it's as bad as it is out here?"

"Well shit, I can take a donation. Nobody here cares about money."

Thunder pulled out a wallet and offered Steele a couple of twenties.

Steele waved him off. "We'll go start a give me money to pay the toll campaign."

"Could be something else? Let's see. Give me mercy, give me monkey, give me Michelle, give me macadamia nut," Kevin said.

"Jesus." Steele shook his head.

"What do we do with it?" Thunder rumbled.

"I suppose we can't do anything with it. Those assholes over yonder still won't open up the bridge and we are stuck over here between a rock and a shell case."

Kevin continued on. "Monster. Micky. Martyr. Movie."

"We have to get ready to fight. We've been here for days and it's only a matter of time before Jackson tracks us down."

Thunder's gray beard moved up and down. "True."

Kevin droned on nearby. "Martian. Maryland. Mopey. Dopey. No. Man. Give man?"

Steele looked back at him. "Give man? What man? Which man?"

Gunfire kicked off and the sound carried clear over the rushing water. Shots rang out in quick succession. Big booming shotgun blasts followed by the smaller pops of a pistol.

Steele stared hard into the night, trying to penetrate the darkness with his care for Gwen. Gwen had been replaced by gunfire. He sighed, his heart fearing for her.

Kevin patted his shoulder trying to comfort him. "Come on, Cap." He steered Steele back toward the camp. "If the light comes back on, we'll see it."

They all walked back to their bonfire blazing away in the night. They joined some of the Red Stripes, Garrett, and Half-Barrel, along with Tess, Margie, and Tony. Steele took a seat next to Kevin who continued to drink and prattled on with words that started with M. Steele tried to ignore him. Tess lounged in the back of the Ranger pickup, her head poking out of a sea of blankets.

"What was going on?" she called down to him.

He gave her a side-glance irritated to be reminded of the situation that was dominating his thoughts. "Someone was trying to send us a message from across the river."

"Who?"

"We don't know, but somebody cut them off before they were done."

"Gwen?"

Steele eyed her. "I think so, but the first part was clear. They aren't letting us across."

Steele walked to the back of the red Ranger and opened the passenger side door. He unzipped his bag, and grabbed an atlas that sat on top, and brought it back over to the firelight. He flipped it open to Illinois. He bent the other pages around to the back so it was only open to a single state. He pointed his finger on the map to the far western point that touched Iowa.

"We are here right on the southeastern tip of Iowa but across the border. We have no choice but to try and find another access point."

His finger dragged down the river bend. "The next bridge is about thirty miles south of here," he said and tapped his finger. "Keokuk, Iowa."

Thunder nodded. "Our fuel tanker is running low, but I think we can make it."

"We'll need to consolidate everyone in the vehicles. Get all the fuel we can." Steele stared at the map. "We'll move down the river and set up ambushes here, here, and here." His finger jabbed the map. "Each group will retreat early in the fight, stringing Jackson's forces along and hopefully slow him down as his men become more cautious. If he does reach our main convoy, his men will be tired and spread out. Once we get across the bridge, then it's another race back to Hacklebarney."

Thunder's lips pressed tight together before he spoke. "That's a lot of ground to cover. Over sixty miles over open terrain with no idea who or what is out there."

"We have no choice but to avoid a head-to-head conflict until something swings in our favor."

Tess chimed in, her voice sneaking out from her pile of blankets. "What if that bridge in Keokuk is blocked or destroyed?"

"If we're that unlucky, then we have to stand and fight." Steele pushed air out of his nose and gave a curt nod to his people.

Kevin stopped saying M words and muttered, "Sounds like suicide." He averted his eyes down to his drink.

Steele's eyes focused on him, searching the man for more than an opinion. "Our only option is to run."

Kevin's eyes drifted up to Steele and he wiped his mouth. "I wouldn't put my trust in luck. I'd put it in well-thought-out plans with impeccable execution."

"I'm working with what we got and it ain't much." Steele turned to Thunder. "Do you think the clubs will see this thing through?"

Thunder poked at the fire with a stick. "I suppose. They don't mind riding, especially if they will get something out of it. I don't see them sticking around too long if the enemy catches up to us."

"That's when we'll need every gun we got." Steele stared at the flames, watching them burn and waver. If he got caught, he was going to die.

Thunder kicked a hot coal that rolled out of the fire back near the edges. "Let's hope it doesn't come to that."

The blaze licked the darkness with serpent-like orange and yellow tongues. The fire mesmerized Steele as it crackled and popped in the night.

Steele broke the silence. "Kevin, can you handle the first ambush?" Steele eyed the drunk man. Kevin was no coward and he could fight, but he was usually with Steele and not commanding his own team conducting an ambush on trained United States soldiers.

Kevin took a shaky swig of booze. The fire flashed off the metal flask as he tilted it back. "Me? Why me?"

Steele had expected him to be anxious. "Because I trust you to get the job done. You heard Thunder, the gangs are tepid allies at best. The Chosen people were once our worst enemies. That means things of importance fall on us."

"I'm not sure."

"I'll do it," Ahmed nodded to him from across the fire. "I can handle a gun, and I learned enough in Pittsburgh to hopefully troubleshoot explosives if need be."

Steele grimaced. "My plan was to send you south with one of the gangs to scout the bridge near Keokuk." He glanced at Thunder and back to Ahmed. "Hopefully, having you with a team of volunteers there will keep them honest."

"I can do that. I'll take Ollie and Weston."

"That's a fine crew. They have some good situational awareness."

Steele's eyes shifted to his next compatriot, one of his only living friends. "That leaves you, Kevin. Can I count on you?"

Kevin wiped his mouth with the back of his hand. "Yeah, I can do it, but what exactly do you need me to do?"

"I need you to ambush the scouts at the head of Jackson's column. Basically, you are going to hit them with some roadside bombs and retreat. Shouldn't even need to fire a gun. Then you'll retreat south to the main convoy. I want Jackson to think we are behind every rock, every tree, and every hill along the river." Steele turned toward Thunder. "You think you could put together a few IEDs for me?"

Thunder grinned. "Not a problem."

"Kevin, let's get you paired up with Tom and O'Hara. They'll both do what they are supposed to.

Kevin slugged back more of his flask's contents then wiped his mouth. "As ready as I'll ever be. Here's to a long life." He raised his glass to Ahmed who laughed and raised a bottled water in the air. "It's bad luck to toast with water, but I'll let it slide." He held his flask up higher in the air. "Here's to a merry one. A quick death and an easy one. A pretty girl and an honest one." He nodded to Tess. "A cold pint and another one." Kevin turned his flask bottoms up with a drunken smile and the sound of muted cheers from the people around him.

KINNICK
Warden, IA

Kinnick's hands shot out from under his blanket, his fingernails scratching the smooth wooden floor in a sleepy haze as he grasped for his M4. He planted the muzzle into the floor and used it to crutch himself upright. He half-walked, half-jogged for the barricade, his muscles in his back and legs tight from sleeping on the hard floor. He knelt down next to Hunter, his heart pounding in his chest. He edged his head just above the barrier, peering out.

A cluster of people marched down the street. Others ran from house to house with guns.

Hunter tracked one through his optic. "They will surround us quick. Get Coffey on the line," he said over his shoulder. Duncan set his M249 SAW on the barricade. Ramos dropped a box of ammunition and it jiggled like a cluster of brass bells.

Sergeant Volk held a radio to his snarled lips. "Volk to Hamilton One. Volk to Hamilton One."

"Hamilton One is up."

"Hamilton One, get close to the brown building on River Street. I want visual on a crowd of hostiles fast approaching for engagement."

"Copy," cracked out of his radio.

Kinnick knew as the seconds passed, the SURC was closing its distance to the shore, guns ready to blaze. Soon the Hamilton One's minigun would be trained on the mob of people gathering outside. A minigun would eat through the cluster of people in a fraction of a second with thousands of bullets.

Townspeople with guns took cover around houses, but many more marched down the center of River Street in an angry rabble. They waved guns in the air alongside fists.

Washington glanced over the barricade. "Looks like a riot."

"A riot about to get fucked up," Whitehead said over his shoulder. He turned and stared back down his sights.

"Prepare to engage!" Volk yelled.

"Hold your fire, Marine," Hunter said. He gave a quick eyeshot toward Kinnick.

"You are not clear to engage, Marine," Kinnick confirmed.

Volk glanced at Kinnick, anger in his eyes, and hissed. "Sir, they shot at us."

"Do not engage," Kinnick repeated. The mass of angry people gathered and shouted at the building.

"Fuck you," shouted a man.

"Come on out, you cowards," cried another.

A man and woman emerged from the middle of the pack. The woman was in her forties with heavy hips and shoulder-length blonde hair. "Look at what you've done to my baby." The young man between them could hardly stand. His eye was black, his cheek sticking out, blood stained the front of his shirt in a thin red line.

"They killed my boy," said a lanky man with salt-and-pepper hair. He clutched a shotgun to his chest. He shook his head, tears of anger rolling down his cheeks. "They killed my boy."

"Justice," cried another man.

Kinnick's eyes darted from his Marines to Hunter.

"What are they talking about?" Kinnick asked. The Marines perused one another.

"What are they talking about?" Kinnick repeated. He gritted his teeth. "Goddammit." He stood up and pushed his way through the Marines.

"Colonel!" Volk exclaimed.

Kinnick ignored the sergeant's pleas and placed his hand on the door handle and twisted. The door creaked open, revealing the angry faces of the mob. Their anger surged when he stepped outside and he was met with a chorus of boos and jeers, buffeting him from every direction.

After a moment, he raised a hand in the air. "Hear me." He waited ten seconds and repeated himself as the shouts settled to a dull angry murmur. He let his voice boom. "Hear me." He felt the presence of other men standing around him. Hunter and Hawkins, Volk and his Marines, all took their place next to him. A thin hard line of military men shoved up against the restaurant with a sea of people waiting to crush them into the walls.

"We come in peace," Kinnick said.

"Sure looks like it."

"Liar," spit an old man.

"Is this your version of peace, Colonel?" the mother of the victim screamed. "Look at what your men did." She lifted her son's chin. The young man let his face be turned so Kinnick could see his battered purpling cheek. "Open your mouth." The boy tried to lift his lips but couldn't, so she forced his mouth open. Only a few bits of white teeth were left inside.

Kinnick held up his hand. "I'm sorry, but none of my men did this."

The boy's father was a short robust man with only a wisp of hair hanging on atop his skull. He spit at Kinnick. "They beat them in the street like they was a piece of trash. The boys didn't even do nothin'."

The people parted and an older woman was led forward. Her hair was in perfect curly as if she had been perming it the night before. She wore a sweatshirt and jeans. She gestured toward the end of Kinnick's line. "I seen them. Yes, I did." A bent finger directed itself at Sergeant Volk. "That one there. I couldn't forget his mean face."

Kinnick glanced at Hunter. Hunter's single eye darted at Kinnick. Kinnick turned his head slowly in Volk's direction. Volk faced him.

"Sir, they're lying. We didn't do anything wrong."

The old woman's voice crackled. "He's the one that knocked Andrew's head on the pavement. Sure of it and his friend was wit' him. There."

Whitehead's face paled underneath his helmet. He gripped his gun tight. He threw his gun up to his shoulder. "You lie," he screamed, his voice rising octaves.

Guns were aimed at one another and the crowd held in silence.

The old woman didn't shy away. "I saw 'em. I was watching those boys check the lines on the docks when those two walked up on them." She pointed with a gnarled hand. "The big one there knocked the line out of Doug's hand and pushed him down. When Andrew tried to help, that one there hit him with the butt of his gun." She nodded at Kinnick. "He kept hitting him over and over again. I knew he was dead with the way he was just laying there."

Kinnick put his hand up. "Everyone stay calm." He turned to Volk.

"There ain't nothing to figure out, Colonel. Your men are to blame."

Kinnick kept his hand in the air and weighed Volk up and down, trying to glean anything that might prove him innocent or guilty. His voice hovered above a whisper. "Did you do this?"

"It was him," the boy cried. The boy's mother hugged the skinny teenager closer to her chest.

Kinnick glared at him. "You're sure?"

The boy squeaked out, "Yeah."

Kinnick turned back to Volk. "Tell me something. Tell me you were anywhere but there."

Volk's eyes drifted toward the ground. "No. It wasn't like that."

Kinnick's face turned into a frown. "What happened?"

Whitehead pointed out at the battered young man. "Sir, they fucking jumped us and they got what was coming."

"Shut up, Whitehead," Volk said with a glare at his fellow Marine. "We stopped them on the dock while we were on patrol. One of them drew a knife on us. It was quick. We reacted."

"Why didn't you report this, Sergeant?" Hunter said to Volk.

Volk snarled. "Because of what they done to Gore. That little fucker was laughing about it." He shoved a finger out at the battered teenager. "That bastard's lucky he didn't end up like his little buddy."

Kinnick couldn't believe the words flowing from this man's mouth. He felt the treachery deep in his gut. "Damn, son, what have you done?"

Volk turned back to him. "I did what you do when one of your brothers is assassinated by a town of treasonous filth."

An uproar of angry yells erupted in the crowd, their balled fists punching the air.

The soldiers and Marines put their firearms up to their shoulders but kept them in the low-ready.

A bottle smashed on the restaurant behind them, sending glass flying through the air.

"Sir, we should duck back inside before this gets ugly," Hunter said loud into Kinnick's ear.

Kinnick eyed the people. *What have we done here? Why did you put me in this spot?* He glanced at Hunter. He appeared calm on the outside, a stoic, but Kinnick knew he was ready to gun down the front ranks and make a break for a building.

This could be the end of the greatest experiment ever made. On the beaches of a small island in the Mississippi River, the entire operation could fold because people couldn't work together to keep the dream alive. Instead, they dug themselves into the ugly shallow grave of revenge and vengeance.

Kinnick pulled his firearm out from his holster and spun on the Marine sergeant. He pointed his M9 at the Marine's head, whose face broke into an outright snarl.

"Colonel? What the fuck are you doing?"

Hunter pointed his gun at the Marine sergeant. "Drop the gun, Volk." His gun bounced toward Whitehead. "And you Whitehead."

"Sir?" Whitehead's face twisted in confusion.

Kinnick ignored the young Marine's pleas. "Sergeant Volk and Private Whitehead, by the power vested in me by the executive branch of the United States of America, I place you under arrest for murder."

GWEN
Hacklebarney, IA

The doors to the American Legion were propped open. Someone had draped an extra American flag over the doorway leading inside. Gwen stood with her grandfather and grandmother outside the building. The Hacklebarney townsfolk made their way inside in twos and threes or entire families of parents and children. Most were multigenerational families of farmers: great-grandparents, grandparents, husband, wife, and children.

John Reynolds grunted. "Best get inside before we have to stand in the back." He had on a pair of fine jeans and a nice Wrangler button-down shirt topped off with a John Deere ball cap. Gram wore a dress that Gwen had only seen her wear to church on Sunday. It had a floral design with a ruffled white lace neck lining.

Gwen had elected to leave the Little Sable Point refugees back on the farm. Bringing them would only make the people of Hacklebarney dig their heels in even more.

They walked inside the American Legion hall. Hundreds of black and gold stackable chairs stood in neat even rows, all leading to the front stage. An old worn podium stood in the middle, adorned with a washed out seal of Hacklebarney on the front. Mayor Dobson watched her enter and smiled. The sheriff sat on stage with him, his hat pushed high on his head, his shotgun leaning on the corner wall.

People turned to watch them walk in. Betty Grant turned to her sister,

Violet Crenshaw, and whispered something. Violet narrowed her eyes at Gwen. Gwen hadn't gained any popularity points at the town dance. *I'm about to lose some more points here.*

Gwen walked with her chin held high beside her grandparents. Becky labored in, pushing Haley lightly in the back to keep her moving. They all took the last seats in a middle row.

"I wanna sit by Gwenna," Haley exclaimed. Becky shook her head and pushed Haley into the seat next to Gwen. Gwen put her arm around the little girl.

From a few rows over, Jake gave her a little wave and smile. He sat with a tall man and woman, his parents, Tyler and Cindy Bullis. They gave Gwen kind smiles. His father wore a dirty red and white International Harvester hat.

People continued to file in and took places standing around the edges of the room.

"It stinks in here," Haley complained.

Gwen smiled, ignoring the girl's complaints.

"And it's boring." Haley alternated kicking her legs right leg and then left leg back and forth.

Gwen leaned down close to her. "Let's play a game."

"Really?" Haley squealed.

"Shhh," Becky said, putting her finger to her lips.

"Come on, Beck, she didn't mean it."

Becky sighed, raising her eyebrows. "Indoor voices. Both of you."

Gwen bent closer to Haley. "I want you to count the number of guns you see in the hall."

Haley pouted, the fun of a game disappearing. "Counting? Ew."

"Just try it out. You can start with mine," Gwen said and pointed to her hip.

"Wow, Gwenna. I didn't know girls could use those."

Gwen pursed her lips and gave her niece a cool gaze. "Girls can use them just as good as the boys, but you should never touch a gun without an adult there to make sure it's safe. But right now, look at all the adults and count how many have big guns and little guns."

Haley nodded. "Okay, Gwenna. I'll try." She stood on her seat and studied the crowd.

The sheriff mean mugged Gwen from the stage. He had begrudgingly let Gwen keep her firearm when she had used it to kill the infected that had wandered upon them by the river. A shot over his shoulder into an infected head had changed his mind, but others weren't as lucky.

Mayor Dobson stood up and walked over to the podium. He waited for a moment, mouthing words to people in the audience and smiling. He made short waves at a few people. It made Gwen want to vomit.

"Can everybody hear me?" he said loudly. He waited a moment for a confirmation. "No microphone tonight, so all you get is my real voice."

"Can't hear ya, George," Brian DeVault shouted from the back.

Mayor Dobson walked out from behind the podium. He smiled again, spreading his hands wide. "I'm not sure you could hear me if I was right next to you." The people laughed, and Brian smiled and nodded.

"How about now?"

Brian gave him a thumbs-up from the back and leaned back against the wall. "We're good."

Dobson clasped his hands together, shaking them a bit as he spoke. "Perfect. I want to start out by giving my condolences to the Newbold family. Sue, Gerald, and Katherine I am sorry for your loss. Red was a great member of our community and will be sorely missed. He died a local hero, fighting against the infected last night. Let's bow our heads in a moment of silence. Let us not forget the Macintosh family. We must hold them in our prayers as well."

Everyone dipped their heads, including Gwen. *That idiot, Red, shouldn't have froze when he did or he would be here today. They aren't ready for what's coming.*

"I know these last few months haven't been great. We've seen a lot of scary things going on out there. Most those things have happened far away and we're blessed for that." Ayes sounded out from throughout the audience.

"I won't say we've been lucky, but we've stood tall and done a good job preparing for the winter months. Although we've had to cut down on production, we should have plenty and be able to plant again come spring. We might need to use some of the old methods, but we'll grow as much as we can. I spoke with Elder Leroy down the river, and he will exchange teams of draft horses in exchange for protection and medical care."

Sheriff Donnellson stood, hoisted his pants farther up, and joined Dobson. He hooked his thumbs through his belt. "I can rotate some men down there in groups of three or four every other day."

The mayor nodded. "That should suffice. Dr. Miller, would you be willing to see some of their people on the house?"

"Yes, I will, Mayor," the gray-haired glasses-wearing doctor said. Van Fogerty patted the thin doctor on the arm. The doctor gave him a smile.

"You all are such generous people, I truly feel like this community is special, but unfortunately our problems don't end here." Mayor Dobson walked back and forth on stage. "There's an even graver threat lurking at the gates of our small town." He thrust an arm out and pointed toward the door. "As we speak, a band of hooligans, ruffians, outlaws, and outsiders are attempting to gain access to our beautiful town." He leaned closer to the crowd. "They are about as welcome as an outhouse breeze."

People booed and yelled, "No!" Gwen's heart beat hard in her chest as she knew she prepared for an uphill fight. The mayor glared right at her as if he dared her to open her mouth. "They bring with them the disease that plagues this great nation. They bring rape, theft, and murder. All they will do is take until there is nothing left, and then they will move on, leaving us stripped of our livelihood and dignity."

Gwen clenched her fists and stood up. She couldn't help but bite on the mayor's bait. "That's not true." The room went dead silent. All heads turned in her direction. Even Gwen herself was startled by the force of her outburst. She pointed a finger at him. "And you *know* it."

The mayor smiled at her and gestured in her direction with one of his hands. Then he clasped both hands behind his back. "Gwen Reynolds, everyone. It's been awhile since she's lived here in Hacklebarney, but our prodigal daughter has returned. And with her, those people."

Gwen took a moment to smooth her clothes and pull down her shirt. She could feel all of their eyes on her. "I'm sure most of you know me. I went to school with the Thornburgs and the Geberts. I've filled sandbags with you in the big flood of '96. I moved away a few years back, but you know me. I wouldn't lie to you. Those people across the river are not criminals. Those are good people, down on their luck and in need of our help."

A susurration swept through the people in the tiny hall. Her grandpa gave her a proud nod.

"Gwen's not wrong," the mayor said. "How many people did you bring with you?"

"One hundred and three with two infants." *And one in my belly.*

Mayor Dobson whistled. "One hundred and three people she brought with her. One hundred and three hungry mouths. One hundred and three beds. One hundred and three people who need protection."

"We can take care of ourselves," Gwen started before she was cut off. Her voice sounded like a whine instead of the voice of someone stating a hard fact.

Mayor Dobson held up a hand. "I'm not finished."

Gwen's mouth clamped shut.

"Who's going to feed these people? Who's going to clothe these people when winter comes?"

People murmured to one another. Gwen could hear the concern in their voices.

"Sheriff, how many people live in Hacklebarney?"

The sheriff thumbed his mustache while he thought. "About one thousand, one hundred and sixty-three souls."

The mayor nodded and pointed out at everyone. "We just added one hundred and three more. We just increased our population by almost ten percent in one night. We don't know when we'll find more fuel. We don't know when we'll get help. We don't know anything, and now, we have to provide for a bunch of new people that we're not even sure can contribute anything to our community." He dropped his chin, letting his words soak in. "What they are is leeches." People nodded their heads.

"Luckily for us, John has taken it upon himself to house these people. Isn't that right, John?"

Her grandfather stood up next to Gwen. He took his hat off and held his ball cap in his hands, nervously rubbing the brim. His voice came out shaky and tired, and it cracked near the end. "I have agreed to take them in."

"And to clothe, feed, and house them?"

John nodded. "I will. With some help hopefully." Gwen knew her grandfather was a proud man. He wouldn't say no now, even if he couldn't do it.

"Mmm. John, that was not the agreement, but I will not have them expelled. We're not monsters."

People murmured their agreement. "What about all the others? Not just the old and the young. There are hundreds of bikers along with men and women who can fight across the river. You'll need them to help farm. You said it yourself, we have to farm the old ways and will need the extra help."

"They don't know farming," B.B. said from across the room.

The mayor shook his head. "No, they don't."

"They could help us against," she stopped herself.

"What can they help us against?" the mayor said. His eyes narrowed.

"There's the infected."

The mayor's mouth tightened. He had her on the ropes. "The sheriff has that under control. What *else*?"

Gwen's voice came out smaller than she would have liked. "A force of renegade United States military forces is hunting the group."

The crowd in the town hall erupted into shouts and cries of dismay. It was hard to pick out who said what, but none of it was positive.

"The United States military!"

Gwen's head spun in circles as she watched them all voice their disapproval.

Gerald shook his head repeatedly. "We can't help them wretches."

Sue Newbold threw her short arms in the air. "Fugitives! They're fugitives!"

"There may be all kinds, but I'm not sure it takes all kinds."

The mayor lifted his hands in the air. "People of Hacklebarney. Please quiet down."

Gwen stood, shaking at their calls of traitor and criminal. She felt sick to her stomach as if every word were a blow to her soul.

"Now, Gwen, we know you have loved ones over there," Dobson said. People gasped, the thought of loving one of those people disturbing. Dobson turned his head to the side, raising a hand toward them. "We should cut her some slack. Even good people get caught up with a rough crowd in times like this." He nodded. "It's okay. We forgive you for that."

Gwen pointed behind her and out the door, her voice rising in anger. "Those people are not traitors. They are as red-blooded American as you and me. Colonel Jackson is the traitor."

Dobson's eyebrows rose on his face. "Now, now, Gwen. Nobody took you for a traitor, but listen to what you are asking me, no, what you are asking this community to do. You want us to harbor a massive group of people that the military is hunting. How could we do that? Many of us have served in the military and would never even remotely consider taking up arms against them."

Grady McAllister cleared his throat. He stood on the wall, arms crossed, wearing his mechanic coveralls and his signature mellow-orange Allis Chalmers hat high up on his head. "We had a couple of birds in weeks ago. Military folk."

"Birds?" Dobson said.

"Helicopters. A bunch of Special Forces soldiers and an Air Force colonel. Their chopper was banged up. Bunch of bullet holes in them. Looked they been fighting each other out there." He nodded. "They looked like the good guys. Gave 'em fuel. Supposed they would have taken it if I hadn't. I never would have thought I'd see the day when we'd fight each other, but Miss Gwen could be tellin' the truth."

Dobson's brow furrowed. "That evidence is insubstantial at best. Anyone could have shot those choppers, including those people over there." He pointed toward the doors.

"Meant no offense. Just my two cents." Grady leaned back on the wall.

Gwen turned, pointing in the same direction. "Mayor, if you don't let those people across, they will be slaughtered by a madman and his men on the banks of the Mississippi. Then when they are done, they will find a way across." She shook her head, knowing she spoke the truth. "And believe me, they will find a way. If the mood strikes them, they will ravage this town." She turned and stared at the people of Hacklebarney. She eyed Kenny and Jenny Hamlin then let her gaze fall on Nowlton and Millie Gebert, who gripped Roland's shoulders. "If you don't give them everything they want, they will murder the men." She locked eyes with wrinkle-faced B.B. "They will abuse the women and burn this town to the ground. I've seen it in their last camp. They abuse their power and do whatever they want to the civilians, and the civilians have no choice but to let them." Everyone's eyes grew wide, including the mayor's. His jaw dropped a bit, but he quickly composed himself.

"That is a tall tale, but as the leader of this community, I have to take such accusations seriously. Sheriff Donnellson, can we double our patrols on the bridge?"

The sheriff stuck his belly out. "I think I can manage to scrounge up a few more men."

"There are some men from Sable Point who can help," Gwen offered.

The mayor leaned over to the sheriff and they spoke in low tones for a moment. "I don't think that's a good idea."

Gwen nodded. *Getting nothing.* Integration was key in winning the town's trust and they resisted her every step of the way.

Mayor Dobson stepped back forward and shoved his hands in his pockets. "Gwen, you can take a seat." Gwen did as he asked, feeling that somehow he had tricked her.

"We've discussed some really important things tonight about the future of Hacklebarney. I don't take these things lightly. It would be easy for me to step in and just say this is how it's going to be, but you elected me to represent you and not giving you a say in the future of this community is downright undemocratic. So let's take a vote."

"But we don't have ballots," Van said loudly.

The mayor waved him off. "We don't have time for anything formal. The old-fashioned way. A raise of hands will do."

The people of Hacklebarney nodded their heads in agreement. If they liked anything, they liked things that they were used to.

"I want you to think about what was said here tonight." Dobson looked down and back up, ever the contemplating manipulator. "Those of you who want to allow the people from across the river entrance to our community, giving them refuge against the U.S. military, say aye and raise your hand high."

Gwen found her hand shooting up. She nudged Becky, who rolled her eyes and raised her hand. Her grandparents did the same. Gwen glanced around the room and saw a few hands here and there.

"Aye," Gwen said loud.

"You may put them down. And those who would like to keep our community secure and barricaded to the outsiders, say nay."

Hands shot up all around Gwen and a multitude of voices cried, "Nay," loud and clear.

Mayor Dobson clapped his hands together. "So there you have it. We maintain our current posture toward the outsiders and let them find their own place of refuge without us."

Gwen was out of her seat and storming from the hall in seconds. She accosted the people as they walked out with not a care in the world. "They will die," she yelled at them.

"Get outta here," howled a man with a dip of his chin.

"Go home," B.B. said with a comforting arm around Annie.

She stood out in the street staring at the people across the river and hugging herself. The people of Hacklebarney filed out and went to their respective farmsteads and homes.

Her grandfather walked up and put his arm around her.

"They just don't understand," she mumbled into his shoulder.

"I know, honey. We'll find a way. There's always a way."

STEELE
Banks of the Mississippi, IL

Clouds of dust filled the air like a thick fog as the convoy rolled down a single-lane dirt road. Through the billows of tossed-up dirt, lines of trees stood guard between them and the water. A narrow path was cut through the middle of the trees for telephone lines that sagged between poles. On the other side of the trees, the land sloped into the brown waters of the Mississippi. The chocolate water bubbled by, moving faster than it appeared, and across the rapid water was Gwen.

He had stood on the banks for over fifteen minutes before he left hoping that she saw him. There was no way she would miss the dust from his retreating vehicles.

On the other side of the road, trees, and fields of unpicked withering brown corn lay trampled and unkept.

Steele rode with Tess in silence. She had been chilly since their disagreement about the pastor, a topic he did not want to rehash with the slight yet feisty woman.

"When was the last comms check with Ahmed and the Wolf Riders?" Steele asked her.

She didn't look at him and instead picked at the flaking black steering wheel. "About an hour ago."

Earlier that morning, Ahmed and his volunteers rolled out south with Macleod and his Wolf Riders. More and more, Steele felt exposed without his allies close by.

He ran a hand over his scalp. "After we get Kevin set up, let's get him back on the horn along with Thunder. I hate being blind out here."

Thunder pulled the rearguard over a mile behind and would take the brunt of any attack if Jackson's forces caught up to them. *Is it wise to put my most loyal scouts at the rear of the column? But who else can we trust?*

Ahead, the road bent almost ninety degrees following the river. Steele pointed. "There. That's where I want our first ambush."

When they reached the tree-lined point, Tess pulled the small red pickup over to the side of the road. "Why don't you have some of the pastor's men to do it?" she asked. Her voice held a high level of irritation.

"Because you said it yourself: they can't be trusted."

She stared at him with her almost black eyes. "This is dangerous and I don't like Sable taking all the risks."

"I don't like it either, but who else can I trust to do the job right?"

She adjusted her hand on the steering wheel, looking out at the trees. "I can't stand to have us lose any more after Scott's crew got chewed up in Pentwater and Lucas and Greg in Burr Oak. There are only so many of us."

He let his chin drop to his chest. There had been so many more names on his list. He didn't even know them all now. He started going down the list in his mind—*Wheeler, Jarl, Andrea*—each name adding to the weight of his failure to bring them all home. He finished with *Max, Bengy, Scott, Mom*. The last name always stung the most.

"I'm sorry. I wish I could have saved them all. I would trade places with them to keep them safe, but we're at war with the living and the dead. People die in war. Innocent people. The good along with the bad. If I could bring them back I would, but I can't, so I'll fight for the rest of us."

Her look was fierce like a tiger. "Try harder."

He stopped, his hand on the door handle, for a moment before he popped open the door. Kevin's pickup sat behind them idling. The other vehicles went around them. Kevin sat with long-haired Tom and young O'Hara, his baby face making him look much younger than he actually was. Kevin opened his door and stepped out with a slight drunken wobble.

Steele pointed. "This is the spot. Line the IEDs on the road here. Cover them with foliage so they don't spook." Steele pointed back at the power lines. "Park the truck up those lines a ways. Wait for the first few Humvees to go by and hit them with it."

"All three at once?"

"Exactly. That should cause a good amount of chaos through the column. Sprint back to the pickup and drive down the lines until you find another way route to the riverside road."

The lanky man glanced worriedly at the trees. "I hope they don't see us."

Steele eyed the maples and oaks. "Keep your heads down and don't mistake Thunder and his club for the bad guys. We don't want biker Santa getting upset with us, and no need for any heroics. We just need to make them think we aren't worth the effort."

"We'll make sure it's done, Captain," Kevin said with a smirk. His eyes were open a bit wider today.

Slightly more sober than normal.

He stuck out his hand. "Captain Steele."

Steele shook his head and put his hand in Kevin's, holding it for a moment. "I told you not to call me that."

"Too late. You can't pick your own nickname. It's Man Code. The more you try to kick it, the more it sticks."

"You're right there. Stay safe. We'll see you soon."

"Back before you know it." Kevin released his hand and got back in his pickup. Tom gave Steele a salute wave, and they drove off the two-track rutted road and turned over into the power line cut thru. Steele watched them drive away. He walked to Red Rhonda and slid back into the seat.

"Let's catch up before we fall too far behind."

Tess gunned it down the road. In a few minutes, they had reached the rear of the convoy. Rural roads passed them by and took them through a small town. Only the dead greeted them with their decaying hands and white eyes. The convoy didn't slow but shot them down and ran them over in passing.

***

By nightfall, they had gone fourteen sluggish miles. Poor roads and not knowing Jackson's location was making their progress painstakingly slow. Weary people made camp on the banks of the river. Steele hadn't wanted to travel too far ahead of his ambushers, and since he hadn't heard from them, he operated under the assumption they hadn't run into Jackson's unit yet.

Thirty minutes later, he heard the rumble of motorcycles. Steele hopped off the tailgate of his pickup. His leg felt increasingly better every day. It was his arm he was still worried about. Using two hands on his handgun was out of the question. If he wasn't resting the weapon, prone or relatively danger close, the M4 proved difficult to use effectively for long durations. Although he could manipulate the M4 with one hand, it was much slower than using two hands, which was what most of his training was based around.

Thunder stopped his chopper near Steele. The heavy biker dismounted his hog and adjusted his belt beneath his belly, running a hand over it.

"You see them?" Steele asked.

Thunder licked his lips. "'Bout eight miles back. Dust from their trucks gave them away, but it looks like they stopped."

"That should have been past Kevin's ambush point."

"Didn't see them as we rolled by."

"I don't like that."

Thunder picked at his beard. "Just means they was hidin', but we did come across some of these fuckers split off from the main group."

Steele's eyebrow lifted as far as it could go beneath his scar. "Jackson's men?"

"They claim they ain't, but who can tell. Probably just lying to save their hides."

"Show me," Steele growled.

Thunder marched Steele around to the back of a full-sized black Dodge Ram. Two men sat on the tailgate wearing Army Combat Uniforms, their legs dangling beneath them. Their heads were hooded with soiled white cloth bags and their hands were tied behind their backs. Big Garrett stood guard next to them, a pistol shoved in his belt.

"Take off his hood," Steele instructed with a nod.

Garrett ripped the hood off one and the man blinked in the dim light.

Steele rested his hand on his tomahawk. "What's your name, soldier?"

The soldier was young, no more than twenty, and blond. His ACUs were too big for him, making him appear even younger. "Holland, sir." He gulped after he spoke.

"Holland, where'd you come from?"

"I. We." His eyes darted to his comrade.

"Don't look at him. Who's your CO? What's your unit?" Steele rubbed his hand along the head of his tomahawk.

"We were part of 2nd Platoon, 1st Company, 75th Infantry Battalion. My CO was Captain Forester."

"Under Colonel Jackson?"

The young soldier's eyebrows went up on his face and his cheeks twitched in a scared smile. He looked around for someone to believe him. "No. I don't know Colonel Jackson. Was he in Chicago?"

"Sergeant Yates? Ben Mauser?"

"No, sir." With every name, Steele watched the young man's face. His language and facial features showed no signs of deceit. Since his hands were tied, he couldn't do comforting moves like rubbing his hands, stroking his hair, or general fidgeting. Steele relied on his facial features to help determine his truthfulness. Holland made as much eye contact as Steele expected a man scared shitless would do. He didn't over blink. He didn't try to speak away from Steele. He didn't shake his head while he spoke. Then again, it was always possible that the man was a sociopath or a habitual liar, something that would greatly assist him with self-preservation in a dying world.

Thunder swatted at the soldier, cuffing him in the back of the head like a bad dog. He grabbed the back of Holland's ACUs and yanked the boy around. He leaned in really close to the soldier. "You think real nice, 'cause you know what we do with liars?"

"No, sir," Holland's voice shook as he spoke.

"We give him to that man over yonder." Thunder gestured toward the pastor. He stood about fifty yards away watching with a group of his followers, arms crossed over his chest. They walked forward, a gang of religious fanatics with their clubs and guns.

"I swear on my mother's life. I'm telling the truth."

"Where's your mother now?" Thunder grunted.

"I dunno. I only went where they told me to go."

"How'd you end up out here? Pretty far away from Chicago," Steele said. He kept one eye on the pastor's men as they approached.

Holland's eyes darted back to Steele, true fear settling over the man. "You aren't going to take us back, are you?"

Steele frowned. "Back where?"

"To Chicago. Please don't," Holland begged. He began to shake and Steele thought he might cry.

Thunder leaned over to Steele and whispered. "They're deserters."

What do I do with the military's deserters? The thought had never crossed Steele's mind. He definitely wasn't taking them to Chicago, but to release them meant risking giving up his position and relative strength to Jackson. To have them join his group, he added loosely affiliated cowards to his cause.

The pastor and his cluster of followers stood expectantly nearby. "What have you found, Mr. Steele?"

Steele glared at the captives. "Thunder came across some Army soldiers."

The pastor raised an eyebrow. "Colonel Jackson's men?" He loomed toward them, peering down his nose. "I'm curious as to the composure of his men. I'm curious as to what makes them tick."

"They claim they came from Chicago."

Holland burst in. "That's right. We came from the quarantine."

"Quiet, you," Thunder snarled.

The soldier's lips shut but his mouth still quivered. He sucked in air through his nose, trying to keep quiet.

The pastor regarded the prisoners from above. "And you believe these men?"

Holland shook his head in fear. "It's true. We deserted. You should have seen it. We didn't even have a chance. The Zulus kept coming wave after wave. Millions. I swear it." His eyes went wide. "Nothing we did made a stinking difference. All we did was die." Thunder swatted the soldier with his hand again, and the soldier broke down into quiet sobbing, his shoulders shaking.

"I do, Pastor." Steele looked at Thunder, and Thunder gave a disapproving nod.

"As disgusting as it sounds, I believe them."

The soldier nodded his head frantically. "Thank you. Thank you. You are a very generous man."

Steele thought Holland might throw himself at his feet and kiss his boots.

The pastor lifted his chin. "Neither of you find it coincidental that while we are being chased by a renegade military unit, we run into soldiers that don't belong to him?"

"He's just a kid. I believe him."

The pastor brought his hands together in front of him with a small clap. "Deserters or Jackson's men, I say we send a message for both alike. String them up and torch them."

Steele met eyes with the pastor. The pastor was unmoving beneath Steele's gaze. His words were true in his world.

Holland's eyes hopped from man to man, and finding no aid, started sobbing again. "We only wanted to live." The sound of running water pouring on the metal in the truck bed could be heard. "Please, we didn't mean anything by it. Don't do it. Please don't do it."

Steele twisted his head in Holland's direction in disgust. "Jesus, man. Get a hold of yourself."

Holland shook as he cried. "P-Please."

Steele considered the pastor and his armed group with a narrowed eye. He would win a fight against them with the Red Stripes at his back. Once the entirety of the factions became engaged, he wasn't so sure. If it came down to it, he would make sure to carve up the pastor first with his tomahawk.

"Deserter or not, I'm not burning these *men*." He made sure to stress the word "men" in an attempt to stabilize Holland's weak fortitude.

"These men lack the heart for this world, Mr. Steele. Nothing steadies their hand or steels their nerves. They are broken. In my experience, you're better off separating the wheat from the chaff sooner than later."

"They stay with the living today."

The pastor licked his lips as if he had more to say. He nodded his chin slightly and gave Steele a soft knowing smile. "Although I disagree, I concede to your decision, but best keep them in your camp. Accidents tend to happen around mine."

Steele gritted his teeth. Thinly veiled or not, the pastor's threat was just that, a clear warning that these men would not be safe.

Holland shook his head in relief. "Thank you, sir. We'll do anything for you. Whatever you need done, we're your guys." The soldier in the other hood nodded vigorously. Muffled thank-yous eked out from inside his hood.

The pastor and his gang turned and left for their campsite. Oily-haired Luke gave a creepy look over his shoulder back at Steele.

"Damn that man." Steele eyed the two deserters. "Keep these idiots locked up until I can figure out what to do with them." Steele walked back to his campsite, his blood boiling.

TESS
Steele's Camp, IL

Flames danced along Steele's face. "How dare he presume to murder those men. This isn't some medieval crusade. This is the 21st century. We can't just burn people at the stake."

Tess watched the fire. *This guy truly is a slow learner.* "Of course he thinks he can. That's what he's been doing since the beginning."

Steele shook his head, staring out into nothing. "I hate that man. Will someone rid me of this godforsaken priest?"

"Just say the word." She snapped her fingers. "Gone."

He gave her a mean look. "No. We have to stay true to our word."

She glowered over at the Chosen campfires. People were huddled around them. Thunder and the Red Stripes were camped nearby. Rather than risk a fight in the night, they had stayed near the convoy.

"I need to take a walk." She unfolded herself from her blanket nest and jumped out of the back of the pickup.

"Don't go far. We don't know what's out there," he mumbled.

"I'm not an idiot. I'll stick to the campsites."

Steele nodded and scratched at his scar. "Damn this thing itches."

She laughed softly and walked away. "Keep yourself alive." She made a beeline for Thunder's camp.

A Red Stripes patched biker, as wide as he was tall, stood in the shadows near his campfire. She waved at him.

"Who is it?" he commanded in the dark.

"It's just me, Half-Barrel."

A grin cracked his lips. "Hey, Tess. He's over by that fire." Half-Barrel gestured with his sawed-off shotgun in hand. She found the thick, big-bellied biker taking a piss on the fire.

"Never do grow up, do they," she said from behind him.

The man shook his member, jiggling it in the direction of the flames. "Better than losing it to one of the infected." He turned around and waved her over. He embraced her for a moment like she was his daughter. He smelled like campfire smoke and body odor.

He released her. "How are you, my girl?" he said, looking down at her.

"Been better."

"We've all been better. It's an ugly dark world out there. That it is." He took a seat and she folded, sitting with her legs beneath her near the fire. She put her hands closer to the flames, letting the heat warm them.

"What's bothering you?" he said. He rested both of his hands on his knees.

She contemplated the licking flames of yellowish orange. "You know, generally speaking, the end of the world is a joyous place. Infected trying to eat us, those pricks over yonder trying to murder us, and the military hunting us like a pack of dogs." She looked up at him. "So everything is just swell."

Thunder nodded, gazing out. "I take everything one day at a time, but then again, I may be more comfortable with my days being my last. Not so long ago, I was throwing back beers at the clubhouse, making money with imports and exports from Canada."

"Imports and exports? You mean drugs?" She peered at him.

He glanced up at her. "Ha. Done enough drugs in my day. I'm over that. The new trade is in animal trafficking."

She smiled. "Like cats and dogs?"

"Nah, the sexy stuff, mostly endangered species parts, ivory, fur, but we've brought over our fair share of live ones too. One time I snuck over seventy turtles."

"Turtles?"

"Yeah, a real hot commodity. Hundreds of dollars a pop." He nodded at the fire. "It's a lucrative business and a lot less jail time if you get caught."

She snickered. "Thunder, the big bad turtle dealer."

"Laugh all you want, but we were rolling dough." He scratched his arm with a free hand.

She put her head down for a moment. "What do you think of him?"

"Who? Steele?"

Thunder sighed. "The kid has got a lot on his plate, but he's doing all right."

"What about him letting the pastor live?"

Thunder shook his head from side to side like an elder silverback gorilla. "I'd have to say he's a better man than me after what the pastor did to us, but I suppose that's why we follow him."

She peered over her shoulder back toward the Chosen camps. "Look at all of them over there. Brainwashed. They're frickin' disgusting."

Thunder grunted and nodded. "Every man follows something." His brown eyes rested on her. "You want to know something I learned over in Nam?"

She felt he was detracting her from her true purpose. "Sure."

He rubbed his hands together. "I was with the 3rd Battalion 7th Marines. We were based out of Firebase Ross. It was in the Que Son Valley, central Vietnam. I was leading a combat patrol near a small village. No more than sixty people lived there, really only a few families. We had intelligence that they were supporting PAVN in the area."

His eyes grew distant as he remembered. "We went through the houses. Women and kids were crying. Dallas and I ducked into a hut. There was a man with his wife and kid. We kicked over some shit. We were searching for weapons and contraband." He scratched under his bandana. "Dallas pulled up a rug, uncovering a trap door. He flipped it open. Tons of shit down there. Mortars, grenades, AKs, enough shit to outfit a company of the bastards. Dallas was screaming at the father. The guy didn't understand a thing."

Thunder's eyes didn't blink. "Dallas beat him. Hit him the face, I dunno, ten, twenty times before I made him stop. I remember that man's battered face like it was my own. I'll never forget it. I hoisted the bastard up by the scruff of his neck." His voice dipped low. "He was whispering the same word over and over through bloodied holes where his teeth used to be. Món ăn." Thunder shook his head. "Food in Vietnamese. His eyes said it. He was only doing it to survive. He was doing it to feed his family."

Tess gulped. "What'd you do?"

Thunder stared into the fire. A moment passed as he relived his memory. "I stabbed him in the gut. He laid on the dirt floor, crying, and he kept repeating món ăn, món ăn, món ăn, over and over. Then I cut his throat."

Tess's voice came out in a whisper. "Why?"

Thunder's eyes blinked and he stared at her again, having come back from the recesses of his memories. "It was war. It was us or them. I'd be damned if I lost another Marine on that tour." He gave her a faint smile. "There may be misguided people out there, but they're people like you and me. We all have our faults. We're all trying to survive. People will latch onto something if it protects them and provides for their family."

"Then I guess I'm like you. The way I see it, it's us or them. I don't care how they got there or why, only that they are blinded by his lies."

Thunder reached over and snatched a can of beer. He held it up at her. "Want a beer?"

She smiled. She hated light beer. "Sure."

He tossed it over to her and snatched up another. The can cracked as he popped the top. He slurped the carbonated alcohol and pointed with the can at the Chosen camp. "He's a harsh man, but times like this breed harsh men."

She took a swig of her warm beer and it tasted stale yet oddly refreshing. "Or that's all that remains."

Thunder's dark brown eyes reflected the flames, and he tossed a branch into the fire.

She broke eye contact and lost herself in the fire. All she could see hidden in the orange and yellow flames was Pagan's face. His mouth twisting, engulfed by fire. His screams reverberated in her ears. His eyes pleaded for release from his unbearable pain as his ghost faded into dust and embers.

"The pastor deserves to die."

Thunder nodded, his eyes distant. "Aye, he does."

"Then help me," she said quickly. Thunder's eyes skimmed over the Chosen camp where the pastor laid his head in rest, contemplating their demise.

"Tess, I hate that guy for what he done to all of us, but they're on our side."

"Until when? Until he decides he can take us out? It won't be only Steele he tries to take out. It will be us too and I don't blame him one bit."

"What are you trying to say?" Thunder asked. His furry brows furrowed together.

"I'm trying to ask you for help in offing the prick." She pointed. "Assassination. Murder. Execution. I don't care what you want to call it." She pointed toward the pastor's camp. "Those people over there are sheep. Mere sheep without their shepherd will be lost. Vulnerable. Those people follow because they are scared. Without him, they will be normal. Cut the head off the snake, the body dies."

"Or you create a dozen of the little monsters, each worse than the last."

"Thunder. It can't get worse than him."

"I suppose you're right."

She glanced up at him. "Help me off this guy. Steele's too weak. I don't know what he sees in the guy, but it ain't helping us."

"You choose to follow Steele. If the man says he doesn't want the guy hurt, then you should respect that, despite the fact that we don't trust the pastor."

"You too? You won't help?"

"Use some logic here. The guy hasn't done anything wrong since he swore to follow Steele. This isn't a good idea. You could turn us inward on ourselves with Jackson so close."

She shook her head. Pagan's face still stared at her from the flames, begging for retribution.

"I thought you were better than this." She stood up.

His eyes begged. "Don't be rash. We've known each other since the early days."

She lifted her eyebrows. "Apparently, not well enough."

She sulked away, muttering to herself. "These men are such cowards. First

Steele. Then Thunder. Jesus, Mary, and Joseph. These men don't understand a damn thing."

A form staggered from the woods in the darkness of the night. She thought it was a drunk but knew better from experience. It hobbled closer and closer. She wasn't sure if it saw or heard her, but it came her way. She loosened a knife in her belt, a short four-inch blade, long enough to penetrate the brain stem, eye socket, or upper neck.

The gray-skinned demon walked with a hunch, one shoulder lower than the other. A low-pitched moan came from its ugly lips. She gripped her knife tight in an underhand hold. It reached for her and she sidestepped quick, jabbing her knife. It punctured the soft thin skin of its neck and she drove her fist up. She didn't stop until the hilt reached its flesh.

The infected stood for a second, white eyes staring vacantly at her, and then gave out. Its weight grew heavy, and she let it collapse into a heap with a small clap on the ground. She bent down, wiping the blade front and back on its raggedly torn clothes. Its skeletal mouth hung open.

"As easy as that," she said to herself. She was confident she could handle one or two with a knife. Any more than that and things could get hairy.

She studied the still corpse with its slender, pale face. "As easy as that," she said to herself. She watched the Chosen camp, a smile curving on her lips. "As easy as that."

KINNICK
Warden, IA

The ten-by-twelve-foot freezer was no longer cold but only cool in the darkness. Clear plastic bags sat empty on barren shelves and racks that normally held meat, vegetables, and cheese. There was only one door in and out of the walk-in makeshift prison.

Hunter watched the men with wolf-like eyes as they trudged inside. Whitehead's back slapped the wall in defeat and he slid down onto the floor. Volk turned around, his face filled with pure disdain.

Hunter held out a sack filled with water bottles and MREs. Volk snatched it from his hand.

"Thanks," he mocked.

Hunter bent down and picked up a silver-handled bucket. "Almost forgot." He handed it to Volk.

Volk's eyes burned with hate.

The Marines lacked any sort of gear and appeared almost childlike without their vests, magazines, guns, and helmets. Volk looked like a kid about to throw a temper tantrum while Whitehead had the appearance of a whipped dog. Whitehead's head dipped down between his legs.

Kinnick stared at Volk, meeting the man's mean eyes. "We will check on you in the morning."

Volk snorted and shook his head. "If the local yokels don't finish you off in the night."

"Pray they don't, because whatever they do to us, they'll do ten times worse to you." Kinnick walked out of the freezer followed by Hunter.

Hunter put a hand on the door and started to close it. When it was almost closed, he coughed. "Why don't you give a holler when the shitter's full? I'll come in and bring you a new one."

Kinnick ignored the banter and eyed the Marines as the freezer door shut. The desperation on Whitehead's face was one of a man being shut in a tomb alive. Volk didn't appear to care.

The silver metal door clinked as the latch clasped shut. Hunter took a metal rod linked with a chain to the wall and slipped it into the latch.

"Well, ain't that some shit. Nasty business." Hunter shook his head in disgust. "Worse than fighting the Zulus. Now what?"

Kinnick exhaled. "We have to find our perpetrators without getting in a shootout with the entire town. Then we have to figure out what to do with these Marines."

"Can you blame them? Somebody out there shot their squad mate in cold blood."

"Yes, I can. We're held to a higher standard." Kinnick turned around and walked back through the kitchen and into the restaurant dining room with Hunter on his tail.

The dining room was dark and looked like a family campout. Gear and blankets littered the floor. The other Marines either sat at the barricade or in chairs.

"I fully believe men should be held accountable for the deed that they've done," Hunter said behind him. He moved alongside Kinnick.

"As do I." Kinnick stared out at the barricade. "Can you imagine the field day the press would have with a situation like this?"

"Ain't no more press, sir, but yes, I can. I know both you and me would be on the hook for it faster than two shakes of a lamb's tail." Hunter rolled out a tin of tobacco and pinched a wad of the black grainy substance in his fingers, pulled his lip out, and shoved it into his mouth.

"I know we would, but we must continue to operate like we will be held responsible for all of our actions. How we treat these people means something. Volk admitted to killing that boy."

"He also said that boy drew a knife on them. These men were trained to fight a war, not police a small town in Iowa."

Kinnick pushed air through his nostrils. "I know what we are meant to do."

"We need these Marines. We're already scraping the bottom of the barrel for fighters and think about what you're doing to their squad. Right now, three of the nine Marines are incapacitated in a single day, one of them their squad leader. That's on top of this clusterfuck disaster our nation is in."

Kinnick dropped his voice. "A nation that is requiring us to enforce Executive Order 17766."

Hunter's cheek muscles flexed as he clenched his teeth together. "It wouldn't be the first order I haven't followed."

Kinnick glanced at the Marines and Hawkins. "Me neither, but we have to figure out a way to cajole this town to the fight. We are here to prep them for war, not wage war against them."

"Feels like a war that never ends. New places. New enemies. Always a war." Hunter's eyes went distant as if he stared at a faraway place in his mind. He blinked as he came back to reality and scooped up a plastic water bottle in his hand and spit in it. Brown juices hit the side of the plastic and dripped down the side. "That's why they pay you the big bucks, boss."

Kinnick laughed and shook his head. "Or nothing at all."

***

Kinnick and Hunter walked down the middle of the street. Boone, Washington, and Duncan formed a tactical triangle. Boone walked in front, gun pointed downward, his lanky neck twisting as he scanned for threats. Washington stalked on the left flank and Duncan on the right flank. Hawkins had stayed with Gore and the Marines under arrest.

Lining the two-lane residential street were newer sidewalks made of clean white cement. The houses were nicer than most of the others on the island, giving off a lake community vibe. The houses had long-panoramic style open windows and porches, all facing the water with fresh paint in lighter pastel colors. Every block away from the water, the houses became shabbier and more rundown. The lawns were overgrown, discarded junk lay scattered in the front yards, and backyards were lined with broken wooden fences. Kinnick was unable to tell if it was the societal collapse or if the homes were like this pre-outbreak.

Hunter spoke under his breath as they walked past lightless houses. "It's tough to ignore them looking out the windows or when a curtain flutters or the blinds bend. It never sits right in your gut."

Kinnick kept his eyes moving from building to building. "Makes you nervous too?"

"Hells yes. It could happen a hundred times and mean nothing, but it's the time a sniper is waiting in ambush that counts."

"Recommendations?"

"Well, I'd love to point my gun at each and every one." He spit chew onto the ground. *Splat.* "But that doesn't show any trust, and when you point guns at people, you're more likely to find guns pointed back."

Kinnick gulped and rested his hand on the pistol-like handle of his M4 carbine as they walked. Their destination rose in the air like a spire. The top of the water tower was barn red like a rocket, the rest of the tower painted white. Four thin support legs propped up a tall thick silver trunk that went deep into the ground.

Hunter had speculated that the shots had come from the tower when Gore was hit. A ring of metal wrapped around the top provided a railing against someone toppling off. It was Kinnick's time to dig up some answers. If he needed to take a risk to get them, then so be it.

Washington pointed to a leg of the water tower. "Duncan, set up with the SAW that way. Boone, you're over there." He pointed at another leg. Washington rounded out by placing himself outward by the nearest leg. He nodded to Kinnick.

Kinnick and Hunter walked slowly through the grass beneath the tower. Both men knew what they were searching for and there was no need to discuss it while in the open. They searched for anything that might provide some insight as to who had shot Gore.

Kinnick blinked and closed his eyes, trying hard to see every detail in the overgrown grass. Hunter kicked with his boots into the grass. Ten minutes passed and they hadn't found anything but dirt and dying overgrown brown grass that had tipped on its side in thick clusters.

Hunter shook his head. "Ain't nothin here. I'm going to hop up this ladder and see if there's anything up there."

"Carry on."

The Green Beret skipped up the ladder. His boots resounded off the metal rungs and his hands bounded over one another all the way to the top. He disappeared over the ledge.

Kinnick paced below. His eyes weren't particularly great compared to what they were when he flew C-130s, but they weren't terrible either. He also knew the odds of finding something were slim. The evidence could easily hide beneath the long unmown grass until the dead finished walking the earth, or the perpetrator could have scooped up any evidence before their retreat. The shot could have come from anywhere nearby and they were searching the wrong spot. Yet they searched because Kinnick needed answers. He needed something to level the playing field with this town of people. He needed a way to trust them again as much as they needed a way to trust him.

The Marines knelt, warily watching their sectors. He brushed his foot along the grass, digging it through the clumps, trying to kick up something that wasn't supposed to be there. He swept his foot through the dead vegetation swinging it back and forth. It crunched under his boots. He looked back up at the Marines and his boot struck something in the grass.

He stopped, eyeing his tan combat boot. He kicked the toe of his boot around the ground there, feeling with his foot. Something clinked off his foot. Squatting down, he felt the weight in his knees. A bit of shiny brass reflected up at him. He picked up the object. He twisted the round cylindrical tube-shaped piece of brass in his fingers. He flipped it around to the bottom containing the primer. It read *.300 Winchester Magnum Cobra AP* around the edge of the shell. A small symbol of a coiled serpent was etched into the metal.

"Master Sergeant," Kinnick called up to tower. "I think we got something here."

"Nothing up here. Only a few missed shots from us."

The end of the brass was dark with gunpowder burn. *This could be the shell casing we need to match to a gun or it could mean nothing.* Kinnick let the shell casing roll to the palm of his hand and he squeezed it tightly.

"Colonel!" Hunter exclaimed. He leaned over the railing and pointed.

Kinnick looked in the direction Hunter pointed. Abandoned town blocks leading to the water. He shaded his eyes, staring up Hunter. "What?"

"Infected," he screamed. Hunter hopped on the ladder and climbed down quickly. He reached the bottom and marched for Kinnick, his chest heaving.

"How many?"

Hunter snarled. "Fleas on a mangy dog."

"Come on," Kinnick called. He started to run for the restaurant. The Marines fell in behind him, their boots striking the pavement.

Kinnick gasped as he ran, gripping his radio. He placed it near his mouth and breathed, "Coffey."

GWEN
Reynolds Farm, IA

A red and black-feathered chicken raced ahead of her, it's feet kicking up little puffs of dust. Gwen tried to snatch it, but it ran faster and scooted out of her grasp. The chicken squawked in victory and continued to run for its life. It dodged into a corner, lifting its feet, preparing to make another break for it.

"Come on, Haley. Trap it in there."

Haley slunk forward, her hands close to her body but ready to launch.

"Don't be afraid to grab it." Gwen crouched down with her arms, elbows flared and her fingers spread.

"Okay, Gwenna, but its talons look sharp."

"It'll be fine. It's only scared." *It will be fine after I wring its skinny neck.*

Both Gwen and her niece stalked close, pinning the terrified creature in the chicken coop fence. The chicken darted, its head bobbing with fierce determination.

"Get ready. It's gonna run," Gwen whispered. The chicken cocked its head to the side as if it understood her words and bolted. It ran straight for Haley, the weak link, and ducked through her legs. Haley lunged much too late and crashed into the dirt.

Gwen dove to the side, the chicken evading her grasp. "Yow," she exclaimed. She rose to her knees and brushed off her overalls and one of her grandfather's work shirts.

"We didn't get it," Haley whined. She stood up, dirt covering her from

270

head to toe. Gwen helped herself up. She smoothed her filthy clothes.

"My mom is gonna be mad."

Gwen laughed. "Yes, she will. Come on over here."

Haley stopped in front of her and Gwen proceeded to pat her down.

"Gonna need to dunk you in the river."

Terror filled Haley's eyes. "No, Gwenna. Please. That's where the scary people are. I'll take a bath anywhere else. I promise. Please."

Haley's response almost broke Gwen's heart. The fear associated with the broken world touched the young the most. Her breath caught in her chest and tears formed in her eyes. The child stared up at her, quivering in fear like a young sapling in a rainstorm.

Gwen crouched down. "Haley. No one is going to hurt you. I promise." Her little unborn blond boy stomped around the chicken coop yard smashing piles of mud with his feet. She ignored him like she had been for weeks. *I see you, boy. Now, let me deal with the people already here.*

Haley's eyes were large blue orbs. "Please don't make me go there."

Gwen grasped Haley's hands. "You don't have to go down there, okay?"

Haley nodded, still pouting.

A voice called from the fence. "Gwen."

She glanced up. Gregor leaned on the fence with his big arms, his long hair drooped on his shoulders. She stood up.

"What's up, Gregor?"

Gregor tucked his long hair behind his ear. "Hank just got back from town. Steele's convoy is on the move."

"All of them?"

"Yeah, they're gone."

She patted Haley on the back. "Let's get you inside." Haley ran off in the direction of the house. Gwen gave Gregor a worried look. "Mark is an impatient man at best. I thought he would wait for us to figure something out. Can you take Chase with you and track them down the banks? Take one of the trucks."

Gregor nodded. "Yes, ma'am." He hoisted his AR-15 and walked off to find Chase.

Gwen followed Haley across the yard. Women cooked over fires outside the barn. Most of the men had gone off with her grandfather to help with the harvesting of her grandfather's soybean and corn crops. They had finished harvesting the smaller plots of sweet corn and had now moved onto the larger acreage of field corn. If it came down to it, although the people wouldn't be happy, they could eat the field corn. The field corn colloquially known as dent corn was primarily the starchy corn that would be used to feed the cattle. Many of the other Sable Point refugees were pulling security, standing watch with rifles and shotguns.

Gwen patted the top of Rocky's black head as she walked by. The boxy-headed Labrador Retriever accepted her praise and laid his head back down. She stepped onto the porch and pulled off her dirty knee-high rubber farm boots. The smell of food tantalized Gwen's nose as she stepped inside.

Gram's voice came from inside. "How did you get so dirty, young lady?"

"Chasin' chickens, grandma."

"Wipe your hands, dear."

Gwen stepped inside the kitchen. Her gram was there with May Clemens, Harriet, and Joey. They were all working on a massive meal.

Gram smiled. She held a wet rag to Haley's hands. "You too?" She glanced up at Gwen. "Those chickens must be mighty weaselly or somebody's out of practice."

Gwen returned her warm smile with one of her own. "I don't think they're any smarter, but I'm out of practice."

Her grandmother finished wiping Haley off. She handed the towel to Gwen then turned back to her kitchen stovetop, wielding a large wooden spoon like a master alchemist. Four large pots bubbled on the stove.

"I suppose we should be thankful for this old wood stove. With no power, it's been a godsend." Handling the wooden spoon, she stirred one and then the other. May chopped vegetables, her knife banging off a cutting board.

"Smells delicious." Gwen stepped close behind her grandma and squeezed her shoulders, peering over. "What are you all making? Chili?"

Her grandmother regarded her over her shoulder. "Your favorite, but I'm leaving it pretty bland. For the kids." She continued to stir, not looking at her.

Gwen smiled. "That sounds great."

"Hopefully we've enough for the folks outside."

"We'll make do. We'll add water if we need more," May said. She gave Gwen a friendly smile. Gwen's grandmother and she were becoming fast friends.

Her grandmother continued to stir. "When are you due?"

Gwen's heart leapt in her chest, her eyes flying toward the other woman and finally settling on her grandmother. "Gram. What are you talking about?"

May stopped chopping and glanced at Gwen inquisitively. Harriet's eyes went wide and she zeroed back in on the food she was prepping.

Her grandmother turned around, holding a spoon in one hand, her other on her hip.

"Gwen. Even if you didn't have that guilty look on your face, I could tell by the color of your cheeks and the size of your breasts."

Gwen averted her eyes. "Gram, please, you're embarrassing me."

Gram swung her spoon around. "Nonsense. Why should you be ashamed? Just because you ate supper before you said grace?"

Gwen's mouth clamped shut. "I'm not ashamed." Her eyes dipped away from her grandmother. "I didn't want to tell you until I was further along."

"You didn't want to tell me because you were afraid of what I'd think."

"Yeah."

"You love the father?"

Gwen avoided her grandmother's gaze before she could meet her eyes. "Of course, Gram."

"Then it's good. Is it that boy who's stuck across the river?"

Gwen rolled her eyes. "Yes, it's Mark's, but he's gone."

Gram shook her spoon, pointing outside. "Just like a man to run away when the world starts to get real. You should have picked a better baker to throw one in the oven."

"Please, he wouldn't have left without a reason."

Her grandmother's face crinkled in suspicion and Gwen didn't know if it was for her or Mark. "You've been seeing that Bullis boy quite a bit lately."

Gwen tilted her head to the side and gave her Gram a disappointed look.

"It's Mark's child. Jake is only a friend."

Her gram raised a gray eyebrow. "A friend you play kissy-face with?"

Gwen felt her cheeks start to color. The other women were silent. May turned back around to the vegetables and Harriet looked away. Joey made a noise and quickly turned around.

Her grandmother pointed the spoon at her like she was casting a spell. "Mark ain't here. Somebody's got to raise the child. Jake's a fine man. He's got a good down-to-earth family."

"Mark will come back or I'll find him," Gwen said more softly than she would have liked.

Gram's weathered face softened and she set her spoon down. "Come over here and give your grandmother a hug." Gwen did as she bid and hugged her grandmother, the relief of acceptance overwhelming her. "There, there, my girl. I'm only being hard on you because I want what's best for you. Just because these are sad times doesn't mean that we don't have reason to rejoice." She whispered. "This is a special gift."

Her grandmother leaned back and wiped a tear. "How far along, dear?"

Gwen wiped the other side of her face as tears leaked from her eyes. "About three months."

May put a hand on her shoulder. "You have the glow," she said softly.

Harriet smirked. "About time we got that out."

Gwen cried a tear then laughed a little. "Yeah, it is. Will you all do me a favor?"

"Yes, dear," her grandmother said. She reached up and touched Gwen's face.

"Don't tell Pa. I don't want him to worry."

"Oh, Gwen. He would be so happy. You've always been his favorite."

The screen door slammed shut.

"Haley," Becky called as she walked in.

"In here, Mama."

Becky set a basket of eggs on the table.

"Now I remember why I became a teacher. Those chickens are grosser than those little buggers I used to teach."

Gram smiled. "Thank you, Becky."

"Why does everyone look so emotional?" Becky eyed them with suspicion. "Jesus, did somebody die or somethin'?"

"No, no," Gram said. "Times are tough and we're letting it out." She gave a knowing side-glance to Gwen.

"God. Don't scare me like that. You should all pick up smoking. It helps with the stress."

Gram sighed. "You should quit. It's bad for Haley."

Becky avoided eye contact with her disapproving grandmother. "Doc Miller said I could smoke when I was pregnant. What's the difference now?"

"He said that because he knew you wouldn't quit," Gwen chimed in.

"You should talk. I remember in high school you and me would sneak out to smoke."

"A youthful indiscretion."

Becky snorted and held up a pack of cigarettes. "If you need me, I'll be outside having a youthful indiscretion."

Gwen crossed her arms over her chest, watching her sister leave.

"She's always been a stubborn one," Gram said. She picked up her spoon and dug back into the steaming red chili.

AHMED
South of Steele's position

Ahmed twirled the bat between his knees as they drove. It reminded him of riding the bus to an away game in college, all the tension of the upcoming game settling in on him while they burned hour after hour on the road. Part of his routine had been silent prayer and he would use the bat to keep the beats in his mind. *Peace be unto him. May you take all their souls and bring them peace that they cannot find here on Earth.*

His second reason for silent prayer was to stifle the sounds of Ollie and Weston arguing in the front seat over who had the better college football team. He prayed for the lives he had extinguished, knowing that he would be forgiven for the lives around him that had been taken too early. *Too many have been taken before their time here was done, but God has a plan.*

The rumble of motorcycles sounded off ahead of them. They drove at the back of the fifty or so Wolf Riders riding slow down the uneven road. Ahead of their scouting group, three more bikers acted as outriders cautiously looking out. He could barely make out the black wolves patches on the backs of their vests. Ollie flicked on the lights as dusk descended upon the land like a gray blanket.

Ahmed rolled his shoulders and then his neck, trying desperately to tune out the two men bickering like an old couple.

Ollie drove, two loose hands holding the steering wheel. "I'm telling you. State is better than Michigan every year." He glanced at Weston as he talked,

276

gauging his comrade's reaction.

Weston shook his head. Weston was a taller version of Ollie with a bald head to match except Ollie had a beard where Weston couldn't grow a thing. "You've got to be joking." He pushed himself back into his seat. "What's the overall series record?"

Ollie scoffed. "Don't know. Don't care. Michigan's got them on the overall series, but what about the last ten years? It hasn't even been close. Coach D is a hero. A mastermind. One of the best coaches in the country."

Weston nodded. "Sure. Sure. Coach D is a great coach, but we have to talk about tradition. Historically, Michigan has been in control of the series."

Ollie shook his head in disgust. "The tides are changing. The past will only be what it was. In the future, people will look back at the last ten years and say this was the turning point. This was the beginning of the culture shift. I have no doubt Michigan will kick, bite, and scratch to hold on to the idea of being superior, but just like anything that is losing relevance, eventually they will be kicked to the side and everyone will talk about the way it used to be as they are forgotten." Ollie slapped the steering wheel as he thought of something else. "And can we really take seriously a bunch of wins when dudes were wearing leather helmets? It's laughable. Not even the same sport. We were a lot smaller school back then."

Weston smirked. "Whatever. The series is in our favor, so it doesn't matter how many wins in a row you get. We don't even consider you rivals. The Buckeyes are our real rival." Weston got comfortable in his seat, smug victory settling on his face.

Ollie glanced back from the road and back at Weston. Color was rising in his cheeks and Ahmed could visibly see the man's blood pressure go up. "Dude, you're joking me, right?" He glanced back at the road and back at Weston. "You're joking, right?"

Weston crossed his arms over his chest and shook his head.

Ollie exclaimed, "We're one of the only teams to beat OSU in the conference more than once since they split them up. You guys haven't won a game against them in years."

"It's called "the Game." That's the real rivalry."

"Doesn't it have to be competitive to be a rivalry? Hell, we have a better rivalry with them than you do."

Weston's jaw dropped. "Take it back. Our rivalry with OSU is historic."

Ollie shrugged. "Just saying, it has to be competitive to be a rivalry. Hey, Ahmed." Ollie glanced in the rearview mirror.

Ahmed sighed and stopped twirling his bat. "What?"

"Who do you think is better? MSU or U of M?" Ollie said, looking at him in the rearview mirror.

"I dunno. Alabama?"

Ollie scrunched his nose up. "Come on."

Weston waved him off. "Apples to oranges."

"Why do you care? Did you guys even go there? It's not like they are going to play anymore."

Ollie looked back at him quick. "No."

Weston peered down and muttered. "No."

Red brake lights flashed ahead. Ahmed pointed in the middle of the two men. "They're stopping."

Ollie braked the pickup, gradually coming to a stop behind the rear of the bikers. The last biker, the tail gunner, waved them forward, and Ollie pulled the pickup onto the shoulder. Weston rolled down his window and a gust of cold air blew into the truck. Ahmed shivered. *Freezing compared to Virginia.*

Near the front of the Wolf Riders, Macleod waited for them. His black goatee swung down his chest and sunglasses hung off the front of his jacket.

"Hey, guys. My boys in the front say we are going to have some company. Don't know how many, but they're coming up quick, so let's take some cover."

"Shouldn't we get word back to Steele?" Ahmed said.

Macleod smiled. "We will. But don't you think it's a better idea to get him actionable intelligence?"

"Yeah, he'll want to know how many we're dealing with."

Macleod pointed to a short ranch-style house in a field. Windows were dark. "Of course. I'm gonna get my boys behind that house and barn over here."

"We'll follow you," Ahmed said. Weston rolled up the window.

"Jesus, it's cold out there," he said, rubbing his hands together.

Ollie reached over and adjusted the heat on the dash. "Those guys must be freezing on those bikes." He turned the steering wheel and followed the bikers up a dirt driveway. An infected man reached for the bikers as they rolled around to the back. A Wolf Rider swung a pipe one-handed on the way by, striking the thing in the face. Skin and brains streaked into the air and the infected collapsed.

Ollie pulled the pickup around to the opposite side of the barn. Wolf Riders were dismounting their motorcycles. Ollie turned the key and cut the engine. He twisted a knob on the dash and the lights disappeared.

The three men sat in the dying light. "Do you guys get a weird vibe from that guy?" Ahmed asked.

Weston shook his head. "I mean, they're in a gang. It's all kind of weird to me."

Ollie nodded. "Seems real angry all the time but not any different than normal."

"Hmm. I don't know. He just seems weird to me." *Not any weirder than the rest of us I guess.* Ahmed pulled his radio out. "Steele, this is Ahmed, over."

There was a ten-second pause before Steele's voice came on. "This is Steele."

"We might have some company. Don't know how many."

"Keep a low profile and let me know."

"You got it." Ahmed tossed the radio on the seat next to him and cracked the rear passenger door.

Ollie glimpsed back at him. "Where are you going?"

"Steele is going to want to know numbers. I'm going to move closer."

Ollie exchanged a look with Weston. "You don't mind if we just chill in here?"

"No need for all of us to be cold," Weston chimed in with a weak smile.

Ahmed shook his head. "Stay here." Ahmed shouldered up his M4 and gripped his bat. He walked to the corner of the barn and knelt down using the bat to brace himself and waited.

The wind picked up, blowing dirt and weed-ridden yellow stalks of dead crops across the road. The leaves on the stalks rustled as if an army of the dead were trampling through them.

The chill reminded him of how bad it hurt to hit a ball in the cold. The sting in his hands after connecting. He assumed that it would be the same smashing in the skulls of the dead in the cold. He rubbed his hands together, letting the bat hang in the crook of his arm. The cold from the earth was soaking through his pant leg on the ground. *If it snowed, it might stick.*

The bikers spoke behind him, huddled around motorcycles. He couldn't make out their conversation, but they didn't seem worried about whatever came this way. *You should be worried. These guys mean business.* He dipped his chin, eyeing the men behind him.

Macleod stood over with a group of his men almost as if they were in a huddle. He glanced Ahmed's way and gave a smile. Ahmed lifted his chin in acknowledgment. *Looks like a rat, smells like a rat, it's a rat.*

He continued to rub his hands. His skin was starting to turn red and dry with the nighttime cool air. He perked up, eyeing the road and the surrounding trees. The hum became a rumble and three motorcycles sped down the road. They slowed down and cut their lights as they turned into the farm's driveway and raced up between the house and the barn.

"Boss, they're right behind us," the Wolf Rider barked.

"Good work, Pot."

Ahmed spied back on the road. He heard them first too. They weren't as loud as motorcycles and they appeared soon after he heard them. He saw their lights first through the trees. Beams penetrating through any open space.

Three tan Humvees roared into view, cruising. Helmeted men stood in their turrets. They continued driving by, blocked from view by more trees.

"Scouts," Ahmed whispered. "They're coming from the south." Ahmed's mind raced and he continued to whisper out loud. "They're coming from the north and the south." He stood for a moment digesting the information. "We are walking into a trap."

He turned around, observing Macleod for a second. The black-goateed man was near the back of the pickup. Another couple of his men were leaning on the other side, talking.

Ahmed stood up and started to walk toward Macleod and yelled over to him. "They're coming up from the south and from the north." He needed to send word back to Steele.

Macleod cupped his own ear. "What's that?"

"I said they are coming from the north and the south. It's a trap. Steele is walking into a trap."

Macleod cocked his head. "You don't say." He leaned against the pickup.

"We have to tell Steele before it's too late. Let me grab that radio."

"Yeah, we really should." Macleod knocked on the window his knuckles wrapping the glass.

Weston's bald head and smooth face poked out.

"Can you grab me that radio?" Macleod asked. "I gotta call this one in."

Weston smiled. "Sure thing." He reached in the back and snatched up the radio. He handed the radio to Macleod with a smile.

Macleod's mouth curved into a nasty smile. "Thanks."

Weston started to roll up the window.

"Wait. I need one more thing."

Weston gave him a helpful smile. "What's that?"

Macleod whipped his arm up level with Weston's hairless head. Weston's face barely registered danger before Macleod's Glock 17 put a round through his skull. Weston's brains exploded onto Ollie's face. Weston's head kicked back to the side, resting on the headrest. His eyes rolled back into his head and he immediately let out a soft moan.

Ahmed's insides electrified all at once like he was hooked up to a car battery. His body felt like a ghost, ethereal and entirely fluid. He only did what was natural.

The biker chief leaned across Weston's body and double-tapped Ollie. Ahmed ran at Macleod. Ollie slumped onto the steering wheel, blood leaking from his head and neck, his mouth open.

Ahmed sprinted and closed the distance in a fraction of a second. He did what was natural with what he had in his hands. He swung as hard as he could, catching Macleod on the wrist before he could turn all the way around.

The gun clanked onto the ground. "Fuck," Macleod cried. He

immediately gripped his destroyed hand in his other. A bearded biker aimed through the window. Pop. Pop.

Weston's body jerked as he absorbed more rounds, blocking the bullets.

Macleod screamed, "Watch it!"

Ahmed instinctually ducked down near the door, and Macleod lunged for him, trying to wrap his arms around his body.

Ahmed body checked him with his bat and ran. He sprinted off into a defunct cornfield. Adrenaline pushed him into a dead sprint, ignoring the tightness of his almost frozen muscles.

He could barely hear their shouts and curses behind him. It was like they were fleeting memories in a world of fight or flight. He picked the plants as he high-kneed over uneven ground. The soil exploded around him. The bullets whizzed in the air. His chest burnt as he sucked in cold harsh oxygen. His lungs needed it to pump the blood roaring in his veins.

If he was one thing, he was fast, and twenty yards turned into forty yards. He could hear the roar of engines as the Wolf Riders fired up their motorcycles to give chase.

Keep going. Allah, help me. Keep going. He repeated it in his mind over and over. His arms whipped back and forth as fast as they could go. The cornstalks struck his arms and legs, tripping him. Every piece of uneven ground tried to bring him down, but he wouldn't let them. A thick line of trees marking the end of the field became closer and closer.

If you can reach those, you won't be in the open. A little further.

"Allah. Help. Me." He breathed each word as he ran.

He felt it bite him. It was a cold bite like he'd been seared with a frozen poker. The sound of reverberating thunder bellowed in the distance. His heart rate went sky high in his chest. His right side burned.

He kept running, but the pain became too great. He gaped down at his chest. Blood seeped through his ACUs near his right breast. His legs slowed. They felt heavier than normal, like he was running with a parachute holding him back. He stumbled forward and fell, dropping to his knees. He put his hand to his chest, dipping his fingers into the blood. The warm crimson fluid covered his fingers. He still didn't believe it was his. *No. They couldn't have hit me. They were so far away. I was so close.*

Almost out of earshot, he could barely hear their laughter and shouts of the hunt over the thunder of motorcycle engines. He rubbed the blood between his index finger and thumb. His fingers were sticky like he had dunked them in watery honey. He forced himself to stand up.

"Not today," he uttered. His mind overcame the lethargy of his legs and they were forced to obey. Shoving his bat into the ground, he stood upright. He stumbled eight more feet and he heard another boom. Something thudded into a tree nearby. He fell back into the cornstalks. The rumble of motorcycles prevailed over the blood pounding away in his ears. They performed more like dirt bikes in the field.

Ahmed's hands dug into the earth. He crawled. He could feel his mind and soul departing his body, but he forced himself to crawl hand by hand over the earth. He knew the only thing that mattered was getting away.

The earth clumped and fell apart in his hands. He let go of his bat. He was a wounded animal trying to flee the hunter's grasp. His feet were cold and he regarded them as only stumps, although he knew they were still there. Motorcycles raced around the corn. Men shouted. Flashlights scanned the land.

"You see any blood?"

"That fucker's got to be here somewhere."

"Didn't you see him drop?"

"Sure did. 'Bout here."

Ahmed pulled himself over a fallen tree trunk and collapsed. He put pressure on his chest. *Damn my feet are cold. Not just my feet.* The darkness surrounded him and closed in fast, gripping his flesh and soul. *Allah take me.*

KINNICK
Warden, IA

Hunter and the Marines pushed ahead. Their gear jingled as they ran, making them sound like escaped reindeer.

"Yeah, boss," crackled out of the radio.

"Get Hamilton One upriver to Garfield. Zulus are coming down that road. Take them out."

Kinnick's radio buzzed. "You got it."

Hard fought blocks disappeared, and they reached Gary's restaurant and rushed inside. Hawkins stood ready, M4 in hand. Gary and Martha huddled together near the kitchen watching the men.

"Let's go. Infected."

Gary scooped up a shotgun from the kitchen counter. "I'm coming with you."

Martha reached for him. "Be careful," she said softly.

Gary nodded to her. "I will."

"Hamilton One is swinging up to the road, but we're going to head that way to stave them off."

Gary nodded. "Others will join."

Kinnick was surprised. "You sure about that?"

Gary nodded his head, a slight look of embarrassment on his face. "They will."

The zip of the minigun hummed followed by the quick thunder of the M2 .50 caliber machine gun as it fired.

Kinnick wouldn't accept any deviation. If Gary and the people of Warden so much as looked like they were up to no good, Kinnick would have them shot. There was a distinct difference between building trust and not defending oneself, and he intended to keep the rest of his men alive. Too many had been lost since the struggle had begun.

"Let's move," Kinnick commanded. The men filed out of the restaurant and into the street. The faraway hammer of the machine gun and buzz of the minigun was like a low-pitched thunderstorm of bees coming their way.

The Marines' equipment bounced on their torsos as they sprinted. Houses blurred past them as they ran. People came out of their homes to watch Kinnick and his men run by. One block turned into two blocks, and within minutes, they had traversed to the other side of the island. A short bridge connected the island to a far-stretching swampy causeway running between low uninhabitable islands, where about a hundred yards away, a short bridge linked Iowa and Illinois.

Hamilton One bobbed in the water about ten yards offshore. Its turrets swiveled toward the road. Fire breathed from metal barrels. Hanger held the handles of the minigun with both hands. He was slightly hunched over the minigun, twisting and turning the turret for maximum coverage. Every burst sounded like he unleashed a giant hummingbird with the destruction of a T-Rex. Hundreds of infected bodies exploded as hot rounds melted through the rotting corpses.

Hunter pointed at Duncan. "Get that SAW up."

Duncan went from kneeling to prone and flinging his bipod out. He moved the stock into his shoulder pocket, his elbows propped up on the ground. Boone knelt down next to him and dropped his pack. A fast-paced da-da-da-da burst from the barrel of the SAW.

A cluster of disorganized civilians, led by Gary, straggled in with shotguns, AR-15s, and rifles. They joined the Marines.

"Where you want us, Colonel?" Gary yelled over the gunfire.

"Fall in line," Hunter called at them. The civilians haphazardly lined the road, intermixing with Marines. The machine guns on the SURC went silent. The boat bobbed on the water.

"They're reloading," Hunter yelled at Kinnick. He turned to the Marines and civilians. "Wait until they're closer. Don't waste the ammo."

With the lull in the bullet fusillade growing silent, the dead marched along the swampy road for the island. They staggered and stumbled, but they all advanced for the island of Warden as if they knew they would soon be rewarded for their undying effort to destroy them.

The dead reached the edge of the short bridge, claiming it as their own. Duncan fire his SAW in bursts, a repetitive sound of tied together da-da-da-das. Then silence while he acquired his next grouping. The rest of the line reported back. The bullets ripped the gray flesh of the infected dead. The body shots only staggered them, and in mangled determination they marched onward as more rounds penetrated their flesh.

Kinnick aimed high, controlling his M4 with quick single shots. An infected man gave him a skeletal grin through his sights. Kinnick's eyes went fuzzy and the infected face became a blur. Ping. The dead man's head kicked backward and he fell onto his side.

"Coffey, get those machine guns up," Hunter yelled into his radio.

Coffey's voice came back through with urgency. "They're reloading."

Hunter's head twisted as he stared down the line with his single eye. He screamed at the men and Marines. "Keep firing!"

The dead fought tooth and nail over the fallen bodies. When one fell, it did not stop. It crawled over the bodies of the others who had been rendered incapacitated. They gained ground on the bridge. Every foot was bought with their twisted and bullet-ridden corpses. Each toppled foe revealed another in its place.

The faces of the dead were clear now. It was easier to tell that they in fact used to be human. Dead white eyes. Painful moans. Slack-jawed faces. Fingers spread wide trying to grasp the living close for their infected bite.

The hum of the minigun fired up again, and to Kinnick, it sounded like a beautiful bumblebee's song. It ate through the dead on the bridge. The tings and tangs of bullets hitting the metal echoed. In thirty seconds, the battle was over. The dead were decimated into chunks of rotting flesh, strewn about the road.

Hunter lined up a final shot and banged it out. An infected woman four-hundred yards away tumbled down onto the ground.

Kinnick inhaled, feeling like he hadn't taken in a breath in twenty minutes and exhaled loudly. The ringing of gunfire dominated his eardrums with a high-pitched hum. He brought his radio up to his mouth and clicked the side button to talk.

"How are we doing on ammunition, Coffey?"

"Went through about 8,000 rounds here. We got about 32,000 left for the minigun."

Kinnick nodded. They did not have an unlimited supply of bullets like some first-person shooter video game with the cheat codes on.

"Cruise up the road to Garfield. Take out any stragglers, but don't be wasteful. I don't know when we are going to get a resupply."

"Wilco."

The SURC motors fired up and powered up the flank of the swamp road.

Kinnick addressed Hunter. "We should have blown this bridge earlier. At least it will provide us a little gap from the ones crossing."

"On it, Colonel." He turned toward the Marines. "Hawk and Duncan, stay with me." Hunter walked off with the two men.

Kinnick turned back to town and ran a hand over his head. Gary moved alongside Kinnick, speaking quicker than normal. "That boat's got some serious firepower."

The SURC grew smaller as it cruised north for Garfield.

He gave Gary a stern gaze. "Yes, it does." *Remember that, Gary. For all these people's sake. Remember that.*

Gary glanced away in discomfort.

"There's something I need to talk to you about." Kinnick pulled the shell casing from his breast pocket and twisted it in his fingers. "We found this by the water tower." He handed it to Gary.

Gary looked at it for a moment, twirling it between his fingers. He flipped it so he could read the bottom. ".300 Mag."

"High-powered round. Made to take down elk and moose and the like."

Gary gulped. "Or kill a man."

"Or kill a man."

Gary leaned close. "There's something I need to speak with you about." He let his voice dip. "At the restaurant."

Kinnick nodded softly. "I see." *What do you have for me, Gary?* He slung his M4 and started his walk back to the restaurant. Washington and Boone joined Kinnick. The civilians followed them in a disorganized rabble of armed men. The sound of footsteps echoed off the road. They walked in silence back to the restaurant.

Kinnick and his Marines entered the dark restaurant. Martha stood near Gore. She glanced up at him. Her eyes filled with tears and she shook her head as she spoke. "I'm so sorry. He. He. Just stopped breathing. I tried to help him but couldn't." She rushed to Gary and wrapped her arms around him and murmured into his chest. "Thank God you are back."

"Everything is safe now," he said to her. They gazed into each other's eyes.

Martha broke away her eyes from Gary and looked at Kinnick. "I'm sorry, Colonel."

Kinnick walked slowly to where Gore lay. When Kinnick reached his side, his eyes fixated on the Marine. He didn't have the appearance of a hard-nosed steely-eyed warrior, but that of a young college kid with so much more to live for. Gore's face was pale and his eyes were open. They didn't blink and had a glossy gaze.

Kinnick had seen enough dead bodies of late to know the difference, but he checked for a pulse anyway. He pushed two fingers into the side of Gore's neck. He felt nothing but flesh and tendons and the side of his esophagus. He picked his fingers up and pressed them back into the young Marine's neck. No blood pumped through the carotid artery. He pushed harder. Nothing. Kinnick grabbed the boy's blanket and pulled it up and over the Marine's childlike face.

He put both his hands on the table and leaned against it taking in the Marine's loss. "Damn," he muttered. Harsh whispers caught his ears.

Washington hovered over Kinnick's shoulder. Anger seethed off the Marine and he cocked his head to the side. "Fuck, man. They'll pay for what they done to you, brother. Colonel, we have to do something."

Kinnick bowed his head, still staring at the dead Marine. "I understand, Corporal. We will figure this out."

"I've had enough of this shit. We been out there fighting and this is how they repay us?"

The Marine turned toward Gary and Martha. Kinnick raised a hand in the air. "That's enough, Corporal. These are our hosts."

Washington stopped, clenched his jaw, and nodded. "Ain't right."

"We'll figure this out," Kinnick repeated. *Will we? Have we already lost?* "Lashing out in anger will not bring Gore back." *Temperance, young one.*

Gary and Martha argued near the open kitchen. Gary looked worried over at Kinnick. Martha's arms were folded tightly over her chest. She stared at the ground and fear settled on her perpetually worried face.

Gary squeezed her shoulder and walked over to Kinnick.

"I'm sorry about your man." His eyes searched Kinnick for some consolation. Gary eyed outside the restaurant and coughed nervously. "I haven't been completely honest with you."

"I fucking knew it," Washington said.

Kinnick's mouth tightened. "Quiet, Washington. How about you take a seat?"

Washington shook his head and walked across the room. He sat down, back to the wall, gun draped across his lap.

Gary gave the Marine a wary once-over as he walked away.

Kinnick took the opportunity to make the subtle gesture of moving his hand closer to his sidearm by leaning on the table that held Gore's body.

Gary's eyes were wide with worry. "You see, I wasn't sure at first." He shook his gray-haired head. "I guess I didn't want to believe it, but after you showed me the shell, I'm pretty sure I know who shot your man."

"Killed."

A few seconds of silence passed between them.

"Why didn't you tell me before?"

"Well, this is a small town. We look out for one another. Maybe I didn't want to believe it. Maybe I was scared, but you stayed true to your word out there on the bridge. You fought the dead like you said you would. A lot of the people today saw that and appreciate it."

"I was *not* deceiving them when I told them we came to help. Operation Homefront needs their cooperation, or this nation will fall."

"I understand. That's why I'm doing the right thing." He looked down at the dead Marine. "The man that I think did this is Martin Biggs. Real big government conspiracy kind of guy. Been rattling off about the whole thing every time he comes in here or the T and C for a drink. The government infected us. It's the government trying to control the population. It's really never-ending with the guy. He's talked about that stuff for years. Never thought he'd act out like this."

Seriousness dripped from Kinnick's words. "Do you know where he lives?"

"Sure do. 'Bout two blocks from here. Near the water tower."

A huge explosion boomed in the distance. Hunter and his men would be back soon.

"Let's find out what Martin has to say for himself."

STEELE
Steele's Camp, IL

Steele drank his steaming hot coffee. The coffee was on the verge of burning his tongue but warmed his insides heartily in the morning chill. The river swept before him, flowing angrily around rocks and fallen trees alike. The bloated bodies of the dead bobbed like life preservers as they passed caught in the current. The water gushed sounding like a falling cataract that never reached its pool below.

The sky overhead was in a perpetual state of silver-gray gloom. Steele sipped his coffee and crushed the grounds between his teeth, emitting barely audible grinding noises with his jaw. They had been forced to make "cowboy coffee" the old-fashioned way over a campfire by boiling the grounds. Soon the grounds would be forcing him to take actions from the seated position in the woods. Although with his limited food intake, it would probably only result in an upset stomach with not much to put out.

Tess took a mouthful of brew and grimaced with the its bitter taste. He was on edge and she knew it.

"We haven't heard from either of them." He clenched his jaw after he spoke.

Her voice fell away with the utterance of every word. "Could mean anything." She glanced over at her pickup, Red Rhonda, trying not to set him off.

"That's my problem. I'm fucking blind out here and now I don't have any

291

idea where Jackson is." She shifted under his gaze and he blew air through his nostrils before he spoke. "Ahmed said he made contact with somebody, but I haven't been able to reach him since. Kevin should have made contact with Jackson's scouts a day ago. Meaning either they haven't come or something went wrong. Now, I don't know which way to go."

"Ahmed was with over fifty men. I'm sure he's fine."

Steele stared at the white coals of the fire pit. "They've failed to report as well."

Tess blew on her coffee before she spoke. "You know there's a perfectly good explanation for all of this."

Steele shook his head. "We're in bad shape. If I send Thunder back out, I risk losing his men as well."

"I say we stick with where we're going. The last known location of Jackson was northeast. That's the best info we have," she said.

"Stick with it." He shook his head in his own disgust. "Wheeler would have loved this scenario."

"Who's Wheeler?"

"My old team leader at the Division. That guy was actually a captain." He peered out at the river. "We could use him."

"We don't have him; we have you. So make a move."

She's right. Action. Not reaction.

Steele tossed back the rest of his coffee. He glanced over at Tess and gave her a genuine smile. "No day like today."

In an hour, the convoy was moving back south, following the Mississippi River. The southeastern part of Iowa mocked them from the other side.

Another hour later, the convoy came to a halt. The sun made the sky only a lighter shade of drab gray, like a dim flashlight underneath a charcoal sheet.

Tess's neck stretched out in an effort to make herself taller. "All I see are brake lights."

Steele leaned near the window trying to get a view of what was ahead. "The pastor better not be leading one of his sorties against the infected. I swear to god I will kill him."

Tess gave him a sideways glance. Her lips puckered a bit. "You won't let me do the honors?" Her voice was soft as if she was trying to be sweet with him. An action that he didn't believe for a second.

He threw his hand up, shaking his head. "You can do the honors."

Steele snatched the radio out of the center console cup holder and brought the radio to his lips. "What's going on up front, Frank?"

He had shifted the Iron Drakes to the front of the convoy.

Frank's voice edged with a touch of stress. "Steele. We got contact."

"Damn it," Tess cursed.

Steele's hand instinctually went near his gun. He sat up in his seat trying to see the front and settled on handling his radio instead of readying his weapon.

"Contact with what? The infected?"

The radio was static for a moment. "We got U.S. Army blocking our path."

Steele put his head to the microphone. "Fuck me." He shared a look of disappointment with Tess. He ran his hand with the radio over his scarred head, giving himself a moment to figure out what to do.

He grimaced as he spoke because he already knew the answer. "Are you sure? Over."

"Either that or a dozen tan Humvees with civilians dressed in combat uniforms."

Steele looked at Tess, anger strewn all over his face. "This is bad." His anger stemmed from knowing he should be a better leader and the frustration of his situation. The more he thought about it, the more he realized he was angry. He was angry with the Iowans and bitter with Gwen for not securing him access across the river. He pushed all those feelings down deep in his gut. He had no time for it because every minute meant something. Every minute meant people's lives. "Do not engage. Roll the convoy back around. Not sure how Jackson got on the other side of us without the Wolf Riders catching a whiff of it, but we gotta go back the way we came."

Frank's voice was terse. "Copy." The radio cut out.

"Tess, take us to the rear."

She whipped the wheel around hard and they drove out of convoy line.

Tess steered them back onto the road, and she zipped down the side of it, passing the worried faces of the others. They slowed down when they came across an all metal and leather collection of bikers: the Red Stripes.

Steele hopped out quickly, favoring his bad leg, and walked up to Thunder.

Thunder stopped his motorcycle and straddled the beast. The bearded man with a bandana around his forehead frowned. "What's going on up front?"

"Jackson's got the way blocked."

Thunder shook his head in disgust. "You've got to be kidding me."

Both men gazed south, anticipating contact with the enemy.

"Wish I was. Everyone's turning around to come back this way. You're now our vanguard."

Thunder gave Steele a nasty look. "This is bad."

"I know, but we don't have a choice. It's north or east and we know what's east."

Only a moment after Steele had spoken, a rocket of fire screeched past the men and exploded in the field next to them. Dirt and rocks flew into the air. Debris rained down in fits and Steele ducked low covering his head. A crater remained in its place, fire crackling along the edges.

"What in the hell?" Steele shouted. His M9A1 appeared in his hand. He looked past Thunder. About a eight-hundred meters away, near a bend in the road, Humvees had begun to fill it in. Other Humvees took to off-road driving into the cornfields, spreading out evenly like cavalry.

"Holy shit." Steele holstered his gun quick and unclipped his radio from his belt. "Frank, we got company in the rear."

"What was that noise?" Frank said.

"Jackson's men tried to hit us with a rocket."

"East. Lead us east," Steele said.

Steele took out his binoculars. Dust rose up across farm fields. Tiny tan all-terrain vehicles rolled from that direction as well.

Thunder squinted. "No," he said. He made a quick glance behind him and then forward.

Steele's radio fired up with Frank's stressing voice. "We got contacts to the east. Do we have orders, over?"

Steele's head swam with decisions. He was a rat with nowhere to go and the ship was sinking. *Everyone is counting on you. Good people will die based on your decision.*

The Humvees sat, each contingent roughly a half-mile away. They sat like war horses waiting for the order to charge so they could run him down. *The only way is west and west is the river.* A shallow island protruded out in the water like a small barge. A marshy lowland straddled the shore and the small island.

Tess's panicked face leaned out of the pickup, her short hair messier than normal. "What are we going to do?" she yelled at him.

His radio blared with Frank on the other end. "We need orders, now."

"We're sitting ducks out here," Thunder said, holding his shotgun across his handlebars.

We are surrounded with no way out. The ground rumbled as another rocket hit the open field. Steele crouched down instinctively as more earth rained down upon him and the bikers, the little pieces showering from above. Everyone's voices were far-off in his mind. The shouts were distant. His radio fired up again. Someone fired a shot in fear. Steele blinked rapidly, his system overwhelmed with stimulus.

"Steele!" Tess screamed.

"To the island," he shouted. He pointed with his left hand. "Abandon the vehicles. Retreat to the island." He jogged back to the pickup and grabbed his pack, shouldering it over to one side. "Come on," he called out with a wave forward.

"You expect me to leave my chopper?" Thunder yelled at him as he passed by.

"If you want to live," Steele shouted back.

He hit the button on his microphone. "Frank, we are headed to that island. The land is shallow and swampy. Only way in is by foot."

"We'll be pinned."

"We're already pinned."

Tess slammed the door of her pickup and caught up with him.

People fearfully funneled through the trees to reach the waterlogged banks of the Mississippi. The pastor and his followers straggled through the trees. The old man eyed Steele from down the embankment.

Tess stood beside him. "You aren't worried about drowning?"

The wetland was filled with muddy brown water that stunk like an overflowing sewer. Steele tested the bog with his boot. His foot sank through the water and was sucked into the soft cool mud. It slurped as he reclaimed his foot.

"What choice do we have?"

He boldly waded out into the bog. Step by step, his feet sunk deeper and deeper into the stinking sludge. After a few steps, the frigid muddy water slopped over the top of his boot. It was a struggle to pull it free each time. He was twenty yards out before he could hear Thunder breathing heavily behind him.

"This ground won't hold a man like me," he howled at Steele's back. "It'll suck me down."

"Keep going," Steele shouted at him. He kept on trudging forward, heavy step after weighted-down step. Stunted trees and long brown grass grew out of the bog. Fallen trees covered in slime decomposed back into the swamp.

His heart pounded in his chest from the effort and he struggled to catch his breath. Steele chanced a look behind him. His people were strung out in a far-reaching, chaotic mass. Most of the Red Stripes struggled nearby. Tess's tiny form was only a few yards away. He squinted eyeing Margie help Tony and Larry with the Sable Pointers. Trent carried a man on his back in a fireman's carry. His cheeks puffed out red with every step. They only held what they could carry in their hands and on their backs.

Steele turned back, facing the lowland island that the river threatened to take back under its currents at any moment in time. He kept his legs working and churned through the slippery mud until his boots found more solid ground. The earth grew harder and more solid beneath his feet marking his arrival. More of the swamp trees had grown taller here and had clustered in a tangle of wet roots and soft ground.

He stopped. He exhaled, his chest heaving from the effort. His body was covered with the stinking dark brown mud. He looked like he had slipped into a giant mixing bowl of brownie batter but smelled like he'd leapt into the bowels of an outhouse. Tess followed him onto the firmer island shore. She found a sturdy enough tree and leaned on its wet bark, recovering from the exertion.

"You're insane," she breathed.

Thunder struggled, the bog up to his chest. Steele dropped his pack and grabbed a rope from a side pocket. His chilled hands struggled to tie a knot around his waist. He waded back out into the putrid muddy waters.

"Toss me the rope." Thunder's mustache fluttered as he breathed hard from his effort.

Steele swung the rope over his and lassoed it out to the struggling man. It fell short into the mud. Steele quickly reeled it in with both hands.

"Come on, Nancy. I'm sinking," Thunder shouted.

Steele twirled the rope around his head and tossed it out. Thunder's hands slapped the marshy surface. His fingers spread wide and he managed to hook the rope with his middle finger. He grabbed the rope, looping it around his back and shoulders. With the added weight, Steele leaned backward and walked slowly onto the shore. Tess joined him, pulling with both her hands on the rope like they were in a tug-of-war for the man.

"You're one big puppy," Steele grunted. The heavyset biker finally made it to shore and collapsed, falling to his hands and knees.

Thunder spit on the ground, fighting for air. "Remind me to just die next time."

Steele stood on the shore watching his followers trickle in by the tens and twenties until most were safe on the island. His eyes were constantly reading the other trees and road along the other shore expecting Colonel Jackson and his men to line the bog and charge in. If he did, Steele would gun them down in the swamp.

As the last of Steele's followers disappeared into the island marsh, the Humvees began to roll onto the shore. The first Humvee stopped. A door swung open and a soldier in a combat uniform hopped out. He moved to the edge of the bog and studied the mire.

Steele estimated that Jackson's men would have to cover over three hundred yards to reach them. *Shit, I'm way within range.* He retreated into the swamp trees. Finding a thicker tree covered in slick green algae that looked ready to topple over, he crouched down and pulled out his binoculars. He scrunched his nose up to the musty rotting scent of the bog. His hand trembled as he held the binoculars. For the first time, his body was reminding him of what a miserable state of cold he was in. His teeth chattered as he watched the soldiers.

A soldier waved the Humvee forward. It drove straight into the mud. Tires spinning, the heavy mud rapidly converged around the vehicle, engulfing it in a brown mass. It stopped after a few dozen yards. Steele could hear the man work the engine. Reversing and driving forward. Then reversing all the while spraying mud. The Humvee rocked away mired in the muddy swamp.

Steele exhaled. *They won't be making their way over here tonight.*

Soldiers hopped out and high-stepped through the mud back to the shore.

More Humvees arrived along the shore, and soon, a skeletal bald man stood on the other side. His hands were on his hips, a big grin on his face.

Steele dropped the binoculars. "Jackson," he whispered to himself. He scanned down the line until he found a man with red hair. He stared, trying to figure out if it was him or not. His voice came in a whisper. "It has to be him." The man had tattoos on his arms. A tan SCAR-H rested across his chest, but it was the way he stood that gave him away. His stance was different than the others, more casual like he was a surfer waiting to catch the next wave. He favored one leg and stood like he was going to jump into action at any moment. *Mauser.*

The pastor's voice came from behind Steele. "Now what?" Steele had not heard him approach. He turned and glanced up at the man. The pastor's long stern face stared down at him.

"You've led us to the muskeg of defeat. How do we escape?"

Steele stood up and put a hand on the pastor. "It's not safe." He pushed the pastor before him farther into the trees. They slogged through the wet ground. Steele glanced up at the elder pastor. "We should start building some sort of bulwark against them farther back into the trees where they cannot see us. We need to get some campfires going. It will be night before we know it and our people are cold."

Exhausted people emerged among the trees, clustering in fear. "I've already sent men to collect wood for fires. None of it is dry enough to use. Everything's too wet."

"Then hunker down close because it's going to be a long night." He looked up at the older man. The pastor appeared older every day, but there was fire in his eyes even now. Steele scanned his scattered, defeated people. He turned back toward Jackson's command. Enough swamp trees stood between them where he wasn't worried about snipers taking shots at them.

"Let's start the fortification here." He pointed between fallen green moss-covered logs. "We can start stacking. Anything thick. Not just concealment. We want some kind of cover."

The pastor waved to Peter and the thick curly haired-blond man, covered in filth, joined them. "Peter, gather the brothers and start building a cover for our people."

Peter's mouth tightened at the sight of Steele, but he nodded to the pastor. "Yes, Father."

Steele nodded his thanks. "I'll gather up the Red Stripes and the Sable Point volunteers." He left the pastor and squished away.

The night was cold, dark, and miserable. The entirety of his people was in disarray. Their morale was so low that very few people could even manage to speak to one another. Hope had drifted away and now they were stuck facing their executioner with nowhere to go.

When he walked among them, they gave him sorrowful looks of contempt. He supposed he deserved their scorn. He had led them and now they were on the verge of complete defeat.

He met a filthy Margie and Tony. They both had the appearance of beaten dogs. "Margie, can you find Thunder and help the Chosen pile the logs? Soon it will be dark."

Margie nodded silently, and she and Tony walked away.

Steele used a log and lowered himself onto the ground. He wiped the back of his forehead with his good hand then ran it through his hair, touching the tender scar on his head.

***

At dawn the next morning, Steele woke shivering and stuck to the ground. Tess's form was nearby, her slender shoulders shaking in the retreating darkness.

It wasn't the shivering that stirred him. It was the distinct sound of chopping, of metal cutting into wood. His body was stiff and his muscles sore. He pushed himself up with his functioning hand and followed the noise through the trees toward the shore. He crouched down behind a fallen log, joining a few Red Stripes and putting the binoculars up to his eyes.

Over a hundred soldiers labored on the swamp shore. Men with axes, saws, and hatchets carved into the forested landscape. Other men carried wood. The pounding of hammers on nails echoed across the marsh. The base of a square structure was forming.

Steele scanned the shoreline. A short broad man with a bald head stood near the structure, overseeing its construction. *Jackson.* Steele kept his binoculars trained on him.

Steele flexed his hand. It was still and frozen stiff in the cold dawn. He painfully squeezed his fingers shut. His nerves screamed along his arm.

A slender form slid next to him. Tess crossed her arms over her small chest in an attempt to stay warm.

She watched for a moment before she spoke softly. "What the heck is he doing?"

"I don't know. Probably building some sort of siege engine," Steele muttered.

What are you doing, Jackson? Aside from bottling me up with nowhere to go. Steele's gut churned as he watched the men assemble whatever evil Jackson had in store for them.

KEVIN
Colonel Jackson's Camp, IL

Kevin watched the soldiers throw a round log across the top of the structure through only one eye. The other eye had swollen shut where the stock of an M4A1 had come crashing down into his eye socket. Jackson's men must have been watching them set up the whole time. Kevin and his crew had no idea they were even close before he was looking up the receiving end of a carbine.

He shifted his weight on his knees. His legs ached. Locked into place for so long, his knees begged to stand up and be moved around. The woods around him were damp and the ground wet, the moisture having soaked through his pants long ago. His knuckles knocked one another, pinned together at his wrists with plastic zip-ties.

Does Jackson think Steele will lead a nighttime raid to take us back? Steele's brave but not stupid. Any assault he could conduct over the marshy ground would be shot to pieces.

A trio of soldiers secured the top beam down with nails and rope. Two held it steady while the other hammered away. He had known from the beginning but hadn't let on to his partners in crime. Between the platform and trusses, any student of history would have known no matter the crudeness of the structure.

Kevin turned his head on an aching neck toward Tom and O'Hara. The two huddled together heads dipped in defeat. Tom's long hair hung limply toward the ground. Their arms were wrapped around their sides, their hands tied together in the back like Kevin's. Kevin wasn't sure if they had any idea of the means of their destruction being erected right before their eyes.

A young soldier with his helmet pushed up on his forehead watched them. He burned a cigarette in his mouth, staring out at nothing. He inhaled from the cigarette sporadically every few seconds. His M4 carbine lay across his lap lazily.

Kevin's voice was hoarse with dryness. "Water."

The soldier's eyelids drooped, not acknowledging Kevin's request. The soldier said something to himself and smiled, taking another drag off his cigarette.

Kevin called out louder. "Water." His voice came out harsh and dry like a crinkled up piece of paper. He wished the man would at least give him a swig of booze. Anything at this point. His body yearned for liquid more than it did for oxygen.

The soldier blinked. He glanced over at Kevin as if he had seen him for the first time. "What'd you say?" He didn't move, still trying to make out if Kevin was part of his reality or his daydream.

"Can we have some water? Whiskey if you got it." Tom lifted his long-haired head up, hoping.

The young soldier didn't move. "No water for insurgents."

Kevin sighed. "We aren't insurgents."

"What' ya call setting up roadside bombs to blow up red-blooded American troops? Figured Sergeant Yates would have put you down in the dirt where you belong when we's found ya. Cause that's what he does. Sets things straight." The young man flung out his cigarette and another found its place in his fingers. "I can't even believe the colonel let you live this long."

Kevin supposed the young guard had a point. In the soldier's eyes, they were the enemy. A group that had actively fought them and tried to kill and injure his brothers and sisters. "We're still Americans. We have rights."

The young soldier burned his cigarette, the end lighting up orange and laughed out a puff of smoke. "Rights? You've got to be joking, man."

Kevin shook his long face. "I'm not. It was written in our Constitution that we have a right to a trial judged by our peers." *A document put together by a group of rebels, vagabonds, and back-country lawyers in the face of an empire's opposition. The cost was great then. The cost is greater now.*

The soldier rolled his eyes. "You'll get a trial all right. In fact, that's why Colonel Jackson wanted you alive. So he could administer justice."

Kevin glanced over at his comrades. *A trial by a madman while we pray for justice.* The soldiers on the platform were throwing a rope over the beam now. They wrapped it around the beam a few times, letting the knotted end dangle. A soldier tied the other end to the edge of the structure.

If it hadn't been clear for Tom and O'Hara what was going to happen, then it was now. O'Hara's body began to shake as he cried into the wet leaf-covered earth. Kevin wanted to comfort him, but he knew it wouldn't do any good. They were on the hook.

***

Hours had passed and the earth had warmed a few degrees, even though the sun was trapped behind the clouds. Kevin didn't know why Jackson waited. A new guard replaced the old. This soldier had graying temples and a beard. His gaze was much harder than that of the first guard. He held his carbine in his hands as if he expected to use it at any moment.

The primitive gallows, like the ones erected to administer frontier justice, rested before them unoccupied and looming. The wood wasn't uniform. Instead, it was rough with axe and saw cuts exposing interior trunk. The pieces were lashed and nailed to each other. The rope dangling from the crossbeam wasn't thick hangman's rope but some sort of black climbing rope. He guessed the kind of rope didn't matter. It would do the job as intended one way or another.

Through the trees, Kevin could barely make out people moving along the island shore. *Steele must have seen us by now.* Kevin knew he was devising a plan. *Steele didn't leave his people high and dry.* After a moment, reality kicked him in the gut. *What could he possibly do in this situation?*

Around noon, the tramp of boots squishing the soft surface came their way. A cadre of military men entered their area led by a short bald man. *Jackson.*

Jackson's ACUs were covered in mud up to his knees and his collar was in need of adjusting. He was flanked by a stocky man with a necklace so full of rotting ears it might snap at any moment. On his other side was a fiery red-haired sergeant. Other men lined the back of the group. Kevin's eyes scanned them briefly and settled on one in back. *Mauser.*

Mauser's gray eyes connected with Kevin's for a moment. Kevin shook his head at the man very slightly. *Shame,* he wanted to yell at him. *How dare you choose them over us? You betrayed us when we needed you the most.* Mauser broke eye contact.

"Look at this sorry excuse for an enemy," Jackson said. His mouth formed a spiteful sneer. "To think that you men, and I hesitate to call you even that, actually thought you could ambush *my* soldiers."

The fiery-haired sergeant with a cross on his forearm stepped forward and spit in their direction. The glob splatted into the earth in front of them, breaking apart and disappearing. "Pathetic."

"You're correct, Sergeant Yates. This is the lowest scum this earth has to offer. Men that would not only betray their country but stand against those that defend it."

"You came for us. We had no feud with your men," Kevin said.

Jackson's almost nonexistent eyebrows bounced upward. He bent down in front of Kevin.

"But I have a feud with you." Colonel Jackson stood up. "Stand 'em up. We have a trial today."

Kevin found himself being pulled up by Mauser and the sergeant with the ear necklace. It stunk fiercely.

The soldier grunted and pointed to Kevin's ears. He gave Kevin a crooked smile and a sharp elbow in the ribs.

Kevin's legs worked begrudgingly beneath him. They felt like tired old things that had corroded from neglect and lack of use, the legs of an ancient tin man left to rust out over time. Mauser and his partner carried him more than his legs did. Kevin watched Mauser from the corner of his eye.

"The only traitor I see here is you," Kevin spat, quiet enough so Ear Necklace couldn't hear him.

"Shut up." His reddish-beard had grown longer since they had last met.

The ground slurped as they trekked over the slick mud leading to the gallows.

"You should be ashamed. Look at the man you follow. He's insane. He's a Nero and you are watching Rome burn," Kevin hissed.

"I said shut up. You did this to yourself. You never should have raised arms against us. Jackson wanted to bring Steele in, not murder everyone."

"You actually believe that? He's about to hang us."

"You dug your own grave when you took up arms against us."

"You dug your own grave when you joined Jackson." His mouth clamped shut. *How could Mauser be so far off the reservation?* He had been a stand-up guy. Now he was a blind man.

They stopped at the rickety gallows. The structure was taller than two-and-a-half men, over fifteen feet high. Three ropes hung off the top beam. Ear Necklace shoved Kevin in the back.

"Easy, Lowry," Mauser said.

The soldier with the ear necklace clicked his tongue and mouthed "fuck you" to Mauser. Mauser wrapped an arm around Kevin's and led him to his rope like he was his prom date. Their boots clopped off the wood as they traversed the platform until Mauser stopped him at one of the ropes. He adjusted Kevin's shoulders manually as he squared him outward.

Steele's group lined the other side of the swamp. Men in leather gear, Michiganders with rifles, men and women with clubs and guns. He could see the tall pastor clad in all black among them. A bearded man stood at the center of the people. Kevin could tell by his strong stance it was Steele.

Mauser looped the noose around Kevin's head. The rope scraped Kevin's face as he forced it down and around his neck, cinching it tight. He dragged the noose around, rubbing it roughly over his skin until the knot was in the back of his neck.

The click of claws sounded above Kevin. He glanced up and backward. Two ravens crowed above him, settled upon the rutty, bark-covered crossbeam. Their feathers shone dark as night and overlapped one another like a jaggedly made metal sculpture. Their heads flittered side to side, and the raven closest to Kevin let out a rolling guttural, "Rock-Rock-Rock." It's partner joined in with the same tune. "Rock-Rock-Rock-Rock." If they could speak, their words would be: "Free food coming up. Come and get it, boys."

"Ha," Jackson called up from below. "Look, boys, the birds smell fresh meat." The hundreds of soldiers surrounding the gallows laughed. Even civilians were intermixed among them. A few hooted cheers of excitement.

"You can do it," shouted one.

Kevin's heart pounded in his chest. His mind knew his moments on earth were numbered. His body was preparing to fight or flight. Kevin doubted if he would have the opportunity for either. O'Hara sobbed outright next to Kevin. His body shook uncontrollably, his chin to his chest. Tom stood with his chest puffed out, chin held high.

"What fine craftsmanship," Jackson said from below. He ran a hand down a still-barked log, testing the sturdiness of the gallows. He moved in front, facing the condemned men from below.

"You three men are being charged with high treason against the United States Armed Forces? How do you plead?"

The ravens cawed in response. Kevin glanced up at the black bird above him. He let his eyes meet the raven's beady sable eyes. It bounced back and forth, never resting, always taking something new in. In guttural sounds, the raven emitted slow words of death. "Rock. Rock. Rock." *You. Will. Die.*

"How do you plead?" Jackson demanded.

"Not guilty," Kevin yelled out.

Everyone's eyes were on him, including O'Hara's and Tom's.

"Not guilty," Tom said.

"Not guilty," O'Hara mumbled. He sniffled, snot dripping from his nose.

Jackson smiled at them. "As I suspected. Unrepentant bastards." He paced, his feet squelching with every step. "You deny that you placed roadside bombs in an effort to harm, maim, and kill soldiers within my command?"

Kevin peered over the marsh, his eyes begging for rescue. Steele stood at the center of his people. His hand rested on his sidearm, motionless. "I do not deny it."

"So you admit that you planted the IEDs and waited in the shadows to unleash them on my men?"

Kevin licked his dry lips. "It's true."

"Then what possible defense can you make for yourself?" Jackson peered hard at Kevin, eagerly awaiting his answer.

Kevin collected himself and spoke. "You've hunted us and persecuted us across hundreds of miles. Innocent families. Little boys and girls. Old men and women. And for what? Because someone slighted you? What we did was in self-defense. We only defended ourselves when we were ruthlessly persecuted by a force of soldiers that should have been shielding us from the dead instead of trying to force us to join them."

Jackson shook his head. "Tell everyone what happened in Youngstown, Kevin. I remember your gangly ass on the video. I saw what you did to those men. My men," he screamed.

Kevin audibly inhaled. "I was there at Youngstown. I was an accomplice to murder."

The group gasped. "Hang him," came a man's voice.

"Let 'em do the hangman's jig," came another.

Jackson waved his hands at them. "So you admit to killing in cold blood?"

"I do," Kevin croaked. The crowd murmured to one another. He perused the bog and the people on the other side. "And I'd do it again," he growled.

The soldiers booed him. A rock sailed past them. Shouts of violence rose up from the angry mob.

"You were supposed to protect us!" Kevin said.

Another rock struck Tom. He cried out, "Shit."

Kevin stared back out at their angry faces. "You turned your backs on the American public. You're the ones who should be ashamed. All I did was fight for our people."

The boos continued. More rocks soared angrily through the air. The ravens above Kevin complained. They flapped their wings rapidly and took flight. They circled the gallows overhead, waiting for their fill.

"By your own admission, you've all committed high treason against the United States by taking up arms against her. I sentence all you men here to die by hanging until you are dead, dead, dead."

Kevin gulped down his fear and stared down at his muddy boots.

307

"Do you have any last words?" Jackson said. His mouth curved into a nasty smile.

Kevin peered out. "Don't have any whiskey by any chance, do you?"

Colonel Jackson appeared amused. He blinked rapidly. "Not for the likes of you."

Kevin nodded. He had never put any faith that his last request would be granted. His voice started subdued but grew with every word. "Then I regret only one thing."

"What's that?" Jackson turned an ear toward Kevin.

Kevin made sure to look toward Steele's camp across the way. *Not coming today, are we. It's been a good run. We didn't make it all the way, but we gave it a shot. I guess I won't be recording our history. Maybe you can record mine. Never give up. Never surrender.*

Kevin cleared his throat. His mouth was beyond dry and his words came out as more of a caw than a conviction. "That I have but one life to give for my country."

Jackson's mouth snarled in anger. "Let 'em rip."

Kevin felt a hard boot in his back and he was launched off the platform. His body was light for a moment before the rope held him back from falling. He felt the intense pressure of his entire body suspended from his neck. His windpipe ceased to function as the rope bit into his skin, blocking it from stealing more air. His feet kicked desperately searching for something, anything to relieve his neck from so much pressure. He couldn't breathe.

The shouts of joy from the people below were almost inaudible over the blood pounding in his skull and eardrums. He felt pressure in his eyes, and they enlarged as his body realized he wasn't going to take another breath. The rope twisted, spinning his body around. He spun past Tom and O'Hara. O'Hara's body was limp his tongue dangling out the side of his mouth. Tom fought like a fish out of water, flopping every which way he could. Out of Kevin's darkening peripheral vision, he could see Tom's hands free, gripping the tight rope around his throat.

Darkness crept in around Kevin's eyes as if it hesitated to take him. He was met with the smiling faces of the soldiers. They pointed and laughed as he wet himself. He had never read anything about that and he didn't care.

He kicked his legs, searching for the ground that he would never find. Searing pain shot through his neck and spine, but it was nothing compared to the panic of not being able to breathe. He tried to gasp for air, but the rope wouldn't let him. Crushing all resistance, it sealed his throat from the only thing he desired: sweet air.

Kevin's body twitched and he was gone. His foot moved, his body's final effort to rescue itself, a distant nerve still struggling to respond that didn't know it was already dead and gone to the next world. He swung next to the other two men. The rope gently creaked against the rough wooden gallows. The shouts of the soldiers died down, and now, it was the ravens' turn as they called out from above, finally ready to get their fill.

TESS
Steele's Island Camp, Mississippi River

No moon shone in the nighttime sky. No fires were lit among the people huddled together in the gloomy marsh for warmth. No flashlights danced in the night. The only light came from the distant campfires of Jackson's men across the muddy mire, the faint glowing tendrils shying away from the center of their murky island.

Her form emitted no shadow when she stepped close to the man. She gently placed one foot down, using her tiptoes to softly pad through sleeping men and women. The faint cough of a man penetrated the darkness. She had been a silent apparition, drifting through the sleeping bodies of their camp.

Tess had watched the men from nearby before she moved in close. Even if they had seen her, they would have thought she was one of their people relieving themselves in the night.

The cowardly talk from both Steele and Thunder proved nothing to her. She was the only one with big enough balls to get the job done right and his death would satisfy her need for revenge. If she waited any longer, she would never have a chance with Jackson's forces poised to strike their death blow at any time.

She stepped over a man, envisioning her sweet vengeance with every foot closer to her victim. Sweeter than anything else she'd had of late. She could practically taste his death on her tongue. She stalked closer to his tent. Two men stood outside, surely armed and aware of their surroundings. She peered from around a tree at her target.

The tent was makeshift. No one had much, most of the gear sat in the abandoned convoy. Tarps were pieced together in a square, using trees as a foundation, forming the roof. A loose tarp end ruffled as the wind flowed through the trees, knocking brown leaves to the ground. It flapped for a moment and lay still.

The shorter of the two guards said something and walked off into the night. She crept closer. He was taller than her. Short hair topped his skull like a freshly cut golf course fairway.

As she inched in behind him, she could smell him over the wet swamp. It was a mixture of mud and shit. Her breathing slowed as she stood directly behind him, her breath shallow. She was so close she could reach out and touch him, but she only watched him. She studied this man's last moments on earth, wondering if he had any clue he was about to die. *Hope it was worth selling your soul.*

Covering his mouth with her free hand, she quickly brought her other hand across his neck. Warm liquid spurted over her knife hand. He convulsed in her arms and his body struggled to remain standing. He dropped his gun. It made a muted slap on the wet earth. His hands leapt up to his neck, but it didn't matter. He could never keep his blood from leaving his body.

Cupping his mouth, she walked him backwards until he was laying down flat. His eyes were wild and frantic in the night, knowing he was fatally wounded. Keeping his mouth covered, she slipped the short blade up under the soft skin of his chin and jabbed it upward into his brain. His eyes widened further and he let out a small dying gurgle.

She tugged the blade free and watched and waited for the other guard. She scanned her surroundings for anyone who may have seen her assault. In the dead of rural night, she was only searching for lighter darkness coming her way. Nothing presented itself, so she checked her six o'clock. She stole forward, squatting on the ground.

Softly, her fingertips touched the edge of the plastic tarp. Waiting for a moment, she gently pushed the tarp to the side. It creased and crinkled beneath her hand. With the tarp open, she peered hard inside, waiting to see if the tent's occupant had been alerted to her presence.

She stood silent and still in the opening of the tent. A slender mound lay on the ground. It sucked in air heavily. Tess held her breath, watching. The old man rolled over and groaned. She steadily exhaled, letting the air escape her mouth.

She crouched inside, letting her feet be soft and nimble beneath her. She hovered over him, peering down at her victim in disgust. *This bastard. He thinks he can murder us. He thinks he can deceive us. He wants heaven so bad, I'll send him on his way.*

Squeezing the knife in her hand, she bent near the ground. Her hand wavered over his shoulder as if some divine intervention would not see her forward. She listened to his calm breathing. *Can't back out now, sister.* Slow and methodical, air entered and exited his body. Her knife inched closer to his neck. *No. I want him to know it was me. I want him to see his executioner.* Placing the blade to his throat, she covered his mouth with her other hand.

He awoke with a start, his eyes blinking in recognition.

"Don't move or it's over now," she uttered. She stuck the tip of the knife a mere millimeter into his neck. Not enough to harm him, but enough to let him know she meant business. She pressed it until she knew fresh blood had formed at the tip of her blade.

He raised his hands up slowly in surrender. His eyes still hadn't recognized her.

A thin smile crawled over her lips. "I wanted you to know it was me." She licked her lips. "I wanted you to know it was me that brought you down. It was me that ruined your little kingdom, and it was me who got revenge for Pagan."

His hand gently touched hers and she let her hand be shifted away. "I won't call out, my child," he uttered. His voice wasn't worried or rushed but seemed to come out at its own confident pace.

"Good." Then added, "It would only end faster for you."

"If he calls me to his table, who am I to deny him?"

She leaned closer to his face. "Quit with your religious bullshit. I don't buy any of it."

His mouth grimaced in the dim light. "You have so much anger. If you surrendered to him, you would be free."

"Anger?" She shook her head. "Anger is only a fraction of it. You burned my friend alive. You killed my people. You conspire against Steele while he showed you *mercy*. One might call it anger. I call it making a cold break."

He closed his eyes for a moment and she reveled in the fact that she caused him pain.

When he spoke, the tone of his voice was not harsh but mild. His confidence rattled her insides, making her unsure of what she did. "Our peoples were at war once, but Steele taught me a valuable lesson. He taught me that we can work together, both believers and nonbelievers for a common purpose. If only he taught you that lesson, Tess, maybe we would be better off."

"You murdered my people," she repeated. "You're a monster."

"I am what God has made me. I have given a downtrodden people hope."

"You've made them into mere zombies."

"Zealous though they may be, their hearts are pure. We were all put here for something. Even you, Tess. I hardly believe it was to martyr an old man."

"That's exactly why I was put here." She pushed the blade harder into his skin. His head leaned farther away from her. His hand drifted away from hers.

"Then why don't you finish the deed? I've done all I can to help my people on their journey. I'm ready to meet him. I've waited for that moment my whole life." He closed his eyes. "Our Father," he started. His voice, while muted, carried power inside it.

She twisted the blade in his skin, but something held her hand like she wanted a better ending or a more gratifying revenge.

"Who art in Heaven."

"Shut your mouth," she growled, frustrated by her lack of conviction.

"Please, send me to him. I am ready. Push the blade into my neck and it will be done. That is what you and I both want," the pastor said.

She twisted the blade a bit more. She knew blood trickled down his neck. "You hear me. This is for Pagan."

The pastor ignored her and closed his eyes. "Hallowed be thy name."

She pulled her arm back to ram the blade into his throat, ending the devious man once and for all.

But pain exploded on the back of her head with a loud crack. She fell onto her backside. Her eyes went haywire like she had gone on a merry-go-round a few hundred times too many. She tried to blink them back straight. Flashlights flicked on, illuminating the half-tent. The pastor sat up, rubbing his neck.

She slashed out wildly and a short stick wrapped her hand hard on her wrist. Her fingers seized in flection and she dropped the knife.

Rough hands tossed her on the floor and a heavy weight pushed down on top of her. The pastor stood, still massaging his throat.

"Good work, Peter."

"Thank you, Father," Peter breathed onto her neck. Her resistance was slow and her head foggy.

Her arms were pulled behind her and she heard the sound of duct tape scratching free as it was wound around her wrists.

"She is a very troubled young lady," the pastor said.

Her vision was doubled. More men poured into the tent with guns and weapons.

"Should we brain her and dump her in the river? No one would ever know."

The tall wraith-like form of the pastor now towered over her. "No, Peter. That is not necessary. Her soul can yet be saved."

"Father, she's but a wild animal."

The pastor lifted a hand at his follower. His mouth curved into a smile. "Her body will suffer, but we will save her soul."

STEELE
Steele's Island Camp, Mississippi River

Gruff shouts sounded through the trees, traveling wide over the small island. Steele's hand went to his M9A1 Beretta instinctively. He eased it free from its holster. He rolled up onto his bad leg and grimaced as the pellets lodged deep inside made their presence known. He scanned the marshy forest, gun punched out. The trees grew lighter by the minute as the day broke the night.

Forms moved through the trees. He knew they must be Jackson's men or infected.

With one hand, he trained his sights on the nearest one, tracking them through the trees.

"Tess," he whispered. "Wake up." He chanced a glance where she normally lay. The ground was empty of her sleeping form. More shouts carried in and out of the trees but no gunfire. "Tess." He scrutinized their area, but she wasn't there.

Flashlights bounced in the boggy woods. Keeping his weapon in the high-ready, his weapon compressed near his body and close to the center of his chest. He was ready to punch out to address any threats. He stalked toward the shouts with caution. A heavy person trudged in the dark nearby.

Thunder's voice boomed. "Steele."

Steele turned his way. "What's going on?"

Thunder's shadowed face angered. "They've got her."

"Have who?" Steele's heart jumped for a moment. *Gwen? Tess? What has Jackson done?*

"The pastor has Tess."

Steele watched the dark forms congregating far away. Their shouts drifted over the air to him. Flashlights bounced in the Chosen camp. "Why?"

Thunder waved a heavy hand and Steele followed. "Come."

Steele hesitantly holstered his firearm and followed the thick-shouldered biker through the trees. Near the center of their small island, a mob of people had gathered. Steele eyed the men. A cluster of Red Stripes, a few Sable Point volunteers, and too many of the pastor's men. The pastor's head stuck out of the middle, taller than most others.

Steele pushed his way through the mass of people. He put a hand on a man and steered him out of his way. "What's going on here?" He made his voice loud. Heads turned his way. The pastor seemed amused. Peter had a triumphant smirk on his face. Steele was not oblivious to the way the people had angled themselves. Red Stripes and Sable Pointers on one side, the Chosen on the other.

"Mr. Steele, we've been searching for you," the pastor said over his people. The Chosen people parted ways, splitting down the middle. The pastor walked forward with his disciples—Luke, Matthew, Peter, and others—in tow. Peter shoved a skinny, hooded person ahead of himself.

The pastor folded his hands in front of him. "Last night, there was an assassination attempt on my life."

Angry cries and murmurs came from the Chosen brothers and sisters. More people arrived, and the crowd stepped closer as they realized something big was going down in the camp.

The pastor's eyebrows lifted, his forehead creasing while he frowned. "I know there are many who despise me. It is difficult to lead a holy life and not garner the hatred of others."

Steele pointed with his unaffected hand. "Enough. Who is that? One of Jackson's men?" Thunder folded his big arms over his chest. Frank shoved his way through people.

The pastor shook his head. "I wish it was our common enemy, but alas, it is one of your followers." Peter ripped off the captive's hood revealing Tess's face. Her cheeks were puffy where she had been hit. Her eyes were downcast.

Dried blood was plastered down the edge of her mouth to her chin.

"There must be a mistake," Steele said softer. Inside his chest, he already knew. She had spoken about it. Endlessly she had professed her hatred of the man. It was only a matter of time before she acted.

"I wish it was, but she slew one of my men and attempted to take my life with this very knife." He tossed a blade onto the ground. When it hit the boggy earth, it made a squishing noise.

Steele approached the weapon and bent over, wrapping his hands around the hilt. Blood still stuck to the point. Steele stared at the blade and back at Tess. Her eyes betrayed her and she met his gaze in anger.

"It's hers," Steele said.

The pastor gave Steele a disappointed gaze. "I didn't want to believe it myself. I thought we brought peace to our peoples."

Peter threw a fist in the air. "We want blood."

"String her up," long-haired Luke howled. He joined Peter, raising a fist in the air.

"String her up. String her up." The pastor's men took up the chant.

Steele stared at the knife in the palm of his hand. *How could it have come to this?* His fingers wrapped painfully around the knife hilt.

The pastor met his eyes. A small smile crossed his lips. *He's got me by the balls and he knows it.* The pastor raised a hand in the air and his people quieted down.

"I do not think it fair to let such egregious acts of violence go unpunished. Murder and attempted murder is a serious thing. As a former lawman, do you not agree, Mr. Steele?"

Steele clenched his jaw. "I agree."

"I thought you would. But God also teaches us forgiveness. I leave this poor soul in your hands, Mr. Steele, for you to decide her fate. I trust you will do the right thing."

Peter shoved Tess in the back and she grunted as she took a step forward.

"String her up," someone shouted.

Tess took a few more steps toward Steele, joining him, her head still hanging low. Steele put his left hand in the air.

"At noon, we will reconvene and discuss her fate."

The pastor nodded with a slight bow of his head.

Thunder untied Tess's bindings.

"Come on," Steele waved at them, storming back to his camp.

The groups faded into their respective parts of the small swampy island.

Steele stood with his back turned toward her. "I told you not to do anything." He paused letting his anger subside. "Yet here we are. Our backs against the ropes." He glanced over his shoulder at her. "Kevin has been hung. We haven't heard anything from Ahmed or the Wolf Riders, and Jackson could lead a crushing assault against us at any moment."

She answered him with silence. Her demeanor reserved, she sat on a mossy log with her hands clasped in front of her.

He turned around. "Our people are on the precipice of annihilation and you decide it's time to settle an old score with the pastor?"

Her eyes lifted up. "He had it coming." Her puffy face peered up at him. Her eyes were unrepentant.

He shook his head at her. "He's our ally and you tried to kill him in his sleep."

"He's never been our ally, only a viper in a clergyman's clothes. A manipulator. A deceiver."

Steele continued to shake his head. "This is how you repay me? With this day's lawlessness? I'm sorry, you've forced my hand."

They locked eyes before she spoke. "Do whatever you have to do, but the only regret I have is not finishing the job."

***

Noon came too fast. The sky was a dreary fall slate. The temperature hadn't gone up through the morning. In fact, Steele was sure it was dropping. Any colder and he would be able to see his breath.

Soldiers still stirred on the other shore, and the clock ticked away as Jackson planned his next and final move. Steele had been outgunned, outmaneuvered, and outmatched at every turn. Now, his friends were either dead, gone, or against him.

The Chosen had come out in full force to witness his judgment. There was no doubt that they could easily turn into a lynch mob. It would only take a spark to send them into an inferno of violence. They lined the trees before him. In their center was the pastor flanked by his most loyal disciples: broad Peter, slimy Luke, and handsome Matthew. The pastor's long face watched Steele's.

Steele's volunteers stood near him, armed and tired. Margie rested her gun on the ground with Tony looming over her shoulder. Next to her stood bald-headed Larry. Beside them was Trent in his hunting gear and Nathan. Thunder and Garrett stood with the remainders of the Red Stripes, Frank with his Iron Drakes, fiery-haired old Red Clare with the Seven Sisters, and the crotchety gang leader War Child with the War Machines were mixed in. If things went south between the two factions, Steele didn't know who would put a bullet in him first, the Chosen or one of the biker gangs.

Steele walked into the middle of the clearing between the two groups. He flexed his right hand a bit. Peter smirked at him. Steele gave him a glare and the man averted his eyes. *You still remember our time together, don't you, Peter?*

He cleared his throat. "As you all know, our groups have had problems in the past." He spun as he walked, eyeing people face to face. "We've also joined together becoming allies against a common foe." He saved a special look of disdain for Tess.

"We must stay together if we are to overcome this storm, both Colonel Jackson and the dead." His eyes shifted over to the pastor. "I will not stand for any more violence between our groups." He flexed his weak hand. "Any person who commits violence will be dealt swift and severe justice."

He gave Tess a crisp wave forward. It was all business until it was over. His actions would be on a structured autopilot. Thunder's face was one of disgust, his eyes were alight. He hadn't agreed with Steele's conclusion, but he gave deference, barely.

Tess walked forward into the middle between the groups. Her steps were short, but her chin was held high. She sidled up in front of him. Her eyes said she cared little for anything he was about to say.

Steele held his chin up higher. "Tess, do you deny assaulting and attempting to murder the pastor?"

"I do not."

"Do you deny murdering one of the Chosen men?"

"No, I do not."

He stared down at the ground for a moment then back up, his eyes connecting with her fierce, almost coal-colored, eyes. "I will not stand for violence between our groups." He would not back down. "I sentence you to thirty-nine lashes."

Steele turned and glanced at the pastor, waiting for the elder to decide if the punishment met the crime.

The pastor regarded him with neither acceptance or denial of the sentence. After a few moments, the pastor lifted his chin up. "In the spirit of forgiveness, we accept the punishment for the crime."

"No!" the pastor's men cried out. Peter's voice rose with fervor. "String her up!"

"Quiet," the pastor commanded. His men grew silent.

Tess gave him a small smile. "That all you got?"

Steele ignored her. "Thunder, tie her to the tree."

The heavyset biker led her to a grooved, dark gray tree. He swung a rope around and around her wrists then knotted the rope around the tree. He turned and glared at Steele. Steele nodded to him.

Thunder released a knife from his belt and gently cut down the back of her black shirt. Her shirt flipped out to either side, hanging free. Her back was bony and each rib visible through her skin.

Thunder marched away back to Steele. "You're making a mistake," he said on the way by. Steele ignored him. Her fate was sealed.

Steele gave Rick a nod and the average, curly-haired man brought Steele a thin pliable reed and handed it to him. The reed felt wet in his hand but heavier than a thin branch should. Steele nodded to the man. Rick gave him a short nod back and rejoined the volunteers.

Tess slipped her chin onto her shoulder. "Come on, Steele. Give it to me."

Do you think I want this?

Steele moved close. He let the reed bend back and forth in his hand for a moment.

"Go on," she said.

"Come on," Luke hissed.

Steele tightened his mouth, and swung his arm back, and whipped the reed onto her flesh. She sucked in a sharply. He surveyed the work at his hand. A thin red line appeared diagonally, biting into her skin.

"One."

Whip. She cooed this time. She turned her head back to him. "Stings."

"Two."

Whack. She breathed heavier now.

"Three." Blood trickled down her back.

Again and again he whipped her, each blow taking more and more fight out of her tiny frame. She didn't cry out until he had hit twenty-three lashes. By thirty-three, the tree held her up. By the last lash, she knelt on the ground whimpering, her face resting against the tree's trunk, the flesh of her back chewed up and raw, blood soaking into her pants.

Despite the cool air, sweat ran down his face. His armpits were damp. His chest heaved. He threw down the tool of her punishment. He approached her and loosened the tomahawk from his belt, pulling it free. Swinging it, he chopped through the rope binding her. She fell back into his arms. He gently wrapped them around her.

"I am sorry," he whispered. Thunder handed him a blanket and he covered her front with it.

Her eyes opened a crack and her voice came out, a weak whisper. "Is that all you got?" She gave him a short smile. He picked her up in his arms and carried her. The people parted before him. They avoided eye contact with him, not wanting to meet his gaze.

He laid her facedown near a fallen tree. Folding up his jacket, he placed it beneath her cheek. The faint sounds of Jackson's men eating, drinking, and hollering at one another around fires taunted them from the opposing shore, penetrating the island trees.

Steele's men and women had no fires. They were wet and cold, tired and defeated. He sat down next to Tess. "One more push and we're done," he said to himself.

"Everyone's gone. Gwen's trapped in Iowa. Kevin hung. Ahmed and Macleod are missing, most likely killed by Jackson."

She coughed. "You still got." He leaned down next to her face.

"What was that?"

"You still got me," she squeezed out. She groaned as she turned her head in his direction. "Even if you take me for granted."

He bent down, giving her some water, and said softly. "We'll get you cleaned up." *My only friend left and I beat the hell out of her.*

GWEN
Reynolds Farm, IA

A fire crackled in the stone-encased fireplace in her grandparents' parlor. Gwen leaned forward, studying the black-and-tan square-checkered board, her elbows resting on her knees. She gently let her hand settle upon a hard chess piece the shape of a horse. She glanced up.

Her grandfather sat across from her. His eyes were cool as if he'd been here a thousand times before. A smile quivered underneath the surface. She pulled her hand back as if the horse had bitten her. She studied him for a moment. He folded his hands in his lap impatiently.

"You're lucky we're not playing with a timer."

She narrowed her eyes and definitively placed her hand on a crowned white piece. She slid it diagonally over the board and tapped a pawn. She put the piece on her side.

Her grandfather gave her a small smile and slid his rook into her white knight, scooping up the piece. Both of her white knights sat on his side of the board, one standing and one on its side in a haphazard pile of defeat.

"Check."

She stared at the board. *How could he have snuck that by me?* She picked up her king and moved him over a single space. Her grandfather rubbed his hands together. He plucked his other bishop in the air and placed it on her side of the board.

"Checkmate."

"Wait." Gwen held up a hand. She lifted her king and shifted him up a square. The black rook took him on that move. A pawn blocked one way and his knight mated alternative squares of retreat.

She shook her head in dismay. "Pa, you always win. One more?"

Her grandfather checked his watch in the dim light. The fire was dying. He slowly found his feet and placed a single log on the fire. "But when the fire goes out, we have to be off to bed or Gram will be mad at us."

"Of course," she said with a smile. She tightened a blanket around her shoulders. The fireplace provided them with extra heat, but the furnace was no longer running.

He sat back down and set the board up again. She had always been the white pieces growing up. As a child, she thought they were prettier, and over time, it stuck. Her grandfather always had the black pieces. He set his pieces in a row, the small pawns up front, and the specialty pieces in the back row. He gave her a cautious glance.

"Gwen, you've always been too hasty. Remember, your queen protects your king." He tapped the top of the queen with a weathered finger.

She followed along, setting up her pieces.

"She's the best player of the game."

Her eyes leapt up to his. His eyes crinkled in kindness. "Ah, and the most valuable to the king. The longer you keep her around, the longer he will stay in the game. Most of the time, anyway." He straightened his back row. "Two rooks are probably just as good, but don't be in such a hurry to get her in the game. Best to let your knights, maybe a bishop, feel out your opponent's defense. Be patient."

"I did beat you once," she reminded him.

"You did. I didn't let you win either."

The dry wood cracked and popped in the fireplace, sending embers up the chimney.

He smiled. "Shall we begin? White always leads."

"I know, Pa," she said.

"Just checking." His brow furrowed a touch. "How've you been feeling?"

She picked up a white pawn from in front of her king and moved it two spaces forward.

"I'm feeling all right," she said cautiously.

He picked up a pawn and moved it two spaces forward. "I know that yesterday was hard on you. You've been under a lot of stress. I don't want you straining yourself."

She moved her knight diagonally back from her pawn. "I'm not."

He moved his knight right behind his pawn.

"Did Gram tell you?" she asked.

He was taken aback. "Honey, please. Tell me what?"

She rolled her eyes. "I told her to keep it a secret. Should have figured she'd spill the beans."

Her grandfather gave her a knowing smile. "Your gram is leakier than a sieve." His bushy eyebrows rose in mirth. "But don't tell her I said that."

"I won't. You know, I didn't tell her. She already knew."

John shook his head in a knowing manner. "She knew when Becky was. She knew when your mother was with you. Hell, when she was with your father, she told me the next day. That woman has a sixth sense about these things."

"Just don't tell Becky." She stared off into the fire. "All I need is her reminding me that I got pregnant out of wedlock."

"Like a steel trap." He twisted his fingers in front of his mouth like he was locking a key.

She moved her bishop out and across the board directly diagonal to his black knight, threatening to take him.

He leaned in. "So it's really true?"

"Yes, Pa." She eyed him, worried that she might be disappointing him.

A wide grin spread over his wrinkled face. "Wow, that's just great."

"You think?" Her voice felt small and weak like a child's in front of him.

"What's not to be excited about? More grandbabies? That's fantastic," he said, his voice too loud. Haley rolled over on the couch and she snuggled deeper into her blanket. The phantom blond boy slept next to her. He still haunted her, always lurking in the shadows of wherever she was.

Gwen gave a laugh and held a finger to her lips. "Shh, Grandpa."

Her grandfather smiled. "The Rossolimo Variation. An excellent attack to the Sicilian Defense." He slid his pawn up on the other side of the board. "That's a good start." He paused a moment, taking in the miniature battleground. "So I guess I can run Jake off then?"

Gwen glanced away. "Please don't."

She slipped her white bishop over a square and took his knight and he quickly took her bishop with his pawn.

He set the piece on the side of the board. "He's not the father. He shouldn't be coming 'round these parts if you're bearing the child of another man. You can't be running around town with every Tom, Dick, and Harry. It ain't right for neither of ya."

She pushed a pawn up from her back row creating a diagonal chain of pawns in defense. "Just don't."

"It ain't right to be feeling another man while you carry somebody else's."

"I know that." Her voice came out sterner than she would have liked. She peered back at the dancing flames in the fireplace. "Jake just reminds me of home. Like you and Gram."

He nodded. "You'll always have a home here, but remember, home is where your heart is. If it's not with Jake, then don't be with him. He's a decent man. I think he'd treat you well, but I can tell your heart isn't with him." His fingers touched his bishop and moved it a single space.

"Thanks, Pa."

"You know, your grandma wasn't the only lady in my life." He paused, letting her absorb his information.

Gwen's eyes widened. "There was somebody before Gram?"

Grandpa Reynolds nodded. "Beverly Henkins. A real looker too."

Gwen gave him a disbelieving frown. "No. I thought you dated Gram since high school."

He gave her a mischievous smirk. "We did, with a short break."

"Short break?" Gwen's eyebrows shot up on her forehead.

"Not my idea, Gwenna."

Gwen set her pawn back on the board. "Wait, Gram didn't want to date?"

Her grandfather's bushy eyebrows twitched. "Taking a break, I think you kids call it."

Gwen laughed, a smile settling on her lips. "I've heard of it."

"But I met Bev at a roller rink over in Burlington. We skated the night away," he said with a far-off gaze. He leaned back, his chair creaking. "We even kissed on the first date. For back then, that was fast."

He nodded his head, impressed with himself.

Gwen laughed. "What'd she look like?"

"Curly brown hair. Stunning blue eyes. Not as pretty as Lydia. But she would make men's heads turn."

"What happened?"

"Well, over time, my heart wasn't in it because mine never really left your gram. I came back to Lydia and begged for her back. She wasn't quite ready but I waited until one day I came home from work and my Mama said Lydia had called. Didn't even call her back. Jumped in the shower and then drove to town as fast as my old pickup would take me."

"Why?"

Her grandfather laughed a bit. "Because she was my heart and I was hers. We only needed a little time apart to see that." He blinked his eyes, caught up in his story. He pointed to his chest. "Your heart knows. Your mind will try and make sense of it, but the heart always knows."

Gwen scooped a tear from the corner of her eye. Hearing her grandfather talk about how much he loved her grandmother touched her soul and made her ache for Mark. She sniffled.

"I wasn't trying to make ya cry, sweetheart."

She sighed. "I know, Pa, but you made me remember everything I love about Mark."

As they had talked, the fire died low. They sat in the almost totally dark room. She could only see the gray outline of one of the greatest men in her life.

"I know he's your man," Grandpa said with a nod. His fingers stopped. "But I have to say, check!" His fingers left a rook in line with her king.

She studied her pieces. Her white soldiers had dwindled, one of her knights and bishops lay slain off to the side, but her queen was still on the board. She tapped it with her fingers before she brought it diagonally and swiped his black rook.

His eyes grew wide. His jaw dropped open a bit. He knew what was coming.

"Checkmate," she said.

He stared at his pieces and brought a speckled hand to the top of his head and scratched. "Would ya' look at that." He folded his other arm over his chest, using it to prop up the one holding his head up. He pointed from one move to the other, trying to figure out how he got bested at his own game.

She let a smile curve her lips up at the corners, watching him.

"Pa, you're going to have to accept you've been bested."

He held up a finger, shaking his head.

A loud knock echoed from the front of the house. Gwen stood up and released her Glock from her hip holster. Her grandfather used his chair arms to help himself up, the chair protesting the entire way. He hobbled over to his shotgun sitting in the corner.

"Gwen, it's me," a man shout-whispered.

Her grandfather pointed his shotgun at the door.

"Who is it?" he grumbled at the door.

"Hank. We got a problem."

Gwen put a hand on her grandfather's sleeve. "Pa, it's okay."

He lowered his gun with a nod and she opened the door.

Hank stood awkwardly, holding his hunting rifle in both hands. He bounced from foot to foot in nervousness. He ripped open the screen door.

"We found Steele's group. It's bad." He looked back out into the night as if he heard something.

"No need to yell, son. Come in," Pa said.

Hank stepped inside. "Take a seat and tell me exactly what happened." She waved him into the parlor. Pa walked to the fire and bent over gingerly, tossing a log on the dying flames. He poked at the hot embers with a black iron poker like he was in a duel. "Can I get you anything?"

"No, thanks," he said, looking at Gwen.

"What happened?"

Hank gulped, his skin hanging relatively loose around his chin. His belly had rapidly shrunk since she'd known him.

"Me and Chase were tracking the convoy down the river." He paused to catch his breath.

"And?" Gwen said.

"Colonel Jackson caught up to them."

"What do you mean? Like a portion of his followers?"

"It looked like the entirety of his forces. We couldn't tell from so far away, but Steele's group got pushed onto some island out in the Mississippi. There's no way off. They're trapped."

Her grandfather's eyebrows pushed together in the center of his head. He clamped his mouth shut, not knowing what to say.

"About how far away?" John asked.

"The river bends, 'bout two miles down the road?" Hank said.

"Sounds like Harlem Island. Only a mile or so by water. Filthy swampy island filled with mosquitos all summer. This is not good."

"What do we do?" Hank said excitedly.

Gwen stared at the chessboard. The white queen stood tall on the board across from the white king. The black king lay on its side, effectively checkmated.

"Pa, let's get the horses saddled. I've got some house calls to make."

"It's late to be a callin' on folk."

"We're in our darkest hour." She turned back to her grandfather. "Not everyone agrees with the mayor. They'll listen."

Grandpa Reynolds frowned. "What's your plan?"

She stared at the tan-and-black checkered board. The flames leapt in the background, reflecting the glossy chess battlefield with fire. "It's like you've always taught me. A queen always protects her king."

KINNICK
Warden, IA

Only a sliver of the moon peeked from behind the clouds in the night. It left a waning light upon the dark pavement, a sky candle threatening to go out. The boot treads were light along the residential road.

Kinnick's boots padded only as softly as a military boot could strike the ground. He kept his M4 carbine tilted down and to the right of Hunter in a low-ready. Washington's large form loomed behind him and to the left like a dark shadow and Ramos's smaller frame hung a little farther back than Kinnick's gun pointed to the right. Their gait was quick but not any faster than Hunter could shoot effectively. Kinnick was not so sure about his accuracy moving and shooting at his current speed, but speed and surprise were their goals.

They moved without night-vision goggles, making their vision equally as poor as anyone else in the night. The difference between them and their prey was that they were on the offensive. Kinnick's mind raced. It had felt like an eternity since he was moving toward an answer instead of reeling from the never-ending conflict that only ever felt like they lost every battle.

The small unit reached a four-way intersection and slowed. A two-story house loomed on their right. The white siding was a smoky gray in the night. Hunter lifted a hand off his SCAR-H and gave a silent point of a finger at a single-story ranch that stood shrouded in darkness.

The four military men crossed the street, silent shadows in the night. It was almost completely quiet. It was too cold for insects and only the sound of running water trickled through the air.

A large wooden fence stood over eight-feet high, surrounding the back of the ranch. Hunter drew them to a halt near one side. Kinnick knelt down in the overgrown grass and waited. The dew on the nighttime grass soaked through his pants.

Kinnick's eyes drifted up to a black-and-orange "No Trespassing" sign on the fence. The soft rattle of the gate latch on metal announced the denial of their entry. Hunter ducked back behind the corner of the fence and knelt in front of Kinnick, facing out.

Hunter twisted his head a bit to the side and spoke over his shoulder. "Gate's locked. I can lift a side window."

"Affirm," Kinnick whispered back.

Hunter disappeared around the fence. Kinnick was forced to stare out into the night, where monsters stalked on the fringe of his eyesight.

A low *hoo-hoo* sounded out softly. Kinnick pushed his legs straight and stood. Keeping his back bent, he cut the corner off the fence. Hunter crouched down next to an open window. Kinnick's feet crushed the dying grass below him until he reached the metal siding of the house. He pushed his gun through first and breached the threshold of the vacant window.

His foot unable to find solid ground, caused him to trip and tumble onto the floor. His gun made a muffled thud as it landed next to him. The muted noise was a blaring of trumpets announcing his arrival. *I should have let the Marines go first.* He lay still for a moment, trying not to make the tiniest of sounds while listening intently for movement in the next room. A musty stench seeped into his nose. The place hadn't been touched by fresh air in weeks.

Kinnick's eyes adjusted to the dim light of the room. A ceiling fan hung overhead. Red, yellow, and pink flowery artwork decorated the walls. His head lay next to the leg sewing table and short wheeled chair.

Washington stepped inside the room, pointing his gun at the door. He was followed by another smaller form that turned into Ramos. Kinnick used the table to help himself into a kneeling position and he felt Hunter's hand on the back of his shoulder, assisting him upward from the floor.

"Always here in a pinch, sir."

Kinnick nodded. The Marines and Green Beret stacked on either side of the door, armed men in a single file line along the wall ready to rush in. Hunter twisted the knob slowly, letting it groan with every centimeter he rotated it. Metal slid inside the door handle removing the latch from the doorjamb catch.

The door slipped open and Hunter checked his angles inside the room. He placed two fingers in the air and pointed one way. His finger pointed in Kinnick's direction and his thumb pointed back at himself then he gestured in the opposite direction that he had indicated to the Marines.

In a dark blur, Hunter curled into the hallway, the Marines hard on his back. Kinnick took up the rear and had to take large steps to catch back up to the outline of Hunter. Leaving too much space between stack members was a recipe for a gunned down team. No sounds came from the rooms, and for that, Kinnick thanked God.

Hunter's SCAR was up to his shoulder and he tilted it to the side as he took small steps across, slicing the pie of an open doorway. He finished his cross and turned the other way to the next door down the hall. Kinnick checked his six o'clock and the Marines were making their way down the hallway back toward them. Two closed doors rested at the end of the hall.

Kinnick gave the doorway that Hunter had successfully passed a quick glance and pointed his gun in its direction. It was a dark bathroom that stunk as if people were still using it regardless of the plumbing situation.

Kinnick stacked near Hunter and the two Marines moved to the other doorway. They would do a simultaneous entry. Hunter put a finger to his lips. He wanted to go in quiet, not guns blazing, something Kinnick had made clear before they had left the restaurant. *What good are dead bodies? I need to show these people that they can still have justice in a chaotic world.*

Capturing someone was a much more dangerous mission than killing someone. If Kinnick had wanted the people in the house executed, he could have set Hunter up in a sniper's nest and let him pick them off, or even easier, have one of the Marines toss a few grenades through a few windows, but then he wouldn't get any answers. He wouldn't know if there were more compatriots throughout the town. Then they would be overrun by a mob angered by the murder of their own townspeople. People could only begin to trust if they felt safe, which meant that Kinnick put his men in the line of fire.

Hunter lightly pushed in the door. The room opened up to a master bedroom with a king-sized bed. Kinnick crept behind Hunter and split off from behind him once the room broadened to its full width.

Two forms lay in the bed, mounds smoothly rising up and down in sleep. He pointed his M4 at them.

Hunter crept along the bed until he loomed right above one of the people. His eyes narrowed in guile and he flicked on his tactical light.

"Good morning, sunshine," he cooed. The man in the bed bolted upright. His eyes were wide with fear, and if his hair wasn't gray already, it would have turned right then. He shied away from Hunter and the gun.

Kinnick flicked the light on his carbine and pointed it at the other form. A woman sat up on her side and let out a fearful wail. Her back shoved up against the headboard and her legs kicked as she tried to scoot back even farther.

The man shaded his eyes with one hand and the other felt behind him. "Wha-what do you want?" he cried. His hand inched near the headboard.

"Not so fast, sunshine. If you don't move those hands away from that shotgun hideaway behind you, I'll put more holes in you than a Wiffle ball. Put 'em on top of your head. Nice and slow like."

The man's face glowered as he placed his hands on the top of his head. Hunter grabbed him by his fingers and yanked him out of the bed. After the man was standing, Hunter kicked the back of his knee. The man cried out and his knees banged onto the floor.

Kinnick turned his hand palm up and gestured for the woman to stand. She did as he requested. Her neck leaned forward and her shoulders slumped in fear.

"Put your hands behind you," Kinnick ordered.

"Why are you here? What have we done?" she demanded.

The sounds of someone kicking a door vibrated outside the room.

"Don't tell him shit, Vicki," the man said over his shoulder.

"Quiet," Hunter ordered with a shove that forced his face into the wall.

"Washington, status?" Hunter called out.

Kinnick finished handcuffing the woman with zip ties.

A boom reverberated off the walls.

Ramos's voice rose in distress. "We got a gun!"

Hunter knocked his restrained captive all the way to the floor and sprinted for the door. He angled off the doorway, looking down the hall.

"Don't shoot," Kinnick screamed. "We want them alive."

"Never surrender, son," the man yelled from the floor.

Kinnick moved up behind Hunter, pointing his gun in the direction of the captive man.

"We need him alive. No casualties."

Hunter cocked his head, taking in the hallway. The shotgun boomed again and Hunter spoke out of the side of his mouth. "He's got Washington and Ramos pinned near the doorway."

The man on the floor continued to holler. "Don't let them take you alive, boy. They only want to oppress us!"

Hunter's SCAR sounded like thunder with fiery lightning flashing from the barrel. Boom. Boom-boom. Hunter took a step to the side and a half-second later the Marines burst into the room.

Washington breathed hard. "Door was barred with some sort of reinforced lock."

"Then that fucking pendejo started slinging slugs through the door," Ramos said, bent over at the waist.

"Come on out, kid, and no one has to get hurt," Hunter yelled.

The father lifted his head up and rolled onto his shoulder. "Kill the bastards. They've no right to be here. We do not recognize their authority."

Hunter ducked back into the room.

"Colonel, can you look downrange while I take care of something?"

Since Hunter had given up his viewpoint and control of the hallway, Kinnick took it back by stepping in short steps, gaining degrees of angles with every movement yet keeping his profile as small as possible. He slid into

Hunter's place, his gun aimed down the hall.

A door with six-inch holes in it stood intact down the hall.

Hunter crouched down next to his captive. "Now if you don't quiet down, I'll give you a three-dollar haircut."

The man twisted his neck and glowered up a Hunter. "Fuck. You. Pig. You got no right to be here."

Hunter's fist slammed into the man's cheek and his head thudded off the carpet. He angled down. "I warned you." He slapped his cheek with a few taps to make sure the unconscious man was completely out.

He walked back over to Kinnick. "Now, where were we?"

Kinnick felt Hunter's hand on his shoulder. He whispered under his breath, "No." He waited a moment, staring down the dim hallway. "What's his name? Lady, what's his name or he dies."

"Randy," his mother said softly. "Please don't."

Kinnick spoke louder. "Randy?"

The shotgun exploded again. A piece of drywall crumbled from the wall next to Kinnick.

"Jesus," he said to himself.

"You can take it from my dead body, pig."

"Should we oblige him?" Hunter asked.

"No. Give me a chance." Kinnick tried to see through one of the holes in the door. "Nobody has to die today. Not you. Not your parents. Not any of us."

"Go to hell," a teenage boy's voice shouted.

"We aren't here to hurt anyone in this town. We're here to help you, to train you to fight the dead. We're allies, not enemies."

"We don't need nobody to teach us how to fight. My Pa did that enough."

"I see that. You have a good shot, Randy." *Thank god it's not better.* "We could really use a shooter like you in the Marines."

"Marines?"

"Yes, sir, Randy. I've got Marines with me right now. Two of the finest I've ever met."

"I thought about joining before."

335

"That's good, son. It's a very fine career. A lot of pride."

"Shut up. You're trying to trick me. I do not recognize your sovereignty here. You're here to enslave us!"

"We didn't come to harm you or force you into labor. I know it may have felt like that, but if we were trying to harm you or kill you, we would have tossed a grenade through your window and been done with it. Why do I have your parents sitting here if I came to kill you?"

"Let 'em go then."

"Randy, you know I can't do that. They are suspected murderers."

"We. Those laws don't apply to us. We defended our town and then you had Andrew killed."

"Randy, we came to help your town and Andrew's death was an accident. Those men have been detained. I don't think you're a bad guy, Randy. Everybody makes mistakes. Put that gun down and we can talk about getting this straightened out because—." He took a deep breath. "You want to know something?"

Randy was silent for a minute. "What?" he said, barely audible from down the hall.

"There are a lot of really bad things that are coming our way, and if we don't get our act together—." A bright white flash exploded. The holes in the door beamed light like the room was atop the sun.

Kinnick covered his eyes and ducked back into the bedroom. He felt people rush by him. His ears squealed with high-pitched ringing that only would have been worse had he been closer. *Must have been a flash bang*, he thought as he squeezed his eyes shut and crouched down to the floor.

He opened and closed his mouth trying to stabilize the ringing in his eardrums. His vision began to settle, and he felt less like he was going to throw up.

Lifting his M4 up to his shoulder, he took back his headspace, aiming his weapon down the hallway. A handcuffed teenager was pushed in front of Washington. Kinnick let his carbine lower and he shook his head.

Hunter peeked out from behind Washington. "With all due respect, sir, I love a good chitchat, but we don't have time for this shit."

GWEN
South of the Reynolds Farm, IA

Wind howled down the river. It froze her face, neck, and hands. Ice-cold rain poured down, stinging any exposed skin on her body. Cold breaths fogged from the covered faces sitting around her.

The trees shuddered beneath the rain and wind onslaught along the shore. The water bubbled as it rushed against her boat. As she rowed, droplets splashed up onto her hands, freezing them onto her wooden paddle permanently.

Gwen dug her paddle hard into the chilly water. She shook her herself, trying to keep in whatever warmth she had left inside her layers of clothes. Harriet coughed next to her. They let the water guide their craft down the river, but she was nervous about what else the river would push along with them.

The moon gleamed across the surface of the rushing water. Shapes darker than the water floated in the dull light all around her boat. She twisted around. The shadow outlined pontoon boats, canoes, rowboats, and shallow-hulled fishing craft floating behind her in a small flotilla.

She stuck her paddle back in the water with some force. A jagged shape jutted out of the water a few feet away, rapidly approaching them.

"Watch that tree," she hissed. Gregor put his paddle out and used it to push off. Branches screeched as they scraped the side of her fishing boat. Gwen ducked as a branch swung over her head. She spun, looking back.

"Tree," she cried out, but it was too late. The canoe behind her tipped on its side unloading the passengers. Two people went into the freezing water.

They splashed as they tried to stay afloat. "Help!" they called out. A boat behind them shined a flashlight and voices of alarm went into the air. Gwen watched over her shoulder as a pontoon slowed down and the people were hauled aboard. She exhaled. *But now there are six less spots.*

In the darkness, it was treacherous. In the cold, you could die quick of hypothermia. They let the water take them down the Mississippi for another half-mile, navigating with as much caution as they could. A small light flashed in the darkness from a nearby island. Gwen's heart sped up in her chest, causing her to breathe hard.

The pin-like light blinked before going dark.

She took out a pen flashlight and clicked it on and off at the other light three times. It responded with four flashes. She responded with three, followed by the other light flashing three more. *I. And. Love. And. You.*

"Make for that island," she said.

They all softly dunked their paddles, taking turns in order to keep their craft headed straight for the island. It wasn't long before her fishing boat scratched the muddy bottom of the shore.

She jumped onto the shallows. *Sploosh!* Her boots were sucked down into the mud and she was forced to strain to free them with every step. The frigid water soaked into her boots and pants, not willing to be deterred. Gregor, Harriet, and Jake followed suit.

They pulled the fishing boat ashore. A canoe ground its bottom next to them followed by a pontoon boat. Men and women hopped down into the water and pulled the boat to shore with a rope. One by one, the rest of the boats drifted in.

Gwen slogged up an embankment, bending to use her hands to help herself up. A man-sized shape emerged from the trees. She drew her weapon. It moved like it was unafraid and had a shoulder sway that she instantly recognized.

"Mark!" she cried. His arms engulfed her, squeezing his body into hers. He stunk like dried mud. She ignored the stench and savored his touch.

"I knew you'd come for me," he said into the hair. He shook in the cold, his clothes saturated with water and filth.

Mark turned away and made a low-pitched call out into the trees like an owl would make. "Hoo-hoo." Timidly, other forms struggled from the trees, huddled together. Bikers. People from Little Sable Point. A tall man walked down the muddy slope. He was dressed in black and almost glided onto the shallows. He tilted his chin down to her on the way by, his long face regarding her with a positive indifference.

His voice was rich and practiced. "Many thanks, my daughter." He nodded and made for the pontoon boat.

She read Mark's face. "Was that?"

"Yes." He avoided her eyes. "I let the pastor go and he has joined with us."

"Jesus Christ Almighty," she said, looking back. His entourage of followers loaded onto the pontoon.

"We can only fit about a hundred people per load and we already lost a canoe on the way down."

"All right. Let's try to get a hundred twenty. Pastor and his people first." He waved people forward before he turned back to her. "Thank you."

"You should come with me, now," she pleaded.

His shaded eyes wouldn't connect with hers. "I'll go later."

She could feel someone's presence behind her. A hand touched her shoulder.

"Gwen, is that it?" Jake said behind her.

She could see Mark tense in front of her.

She licked her lips and swallowed, her throat suddenly dry even with so much moisture in the air. She glanced over her shoulder at Jake.

His hand held in place, his fingers firming up. His hand felt like it claimed ownership over her, protecting her and holding her at the same time.

Her eyes leapt for Mark's. She wondered if Mark could see her guilt in the night. In order to cloak her own deceit, she ignored her instinct to stay between them like a boxing referee and took a step back. "Mark, this is Jake Bullis."

Her mind's eye drew a boxing ring around them, the bell dinged signaling the beginning of round one. *In the right corner, is Mark Steele, love of my life, baby daddy, and leader of a band of desperate people in the apocalypse. And in the left corner is Jake Bullis, my forgotten high school sweetheart, farmer, and the one currently trying to win me back by going against his own town and self-interest to help my people.*

Jake stuck out his callused hand with a smile. Mark appeared less than amused, but took Jake's hand.

"Great to finally meet you, Mark."

"I've heard a lot about you," Mark said in turn. She wondered who was winning the match of alpha-male handshakes.

After a tense moment, the two bull-like men released hands.

Mark called to her people manning the crafts. "Let's move, people. We're in danger here."

"You aren't coming?" she said. The rain continued to fall, unimpeded by leaves. It was as if the clouds huddled over Gwen and dropped all their precipitation just on her.

His face was set like the stone of a forgotten statue. "I will be the last one."

Twenty minutes later, Gwen and Jake shoved their boat off into the water. Eight more people were aboard. She jumped onto the gunwale and hands helped pull her aboard. She took a paddle, dipped it into the water, and they heaved away into the darkness.

***

The night was never-ending. The drudge of paddling, up and down the Mississippi River was literally sucking the life from her. Every single muscle in her body ached, hurt, and she was sure she would be sick from all the cold, the rain, and the exhaustion.

This was her eighth trip between Harlem Island and grandparents' land, and she didn't know if she could do another. Jake was still with her. He had a tireless farmer's work ethic. She was sure he could do this labor forever without breaking. He was like Mark in that regard, but she thought even Mark could be outworked by this hometown countryman, who knew nothing more than hard work. He might be a simple man but his values were unwavering in the face of struggle. Keep your head down and don't complain, work hard, love hard.

They had lost Harriet to the elements. After the third trip, the woman was more of a liability than an asset. She trudged back toward the barn in a daze. Huge bonfires blazed on John and Lydia's property. People huddled for any and all warmth they could steal in the wet night.

The sickest went into her grandparents' house or the barn. The rest were trying to set up some sort of cover in the rain. Their porch was awash with bikers and Chosen alike. She thought her grandparents might have a heart attack, but they welcomed everyone the best they could.

There were plenty of volunteers from the people she had rescued. Margie and Tony filled in. The exhausted, starving woman lasted two runs before Garrett from the Red Stripes replaced her. The big man pulled hard on his paddle.

The last load should have been the final trip to the island, but organizing hundreds of the people to do anything timely was difficult, and more and more people emerged from the trees like ghosts of a forgotten battlefield in need of rescue.

Gwen's shoulders were numb but still managed to ache with pain as they neared the island for what she hoped would be the last time. They manually propelled the fishing boat right up onto the embankment. Mark was waiting. She climbed out of the boat. She ignored the water. She hadn't felt her feet in hours.

"Why are you waiting? Let's go!" she half-yelled.

His voice was deep and gruff. "I need your help." He had the appearance of a wet wounded wolf badly in need of a meal. He motioned her forward with his functioning hand. The midnight trees embraced his faint form and she hurried behind him, her feet squishing in wet marshy mud. The heavy scent of organic decay dominated the air, and she ignored the weight of her waterlogged boots.

She followed him through the marshy woods. As they got closer to what she thought was the center of the island, a bright flash took her by surprise.

The bright light shot up in the sky like a firework, but it was a single light. It hovered over the island, illuminating their area. Mark dropped to his knees.

The earth squelched as she fell beside him. He eyed the sky with suspicion. The burning light drifted down over the top of them. His face was more haggard than she had ever seen it. It was as if the fight against Jackson had aged him twenty years in a matter of weeks.

"Shit," he cursed. His eyes flicked back and forth as he read the flame in the sky.

"What's that?" she asked, her voice hurried.

"They know something's wrong," he hissed. His cold hand grabbed hers, pulling her up. "We have to hurry."

The flare radiated downward on the swampy forest, forcing the shadows into the swamp. Bump. Another flare snaked into the sky. Bump. Then another trailed behind it, each casting more light over the trees. Mark ran in front of her, meandering through dead timber and sodden earth. Ahead of them, a low-hanging tarp covered a fallen log. It rippled in the wind and rain.

Mark bent down in front of the tarp. He turned back to her.

"I need help," he grunted.

Gwen hurried forward and gasped. "Oh, my God." A crumpled, blood-soaked form lay facedown on the ground. "What happened?" She bent down next to the skinny woman. *Tess.* Gwen had never loved the woman, but she was a part of their lives.

Mark stared down at Tess, his eyes blank. "I did it."

Gwen laid a hesitant hand on Tess's shoulder. Tess flinched beneath her and coughed. "What have you done?"

Tess's voice was gargled and weak. "He hits like a wimp."

Gwen lifted a bandage and Tess groaned. Her eyes shot for Mark.

"Healing up well?" Tess muttered.

Mark came to. "I had to keep order."

Gwen's brow creased. "Keeping order? Are you insane? The poor woman's been beaten to a pulp."

Mark closed his eyes for a moment. "It had to be done."

Tess coughed. "Pah, if I'd succeeded, you would've given me a handjob as a thank-you present. That man is the devil." Her speech broke into a wet cough.

Gwen's eyes narrowed in concern.

Crack. Wood splintered in the trunk of a nearby tree. Both she and Mark ducked. Semi-automatic gunfire popped from across the swamp separating the island from the shore. Humvee lights flicked on, high beams exploding in the night like spotlights.

Mark scooped up Tess's things. "Come on. She's the last one." He wrapped his arms around Tess. Gwen did the same.

"This is going to hurt," she whispered to Tess.

They hauled Tess upright and she cried out in pain. "Aggghhh!" she screamed. Bullets whizzed into the trees around them. They stumbled, their backs bowed to the river shore.

Tess groaned and gritted her teeth as they ran. They clambered over sunken logs and dodged watery pools. Garrett and Jake's forms grew larger on the shore. Garrett grabbed Tess in his arms like a child and ran her to the boat.

The distinctive sound of a mortar thumped faintly from across the swamp like someone had dropped a heavy book onto a carpeted floor. Mark turned and an explosion erupted from the island. He watched the fire and smoke rising up into the air.

Gwen didn't realize she was shaking violently, her teeth chattering. Jake wrapped his arms around her. "Come on. Let's get you on board." He led her down to the boat then lifted her onto a bench like a child.

Garrett gently set Tess in the back. Gwen held herself with her arms, looking out at Mark.

His eyes narrowed into vengeance through the icy rain. His beard lay wet and hung limp off his face. He tucked his bottom lip up, tightening his mouth in anger as he stared in the direction of Colonel Jackson and his men. His hand flexed at his side.

"This is not the end, but only the beginning." He walked determined down the embankment then shoved the fishing boat back into the Mississippi.

STEELE
Reynolds Farm, IA

In the darkness, the flat-bottomed fishing boat scratched the embankment and dug into the muddy earth as it slid onto the shore. The rain was starting to lighten, and dawn was hiding beyond the horizon.

Two dozen other small watercraft—canoes, pontoons, fishing boats, and kayaks—lay strewn about a small dock and shore. He jumped into the freezing water with a splash and was followed a second later by Jake. Gripping the sides of the boat, they hauled it farther onto the riverside bank where it wouldn't be swept away.

Steele quickly offered Gwen his hand before Jake did. Even though his body felt like it was about to die, he acted like he could go on for another six hours.

He grasped her cold wet hands and helped her down onto the muddy embankment. She gave him tired, worn-out eyes and a flat mouth. He glanced back at Garrett.

"You got her?" He gestured with his head to Tess's crumpled form.

"I got it," Garrett grunted. The tall biker crouched and gently hefted Tess up in his arms.

Steele slipped up the wet ground, following Jake to a narrow foot-trodden trail. The hard trail had become slick with the rain and they walked in silence, trying not to fall, the only sound boots sucking in the mud. Jake led them to the edge of Gwen's family farm.

The field before them was filled with people. Groups of them surrounded bonfires. Some hovered near and others sat beneath an old yet sturdy barn in an effort to stay dry. The white farmhouse stood in the distance. It too was covered with people like an old farm dog with fleas.

They walked around the campfires. The flames persisted through the sprinkling rain, sizzling with smoke. Steele turned back toward the river, wondering if Jackson could see their smoke. He bet he did but was too tired to worry about the man.

Bedford and Half-Barrel nodded as he passed their fire. The Chosen gave him curious stares as they warmed their hands over orange flames. They appeared conflicted over whether they should burn him alive or thank him. In everyone's current state, he couldn't give two shits. He reached the steps of the old farmhouse. He could feel the eyes upon him, so he brought himself to a halt.

The sun was coming back to his side of the earth and light was encroaching on this field of diminishing darkness. A graying man sat in his rocker on the porch with a thick brown coat on. He was a sentry, the one that decided who entered his home. He stood with his shotgun in his hand. His wrinkled face squinted down at Steele.

"House's full." He gestured with a speckled hand. "May be some more space in the barn."

"Pa," Gwen said from behind his back.

"Oh, God," the old man said. He hustled down his steps and embraced Gwen. "I know you got a piece of Ma in ya, but gosh darn it, you had us so worried." He glimpsed over at Jake and then Steele and released his granddaughter.

"Jake." He nodded. "Who's this young man here?

"Pa, this is Mark."

Her grandfather's eyes inspected him.

"Looks like a wet dog that's seen better days."

"I feel like a wet dog that's seen better days."

The grandfatherly man eyed him with more than an ounce of mistrust but gave out his hand. Steele shook it.

"Heard you've been having a rough time across the Big Muddy."

"Yes, sir, we have."

Gwen's grandfather frowned, bobbing his chin. "You can call me John." He gazed up at the sky. "Lightenin' up a bit, but you two look miserable." He gestured to them. "Come on in." He stopped, eyeing Jake. "Give me a minute and we'll find you some dry clothes and a place to sleep."

"Thanks John." The exhausted farmer took a seat on the porch steps. Rain dripped from the tips of his hair. "See you in the morning," he said to Gwen. His eyes regarded Steele with no fear. She was quiet at Steele's side.

John opened the storm door and pushed open a squeaking door, letting them inside the house. People lay on the floor with blankets and on couches with quilts. A fire burnt low in the fireplace.

"I finally got Ma in bed an hour ago. A lot of excitement tonight." The old man struck a match and lit a candle. He waved them forward to his stairs leading to the second story.

"Gwen's old room is upstairs," John said to them.

Each step complained as they walked up. The candle flickered along the walls lined with old black-and-white family pictures.

At the top of the stairs, John led them to a room on the right. The door clicked open. "Becky and Haley are over there," the old man hushed. A mound of blankets lay bunched together.

"Thanks, Pa," Gwen whispered with a hug. John gave Steele a knowing glare as if he already knew Steele had been intimate with his granddaughter. It was equal parts mistrust and affection for a new man hanging around his beloved family.

"Get some rest now. We'll figure this out in the morning."

Steele nodded. "Thanks, John."

"Don't thank me. Thank Gwen. If it weren't for her, you'd still be stuck over there."

Steele ducked his head in respect. "I know."

"Too good for the likes of you or that other one down on the porch."

Steele gave him a grim smile. "I know."

John lifted his chin a bit. "Good. Goodnight, son."

"Goodnight, John."

He closed the door and softly walked across the floor. Gwen was stripping off her wet clothes and tossing them. Their wet fabric slapped the wood floor. Her wet hair hung stuck to her face and neck. She was thin, bones showing in places he didn't remember, despite a slight bulge around her midsection.

"Come on. Take those off. I'm exhausted," she said in hushed tones.

He stripped off his filthy Army Combat Uniform and tossed it in her pile of clothes. One of the mounds in the other single bed moaned and rolled over. Steele stopped unzipping his pants and gestured with his head.

Gwen nodded and grabbed a quilted-blanket. She held it up to give Steele privacy while he undressed.

"Didn't mind the view from over here," mumbled Becky from the other bed.

Gwen snorted. "Quiet, you'll wake her."

"Just saying," Becky mumbled.

He tossed the rest of his clothes on the ground and slipped on a pair of white boxers John had left. He bounced into the single bed and Gwen joined him. She draped the quilt over them and snuggled into his chest. In moments, as the sun cracked the horizon, they had fallen into a dead sleep.

***

Red shone thru Steele's eyelids. He forced open eyes that wanted to be shut for the next eight hours. Bright light penetrated the white curtains with ease. He shifted Gwen off his healthy arm, regaining feeling against the pins and needles. He flexed his fingers of his damaged arm. The tissue of his upper arm was new and fresh and ached.

"No," she muttered. He eased himself out of the bed. Becky and Haley were gone, only a pile of blankets left in their place. He lifted the curtain with a finger and peered out the window. Almost a thousand people were scattered below. Bikers in leather. Little Sable Pointers. The Chosen. All intermixed. All grouped into one refugee camp. All alive for the time being.

He glanced back at Gwen. She was awake and watching him with her green eyes. "I wonder how far he got in the night." He turned back from the window to view his refugees. *You banded these people together. Now how are you going to protect them?*

"It's almost twenty miles down south to the next bridge. Then he's got to drive all the way back up. That's saying he knows where we are. We have time."

"Not much time. And what if he goes north toward Hacklebarney instead of south to Keokuk? Then it's a lot shorter drive."

She stuck her bottom lip out a bit. "That bridge is blocked."

"He'll easily destroy those vehicles. How many men does Hacklebarney have?"

She frowned. "There's over a thousand people in this area, but there's something I have to tell you."

He hated surprises especially in his exhausted state. "And what's that?" He flexed his hand as he waited, trying to work some function back into this arm.

"Not everyone in Hacklebarney helped last night."

"What'd you mean?"

"I was only able to convince a few sympathetic families to help. Mayor Dobson and Sheriff Donnellson don't want anything to do with you."

Steele shook his head. "Those assholes. Like it or not, we're here, and we need them."

"I know, but you have to understand. These are prideful folk set in their ways. You push them too hard and they'll act like mules."

He smirked at her. "I had no idea."

She raised her eyebrows. "Don't you say it."

He laughed. "Lucky for the both of us I have a lot of experience in dealing with people like that."

Her eyes narrowed in a playful manner. "I'm not stubborn."

He grinned at her. "The apple doesn't fall too far from the tree."

Her mouth gaped open. "That makes you an ungrateful ass 'cause this mule rescued you when you were trapped."

He sat back on the bed and touched her face. "Wrong. That makes me a grateful ass." He kissed her lips, letting his hand fall onto her belly. He looked down at her growing abdomen and back up into her sparkling green eyes. "Is it okay?"

She smiled. "Yes. It's great. Gram's been feeding me plenty."

"Very good." He pecked her lips again. Standing, he walked over to his ACUs and pulled on his pants, securing his belt, firearm, and tomahawk.

"I'd like to meet this mayor and sheriff. I've heard so much about them. It'd be great to put a name with a face."

Gwen's brows shrank a fraction in worry. "You're not going to hurt them are you?"

He threw on his jacket, draping it gingerly over his bad arm. "Nah. I just want to talk to our newest allies."

"But they don't want you here."

He buttoned his jacket, struggling with one hand. "I'm sure we can work something out."

GWEN
Hacklebarney, IA

Patsy's hooves clopped on the road. Gwen felt silly riding the horse alongside her grandfather while everyone else either walked or rode on a hay trailer pulled by horses, but Mark had insisted. It wasn't that her body didn't feel like she had wrestled a bear the night before, but she felt like she was being treated like a porcelain doll. Small painful fluid-filled blisters dotted her hands and every muscle in her body felt torn. She held the reins loosely in one raw hand, not wanting to put too much pressure on it.

Mark walked in front of her by himself. The leaders of the biker gangs and their enforcers followed close by, but not with him. Santa-like Thunder and tall Garrett were the only ones she recognized. The pastor strode with curly-haired Peter and handsome Matthew, whose flail clanked around at his hip as he walked. Gregor and Hank flanked her horse on one side, Jake on the other. The men were quiet as they walked, only the rattle of magazines or guns and the faint sound of boots marching over the ground. She knew they were tired from the nighttime retreat just like her.

Her grandfather gave her a sad smile as he rode next to her. A cool wind buffeted his stringy white hair atop his head. Thirty minutes later, they were upon the small Iowa town of Hacklebarney. They marched right down the center as if they were an apocalypse parade.

Doors shut. Windows closed. Curtains fluttered and shut. The American Legion was closed up, dark, and deserted. They stopped in the center of town in front of Mayor Dobson's office. Steele gave her a rearward glance, questioning their next move. His hand rested on the pistol handle at his hip. She gave him a gentle shake of the head. *No.*

She lifted her eyes up to the windows of the mayor's office, studying the dragon's lair. The shade dropped and closed. The residual movement left it shaking in the window.

She cleared her throat. "Mayor Dobson," she called at the window. "I have some *men*," she made sure to emphasize that, "that are here to talk to you."

The blinds moved, but nothing happened. She turned Patsy in a semicircle. "Hacklebarney, I bring to you the good people who needed your help, but only a few answered the call." She scanned from building to building. A man emerged from the sheriff's office.

Sheriff Donnellson tugged on his pants a bit as he walked, his shotgun in one hand. When he reached the group, he kept his distance, gripping his shotgun with both hands.

His mustached flared. "Now, Gwen. We already had a vote. You turn your pretty little ass around before you's get a spankin'. Take your little gang and mosey on out of here or I'll call the posse up."

Gwen's jaw dropped. *The nerve of this imbecile.* Steele gave her a small smile beneath his beard and nodded. "I got this, babe." He gave her a pat on the leg before leaving her side.

Steele squinted as he approached the sheriff. "Sheriff Donnellson, is it?"

The sheriff's mustache fluttered with anger. "Yes, it is."

"I'm Agent Steele. I believe we spoke the other day on the radio."

"Is that so?"

Steele took another step forward. "We're the ones who asked nicely to come across and I believe you said 'no.'"

"Now, son. Don't you be puttin'—."

"Sheriff." Steele's voice was iron.

The sheriff's mouth snapped closed. His lips twitched in anger.

"I think you owe Gwen an apology."

Stubbornness settled on the sheriff's face. "I will not."

Mark tapped his finger on his gun. "I'm not sure you understand the situation at hand."

"Are you threatenin' me, boy?"

"I sure as hell am, Sheriff. Now, you drag that coward mayor of yours down here so we can talk to him or this town is gonna have a new lawman in these parts."

"I'm—" The sheriff stopped. He frowned and glanced up at Gwen and then cautiously looked at the bikers. "He's in his office." The sheriff hobbled over to the mayor's door. He pulled out a ring of keys. They jangled as he searched for the right one. He tried one and then another.

"Sheriff, need I remind you, time is of the essence," Gwen said. She dismounted her horse with a hand from Jake.

The sheriff gave her a weak smile. "That's it." The door clicked open. Steele put his hand on the sheriff's shoulder. "I believe you forgot something."

The sheriff's mustache twitched furiously. Gregor inched closer along with Thunder. Garrett gave the sheriff a wicked smile, overshadowing the lawman.

The sheriff turned around, facing the group. "I'm sorry, Gwen."

Thunder put his arm around the sheriff. "You'll have to forgive me, but me and my boy Garrett don't hear too well. You see we've been riding way too long to hear such a soft voice. What'd you say?"

The sheriff's eyes searched for a way out. "I said, I'm sorry."

Steele reached in and soft patted the sheriff's cheek. "Now that's how you speak to a lady. You know, I'm glad we had this talk."

The party of people surged past the bewildered sheriff and walked up the stairs. At the top, Steele tried the other door. It too was locked.

Steele shouted down the steps. "Sheriff?"

Sheriff Donnellson stretched his neck while scrutinizing his keys in one hand. "Don't think I got a key to that one."

"Jesus," Steele cursed. He took a step back onto his bad leg and planted a foot into the doorjamb. Once and then twice, he kicked against it with his good leg until the door burst inward. Mayor Dobson shrank down in his chair. The entire group filtered into his office, filling every available space with dirty, angry men and women. Thunder leaned on the mayor's desk.

"So this is the prick who wouldn't allow us to cross the bridge?" Thunder sneered down at him. "I oughta skin him alive."

The pastor weighed down upon the mayor from the other side. "God's people deserve better than they've been given, Mayor. You must repent for the sins you've committed."

Dobson's head bounced from threat to threat. His office brimmed with men and women who would love to see him suffer. He gave a nervous laugh and smiled, spreading his arms wide then brought them together. "What's mine is yours. You can't possibly hold me accountable for something that was done democratically? It was a vote."

"People died because of your vote, Mayor," Gwen said. The group parted, giving her unimpeded access. She walked through them with her grandfather at her back, taking her place near Mark.

"I was only trying to protect my town. Surely *men* of your caliber understand that."

Steele leaned in. "My best friend got strung up and hanged trying to help us find a way across."

Dobson rubbed his hands together. "I'm sorry for your loss. Many have lost much during these terrible times. Just the other day-"

Mark cut him off. "I'm not here to barter with you, Dobson. I come with a warning."

Dobson blinked. "Carry on."

"There's a madman on the other side of that river. He has hundreds, if not thousands, of American soldiers under his command and he wants us dead."

"I don't see what that has to do with Hacklebarney. This is a community that serves. We support our military."

"Those men across the river have gone bad. They look like the military, but they are rotten at the core. There may be good apples in the barrel but the barrel's rotten."

Dobson sighed. "I'm sorry. Hacklebarney cannot help you. Please carry on and don't come back. Plenty of land west."

A voice came from behind Gwen. "Then maybe Hacklebarney needs new leadership," Pa said. Heads turned toward the old man.

Dobson gave Pa a slimy smile. "John, please. You're far too old to lead our wonderful town through such a turbulent time. The stress would be horrible for your health."

Pa nodded. "You're right, Mayor. I am too old. If I was a younger man, I'd take you out back and whip you with the hose. That's what we used to do with a cheating darn son of a bee like yourself." Gwen reached out for her grandfather's arm. He shook beneath her hand.

"Pa, it's fine," she said with a proud yet sad smile.

He gave her an understanding nod.

Dobson smirked. "You can't possibly suggest one of these. These *outsiders*. The town would never stand for it. And, by God, we will fight for our town. Sheriff?"

"I reckon that be so," Donnellson said from the doorway. Steele eyed the local lawman with disdain.

Her grandfather's voice rose up and crackled a bit with age. "Mayor's right. There ain't no need to fight, and with no offense to our guests, it can't be one of y'all neither. Nor me."

The mayor smiled. "Of course not."

Pa held up a hand. "Now, hold your horses. I lived here a long time. Longer than most, not as long as some, but I've seen a thing or two. We got some good hardy folk here. Strong stock. Some ain't too bright, but they ain't bad people." He pointed a finger at the mayor. "But since you been here, Mayor, I seen some ugly times. It ain't all your fault. I might even have agreed with ya once or twice, but it wasn't until my granddaughter arrived did I realize what kind of man you are."

"John, my good man, please. This is hardly helping anything," Dobson said.

John's voice grew stern. "Now you be quiet and listen. Gwen here. She did something amazing. She organized and rescued all those people trapped across that river. Something she never should have had to do. But you know what? She did it anyway because she's got a gosh darn spine and a heart to match. She done more for people in a few hours than you've done for this community in six years. So I think it's time you turn over the key to the town and make Gwen the mayor of Hacklebarney."

The room was silent. A slow smile stretched along Dobson's lips. "John, you know I value your opinion, but I don't see how that is democratically possible."

Pa pressed his lips together and raised his chin. Gwen had seen that expression a hundred times growing up. The old man had become a human mule and nothing would budge him from his course.

Dobson carried on, not noticing or caring, his voice patronizing. "John, you see, this is America. We have *elected* officials. I ran for office and the people *voted* me in. What you're proposing is a dictatorship, ruling by force and fear. Whether you like me or not, I'm elected. And we won't hold another election for two more years. She'll just have to wait until then and run like it says in our town charter."

"What happens if the current mayor is *incapacitated*?" the pastor said. His mouth stayed taut, a bowstring ready to hurl verbal arrows in any direction.

Dobson gave him a curious glance.

Thunder leaned over the desk. "Or missing?"

Dobson leaned away from Thunder. "No need for threats, but I assure you this town will never lay down for the likes of you."

Gwen spoke up. "Mayor. I'm flattered by my grandfather's proposal, but I don't think it's right to depose the mayor by force. He was elected and however much I disagree with his politics and general attitude toward everything, I can't accept a position by force."

"Now hold on a second," Pa said.

She reached for him. "Pa, it's okay."

"Now don't you tell me it's okay when it ain't." He pointed at the mayor. "That man there has got to go and you're gonna take his place."

"Sorry, John. It's not possible," Dobson said.

Steele grew tired of the back-and-forth bickering. "We don't have time for this debate. Jackson is looking for a way across the Mississippi as we speak, and we need your support."

Dobson shook his head. "Like I said. If the United States military requires our assistance, we will be more than happy to assist them in any way possible."

John's voice grew strong. "You're wrong, Mayor. Section 12, Amendment A of the Hacklebarney Town Charter, reads something along these lines: In times of great crisis, a special election can be held to ensure that the immediate survival of the community is maintained."

"Bull hockey," Dobson said.

Pa nodded. "I don't lie. Read it yourself."

Dobson stood up and walked over to his bookshelf, trying to avoid touching the bikers waiting to beat him to a bloody pulp. He flipped open an old worn yellow book. He licked his fingers before he turned the page. "Here it is." Dobson held the book up.

"Section 12. Elections are to be held on the first Tuesday in November every fourth year. I don't see anything else."

"It was an amendment." Pa pointed impatiently with his index finger. "It would be in the back."

Dobson flipped to the back and ran his finger down the page. He stopped and his eyes blinked. "Amendment A. In times of great crisis such as war, famine, drought, etc., the community may hold an emergency election. It may be called by any member of the community and the duration of special appointment may be at least ninety days or until crisis has been mitigated. Although not every able-bodied community member must attend, a super majority of those in attendance is needed to enact an emergency duty official. Enacted by Mayor Fulton Reynolds, December 8th, 1941." Dobson stared at the book and back at Pa.

Pa nodded his head slow. "He signed that decree right before he left for the Army."

"Pa, I never knew that your father was the mayor of Hacklebarney."

Her grandfather stared at Gwen for a moment. There was pain there and pride. "He was. Damn fine man. Makes me just about as proud as you do."

Dobson dropped the book on the table and spread his arms wide. "This is preposterous. This hasn't been used in ages. There's no reason to start now."

"No, Mayor, this is exactly what it was meant for." Her grandfather stepped up next to her. "As resident of Hacklebarney, I hereby call an emergency election in accordance with the town charter." Pa reached out and gripped Gwen's hand and smiled, "And I respectfully put Ms. Gwen Reynolds forth as an emergency mayoral candidate."

KINNICK
Warden, IA

Howls for justice penetrated the restaurant. Only the light machine guns stopped them from rushing inside and tearing the Marines to pieces. Gary and Martha stood with Kinnick back from the barricade watching them.

"We need more time Gary. The boy admitted that he was with his father when he took the shot."

Gary's brow creased. "All they know is that you rounded up their fellow law-abiding citizens in the night. There were gunshots and people from their community were gone in the morning. How can they settle for that after what's been done to poor Andrew?" Gary paused, looking over at Kinnick. "He was a good kid. Worked hard. He prolly would have graduated and went to University of Iowa next year given the chance."

Kinnick sighed. "It's not something I can change." He glanced over at Gary. "We need one another if we're going to survive the coming days."

Gary spoke softly. "I believe you, Colonel, but how will you fix this?"

"I'll give them a choice and their fate will lie in their own hands." *If they don't fall in line, the executive order states I must execute them as traitors to the United States. It's not only the dead they must fear but their own government. It can't be that way.* He nodded to himself. *They hold their own fate in their hands.*

The Marines lined the front of the restaurant, weapons pointed out. "Hunter."

The master sergeant rose to a crouch and jogged over to Kinnick. He

357

rotated a thick wad of chewing tobacco from one side of his mouth to the other. "Folks out there are more ornery than a gator without a toothbrush."

A brick went through the front window. Glass shattered and tinkled onto the floor in shards. Gary ducked and Kinnick flinched. Hunter only turned his head a bit.

"Hold your fire," Hunter said behind him. He turned back to Kinnick. "Figured that was coming. Whataya think, Colonel? A few warning shots scare them off?"

Kinnick eyed his gritty master sergeant. Hunter shoved his tongue down on his tobacco.

"You want to go talk to them?" Kinnick watched the soldier's reaction, but Hunter didn't back down. Instead, he laughed.

"We seem to have been doing a lot of talking lately and they're still getting all worked up. Just like a bunch of damn snowflakes."

Kinnick glanced at Gary. The restaurant owner's eyes were wide with fear. Whether that fear was for himself, the people outside, or Kinnick, he couldn't tell. Hunter looked impatient as though he would hit the next person who talked to him. "Whether we like them or not, these are the men and women we swore to protect and I mean to do it. Put on your talking face."

Hunter squeezed the chew into his lip, and Kinnick wasn't sure if it was a smile or an effort to extract the most buzz out of his chewing tobacco. "Talk isn't my forte, Colonel, but I've charmed a few angry women in my day. Can't be that different." He gave Kinnick a wolfish grin.

Kinnick grinned back. "Me too." He turned to Gary. "You can come with us if you please?"

Gary gulped. Kinnick firmly placed his hand on Gary's shoulder. "They're probably less likely to throw more rocks if you're there."

Gary's face grew red and dropped his chin to his chest in defeat. "I'm not sure of that, Colonel."

"Let's find out together. How lucky is Sheldon's Lucky Number Seven?"
Gary licked his dry lips.

"How'd you come up with that name anyway?" The three men slowly walked to the front of the restaurant as if they were on death row.

"I. Umm. I was one of seven kids growing up. I was the only one who didn't end up in jail. Figured it was more luck than anything else, considering the other six of us."

"Let's hope it stays that way," Hunter said.

They reached the front of the restaurant. The shapes and forms of the angry mob were outlined outside. The wind blew their hair around atop their heads. Their cheeks were red either from the bite of the cold or the heat of anger. Kinnick couldn't tell, and it didn't matter. They demanded answers and he would give them. If they didn't accept his answers, then they would be forcing his hand on something he knew he could not order. *Their deaths would be on the Commander in Chief. Or would it fall on the man who pulled the trigger?*

Gary turned the knob and they walked in front of the store. The people grew quiet. He raised his hands up in the air. "Now, everyone. Hear what Colonel Kinnick has to say. He means no harm."

"Get out of the way, Gary," screamed a woman. "Fucking coward."

A chorus of "yeahs" went up.

"How can we trust the word of a man who is harboring these murderous cowards?"

"He's prolly in on it!"

Gary waved his hands and shook his head no. "I'm not in on anything. I'm just trying to help the colonel figure this all out."

"What happened to the Biggs?" shouted a man. It was not lost on Kinnick that the man held an AR-15 in his hands. Kinnick watched Hunter from his peripheries. The Green Beret's form was relaxed as if he faced a mob on a daily basis. *Can we afford to leave hostile people in control of critical points in our defense?*

"Not a problem, Gary. I'll answer them."

"The Biggs have been detained as suspected murderers."

"What?"

"Where's the proof?"

"The boy, Randy, admitted to being there when his father shot Private Gore."

A man stepped out of the mob. "You're trying to tell us that you're taking the word of some scared kid that you probably threatened to kill if he didn't fess up to it? Probably waterboarded him too. You're a liar."

Kinnick shook his head. "That's not true. He admitted it. We have a rifle that matches the caliber of the bullet that killed the Marine along with the specific kind of bullet used in the attack."

"You want us to just take your word for it? What are you going to do? Put them to death? What about Andrew?"

"Justice for Andrew! Justice for Andrew! Justice for Andrew!" a woman howled. She turned her back to Kinnick and started pumping her hands in the air as she riled the crowd up.

The mob joined her in yelling for justice. *What about the justice for Private Gore? Where is his justice? He came to train these people, not to occupy their town.*

Kinnick tried to swallow his feelings of injustice. He had to be above it, at least here. *I must treat this like a job or I will get swept up in the whirlwind of the mob.* He closed his eyes for a second and raised his hand in the air. He held it there while the people screamed for justice for their fallen.

"We'll give them a trial and a jury of their peers will decide their fate."

The group quieted down. A few shuffled their feet. Others stood on their tiptoes to see Kinnick.

The man with the AR-15 spoke. "You'll let us decide?"

"It will be a trial by his peers, but I will be the judge, and we will only do this if there is no more violence."

The crowd erupted into conversations amongst themselves and a soft hum filled the air.

The man with the AR-15 nodded as he spoke. "We'll take you up on the trial only if you put the Marines on trial for what they done."

Kinnick could feel Hunter tense next to him. Hunter hissed. "Don't. You know what's at stake."

All eyes were upon Kinnick, awaiting his ruling. He looked at the broken glass on the ground. Hunter's voice buzzed in his ear, but he ignored the soldier. The people were silent. He could feel his heart pounding in his chest. People would live and die based on his decisions. The wrong move here and he could be folding his entire operation. *Is the American cause enough for them? Is it enough for me? It must be.*

He eyed the front row of the mob. "The Marines will be put on trial for their actions."

GWEN
Hacklebarney, IA

Everyone in town and all of the leaders of Steele's band were wedged inside the American Legion hall. No chairs were put out and the townspeople stood shoulder to shoulder. There was a clear partition between the townspeople and the newcomers. In the middle were the sympathetic men and women who had helped Gwen rescue Mark.

Gwen stood near the front next to a nervously pacing Mayor Dobson. He held the town charter like a Bible, massaging the cover over and over. He gave her a glance and a snort. "They won't go for it. They already voted against what you did unilaterally without the community's support. Why would they vote for you now?"

"Because they're going to realize that what I did was right."

"Ha. Then you don't know them."

She turned, eyeing the weasel of a man. "I know them better than you do. There may be a difference between nice and good but some are both."

Dobson snorted.

The sheriff joined them. "All right, everyone. Let's quiet down." He waved his hands in the air to gather all their attention. The quiet murmur of hushed conversations died down to nothing. The newcomers had made them nervous. She could see the scared glances at the rough-looking bikers and Steele's military gear.

"Apparently, in our town charter, there is a special election clause that in times of emergency we may elect a temporary mayor to navigate a crisis. John Reynolds has called for a special election and proposed running his granddaughter, Gwen Reynolds, as a candidate." People spoke softly to one another.

"Are there any other candidates being nominated?" the sheriff asked.

No one raised their hand.

"That's fine. Ms. Reynolds must receive sixty-six percent of the vote in order to assume the role as emergency mayor. Each of you has a piece of paper in your hands. At the end of the nomination speeches, you must pick one candidate and write it on the paper or pick none at all." He nodded his head and stepped to the side, assuming a place along the wall. He crossed his arms over his belly and watched.

Gwen took a step forward. "I-," she started.

"I'll begin," Dobson said waving her back. He walked near the front row of people. Gwen bit her tongue but kept her composure. *If I look too eager, or angry, I will just be perceived as a shrill pregnant bitch.*

She gestured out to the people. "Please," she said with all the poise she could muster.

"Thank you, Gwen." His voice was that of a snake in disguise fighting for survival. "People of Hacklebarney, let me start by thanking you for coming. Although, I feel this is a waste of our time. Only a few days past, we were here and voted to keep these rough, uncouth people outside our city gates." He spread his arms wide. "Not because we don't care, but because we didn't know them and they could be dangerous. And you know what happened earlier today?" His eyebrows lifted. "They kicked in my door today and held me at gunpoint."

Gasps were audible throughout the attendees. People shook their heads in disgust. Evil eyes went toward the bikers and the Chosen.

"It's true. They basically forced this vote upon us and for what? So we could feed them and clothe them and harbor them from their enemies? Why us? We're only a few simple folk. Making do with what we have. Their presence weakens us and threatens our very existence. Even as we speak, the United States Army hunts for them as *traitors*."

More gasps protested from the crowd. Angry yells burst from Steele's contingent. She glanced over at Mark. He stared hard at the man from beneath his eyebrows. He looked like he would spit fire and burn the mayor to ash.

How am I going to get these people to vote for me?

Dobson held a hand up. "Not proven, but nonetheless, they confirmed that the U.S. Military is after them." He shook his head in disgust. "Helping these people is not the right choice for us. Since they are here already, a dastardly deed that Ms. Reynolds orchestrated, we should let them carry on and travel away from here."

People nodded their heads in affirmation. "Get 'em gone," said Colton Clark. He punched a fist at the stage.

"I agree, Colton. Let's get them gone, but the *first step* to that solution is voting for me to continue to be your mayor. Thank you." He nodded his thanks to the people.

Gwen bit down the anger boiling into her stomach. *This lowlife is preying upon these people's fears. Pathetic.* She gave the entire group a big genuine smile. "You all know me. You heard my impassioned plea to bring these men and women across the river, and you voted no." She took a step toward them. "I understand that. I asked too much. Yet here we are. Look at them." She pointed a finger at Mark. His eyes grew large and he glanced from side to side. He mouthed, "Me?" She smiled at him.

"That man right there. He's the father of my child. A decorated counterterrorism agent. He has saved more lives than probably all of us in this room combined. He's done more than I could even think possible to protect all of his people from me down to a boy he just met." *Max.*

"But, as a group, you turned your back on him. You turned your back on Thunder and the Red Stripes. Sure, they look rough and like to party, but they're survivors, and they protected innocent people trying to survive against the living and the dead alike. You turned your back on them." She pointed at Larry. "Larry served in the National Guard for eight years. You turned your back on him. Margie was a stay-at-home with two kids at university. You turned your back on her. Kevin was a history teacher from West Virginia." She bit her lip. *His body hung from the gallows.* "You turned your back on him and Colonel Jackson hung him for it. We're better than this. We're Iowans."

She shook her head, trying to rid her mind of Kevin's corpse. "People joke that we're nice, but nice isn't the same as good. Nice and polite are just superficial things people do. We're better than that. We need to do the right thing. The right thing is to aid these people on the run for their lives. Give them food. Give them shelter. What happened to give me your sick? Give me your weak? And give me your poor? These people are people like you and me. And just because they didn't grow up here doesn't mean they aren't like us. I'm here to tell you that what's across that river is more terrible than any war we've ever seen. Thousands of the infected. Criminals. Rogue military. One, or maybe all of them, are coming this way. And those men sitting over there." She paused and pointed at Mark. "They can fight. You need them as much as they need you if we're going to make it through this. Don't lay down and hide with Dobson. Stand for something. Be the good that I know you are." She stopped talking and greedily sucked in oxygen. Eyes stared at her. She could feel Dobson's eyes boring into her.

B.B. Palmer stood up and removed his cap. His voice was like gravel. "All well and good, but what about the military? Those are our boys. You expect us to commit treason against this great nation? That might be okay for you city folk, but that's not how red-blooded Americans do it."

Mark walked forward. "Colonel Jackson is not U.S. military anymore. I've fought with the real military against him. He's gone mad. He's murdered dozens of our people for no reason other than he's out for revenge. His unit is no more than a legion of AWOL mercenaries. He murdered U.S. troops trying to track down a doctor to find a cure. They're nothing but wolves in protector's clothing."

B.B. nodded. "That's a lot to swallow." He sat down and said something to Annie.

Mark gave Gwen a nod and continued. "Gwen is a true wonder. She rescued us from the jaws of defeat. We all owe our lives to her and the people here that loaned their boats, risking their lives to help us. You have our deepest gratitude. Thank you." He paused letting his words sink in. "We'll respect your vote no matter how it goes. We are men and women of our word." He stepped back and leaned back against the wall.

"Well, I think we've heard enough from the rebels," Dobson said. He waved to the sheriff, composing himself for a moment before his rebuttal. "I think a quick vote will do fine for this referendum. I bid you one final warning. If you pick Gwen, you'll suffer whatever crazy schemes she has concocted for you. Stick with someone that has dedicated his life to this community. Someone who's been here. Not some girl who shows up pregnant in the night to this place that wasn't good enough for her after living in the city for years."

The sheriff ambled onto the floor, pulling on his gun belt in an attempt to keep his pants from sagging. "Everyone place your ballots in the basket." He handed out a basketball-sized wicker basket to people in the front like he was in church collecting alms. The basket passed hand-to-hand through the attendees.

"Dr. Miller, in the interest of transparency, will you count for us?"

Dr. Miller smiled. "Of course." He joined the sheriff, dragging a table and chair from near the wall.

Gwen wrung her hands together. It was her turn to be nervous. She stared out vacantly at the crowd. Dobson's mouth turned out a smug little smile in his assured victory. *Do I even want this?*

She felt a hand removing hers from their tight mess. Mark's eyes read hers for a moment. "It's okay," he said softly, trying to reassure her. His kindness and gentleness surprised her, but she knew that it shouldn't. Even after all this time, he was the same man.

Emotions were welling up in her, but instead of going for his comforting shoulder, she stood tall squeezed his hand and let go. Leaders don't cry at the podium and they don't need their hand held.

Time ticked by slowly as the basket went from person to person until it ended up back in front. The sheriff handed it to Dr. Miller. He began removing the papers one by one.

"Dobson," he read setting the piece of paper in a pile. "Reynolds." He set them in separate piles. "Dobson. Dobson. Dobson." With each Dobson, she grew further and further from becoming an emergency mayor. The doctor read every single ballot aloud.

She lost track of how many she had gotten and how many Dobson had. She swallowed, trying to coat her drying throat. She looked at the doctor. The doctor scratched his head.

"That's all of them." He took his arm, laid it flat on the table and separated the two piles of tiny paper even farther apart. He studied the piles. "We have 203 votes for Dobson." He stopped and licked his lips. "And we have 398 for Reynolds."

The words barely registered with Gwen. "Fraud!" Dobson exclaimed. "The newcomers must have added votes. That's the only way." He took a swipe at the piles. "Recount!"

Dr. Miller stood. "Now, Mayor Dobson, I stand by my count."

"No. You. Backstabber. You were on her side the entire time. How could you people vote for her? You stupid inbred dipshits." Spit flew from his lips into the audience. "I pretended to care about all of your pedal-pulls and fairs and goddamn parades. You got a parade for the goddamn corn harvest for Christ's sake. You got the Pork Queen contest. Jesus F-ing Christ. But then you let some knocked-up whore come in and play on your do-gooder emotions." His voice grew mocking and nasally. "Help the poor. Save the refugees. Blah, blah, blah. I'll tell you one thing. When that Colonel Jackson comes this way, I'm going to him and telling him what you done." He pointed at all of them. "You-you'll see. You made a mistake." He screamed. "Fatal mistake."

Gwen walked over to where he stood. He shook in anger, his face redder than a ripe tomato on the vine. "What are you gonna do?" he hissed.

She wound up and punched him square in the nose. His eyes went wide and blood started to pour from his nostrils. "You broke my nose."

"The only regret I have is not doing that earlier. You're a coward and a scumbag and these people deserve better than you." She finished her statement off with an affirming nod. Dobson took a step in her direction. Mark appeared at her side. He pulled his tomahawk halfway from his belt loop and shook his head.

"Don't be foolish, Dobson. It's been a long day."

The sheriff pushed Dobson toward the door. "Come on, George, we should get you home."

"Take your hands off me, you ingrate."

Dobson walked quickly through the multitude and out the doors.

Gwen watched him leave. The crowd stared back at her and they erupted in furious clapping. After a moment, they quieted down. She smiled at them, giving them the fullest smile she could muster. She gave Steele a glance from the side.

"Let's get to work."

STEELE
Reynolds Farm, IA

"Here you go," John said with an unsure smile. He handed Steele an old faded map. Steele nodded his thanks.

"Things haven't changed much. The bend in the river's widened a bit over time, but the elevation should be right."

"Thank you." Steele blew the dust off and carefully rolled out the map on the Reynolds' parlor table. He set an old brown book with yellow pages he'd been reading on one end. The only legible portion on the spine was scrawled in attractive cursive: *Morgan.* John handed him another tome of literature and Steele placed it on the other side of the map. He scrutinized the topographical landscape.

The Mississippi River meandered in and out over the map of southeast Iowa. A couple of gray squares on the map represented Hacklebarney. A thin gray line crossed from Hacklebarney to Illinois.

His eyes scanned down the coast of the river, looking for more bridges. A dotted line down the center of the river represented the division between Iowa and Illinois.

Steele peered up at Thunder. The big biker ran his fingers through his beard untangling snarls. The fire emitted a low crackle in the background with an additional pop every few minutes.

"We can't let him cross or it's a toe-to-toe fight against Jackson's superior forces."

Thunder shook his head. "And we can't run. All our vehicles are abandoned on the other side of the river." Steele knew that of all the things that irked his big biker ally, it was the loss of his motorcycles that stung the most. All the gangs had lost their freedom of mobility, and at the same time, severely limited their scouting usefulness to Steele.

Steele sighed. "Hacklebarney doesn't have enough vehicles, and if it did, how long before he catches us?" He ran a hand up and over his scarred head. "Gwen, do you know anyone in these towns down here?" He tapped a finger on Keokuk the furthest southeast point of the state.

"Sure. Don't know if they're still there though. I know more people through here." She pointed.

Tiny dots littered the interior of Iowa west from the Mississippi. "How many people? And do you think they will fight?"

Her long blonde hair was around her shoulders today and her skin glowed. "Those are the villages of Van Buren County. Each village less than a thousand. Stand up against the might of the U.S. military? I dunno. You saw how difficult it was to get Hacklebarney onboard."

Steele nodded and placed a hand on his beard.

Frank grimaced. "We need to sink those bridges and hope we can play defense."

"My girls can handle it," said Red Clare. The old female biker frowned. "Gotta keep on the lookout for those dog fuckin' Wolf Riders."

Steele turned toward her. "I wish I knew what they ran into, but I'm assuming it was bad." He glanced at Gwen. She pored over the map trying to hide her worry about their mutual friend.

Frank eyed Red Clare and then Steele. "We need a plan in case we can't blow them in time."

"I sent War Child this morning. That old fucker was excited about getting to blow something up. Thunder has the bridge into Hacklebarney ready to blow. I'd figure maybe we'd wait until somebody we didn't want to cross decided to cross."

Thunder smiled, looking like a sinister Santa Claus.

"Smart," Frank said.

"Only if it works. Otherwise, I could have sent War Child into a nasty scrap."

His eyes darted up. "But we need to take care of the bridge near Burlington in case Jackson goes north." He looked at the leader of the Seven Sisters. "Red Clare, can you head that way?"

The leathery reddish-haired biker nodded her head. She flashed him some yellow-stained teeth. "I'll get some of the girls going that way, sweetie."

Steele sighed. "Back to our worst-case scenario. This is what I got. If Jackson comes from the south, we'll set up here. It's about a mile south of where we stand now. Close enough where we can deploy quickly and it's between both us and Hacklebarney." He tapped the map.

Two small circle hills stood near one another with a low-lying saddle between them. Another hill stood a few hundred yards north toward the Reynolds' farm.

"John, do you know the names of these hills?" Steele asked the old man.

John scratched his cheek. "Don't suppose they'd be on a map now, would they." He glanced at the map. "But I know 'em. The two furthest south are Sauk and Fox Hills and the bigger one is Black Hawk Hill."

"Thank you, John." Steele's finger tapped the edge of the map as he thought. "They're mobile and we're not." *Advantage Jackson.* "He's flanked us in the past, but I think he's gunning for us. His victory was stolen from him on the island. Now, he wants it even worse."

He glanced at the small black-haired woman. She stood, but the hunch in her shoulders gave her an uncomfortable appearance. She gave him a pained smile. His eyes said he was sorry, but he couldn't say it in front of the pastor nor would he say it in private. Tess had to understand to survive as a group she couldn't just off the leader of another group. The tall man in black watched them from across the table. His eyes soaked in everything, weighing the meaning of a single blink.

"Tess. I need you and best shots of the Sable volunteers out in front of the Sauk and Fox Hills. Hunting rifles only."

She smiled. "The sharpshooters will do the trick."

Steele nodded. "I'll keep Trent. I need him."

"He's all yours."

"Okay, you'll likely run into a scouting force. A squad or platoon of soldiers searching for us. You are a delaying action so we can get mobilized. Slow them down and retreat. Back behind here." He tapped the line between the hills.

His eyes jumped to the pastor. The man mirrored a Puritan clergyman at the Salem witch trials. Unforgiving at best. "Pastor, I need your Chosen here between the hills. It's exposed, but Hacklebarney has enough sandbags to construct a protective wall." His eyes moved to Gwen. Her body language was confident.

"We've thousands of bags ready to go," she said with a smile. "Usually we use them if the river's going to flood, but it's not that time of year."

"Perfect," Steele said with a nod. "It should protect them from most gunfire."

The pastor's sharp eyes pierced Steele as he turned toward him. Weeks ago that man had tried to murder Steele and half the people in the room.

"My men are not expert fighters." He paused. "They have fervor, but none of the formal training of the bikers." He said the word bikers as if it was a cigarette butt on his tongue.

Steele nodded. "I only need them to hold."

He was cut off by someone pounding on the farmhouse's old wooden door. Everyone's heads turned. War Child burst in. Blood ran down his face and his white hair fell loose out of its braided ponytail.

"What happened?" Steele asked. His mind ran away with every potentially awful thought possible.

The old biker breathed heavy and his voice came out in a gravely groan. "They're across."

KINNICK
Warden, IA

Kinnick sat behind a square restaurant table. In front of him was a notepad, a pen, and a glass of water. He faced a dim restaurant even during the middle of the day. The windows were still barricaded, blocking most of the ambient light from the overcast sky. The tables had been cleared out and only the dining room chairs remained in short rows facing his direction.

He clasped his hands in front of him, feeling like a mob boss awaiting the townspeople under his protection to pay him tribute. In reality, he was waiting for the people of Warden to finish filtering into the dining room. He could sense Hunter looming near the right-hand wall like a court bailiff ready to jump into the fray at a moment's notice. He only had a sidearm as did Kinnick, and none of the townspeople were allowed weapons inside the restaurant. Washington and Duncan patted people down at the door. Duncan peered into a woman's purse and waved her through. A line formed running along the building.

Kinnick checked his watch. They were fifteen minutes past the agreed start time, so he nodded to Hunter. Hunter waved to Washington and the Marine stepped into the doorway.

"There's no more room."

A man peered around him. "Come on."

The large African-American soldier stood his ground blocking his path. "You can see through the windows." A crowd had formed outside. They looked over one another in an attempt to see inside.

Kinnick picked up his pen and clicked the silver button on top with his thumb. Click-click. Click-click. Hunter positioned himself near his right again, hands clasped behind his back. "Hunter, bring them out." The Green Beret disappeared into the kitchen.

Kinnick stared at the people. They were regular enough. Some were overweight. Others were thinner. Almost all were white. He saw the old woman that had witnessed the Marines kill the boy. *She will surely testify.* An eyewitness did not bode well for the Marines' fate. Volk had all but confirmed that he was guilty. *How can I be fair and see this horrible situation to a successful conclusion? You can't,* his mind mocked.

A cluster of boots thumped the floor in the back, and a moment later, Hunter brought Volk and Whitehead into the main dining room. He escorted them to chairs. The townspeople whispered angrily to one another.

A lanky man with a ball cap on his head stood and pointed with a stiff finger at the Marines. "Fuck you for what you done. My boy's gone."

Kinnick raised his hand. "Enough, sir. We're here for a trial, not a lynching. Next outburst and you're gone."

The man looked like he was about to spit but instead took a seat next to his wife with ear-length blonde hair, who wiped her nose with a handkerchief. He placed a comforting arm around her, his eyes piercing Kinnick.

Kinnick spoke loudly so even the people outside could hear his voice. "You all agreed to a dual trial for the Marines and the Biggs. They will be judged by a jury of their peers, and I will preside over the decision. Is this clear?"

People nodded their heads. Kinnick gave Hunter a single nod. "Bring them out."

In less than thirty seconds, Hunter brought Martin and Randy Biggs out and sat them at another table on the other side of the room from the convicted Marines. The left side of Martin's face was different shades of black, purple, and yellow. Randy was slumped over in his chair, already defeated. He dipped his shaved head and stared at the floor.

"We'll start with the murder charges brought against Sergeant Volk and Private Whitehead. We will begin by hearing Sergeant Volk's story. You may stand."

Volk stood in his spot. He lifted his chin a bit and stared unafraid at the town's people gathered against him. He sneered a bit. "At approximately 0330, Private Whitehead and myself began our nightly curfew patrol. As we all know, a curfew was put into effect after the assassination of USMC Private Gore. At approximately 0415, we came across two civilians near the docks. They were in clear violation of said curfew." He turned toward Kinnick now. "We had strict orders to treat all civilians out after curfew as immediate threats." He turned back to the assemblage with a tight-lipped smile. "However, since they were a couple of kids, we decided that we should just scare them a bit and send them on their way." He shuffled his feet. "I asked the older of the two what they were doing out after curfew. He gave me some sort of bullshit about checking fishing lines. I told him to get lost and he responded by telling me to fuck off. I'll admit I took a swing at him and knocked him down. I mean, come on, we could have executed him for violation of curfew for Christ's sake."

"You did," shouted a lady.

Kinnick pointed at her. "We'll have order or nothing."

The lady plopped back down in her chair and clamped her mouth shut.

"That's when the other civilian took a lunge at us. It took me a second, but he had a knife in one hand. We were so close, he could have killed one of us. I shouted, "Knife!" and I struck him with the butt of the gun. He went down hard."

Kinnick jotted some notes. *Knife? How will we know if he's telling the truth?*

"When I yelled to stay down, he tried to stand up, so I hit him again. Maybe a few more times, but we were dealing with a deadly situation. I guess he hit his head pretty hard."

"How many times did you strike the civilian?" Kinnick asked.

"Once or twice."

Kinnick had watched the man as he spoke. His eyes drifted a fraction when he said the word twice.

Kinnick's mouth tightened. "Which was it? Once or twice?"

Volk gulped. "Twice, sir."

The townspeople probably didn't notice, but Kinnick did. There was more to his story or he was being deceptive or both. Kinnick also knew that a hit to the skull with the butt of a rifle could kill someone, but for that matter, so could falling.

"And he had a knife?"

"That's correct."

Kinnick jotted some notes. "Whitehead, you may stand."

Whitehead was nervous. He was young and had a healthy fear of punishment. His eyes peered down at the floor.

"You may speak, Private Whitehead."

"It's as Volk said, we were on curfew patrol around the dock when we saw the two civilians. When we asked them to go back to their homes, the older one took a swing at us. It was an accident. We weren't trying to hurt anyone, just scare 'em."

"What was an accident?"

Whitehead kept his eyes downward. "His death. Volk was only trying to scare him."

"Did Volk tell you that?"

"Well, yeah."

"What exactly did he say?"

Whitehead glanced at Volk. Volk's eyes were hard.

Kinnick was stern. "Your commanding officer asked you a question, Marine."

Whitehead stared back down at the floor. "He said if you weren't going to do anything about Gore maybe we should put some fear into these rednecks."

Cries went through the crowd. They whispered to one another in hushed tones.

Kinnick clenched his jaw. *I wasn't trying to put fear into them, I was trying to recruit them to fight with us.*

"We was only trying to scare them. Rough 'em up a bit. Let 'em know we meant business. We're Marines, sir."

"Whitehead. Did you see a knife?"

Whitehead's eyes dipped even lower. "Yeah."

"What kind of knife was it?"

"A black folding knife."

Kinnick turned to Hunter. "Do we have the knife?"

Hunter shook his head. "We do not."

Kinnick turned back to Whitehead. "Where did the knife go?"

"I dunno. Fell in the water, I suppose."

Kinnick sighed. He circled knife on the paper. If they had no knife, it was hard to prove that they had any just cause to assault the young men. "Now, Whitehead, was there a knife?"

"I don't understand." Whitehead looked to Volk. A confused look settled upon his face. "Volk said there was a knife."

Kinnick squeezed his eyes closed for a moment. *No knife. Volk, what have you done?* "So Volk said there was a knife, but you didn't see the knife?"

"Well, yeah, he yelled knife and we took quick action. I only assumed."

"The kid had a knife," Volk piped up. He crossed his arms over his chest. "I saw it."

"Where's the knife?"

"No idea. Betcha one of them took it off his body or it fell through the cracks of the dock. But he had one."

Kinnick gave Whitehead a short gesture with his hand. "Whitehead, you may sit."

"Next, we'll hear from Doug." Kinnick scanned the seated people. "Where's Doug?"

A teenage boy stood up hesitantly. His mother leaned in and whispered something to him. He nodded a swollen battered face. The left side of his face was the shade of the sky at dusk. His lower lip stuck out, a fat earthworm twice as big as the upper lip. He was skinny but taller than average as if he had just started his pubescent growth spurt. He walked down the aisle, his shoulders slightly hunched.

He stopped near Kinnick. Kinnick pointed to a nearby chair. "Go on and tell us what happened."

The boy gripped his hands in front of his body. "Well, me and Andrew. We's was checkin' the trotlines like we do every morning. You see, we let out a bunch of trotlines out from the docks every night, and before dawn, we check 'em to see if we got anything. Usually bring about three or four catfish every morning." He glanced at Kinnick for approval.

Kinnick nodded. "Go on."

"Well, we's was almost done, had a real good catch too. Two good-sized catfish had to a been twenty-five to thirty pounds each when those two over there came up on us." Doug pointed at Volk and Whitehead. "You know Andrew was funny. He always was making jokes. Sometimes they was mean, but that's just how he was. A jokester."

"What was Andrew joking about?"

Doug's eyes danced nervously about the people. He glanced at his parents and dipped his eyes in adolescent shame.

"Doug, you can tell us what he said. You aren't in trouble."

Doug looked away. "He was talking about Kat Mulligan."

"What about her?"

Doug frowned. "Andrew liked her. He was talking all big about having sex and stuff with her. About how they did it in his car."

The crowd murmured to one another and eyes drifted to only who Kinnick could assume was Kat Mulligan's father. Blood rushed to his face and it turned red.

"It's okay. Was he *joking* about anything else?"

Doug's shoulders slumped and his lip twitched to the side like he might break down and cry.

"Doug, please, this is serious. Answer the question."

Doug gulped. "He was talking big about fighting the monsters. Said he figured that Marine would be a monster now and that he'd probably have to take him out too to keep the village safe."

"What else?"

"That's when the Marines walked up on us. They asked us what we were doing. We told them we were checking lines like we's do every day. That one called us little cunts and then he punched me in the face. I fell down. That's when Andrew tried to stop them."

"Is that when Sergeant Volk hit Andrew?"

"Yeah, he hit him with the butt of his gun in the face and it knocked Andrew down. Then he kept pounding his head with the butt." Doug's plump lip trembled. "The sound was so bad. It was like a tree branch breaking and his head was. His head was like mush."

Doug took a deep breath, his chest shaking as he tried to control his emotions. Andrew's mother cried in her seat, hands on her face.

Kinnick let the boy collect himself. He leaned a bit closer. "What was Andrew doing when the Marines came up on you?"

"He was untangling a trotline."

"Thank you, Doug."

Doug bobbed his head and quickly stood. He took a few steps forward before Kinnick put his hand in the air.

"Doug, wait." The teenager stopped and his shoulders sagged. "Just one more question."

"Yeah?" The teenager looked like he wanted to shrink away to nothing.

"How was Andrew untangling the trotline?"

Doug gave him a quizzical look, not understanding how Kinnick didn't know how to do this. "He pulls the line in and checks each individual line for fish. If the lines get tangled, he cuts it and lets it go."

"What's he cut it with?"

"His knife."

Kinnick circled the crossed-out word on his paper again. *Knife.* "Wait, Doug. Andrew had a knife on him?"

"I. Um. Yes. Always does."

"What's the knife look like?"

"Bout five inches, black."

"You're released."

If we had the knife, this would be easier.

Kinnick stood up.

"Mrs. Thomas, can you come up?"

The old woman with perfectly curled hair walked forward and sat in a chair near Kinnick. Her head went from person to person. She waved hello to a few people, loving the attention.

Kinnick tapped his paper with a pen. "Can you reiterate your story for everyone?"

She matter-of-factly nodded the affirmative. "Yes, I can. I was getting ready to cook breakfast. I heard some shouting and looked out the window. I saw that man there." She pointed at Volk. "He was hitting Andrew with his gun over and over until he stopped moving."

"Mrs. Thomas, where is your house in relation to the docks?" Kinnick studied his notes. He jotted a long rectangle representing the dock.

"Four doors down."

Her chin rose up slightly as she spoke.

"About how far would you say that is from where Andrew and Doug were standing?"

"I dunno. About forty yards."

"Mrs. Thomas, what kind of vision do you have?"

Her brow scrunched up and her eyes squinted.

"I wear glasses," she muttered.

"Where are your glasses today?"

She seemed taken aback. "I didn't wear them."

"Why didn't you wear your glasses?"

"'Cause I only need them for reading."

He drew a line from the house back to the docks with an arrow and jotted forty next to it. He glanced up at her. "Were you wearing your glasses that morning?"

"No, I was not." Her mouth settled flat.

"Can you do me a favor? Can you turn your back to everyone?"

Her eyebrows shifted to their lowest point in offense but did as he asked. Kinnick waved at Whitehead and Volk. "Go to the edge of the restaurant. Hunter. Washington. All of you." Kinnick's men lined up against the wall of the restaurant.

"Before Mrs. Thomas turns around, does everyone agree that this is about twenty yards? A shorter distance than what Mrs. Thomas claims to live from the docks."

People looked at one another and heads nodded.

"Good." He turned to face Mrs. Thomas. "Now, Mrs. Thomas. You may turn around." Mrs. Thomas spun around. She immediately squinted at the far wall filled with his men.

"I don't see why this is necessary," she said angrily.

"It is. I want you to pick out the two Marines you saw that day. The two that hit Doug and killed Andrew."

She licked her lips. "Let's see here." Her eyes scanned back and forth down the line of fighting men.

"I'll say." With hesitation, she lifted a hand and pointed at Boone. "I'll say." Her hand drifted down the line. "Him. He was the one I saw and him." Her hand pointed to the end. "Yup."

"Are you sure, Mrs. Thomas? This is important."

Her chin rose even higher. "Absolutely positive."

"Those selected, you may step forward."

Duncan and Boone took a step forward. "You selected two Marines that were not there."

"No. You tricked me. Those two men were there."

"They were not. Please have a seat, Mrs. Thomas."

She shook her head no. "I. I swear I saw them." The elderly woman walked back to her seat.

Kinnick exhaled. *It's enough of a finger-pointing match to call it,* he thought, *but the boy is still gone.* Kinnick sat back in his chair and wrote "*no credible witnesses involved*" on his notepad and circled it. He cleared his throat, prepping himself to speak. "Before we move forward, I believe it prudent to hear Biggs's story."

Whispers rippled through the crowd.

"Give us justice."

Kinnick shook his head. "Now, hold. These cases are related."

"Mr. Biggs. Can you tell us your story?"

Mr. Biggs shook his head in disgust and stood. "Not guilty," he said loud at the people. "I didn't do it and I don't recognize your authority here nor the authority of this illegal court."

Kinnick sighed. "Yet here we are. Are you saying your son is a liar?"

381

Mr. Biggs glared at Kinnick. "I'm sayin' my son was confused. He didn't know what he was talkin' about. Listen, he ain't none too bright and all your big words got him all scrambled like in the head."

"So, you did not shoot Private Gore three days ago?"

Biggs pressed his lips together and nodded. "I did not."

"You may sit. Randy, can you stand up?"

Randy nodded and stood. He was about sixteen years old, his frame thicker than average with a shaved head and a snub nose. Acne spotted his face. "Randy, do you remember our conversation a few nights ago?"

Randy nodded.

"What did we talk about?"

"I don't remember."

"We talked about the shooting at the water tower."

"I can't remember."

"We talked about how you felt when my unit came to the town. About how your father made you accompany him to the water tower."

Randy shook his head no.

The packed restaurant grew restless. "You're leading him," said a man in the front row.

Kinnick held up a hand. He pulled a bullet casing from his breast pocket. "We found this below the water tower. It's a casing for a *.300 Winchester Magnum Cobra AP* bullet." He scooped up a baggie in his other hand. "Is Dr. Yentz here?" The doctor stood up, his eyes large behind his glasses.

"I am."

Kinnick waved the baggie. "Can you look at this?"

The doctor walked forward and took the baggie in his hand.

"Is this the bullet you removed from Private Gore?"

"It is."

"You notice anything different than normal?"

"Well, I haven't treated many gunshot victims, but it seems different than a normal bullet."

"How's that, doctor?"

"The metal I found in him was steel."

"Thank you." Kinnick took the bag back.

"Hunter. What kind of bullets are *.300 Winchester Magnum Cobra APs?*"

"Cobra manufactures an armor-piercing round for rifles."

"Is this bullet consistent with what you know of Cobra Magnums?"

"Yes, it is. An armor-piercing round is usually designed with a steel or other hardened core, and with enough velocity, will penetrate body armor. Of course, all of this is dependent on the weapon and the level of body armor. It's not unheard of to have regular rounds go through armor, but Gore's body armor looked like someone drilled a hole through it. To me, that indicates an armor-piercing round was used in the assassination."

"And it matches the casing we found?"

Hunter brought forward a scoped rifle.

Kinnick held it up in Randy's direction. "Randy, do you recognize this gun?"

"Yeah, it's my dad's."

"What kind of ammunition does this shoot?"

".300 Mags."

"There has to be a dozen guns just like it in town," Mr. Biggs said.

"That's true, but how many people have the Cobra rounds?"

Hunter brought a box of ammo and tossed it on the table. The rounds jiggled together in their case. The packaging had a coiled cobra on the side.

"We found those in your closet," Kinnick said. He pushed the ammunition. "Gun, ammo—," Kinnick let his voice trail off. He turned back to Randy. The group was beginning to see the reality of the situation. Kinnick had the bad guy. He had the weapon. He had the placement. He only needed a motive.

"Randy, have you ever heard your father speak badly about the government?"

"I. Um." The young man's brow wrinkled as he thought.

"Go on ahead."

"Yeah."

"Like what kind of stuff would he say?"

Biggs stood up from his chair. "We do not recognize this court!"

"Enough, Mr. Biggs," Kinnick said sternly. He turned back to Randy.

"You may continue. What does your dad say that he hasn't said already today?"

Randy stared down at his hands. "He doesn't like the stuff Congress was doing. He thinks the federal government doesn't represent us. We didn't sign any contract with them."

Kinnick pushed on the boy some more. "What kind of contract?"

"I don't always understand all of it, but we hold our own sovereignty that is given to us at birth." He looked out at everyone and not getting the response he thought he would, peered down at his feet.

"I see. Did your dad like the president?"

Randy kind of laughed. "No. He hated that guy." Nervous laughter sprinkled the crowd.

"Did you ever hear him say anything about the military?"

"Yeah. He said you were the control arm of the government and it was only a matter of time before the government used them against us. You guys showed up just like he said you would."

Kinnick nodded. "That's correct. We came to help. What about when my men and I arrived? Did he say anything about us?"

"He talked a lot about how you were only here to collect food and taxes. You only wanted to take advantage of us. Then leave us to get murdered by the monsters."

Kinnick nodded. "Have we done any of those things?"

Randy glanced around. "I don't think so. I mean you hurt Doug and killed Andrew."

Kinnick paused. "I see. Did he ever talk about hurting any of my men?"

"I guess. I mean kind of like 'I'll take care of them.'"

"Not a crime," Mr. Biggs said.

"You are correct. It's not a crime to talk about something in passing." Kinnick stood and began to pace, hands clasped behind his back. "Randy, have you ever been up to the water tower?" Kinnick stopped close to the young man and stared.

"Well, yeah. We ain't supposed to, but sometimes we climb up there for fun. You can see really far."

"What can you see from up there?"

"You know. Across the river, houses, the school."

"Can you see the building we're in now? Can you see this restaurant?"

"Sure."

Kinnick turned his back and paced the other way. "Your dad ever go up there?" He looked over his shoulder when Randy didn't answer right away.

Randy's leg started to bounce up and down. "I suppose so."

"What about a few days ago?"

"No," Randy muttered.

Kinnick spun around. "Randy, did you go up there a few days ago?"

"Yeah." Randy rubbed his hands on his leg, forcing his leg to stop shaking.

Kinnick cocked his head. "But your dad didn't?"

"I mean, he might have." Randy's eyes drifted back to his father.

"Well, was he there or not?"

Randy licked his lips. "Yeah, we climbed up to the top."

"Why?"

Randy lifted a shoulder as he spoke. "I dunno, to get a better view of the area."

"But not to shoot any of my men?"

Randy regarded his dad and then flicked his eyes back to Kinnick. "No."

"Randy, do you like your dad?"

He kind of smiled. "Of course."

Kinnick paced forward. "He ever hit you or your mom?"

"Only when I was bad."

"He ever make you do something you didn't want to do?"

The young man cracked a small smile. "Yeah. All the time."

"Did he ever make you do something you felt was wrong? Deep down you knew he was wrong, but you did it anyway 'cause he's your dad."

"I dunno."

Kinnick stood up straight and gave the townspeople a sweeping gesture. "Randy, all these people are here to try and fix this problem. We just want the truth so we can make it go away. Wouldn't that be nice, Randy? To make this all go away?" Kinnick got to within a few feet of Randy. "Which one of you shot Private Gore?"

"I." The boy stuttered and looked back at his dad.

Biggs's lip curled. "Don't answer that, son."

The boy stared at Kinnick, watery tears filling his blinking eyes. Kinnick leaned even closer.

"Answer the man," said a man from the audience.

"Yeah!" cried someone else.

Kinnick held up his hand. "Let the boy speak." He stood up tall again. "Now, Randy, I know you're not a bad kid and we all make mistakes sometimes. I get it. We came into town unannounced and it seemed hostile. You thought you had to stand up for your rights, so you climbed up there and shot one of our men. I get it, Randy. I'm a patriot too. I've been fighting for our country and our rights since I was your age. We're the same really."

"You shut your goddamn mouth. You and him ain't nothin' alike."

"Mr. Biggs, I was talking with Randy. You can wait your turn to speak."

Mr. Biggs stood up. "You don't make the rules here. This country was founded on rights and all you've done is stomp all over them."

"Mr. Biggs, I'm going to ask you to sit down and let Randy speak." Kinnick turned toward Randy. "Randy, no one thinks you're bad, but why did you shoot that Marine? This is very serious. He died as a result of that shooting."

Randy's jaw dropped. "But I didn't." His mouth gaped as he stared around the room. "I swear it I didn't do it." He shook his head, begging for someone to believe him.

Mr. Biggs shook with rage. "Quit hammering the poor kid. He didn't do nothing wrong. I did it and I'd do it again. You pieces of shit only ever take. Ya never give. All you do is lie and lie and tax the shit out of us. Electricity goes out, and a few months later after we been doing just fine on our own, a boatload of you guys show up and want to help. Probably here to see how much we have so they can take it from us like the criminals you are! I don't recognize your authority here. I only recognize my sovereign rights as a citizen. Your laws do not apply here."

Kinnick sighed and nodded his head. "Martin, you can sit down now." *Confession.*

Kinnick moved back to his table. "This is an ugly situation. No doubt about that. Not much good has come since we've been here. You've heard everyone's testimonies. I've heard them. I want people to feel like there is justice done here, so I will leave their fates in your hands. Will you hang Volk for murder? Will you hang Martin Biggs for murder? What will you do, people of Warden?"

The restaurant erupted in shouts. Volk's mouth was tight like he wanted to spit. "Fuck you, Colonel. You can't do this to us. It was an accident. It was a fucking accident, and now, I have to answer to the likes of them." He pointed out at the people. "You saw what they did to Gore!"

People pointed and shouted. Hunter rested his hand on his sidearm ready to go hot if things went south. The shouting reached an apex and Kinnick could stand it no longer.

"People, please. Listen." Slowly they calmed and took their seats. "I will admit this has been a disaster. One of my men killed a young person of your community. He did so out of frustration for the loss of his own brother-in-arms, but he seems sincere when he says it was an accident. We also have Martin Biggs, a man who has admitted to murdering one of my Marines in cold blood. Can we come together and say that enough death is enough? Can we recognize that there's a greater threat and we have to stick together or perish? Let these men live and let us fight the greater evil, the dead."

The people eyed one another. Some nodded. They had all seen the dead or the monsters. Others shook their heads no. Too much injustice had been done.

Kinnick dipped his chin and folded his hands behind his back. "I'll give you until tomorrow to make a decision. Everyone's dismissed."

MAUSER
Southeastern Iowa

Mauser's boots crushed dead grass beneath them as he circled a pickup on foot. It was so riddled with bullets it was almost unrecognizable. Fuel leaked out from the truck, puddling underneath. Blood ran out the bottom of the doors and dripped onto the ground below in a tiny crimson stream. The dark blood of the bodies refused to blend with the oily fuel.

He held his SCAR downward. Mauser peered through the shattered window. Four remains were in the cabin. He reached in, grabbing the sleeve of one. He jerked the man, or what he thought was a man, his eyes trying to decipher the gore-stained patch. *Some sort of mechanical gear.* He let the man slump back over onto the remains of his seatmate, no more than another pile of ravaged uncooked meat and bone.

Bullet holes covered the bodies like a sickening plague. Blood seeped from every single hole. Jackson had let one of his .50 caliber turrets open up on the unsuspecting pickup from less than twenty yards away.

He glanced over at the Humvee responsible. "Bengston, you sure there were more?"

"Yes, sir. At least two other trucks that got away." Mauser turned back to the pickup. He moved closer, ignoring the puddle of bodily fluids gathering nearby. He leaned over into the truck bed. Three large packs sat in the back. He picked one up and turned it upright.

He dug his hand around inside, expecting food and water or at least

388

bullets. His hand wrapped around a plastic-enclosed rectangular block. He pulled it out and felt its weight. *C4 explosives.*

He tossed it back down into the truck bed and marched back to his squad's Humvee. He yelled at his firing team as he passed.

"Find out where they went."

"Yes sir," said Bengston. He jumped into the Humvee and they headed north down the bumpy road.

Mauser hopped inside his Humvee. Specialist Brown sat in the driver's seat. "Get me back to Jackson's command," Mauser ordered.

Ten minutes later, Mauser nodded to two soldiers in front of a red-brick two-story building with a white door in Montrose. It was about eleven miles from where Jackson's command had crossed the Mississippi unimpeded by the dead or Steele's group.

He ran up some wooden steps to the top floor apartment. He banged on a white metal door. "Come in," came Jackson's voice. Mauser swung open the door and walked in.

Jackson sat at a white card table. His coat was unbuttoned, and his bald head glinted on the side facing the window. Lieutenant Colonel Davis stood nearby, arms folded across his body, and Major Ludlow glanced up at Mauser with his bug eyes.

Jackson grinned when he saw Mauser. "The noose continues to tighten on our mutual acquaintance and his rabble of misfits."

Mauser glanced away in irritation at the mention of Steele. "The men we shot on the road appear to be a part of his group. The back of their pickup was filled with explosives."

Ludlow's eyes grew even larger. "Vehicle-borne IEDs? It feels like Iraq out there."

"It wasn't rigged to anything, but they were planning something," Mauser said. "If I was a betting man, I would say they were coming down here to blow the bridge over Keokuk."

Jackson shook his head with a smile. "That boy's clever but not quick enough. Tomorrow, I want our entire unit on the move straight north. That's where they were coming from?"

"That's correct. I sent Sergeant Bengston's fire team north to see what they could find."

"Can't be far now."

Davis spoke. "Based off where they were last seen, I'd say somewhere south of Burlington." He pointed a long arm down at the map on the card table.

"They couldn't have gotten far from where they evaded us on the river without transportation."

Jackson smiled, a skeleton face grinning. "Which means our little renegade boy is near the end of his rope. Wonder if he'll do the hangman's jig like the rest of his friends? Maybe I'll give him a choice. A firing squad?"

Ludlow smirked. "Waste of bullets if you ask me."

Jackson tilted his head to the side considering Ludlow's comment. His lips pursed in consideration. "We could line a bunch of them up and see how far a .50 caliber bullet goes through them?"

"An interesting experiment. Now I'm intrigued."

Jackson nodded. "You and me both."

Mauser looked at his boots then lifted his chin and stared back at Jackson. "Sir, if I may speak freely."

Jackson turned his way, lifting his nonexistent eyebrows. "You may."

Mauser moved closer to the table. "Steele's not stupid. Wouldn't we be better suited using some flanking maneuvers to gain an advantage? I don't think charging up the road is the best idea."

"Would you look at this guy?" Jackson chuckled, prompting the other two officers to laugh.

"They have no place to run. They're tired, unorganized, and beaten. I'm done chasing that traitorous bastard. His continued living is boring me. Tomorrow it ends. Swiftly and decisively."

Mauser gulped, He knew at least a few people in that camp. *Like Kevin. One less now.* He blinked the thought away. *They made their choice and you've made yours.*

Mauser's radio kicked off. "Mauser. Bengston here." Mauser ducked his head and walked to the edge of the room.

"Report?"

"Sir, we've come upon a substantial body of people."

"Infected?"

"No, sir. Big farm. I'm thinking up over a thousand. Over."

Mauser licked his lips. "It's got to be him." He clicked on his radio. "Good work, Sergeant. Come on back."

"Copy that."

The radio crackled and went dead.

Mauser walked back over to the table.

Jackson's eyes were expectant.

"Bengston's got eyes on a big farm with a ton of people on it."

"Perfect. The entirety of command will be moving north for battle tomorrow early."

"Sir?"

"What, Mauser?" Jackson's irritation could quickly turn sour. "You're not going soft on me, are you?"

"No, sir."

"That's my boy." His eyes went back to the table.

"Our flanking maneuvers worked well against Steele's force. May I suggest continuing those?"

Jackson hit the table with a fist, his maps jumping in response. "Jesus. You're afraid of this guy, aren't you? This piss-ant piece of shit pretender."

"No, sir, but I know him. He's not stupid. He knows you're coming. I wouldn't expect him to roll over."

Jackson blew air through his nose, calming himself. "Neither do I. I expect him to bend over and take it like a man."

The officers laughed at his crude joke.

Mauser cracked a weak smile.

Jackson shook his head at Mauser. "You used to have a lot better sense of humor, ya know that?"

"I do."

"Do I have permission to flank Steele's forces?"

Jackson shook his head in astonishment. "Yes. Since you are so worried about these bandits, you can lead a platoon around the flank when we engage.

But if we tear them up with HE rounds and the mortars before you get in the fight, don't blame me for you missing out on the action."

Mauser nodded. "I will not. Thank you, sir."

"You may take your leave," Jackson said firmly. He shooed Mauser away.

Mauser turned and left. He jogged down the wooden steps. Dual sets of Humvees were blocking each street, forming a short cross intersection for Jackson's command. Mauser's squad had commandeered a two-story metal-sided green and white house across from Jackson's.

Mauser opened the door. Four soldiers sat around a light brown wooden kitchen table playing cards. Another lounged on the couch with an old CD player. He nodded his head slowly to the beat.

Sergeant Yates slammed down his cards. "Full house, boys. Read 'em and weep."

"Fuck," cursed Vaughn. He tossed his cards onto the table. "I had tens and sevens. Two fucking pairs." He picked up a beer and slugged the rest of the contents back.

"Sir, this is bullshit. What am I supposed to eat tonight?" Brown complained.

"Not my problem, soldier. You're resourceful, go find something. I'm sure one of the survivors around here hoarded something."

Brown shook his head. "This sucks." Brown stood up and walked to the door.

"Find some booze," called Low from the couch.

"And pussy," Jarvis said at him.

"Like any chick is gonna want to get with you with all those little fucking fingers around your neck."

Jarvis's brow furrowed and his hand lifted up the necklace. "This shows my warrior prowess."

"When they take one look at your little pecker, they're gonna want one of those," Campos said. The black-haired tan man with a round face grinned. "Jump in some of that thick Midwestern ass."

Low removed one of his earpieces. "Like those farm girls outside of Houghton or Huffman or whatever that tiny shit town was called. Or how about Ash?"

Brown laughed and gave Low a look of disgust. "Dog, come on. You can't be messing with Jackson's piece."

"I mean." Low cut himself off.

Brown shook his head at him. "I'll be back, you horndogs."

"Don't come back without any chicks," Vaughn yelled at the man.

Brown snatched up his carbine and walked out of the door.

"Yates, can I talk to you?" Mauser said.

Yates gave him a big smile and collected his winnings of food and batteries with wide forearms. "Well, I ain't playing anymore. Don't want to give these peckerheads a chance to win their shit back." He stood up and walked closer to Mauser.

"Bengston's crew chewed up a pickup of Steele's men on the road. They had a buttload of explosives."

"Jerkoffs don't give up, do they?"

Mauser sighed. "No. The colonel wants everyone ready for tomorrow morning. They're camped about nine miles north. He wants this done tomorrow."

"Thank fucking god."

"He wants to move right in for an attack. I don't like it. Steele's not stupid. He wouldn't just wait out in the middle of nowhere to get chewed up by our machine guns."

Yates snorted. "That's about all he's done so far."

Yates wasn't wrong. Jackson had pummeled Steele's forces their entire way across Michigan, Indiana, and Illinois, even when his units had used deception and tried to spread out. Jackson rounded them up too. Jackson was a master tactician and always seemed a step ahead of Steele in this cat-and-mouse game. He always knew where Steele was running to, probably even before Steele did.

"A couple of squads are going to circle around and hit their flank. Maybe we can end it early," Mauser said. He stared Yates in the eyes. There wasn't much feeling inside his orbs, only a ferocity tempered by what he'd seen. The man had seen too much and survival wasn't a huge priority.

"The boys will be ready."

Mauser nodded. "They always are."

Mauser went into a back bedroom he had claimed. He set his SCAR down in the corner next to the queen-sized bed. It had been left untouched by whoever had lived there before. He sat down on the edge of the bed.

He massaged his temples. The chatter of laughter and revelry resounded in the next room as the soldiers continued to drink. He stripped off his ACU jacket and threw it on a rocking chair.

He looked down at his tan boots. They were tainted with mud and grime, making them almost permanently brown. His heart pounded in his chest. He took his Beretta out. The bed bounced a bit as he set it next to him. *What am I doing? How did we get here?*

He glanced at the Beretta. The black handgun rested there, only as deadly as he would make it. He picked it up, feeling the weight in his hand. He held it open-palmed, staring at it as if it held all the answers. He gripped it and pointed at himself in the dresser mirror. He peered over the sights at the man pointing the gun at him. A gaunt, bearded man stared back and his eyes were held little life. *Who are you?*

He set the gun back down. It had been easy to ignore the things that had been done in the name of survival. It came first, driving all other ideas away. Then there were the things that were done. Things that went beyond that. Things that men did because they held the power and had nothing to check their base instincts. The two farm girls in Holton. Private Low couldn't even get the name of the town correct. He wasn't the only man to blame for what happened, but no man had taken a stand against it, so it happened, and nobody seemed to care. After all, there were so many worse things out there. Namely the dead.

Then there were the people they had killed as insurgents. Nobody had given it much of a thought. After all, they had the green light from Jackson. It was us or the other and the other never got picked over us.

The insurgent looked guilty and sounded guilty, but nobody even bothered to verify where he'd gotten the stash of military guns. More bodies in the ground and nobody even asked the question.

Mauser glanced back up at the man in the mirror. A dead man reflected back at him. *I'm not me.* He took both hands and held his head, rubbing his fingertips into his temples, trying to quiet the voices that screamed at him for the decisions he'd made.

His hand found his M9 Beretta and he gripped it tight. In a fluid motion, he pointed it at the side of his head. The muzzle touched the hair of his temple. *Just do it, you pussy. One quick squeeze and you will be released from this hell.* He watched himself in the mirror as if it were someone else. He felt so far away from that man sitting there. So distant and detached from this reality. The man had the same face as Mauser, but he didn't know the imposter who sat in his place.

He dropped his hand and tossed the gun onto the bed. "Jesus." He shook his head. "Not worth the bullet." There are still things to fight for. He just didn't know what they were anymore.

THE PASTOR
Sauk and Fox Hills, IA

The wall of tan sandbags was only about waist-high. The bag wall stretched for forty yards between two low-lying hills divided by a two-lane, gravel-based road. The heavy sandbags were stacked six deep. Red oak, white oak, and hickory dominated the landscape, preventing easy circumvention of the road over land. It would act as a funnel or a bottleneck for Jackson's forces, or that was at least what Steele had told them.

The pastor stood tall behind his Chosen people, watching the road ahead. His followers sat with their backs against the sandbags, cradling guns between their legs. Others rested their guns on top of the wall.

The pastor turned and looked behind him. His eyes ran along the field that stretched on either side of the road and disappeared into the trees and another hill. The hill was taller than the two flanking the pastor's line. Steele and the rest of his men waited in the trees like natives. His former enemy had personally requested the pastor to stand with him in the back, but he would not stand to the side when God's battle was to the front. He was a shepherd and he would not abandon his flock in their time of greatest need.

He grasped his hands behind his back and patrolled down his line. He could feel his shadow, Peter, behind him. Peter wasn't the same man he'd been before his captivity at Little Sable Point. He was still loyal, but broken. The man couldn't make eye contact with Steele.

"Pastor. You shouldn't be so exposed," Peter said behind him.

The pastor glanced at him from his side. Peter clutched his AK-47 tightly in his hands.

"Nonsense. God giveth and he taketh. If it's my time then it's my time. No need to beat around the bush. If he wants me, he will take me whether or not I hide."

Peter's voice dipped. "Yes, Father. But you are our shepherd and our leader. Your flock will be lost without you."

The pastor stopped, considering the man for a moment. "Will you?"

Peter stuttered, his eyes widening. "Why, of course."

The pastor smiled. "Have faith in the Lord and you shall not fear. Do not put your faith in me for I will leave you wanting." *Lord, give us the strength to fight in your name. Let us not all fall here today.* He continued walking.

He passed Brother Adam. The former nursing assistant held a double-barreled shotgun. It did not have a great firing range. The bald man nodded, but his eyes were afraid. "Gather strength from the Lord," the pastor said to him. The goateed man swallowed, nodding feverishly. The pastor continued.

Brother Luke held his AK-47. His long black hair hung limp around his shoulders. He wiped the dirty hair back over his ear and gave the pastor a wicked grin. "When do you think the dirty Philistines will arrive?"

"Soon, my child." *But they are the Romans and we are the tribes of Israel.*

"God will take pleasure in the slaughter." He licked his lips.

Our slaughter? "Stay vigilant for God is with us."

"God wills it," Luke said loud.

"God wills it," the pastor responded.

The pastor continued on, speaking and praying with his followers. He knelt with a group for ten minutes, leading them in prayer. He blessed men and women and absolved them of their sins. He assured them that heaven awaited their obedient souls. Even with the fear of battle, they did not fear death.

He stopped and bent down near a teenage boy. Maybe fifteen-years-old, but no older. His curly brown hair was matted and snarled. His face and clothes were covered in dirt.

"What is your name son?"

"Alec, Father." He clutched his gun like a football.

"Fear not the pain of death, Alec, for an eternity of life awaits you in Christ's Kingdom of Heaven. Be not afraid for God is with us. We are like David before the Philistine giant, Goliath. Faith steadies our hands and fills our hearts with courage against the might of a great enemy, and no enemy shall prevail in the face of God's faithful."

The boy blinked and gulped. He visibly calmed before the pastor. "Yes, Father."

The pastor lifted his eyes to the sky. "Dear God, bless your holy soldier. This boy Alec who has the heart of the lion David. Bless this warrior of God and give him the power to punish those that would do us harm."

The pastor bent down and squeezed the boy's shoulder. "You will fight like David did against Goliath. Remember his story. A boy no older than yourself defeated the mightiest warrior of all the Philistines."

The rumbling of an engine quaked in the distance, the loudest sound for miles defiling the bucolic back road. The pastor turned his head, facing its direction. He stretched his neck and forcibly straightened his back. "Prepare yourself, boy."

The pastor clasped his hands behind his back. His eyes were not what they once were, but he could see the dust cloud and the shadowy tan vehicles emerging in the distance. Single gunshots rang out. The .50 caliber machine gun rippled into the surrounding trees. That would be the Little Sable Point shooters kicking off the battle. One of the .50 cals went silent. He couldn't see if the soldier had been shot but he assumed the devils of Little Sable were doing their dastardly long-range work.

Even as he watched, he knew that they retreated through the timber toward the hills on either side of the pastor's line. Soon their day of judgment would be upon them and all the heavens would rejoice with the songs of angels.

After a stop-and-go, absorbing long minutes, the tan trucks grew larger. He started to be able to make out that they were the standard military Humvee. A helmeted soldier's head and shoulders stuck out from the top.

The pastor released his hammer from his belt, gripping the worn shaft and thrusting it into the air.

"Pastor. They're closing in," Peter hissed. He crouched behind the sandbag wall.

The pastor let his voice command the choirs of angels. It was loud and clear and held no fear of death. "Fear not, God's Chosen people. For heaven awaits all who stand before the wrath of Legion." More tan vehicles lined up. He knew guns were pointed their way but held his place. *I walk through the valley of the shadow of death, but I fear no evil.*

He waved his hammer at Colonel Jackson's soldiers. The rusted carpenter's tool held in place over a military vehicle. He let his voice come out as a shout. *They all must hear this.* "Captain Steele demands we hold for three minutes." His mouth formed into a snarl as he watched the soldiers drive forward, whipping up dust. "I say let's give him ten."

He held his carpenter hammer up in the air and Peter began shouting behind him. "God wills it."

"God wills it!" the pastor shouted. His eyes went from brother to sister down the line of his people. "God wills it. Now send them back to hell!" He let his hammer fall to his side. At four hundred yards, the Humvees opened up. Smoke exploded from their barrels. Fast, furious, and terrible du-du-du-du-du-du thunder clapped from turret guns. The .50 cal cut into his line. Peter dove to the ground. Sand spurted into the air as the bullets thudded into the layered sandbags. Brother Herman's head was too far above the bags and it disappeared. His body collapsed onto the ground, and his neck squirted ruby colored blood into a pool at the pastor's feet.

"Fire! Fire!" the pastor screamed. He watched the enemy press closer. The enemies' bullets whizzed and whistled by him, but none could find him.

"Father, please," Peter pleaded. "Take cover." He leaned onto the sandbags and his AK-47 pounded out bullets into a Humvee.

The sandbags stopped most of the bullets. The densely compacted sand was an effective means of protection as long as his people didn't expose themselves to the large-caliber rounds thundering their way. When they did, his men fell, missing arms, shoulders, and heads, yet the line held.

He walked down the line, the battle raging. Bullets were breaking through the bags. They could only maintain their integrity for so long. In some places, his men fell. He was brazen and unafraid. His body glowed with God's warmth. Leaden smoke engulfed his line like a morning fog. "Fire! Fire for the Lord!"

Bullets winged and twanged and whizzed past him. He turned his face to the sky. *God is with me.*

Men were exiting the Humvees. Using their doors and timber as cover, they continued to rain hell upon the pastor's line. "Fight for our Lord!" he screamed.

The ground erupted in the center of his line. Sandbags and his people flew in the air. He turned, watching his people writhe on the ground. Vince picked up his arm with his other hand. His unblinking eyes stared right at the pastor for a moment in shock. Bullets cut him in half and his torso fell from his legs. Another bomb exploded the pastor's line. They were literally blowing his line into pieces.

"Hold!" he called out. He waved his hammer in the air, thrusting it at the enemy, but he couldn't even hear himself over the roar of battle. The gunfire heightened, deafening him. In a slow-motion moment, the earth beneath him disappeared and his body was engulfed in a weightlessness. His body was in flight along with chunks of earth and debris.

Minutes seemed to pass. The sky appeared above him then his body crashed into the hard cold field. The whole world rung in his ears. The clouds parted above him. He felt as if he were immersed in flames. His mouth barely moved. "Take me, O Lord. I am ready."

The ringing in his ears turned into the glorious trumpets of the Lord. His voice came out in soft whispers. "The Lord has come. Deliver us from evil." He raised a bloody hand in the air. Red blood ran down his finger and onto the handle of his hammer still gripped in his hand.

"Your servant has come home."

Peter's curly head shadowed over him. He was yelling something. The pastor felt himself being lifted like a child off the earth. Peter jostled him as he ran across the ground, trees bouncing around him, as his eyes dimmed.

STEELE
Black Hawk Hill, IA

Steele shifted to the other side of a tree for a better view. He squinted, trying to peer through the branches and trees of the forest. He placed his left hand on his chest, feeling both Thor's hammer and, below that, his counterterrorism badge beneath his shirt. He wore the necklace for his friend Jarl. He wore the badge out of some nostalgic superstition that he had grown used to over the years of being a counterterrorism agent.

The cacophony of gunfire dominated the field in front of him, but closest to him, he could hear the shuffling of nervous men and women laying prone and hidden behind trees, rocks, and downed logs.

A quiet anxious cough was emitted here and there. Then came the screams of the dying on the pastor's line. His followers were in the process of breaking. Craters appeared where once men and sandbags had been. Piece by piece, men and women sprinted for the forest surrounding Black Hawk Hill.

It would be a dangerous two hundred yards for them to run. He knew it when he had asked them to hold the line, but his plan would never work without drawing Jackson's men in. Without the Chosen sacrifice, the battle would be a slaughter and Steele's forces would be on the receiving end of it.

The Chosen ran down the gravel road that twisted right along Black Hawk Hill and cut through thick timber that made good white-tailed deer hunting this time of year.

He glanced to his left. Gwen's contingent of Iowans was closer to the fighting stretching down the sloping left flank. She knelt with her grandfather's shotgun in one hand. John leaned on a tree next to her along with Sheriff Donnellson.

Donnellson had a camouflaged hunting jacket over his brown sheriff's uniform. He pushed his brown cowboy hat up on his forehead. All the able-bodied men and women of Hacklebarney had turned out. Most held shotguns and hunting rifles. Steele even thought he saw a couple with compound hunting bows. Steele didn't know if it was the pride of not being left out or if it was not backing down on their word, but they had come when called, covered in hunting camouflage and with a grim determination to fight.

Steele's force was over half of the Sable Point volunteers. The rest of the volunteers were with Tess, hopefully still alive. Harvey, Trent, and Larry knelt closest to him, hidden in the trees. Every now and then Trent would place his optics up to his eye and stick his tongue out as he squinted with the other.

"I could probably take a few shots from here," Trent said quietly. The goateed hunter glanced back at Steele.

"Sit tight. They'll be on us quick enough."

"What are they doing?" Frank asked softly. His black-and-gray beard jutted out as he watched the firefight with intensity.

The Iron Drakes overlapped on the Steele's volunteers' right flank stationed in the center of the line. They would be the linchpin in their defense as the road curved deeper into the forest at this point.

Frank peered out, pointing at the pastor's collapsing line. "I thought you told him to hold for three minutes. The idiot's been standing up for almost eight."

"I did."

"Well, he's really selling it."

"He's going to kill himself and all his people."

Pockets of people ran from his line. He could see the Chosen wavering. A series of concussive explosions shattered the rest of his line. They made a run for the trees. Bullets cut down the slowest, punching through their backs and out their fronts. Anyone still alive ran for cover.

"Too many bodies are still there," Steele said to himself. The pastor's stand, while admirable, had chewed up his followers. Humvees gunned it for the broken line. It was as if they raced to see who could be the first through the breach.

From a distance, the M2 .50 caliber machine guns hammered out gunfire into the trees and the backs of the pastor's men alike. Steele clenched his jaw as three of the Chosen were shot from behind before they could make it into the relative safety of the forest.

"Keep coming," Steele whispered as he watched the Chosen soldiers die. The farther into the trees they ran, the safer they became.

The remainders of the pastor's men flooded and weaved through the trees up towards Steele's line. Peter's curly-haired head bobbed as he weaved through the trees, carrying a fallen man in his arms. The gray-haired man was limp in his arms. Steele was amazed at the speed in which the beefy man moved. Peter struggled up the hill and collapsed to his knees after passing through Steele's volunteers. His chest pushed up and down furiously, and he went on all fours, fighting for air. The pastor lay motionless, his clothes drenched in brown dust and bloody dirt.

"Is he?" Steele asked.

Peter closed his eyes. "No. He lives." Steele turned back to the enemy racing his way.

Humvees drove through holes in the sandbag line; others drove up and over the collapsing wall. Sand exploded from the bags as Humvees whipped through the meager line. A single Humvee stopped. A soldier jumped out and fired his gun point-blank into the back of a crawling man. They were already savoring the taste of victory. *Keep coming, you bastards. Keep coming.*

Steele blinked back the carnage, swallowing his anger.

"Hold your fire," Steele said to those around him. He touched Larry's shoulder gently. "Pass it along. Turrets first." Larry bent near Nathan and his men played telephone with his orders. Steele turned toward Frank. "It's about time you go back to your line. Turrets first."

Frank slapped his Iron Drakes patch twice and jogged off at a crouch. The Iron Drakes had a bone to pick with Jackson, and Steele wanted them at the center where the fighting promised to be the fiercest. He watched the man fade through the gray trees.

Down on the Iron Drakes' right flank, Steele could barely make out the ancient biker War Child and his War Machines. They were armed with AK-47s, M4s, and at least one Browning M2 .50 caliber machine gun. Where they had acquired such firepower, Steele did not know. All were interspersed throughout the trees, weapons trained on the forest road.

The road cut into the hilly timber near the lower portion of Black Hawk Hill, and if Jackson wanted to give chase, he had to lead his men into the forest. That's where Steele's forces waited.

He watched the road with intense focus, knowing that threats hastened his way. The first Humvee slowed down before entering the forest. A bit of intuitive caution overrode the surge of bloodlust against a defeated enemy. The driver must have seen some of the men running through the trees ahead and sped up again. A second Humvee gunned it close to the first, tailgating behind. The turret gunner showered bullets into the trees, hoping for a random hit. It was followed by the third, fourth, fifth, and sixth Humvees. Steele peered back at the sandbag line. More Humvees followed through in a column. Guns swiveled on turrets, searching for easy victims to annihilate with giant .50 caliber rounds.

Steele peered at the smaller Sauk and Fox Hills on either side of the sandbags. He wondered if the Red Stripes and Seven Sisters were ready for what was about to happen.

One of the last Humvees passed the sandbag line then came the oversized McCone people mover. The giant airport lounge bus with retrofitted steel-plating over the windows bulldozed the gap and came to a halt.

Camouflaged soldiers climbed down from the back and they spread out, approaching the forest. They marched brazenly over the field, putting bullets into the fallen. A minute passed until the dismounted soldiers neared the forest edge. That was his cue.

Steele touched Trent's shoulder. The first ten Humvees were already past their portion of the line. *War Child will have fun with those.*

The goateed hunter glanced back at Steele. Steele nodded. Trent licked his lips and took aim through his scope. Soldiers on foot were entering the woods now, passing between trees like a line of deer hunters "pushing" deer in a fall hunt. In a few minutes, they were within a hundred yards of Gwen's line. More Humvees passed his position.

Steele's arm jabbed out with a knife hand in the direction of the enemy Humvees. "Unleash hell."

Trent's single bolt-action rifle sounded off with a *crack*. There was a momentary pause. The man in the turret seemed to stare straight at Steele, but it was too late for him. He jerked and blood poured from his neck. He slumped onto his .50 cal machine gun, head dipping forward.

Gunfire thundered. Steele's line rained lead into the Humvees. Boom. Pop-pop. Crack. Pop-pop-pop. All manner of gunfire erupted at once in a clamorous encore of battle. The soldiers in turrets unloaded bullets into the trees, not knowing where the shots came from, but that enemies were lurking nearby. There was nothing that massive amounts of bullets couldn't stop in their minds.

Leaning against a thick oak, Steele put his affected arm against the tree and placed his M4 carbine to his left shoulder. It didn't feel right, but he ignored it and worked the trigger with his left hand. The recoil was worse than with two hands, but he was satisfied as a turret gunner directing fire against Gwen's line fell atop the weapon mount.

Gun smoke began to blanket the forest in a thick white smog, the dense sulphur smell of gunpowder dominating the air. Steele ducked low and moved down the line. "Keep firing!" he screamed as he dodged between trees.

MAUSER
Black Hawk Hill, IA

The inside of the Humvee stunk like Jarvis's rotting fingers and unwashed men. Mauser was in the lead Humvee of four, sitting on the edge of Black Hawk Hill in a fallow field. Gunfire vibrated the air from the other side of the hill, like a thunderstorm raging only a hilltop away.

Mauser's radio had been buzzing with communications from the soldiers on the other side.

"—Sir, we are taking heavy fire—" the radio cut out.

A man breathed into the microphone. "Spencer is down. Oh shit. He's fucked up."

Captain Ogden's voice came on the radio. "Keep throwing out smoke screens. Third Platoon provide support. Second Platoon push closer to the front."

For the last few minutes, the radio chatter had gone from hooting and hollering about getting some to concern as the forward units took casualties and the resistance grew stiffer. It made Mauser's gut churn like waves beating an old dock. If he cared about living, he would be worried, but he had surrendered that part of himself a long time ago. He clicked the radio to the channel he had for his unit. He held the radio microphone to his mouth and depressed the side.

"Yates, what do you think?" Yates sat in a Humvee directly behind him.

Yates's voice came through the radio. "We should be up there already.

406

Fuck Jackson. Our guys are getting crushed out there."

"We're still waiting on the go ahead from Jackson."

Anger-seethed in Yates's voice. "Copy." The radio clicked off. What Yates hated the most was losing men. It drove the man into a rage.

Once the gunfire started coming from the hill, Mauser would have been up to the top, but Jackson was holding him to help wrangle up any survivors instead of putting him in an overwatch position. The gunfire did not let up like a jackhammer on a busy street.

Mauser tapped his hand on his SCAR-H nervously. Every few seconds, he would lean close to the dash and glance up the hill, trying to see the men on the top through the dying leaves and graying trees.

"Sounds like a lot of fifties are going." Low raised a lip as he strained his eyes. "You think there's more of them up there?"

Mauser scratched at his face. His beard itched terribly today. "I can't imagine there being that many insurgents, but it's possible they all clustered here."

Jarvis leaned in the middle of the Humvee console. "Finally. We can put them all under at once and be done with it." He took a grenade off his vest. "A couple of these should fix the cocksuckers up."

"How you gonna get your fingers then?" Low asked.

A hurt expression crossed Jarvis's face. "There'll be fingers left. I mean, on some of them." He pulled at his necklace, judging how much space remained. "Always room for a few more."

Mauser looked over his shoulder and snapped. "Get that nasty thing out of my face."

Jarvis sat back in his seat. "Fine. You got no respect for the number of kills I got."

Mauser shook his head and glimpsed worriedly up the hill again. *We should be moving.*

"Mauser, what's your status?" Jackson's voice came through the radio. Mauser's eyes studied every inch of the hill, taking in the fall trees.

"Once the gunfire started, we moved up within range behind," he stopped reading and glanced at his map. "Black Hawk Hill." He held the radio away from his ear and waited.

Venom spit from Jackson's tongue. "This fucking rebel thinks he set up a nice little ambush. It ain't gonna work because you're about to ruin his day. Move up the hill and take them from behind."

Mauser stared back up the hill. The dying forest could hold anything. Steele had made the mistake by not protecting his flank. It was Mauser's turn to exploit his weakness.

"We're on it, sir."

"Move your ass, soldier. We're counting on you to break this stalemate."

Stalemate? Mauser tossed the microphone down and clicked on his radio attached to his vest. "You heard the colonel. Let's move!" he yelled at the soldiers in his Humvee. Doors slammed and his men converged near the edge of the hill.

Yates jogged up, M4 across his chest, his team at his back. Campos held his M249 SAW. Jarvis and Low joined them, checking the status of their weapons. Low threw a helmet atop his head haphazardly. Bengston's squad was the last to join.

The gunfire grew fiercer now. The gunshots were becoming more furiously rapid. The battle had gotten closer together.

"Our men are in an ambush. They need us. Let's finish this for the Legion. On the double."

STEELE
Black Hawk Hill, IA

He hoped to god that Thunder and Tess, as well as Red Clare, had pinched the rear of Jackson's column. That was the only way it would work. They had to push all of Jackson's forces inside the kill zone or they would leave too much to chance. He hid, standing behind a tree peering out. Smoke rose up from Sauk and Fox Hills. Thunder and Red Clare were in the fight. Whether or not they were winning was a different story.

Just as he feared, the .50 caliber machine guns were tearing into his line. As the soldiers zeroed in on the enemy, the gunfire became more deadly. It was heavy, methodical, and louder than a SAW M249 banging a repetitive du-du-du-du-du-du. Trees exploded and splintered, shooting wooden fragments into the air and his people. Volunteers ducked for cover, some to never stand again.

"Keep firing!" he screamed. "Turrets! Shoot the turrets!" He had no idea if anyone heard him.

An impenetrable white cloud filled the trees as soldiers threw M18 smoke grenades. Combined with the smoke from the guns their ability to see was severely crippled.

"Smoke screen," he cursed. "Fuck." No one could see anyone now. The enemy soldiers could move forward or backward with little impediment. More canisters were shot into the hills and Steele ceased to see much of anything but the immediate trees around him. Rounds repeatedly exploded into the tree trunks sending splinters of wood into the air. He ducked and moved closer to Frank's part of the line.

Frank stood near a tree letting rounds go off in bursts with his AK-47. "Frank," Steele called at him. Frank gave him a snarl.

"Can't see shit," he yelled at the soldiers.

Steele got closer. "We have to move closer."

"Are you fucking crazy?"

"We can't let them escape." He grabbed Frank's arm. "This ends now."

Frank gave him a crazed look. He barked a loud, "Fuck it." He turned his head and called down his line. "Iron Drakes. Let's fuck some shit up. Move!" he screamed. They stood, leaving their concealed positions. Frank gave him a sneer and sprinted down the hill for the Humvees.

Steele turned back to his people. "Sable, charge!" Steele roared while running down the back of his line. "Charge!"

MAUSER
Black Hawk Hill, IA

Mauser's squads fanned out and they began their trek up the back of the hill at a jog. Jarvis ran next to him, holding his M4 contact ready as he peered just over his optics. His finger necklace bounced on his chest as he moved, the fingers, making an odd tapping noise atop his gear. On Mauser's other side was Campos with his M249. His cheeks puffed out in physical effort.

The first two hundred yards of the hill was a slight incline covered with tall thin brown grass. The farther up the hill they moved, the steeper it became. Trees began to dot the hillside.

Mauser's heart was in overdrive and his adrenaline caused him to ignore the fatigue in his legs as they moved fast up the backside of the hill.

He slowed down as his radio clicked. "Mauser."

"Sir?" Mauser's squads continued to move. He stopped, listening intently.

"We're taking gunfire from the hills here." The voice grew faint as Jackson talked to somebody else with his microphone hot. "I don't give a shit. Pick up a gun and fight." It grew louder again as he spoke to Mauser. "The bastards are charging down the hill. Get your men up that hill now."

Mauser's men had drifted ahead of him. "Copy that, sir. We are Oscar Mike."

"Hurry, goddammit. They think they can win."

Mauser double-timed jumping over logs and pushing his way through branches. If the battle wasn't raging on the other side of the hill, they would have easily been given away.

411

Smoke tendrils curled down the hill. "Stay close, men. No Blue Falcons," Mauser half-yelled at the others. The men naturally slowed as their vision diminished in the fog of battle. Mauser could make out Campos next to him lining up the sights of his M249 SAW through his 3.5x35 ACOG optic.

Darker shapes formed in the hazy smoke. People were among the trees. Mauser took aim with his SCAR-H, his eye filling the scope, a man shape zooming in.

Campos opened up with his light machine gun in six-round bursts with a high-speed da-da-da-da-da-das. The M249's rate of fire was much higher than the .50 cals thundering on the other side of the hill.

Mauser kept his breathing steady and depressed the trigger. His SCAR banged. The extractor ejected a shell casing, flinging it into the air and his target collapsed.

The ghostly fog embraced them and Mauser lost sight of Jarvis and Campos as they were consumed. He pressed forward, gun to his shoulder, both eyes wide and scanning the misty trees for enemies.

STEELE
Black Hawk Hill, IA

Bullets slammed into the trees behind Steele, cracking into the wood like an axe. He dove for the ground. Dying leaves and soft earth met him. *Where are those coming from?* He stooped his head and checked his six o'clock.

A vertical line of bullet holes erupted into the oak where he had been standing. *They're behind us. They're flanking us.* The thought had barely flickered in his mind before he rolled to his side. Shadows advanced from the back of the hill. They dodged from tree to tree. "Volunteers behind us." Harvey turned around only to be struck by a bullet just below his eye. He twisted his head to the side and buckled onto the forest floor.

Steele fired into a form charging for him and the person fell to the ground unmoving. Using his other arm as support, he transitioned from target to target. He scanned the area trying to find friend or foe. The Sable Point volunteers were mostly gone. Only Harvey's dead body, leaking brain and blood into the soil, was left.

Steele stood cautiously. Ashen smoke enveloped the trees, an out-of-place autumn morning fog. Gunfire rippled in the background, a dozen thunderstorms converging at once.

A murky form morphed into a man ahead of him. A predator of men, his rifle was trained on Steele. The form stalked ahead. Reddish-hair emerged behind the sights. Steele's heart pounded in his chest and his breath became shallow as the man took step after step, closing the distance.

"Steele," the man-shape uttered.

Steele's hand drifted to his holstered Beretta. *You'll never beat his trigger with your gun holstered. But it's better to go down with weapon in hand than defenseless on your knees.*

"Not so fast, buddy," Mauser said. He squinted over his sights. He took a step closer and hovered only a few feet away, staring at Steele as if he didn't believe it was really him.

Steele started to sidestep in a circle slowly. Never backward. Step offline or take the initiative. The gun in his face took any initiative. The two men circled around each other.

"Never thought I'd see your traitor ass again," Steele said. He took another step, forcing Mauser to keep rotating.

"Me a traitor? You need to take a look around you, bro. We're what's left of the military and you're up here with a bunch of armed criminals."

"Jackson's a madman!" Steele yelled. His heart pounded in his chest, echoing in his ears. "He's trying to murder us, and for what?!" His left hand felt heavy on the handle of his Beretta as if it had never been there before.

Mauser's brow furrowed. "'Cause you murdered our men."

"Our?"

"What about what you did to Gwen?"

Pain filled Mauser's eyes and his eyebrows lightened up.

The earth exploded forty yards away. Steele dove into the earth and Mauser was taken off his feet from the shockwave. He tumbled onto the leaf-covered forest floor. Steele blinked and wiped dirt out of his eyes. Trees cracked and toppled over near where the mortar round hit. Mauser rolled off his back, using his arms to push himself onto all fours.

Steele pushed himself off the ground. He stumbled upright, his hand finding the handle of his handgun.

Mauser scrambled onto his feet. His hand rested on his sidearm. They both were ready to draw, waiting to make a move.

"Left-handed, now?" Mauser said.

"Took a round through the right. Hand ain't been right since."

Mauser crossed his feet as he moved laterally. "Ha. You couldn't even keep up with me with your strong hand. Let alone your off-hand."

"Don't matter." *Yes, it does. He's fast off the draw. Maybe with my right hand but not the left. I know it. He knows it. Just not enough time to train it up to speed.*

They circled each other. It was more of a wolf circling the family dog. Mauser had every advantage. Steele's crippled arm, healing leg, and off-hand draw all stacked up against him.

The gunfire blurted out behind them. Shouts. Dying cries. They locked eyes, Steele's harsh blue with Mauser's thundercloud gray.

"Make your move, Kemosabe," Mauser taunted. He sneered like he knew an evil secret. "It will all be over soon enough."

"I wish it hadn't come to this." His finger itched for the trigger.

Mauser's finger taunted him, tapping the handle of his gun. "You were my brother," he said softly.

"Were."

How quick are your fast-twitch muscles? How many reps have you put down range? How many times have you practiced getting the gun out of the holster and presented it to your enemy? How many times have you set your sights to shave time off your firing time? Every question was a check plus in Mauser's favor. He simply was going to win the shot.

If I dive to the ground, maybe I can throw him off long enough to get a shot off. Once the firing started, it wouldn't stop until one of them ceased breathing.

Steele went into autopilot. He stopped thinking and went through the motions of what he had done thousands of times, almost all with his other hand. It wasn't that the mechanics were different, but have you ever written with your off-hand? It was just different. Clumsy and awkward at the same time, still practiced and deadly.

He ripped his M9A1 9mm Beretta from his holster. He couldn't hear the gun metal sliding over the hard plastic holster. He pulled the gun up and toward his face. The gun reached his chin. Fire burst from Mauser's gun. The close gunshots made his adrenaline spike of the charts.

Steele punched out his gun responding with sluggish bangs. Mauser flinched. His firearm wavered in his hand. Steele gazed over his sights.

Mauser's gun lowered. He took a hand off his gun and pressed it in the center of his chest. He turned his hand upright and smeared the red liquid between his fingers. He looked back up at Steele and gave him a little smile. He dropped to his knees, his backside resting on his boots.

Steele ran for him. Mauser tipped to the side and rolled onto his back. Steele jumped down next to him, dropping his gun. He grasped Mauser's hand tight and it felt like he wrapped his hand around iron. The blood stuck between their palms, suctioning them together.

Mauser grimaced, his face in pain. "Got me pretty good, didn't you? With your weak hand too."

"Not weak, just not as strong."

Mauser gave Steele a faint smile, his teeth stained red. "You're stronger than you look."

Steele let his chin dip to his chest for a moment, collecting himself. "How did this happen?"

Mauser half-laughed and it turned into a fit of coughing. "No idea, buddy."

Steele stared out through the gun fog. More shapes stirred in the trees. Random gunfire rang out. *I just shot down my best friend.*

"Hold on," Steele said. He pushed onto the bleeding hole in Mauser's chest. Mauser struggled to get enough oxygen with the added pressure. "We'll get you help." Blood pumped out from around Steele's hand.

"Help!" Steele called out. He frantically looked around. Only trees, fog, and gunfire answered him.

Mauser's voice came out soft and he sounded like a totally different man. He had always had a booming voice filled with vigor and life. "Mark."

Steele stared back at him. "Yeah, buddy?"

The crow's feet around Mauser's eyes deepened. "Sorry about Gwen. I never wanted to hurt either of you."

Blood oozed from the corners of his mouth. He stopped moving and his hand stayed gripped in Steele's, firm and uncompromising.

Steele blinked a few times, unable to accept that his best friend was gone.

I did this. "Your watch has ended, but you will not be forgotten, Benjamin Mauser." Steele ripped his badge off his chain and placed it over Mauser's head, letting it rest on his chest.

Leaves crunched behind him as he sat back. He wrung his hands in front of him. He wiped his face, feeling the sticky blood streak across his bearded cheek. Seconds, perforated by gunfire and yells of victory, passed into history. He suffocated in gun smoke and drowned in the blood. The body of his best friend turned enemy lay next to him, pale and unmoving.

The outlines amidst the trees grew closer as if they were hunting him. He could see the guns level in his direction. Three men grew close and stood with their guns pointed at him.

"Mark," came a woman's voice. She ran for him and crashed down onto her knees beside him. Gwen cupped his cheeks in her hands. "Are you okay? What happened?" she said hurriedly, reading his eyes for answers.

He looked over at Mauser's body. "Ben," was all he could muster.

She glanced over at the still body. "Oh my God, Ben." She crawled over to where he laid. She put two fingers on his neck. Mauser was the palest shade of pink. After a moment, she glanced back at Steele. Angry tears filled her eyes.

"He's dead."

"I know."

She crawled back to Steele. Tears streamed down her face. B.B., Gerald Newbold and Sheriff Donnellson peered down at them. Frank topped the hill, a big grin on his face. He raised his AK-47 up in the air. Larry hobbled up the hill with an arm wrapped around Trent. His people emerged from the fog of battle. He couldn't understand what had happened. He turned back to Gwen, his face pleading for an answer.

Her tear-filled eyes softened and she tried to wipe the grime on Steele's face with her hand. With a regard for Mauser, she sniffed back her tears and looked Steele in the eyes. "We won." She cried and laughed at him. "We did it."

Steele eyed Frank and then turned back to her. "We won?"

She nodded her head. "You did it."

He shook his head no. So many people had died for this victory. *How can I live with all the loss?* She wrapped an arm around him and helped him up. They walked over to the edge of the hill. Steele gazed down at the road.

Bodies were strewn over the hill. *You will live with their losses because there is no other way.* He would have to live in a world where victories would be filled with sorrow for the dead and hope for the living. He wasn't even sure if that was a different world or just a shade of the past.

Smoke floated up from the Humvee engines. They were riddled with bullets. Camouflaged men were strewn atop the Humvees and inside open doors. They littered the ground where they had been brought down by a plethora of civilian small arms fire.

Steele trudged down the hill, taking in the carnage he had unleashed upon his people. Their loss filled him with sorrow, but if he hadn't brought them here to fight, then all people would have been run down, enslaved, or murdered at the whims of Jackson and his men.

Gunfire rippled from the sandbag wall. Steele held his binoculars up to his eyes. A half-dozen Humvees drove in the opposite direction.

"Jackson's escaped," Steele said.

"Most of his force has been destroyed," Frank replied.

"True. But I know that man. He will always be a threat."

Steeled watched them drive away. *Had he really won anything at all except a bit more time?*

"Captain Steele," shouted Frank. More and more people flooded in with the wounded. "Captain Steele."

"Victory!" his people yelled. They laughed and cried. They gripped arms and hands and each other in exhausted happiness to be alive.

"Victory!" They screamed holding their weapons up in the air, but all Steele felt was the tiredness of the long road ahead.

He gave them a grim smile and turned his head to the sky. "Victory!" he yelled into the trees.

KINNICK
Warden, IA

Kinnick lifted the pin attached to the chain from the freezer door. The silver handle was cool to the touch and he pulled the lever. The heavy door opened. His candle flickered and the light was slow to illuminate the two Marines sitting inside. Volk gloated, a sneer splitting his face. Whitehead was hesitant to lift his chin, using all his remaining energy to meet Kinnick's eye.

"Come," Kinnick commanded. He waved them forward with his fingers. The two men pushed themselves upright.

"What are you going to do with us?" Whitehead mumbled.

Volk gave him a shove in the back. "Just go."

Whitehead stepped passively past Kinnick. When Volk got parallel with Kinnick, he stopped. He studied the colonel's chin as if he was trying to find a place to punch. His eyes danced up to Kinnick's.

"You know, Colonel." He licked his lips. "I'm not sorry for what happened. Those dumb kids had it coming." A small smile curled up on the left side of his mouth.

Don't make me regret this decision. Kinnick's words came out like a one-two punch. "Move, Sergeant."

Volk stared down at Kinnick's lips then let his eyes return to Kinnick's and gradually nodded his head. He turned away and walked through the dark kitchen. It was just past midnight. Kinnick followed them.

The Marines and Green Berets stood waiting. Every piece of gear was on their person. Their long guns were pointed downward, his men relaxed. They stared at the convicted men and Kinnick alike. Gary and Martha stood to the side. Martha was wrapped in a robe and Gary a thick woolen sweater. They appeared even more tired than his men.

"Volk and Whitehead." The Marines turned and faced him. Kinnick took in the moment, seconds ticking by. "Collect your gear. We're leaving."

Volk gave him his signature sneer. "I knew you wouldn't fall for this bullshit." He elbowed Whitehead. "See. I told you. We ain't subject to that bullshit."

Hunter tossed the men their guns. They caught them and hugged them dearly. Volk checked the status of his quick. "Whew, I missed this little bad boy. Ha, so are we going to leave the Biggs a going-away present?"

"We are not."

Volk shook his head in disgust. "Seriously?"

"That's not all." The men stared back at Kinnick.

"Sergeant Volk, you have been demoted to private first class for actions unbecoming a United States Marine."

Volk snorted. "You can't do that."

"It's done." Kinnick looked at Washington. The muscled African-American Marine was stoic. "Washington, you are now rifle squad leader and promoted to sergeant. Duncan, you're now fire team Alpha leader." He turned back to Volk. "I'll accept your resignation if you want to stay."

Volk seethed in anger and continued to pack his gear.

"Hunter, is Hamilton One ready?"

The bearded operator nodded. "It is."

Kinnick approached Gary and Martha. "I apologize for all of this. We meant to build an outpost and train the people here. Now two people are dead and we are nowhere closer to setting up an outpost. I hope that you will be ready for the dead when they come."

Gary's face was accepting of the facts. "We'll do our best. This wasn't meant to be."

Kinnick glanced at Martha. "Your hospitality has been above and beyond the call of duty. When we meet again, maybe you can whip up some of those world-famous meatballs."

She gave him a sad smile. "I will, Colonel."

He turned back to Gary. "Wait a little while after we leave, but the goods will be on the docks. A dozen carbines, enough rounds to last you, and a crate of MREs. It's the best we can do and not be based here."

"Warden does appreciate the government's assistance."

"Hold the line, Gary. You can do what you'd like with the Biggs family."

The two men clasped hands.

Gary nodded. "We'll handle them."

Kinnick left them and walked for the door. "Hunter, let's move."

***

Hamilton One motored down the muddy waters. The sky was black and the moon covered by bitter nighttime clouds. The boat navigated the river at a slow pace. Once they were out of eyesight from Warden, Coffey flicked on the lights over the pilot's house to assist him in navigation that an errant tree or infected body might hinder.

The Marines were shady, camouflaged forms sitting along the front of the craft. Heads were down and a general quietness hung over them as if the week's events had placed a yoke of exhaustion upon their shoulders.

Kinnick leaned toward Coffey. "We're going to leapfrog the other teams down the river. Take us to Hacklebarney."

"Roger, boss."

"Hopefully, we will have a better time than we did in Warden."

Coffey kept his eyes on the river. "At least we got the bridge blown."

"That should help."

Kinnick maneuvered over and took a seat next to Hunter. The master sergeant's head was dipped, beard running down his chest like a scroll. His head bounced with the boat and he stirred himself awake.

"Colonel."

"Master Sergeant."

They sat in silence for a moment, listening to the motor kick along.

"I know you didn't agree with what happened back there."

"Nope."

"That decision is on me, Master Sergeant."

Hunter answered quick. "I only follow orders."

"I'm gonna need you to watch him."

All of their eyes drifted to the front of the small craft. Newly-made Private Volk sat in the front, his gun between his legs. The decision had been a tough one. Kinnick had weighed all the options in his head over and over. Leave Volk to the public's whim or free him and risk unrest. In the end, it was better to leave his team intact versus letting the mob string up his Marines. *Best not to leave things to chance.* He had left the supplies, knowing the town would need them to survive the coming winter.

"I'll keep an eye on him." He smiled a bit under his beard. "My only eye."

Kinnick gave a short laugh. "You know we've gone directly against an executive order. You know what that might mean in the future."

Hunter's voice came out assured and relaxed. "I do."

"I still have your support?"

Hunter nodded. "You do. I don't disagree with your decision to leave that place."

"What do you disagree with?"

"You left supplies meant for people that will use them in the hands of a group that wants us dead. Not the best use of our limited resources. We don't even know when we're going to be resupplied."

Kinnick nodded and sucked in air. "This situation is bigger than even that. As long as they fight the dead, they're helping us. They're critical to this front whether or not they want to be. If they won't fight with us, then they are on their own, but it doesn't mean we can't give them some sort of support. We are all still Americans."

Kinnick gestured with his head at the Marines. "How do you think they will handle not having justice for Gore?"

Hunter studied the deck. "This ain't the first time we've lost one with nothing to show for it. What's done is done."

"What's done is done," Kinnick repeated. The men accepted the fact that eventually they would have to answer for going against orders.

The woodland banks skipped by them, only dim shapes in the night. All manners of death marched their way and the weight of preparing these people for it was enough to sink a hundred ships. *Do we even have a chance?*

GWEN
Reynolds Farm, IA

She stopped near the faded red barn doors. A deep sigh escaped her. Her feet were swollen and her body near exhaustion. *Just don't think about it.* She used the old wooden door of the barn to steady herself.

"Gwenna," Haley yelled at her from across the yard. The little girl ran up to her and latched onto her leg. Gwen gave her a faint smile.

"Did you take those bandages to Dr. Miller like I asked?"

The little girl's blonde head bobbed up and down. "Yup. All o' dem."

"Good girl. Now take that bucket over there and run over to the pump. Keep filling it and bringing it Dr. Miller, okay?"

"Okie dokes," the little girl chimed in. Gwen stroked her head fondly. The little girl hefted a metal pail by its wire handle and trudged away.

Gwen collected herself and turned the corner into the barn. The wounded and dying lay in shoddy rows. The deceased lined the outside back of the barn. She would have Mark and Pa hitch up a wagon to haul the dead away to be burned. It seemed to be the only way to cleanly handle the destruction of those that had expired.

Dr. Miller stood next to Mr. Uhl, a farmer from north of town. He wiped his brow and gave her a sad smile. "Mayor."

"How's he doing?" Dr. Miller glanced down at the wounded man. He quietly shook his head no.

"Not much longer." He glanced around the room. "I'm running low on supplies. I just—" He bent closer to her. "We can't handle the number of wounded." He rubbed the side of his head. "I can't handle them. I've never treated gunshot victims let alone this many people at once." He stopped. "And inside a barn." He sighed. "Gwen. I've never seen this many wounded. Many of these people are going to die because we don't have access to a hospital."

"Keep doing your best. I sent the sheriff up to Burlington to see if we can find any help at the hospital. I'll send B.B. over to Keo to see if Dr. Farmer can help."

"Thank you," Dr. Miller said. He physically steadied himself. "I'll do what I can." He bowed his head and went back to checking his patients. Becky wiped her hands on a rag, approaching Gwen.

"What'd you do with that little girl of mine?"

"Sent her on a mission for water buckets. Should keep her busy for awhile."

Becky's eyebrows climbed up at Gwen. "Break time? I could use a cigarette."

Gwen smiled. "Me too."

Becky's eyes grew large. "After all those lectures you gave me."

Gwen sighed. "Not with the baby, of course. I'm just saying. It might help take the edge off things."

"Well, I hate to break it to you, but things are about to get even more stressful."

"What?" Gwen breathed.

Becky's eyes shifted toward the barn doors. A solid man stood there, arms crossed over his chest. He leaned on the frame with his red-and-black plaid sleeves rolled up to his triceps.

Gwen saved an evil glare for Becky.

"No one told you to date two men at the same time," Becky reminded her.

Gwen opened her mouth to respond and closed it. "That's not what happened."

Becky angled closer. "I'm taking a smoke break." Her eyebrows bounced on her face. "I'd suggest you make a break as well."

Gwen shook her head at her sister and Becky walked away.

"Gwen?"

Gwen turned around. "Jake." She gave him a smile.

"Hey, there. Just came by to tell you that my dad and I got most of our harvest in. Gotta 'nuff hay for the upcoming winter to feed the cattle. John's going to supplement with part of his corn harvest since there's no one to buy anyway. Most of the farms are going to have to dump part of their crops. Should be enough."

"No, don't. Tell them to store it. Even temporarily. We might be able to trade it and we can eat it if we have to."

He nodded his handsome face and gently placed his hand on her shoulder. She kindly moved his hand away.

He blinked a few times, unfamiliar with her rejection. "What's the matter? You aren't getting too high and mighty now that you're mayor, are ya?"

She chided him with her eyes. "Jake, you know that this isn't going to happen between us. I'm carrying Mark's child."

He chewed his lip and shrugged his shoulders. "I've never stopped loving you, Gwen. I thought that when you came back, we would pick up where we left off. We had something special."

"We did, but as much as we could try to pretend that everything is the same as it was ten years ago, it's not." She peered down at his chest before she continued. "I'm different. As much as you think you aren't different, you've changed too. We were flirting with the past, but we're living in the present. And in the present, there is no us. I'll always care about you, but only as a good friend."

Jake's face drooped in sadness. "Can't say I'm happy about that 'cause I don't think I'll ever change my mind about ya." He took a deep breath and gave her a sad smile, "As much as you didn't want to believe it, I always knew you belonged here. Ha. Now look at ya. Mayor of Hacklebarney, Gwen Reynolds."

She smiled. "I have no idea how that happened."

"Well, I sure do. You're the right woman for the job. Smart. Tough. You love these people. The right kind of woman we need to lead us through whatever this is."

"Thank you, Jake."

"I'll be around if you need me. You know where we live."

He embraced her and walked away.

She gave a small wave. "I'll see you soon."

He flashed her his winning grin. "I know." He tucked his hands in his pockets and walked away.

She spent the rest of the afternoon caring for the wounded. Sometime late in the day, she wandered back to her grandparents' house. She was beyond weary. She dragged herself up the porch steps, petting at Dutch and Rocky who laid at the top. Rocky's tail beat the wooded porch floor. Thump. Thump. Thump.

Grandpa Reynolds sat in his wooden swing. "How about you take a load off?" He patted the seat on the swing next to him. She collapsed on it and he gently moved the swing with his feet. She rested her head on his bony shoulder.

"I'm proud of you."

She lifted her head for a moment and rested it back down. "Thanks, Pa. I don't know where'd I'd be without you."

"Nonsense, girl. You got a good head on your shoulders, but even more importantly, you have a good heart in your chest. You don't need much else with those two working for you. 'Cept maybe a good man." He laughed to himself. "But it seems like you got a good one of those too."

"I do."

The swing creaked as they swayed front to back.

"I talked to Jake about the harvest. He says they'll have more than enough."

"That should do. The winter will be long and harsh. We need to keep the animals well fed. There be a lot more mouths than usual to feed, but we'll make do. We always do."

She could feel his eyes on the top of her head. "Did you talk about anything else?"

She slowly lifted her head off his shoulder. "Yes, Pa."

"He ain't too bright, but it ain't fair leading him along if he's not your cup of tea."

"He's okay with it. He understands."

"I'm proud of you." He squeezed her in his arms. "Your gram's got some hot stew on the stove."

She kissed his cheek and stood up. "Thanks, Pa."

"Go on now."

She placed a hand on the doorknob and turned. Yelling erupted down the drive. She turned around. Her grandfather sat up, leaning forward and squinting down the road. Helmeted men in camouflage marched down the center of the driveway.

"Mark!" she screamed and swept up her grandfather's shotgun.

STEELE
Reynolds Farm, IA

A fire crackled in the Reynolds' farmhouse fireplace. Flames licked the logs with fiery tongues, reaching for the top of the chimney. The heat put out from the fire was small in comparison to the throng of people pressed together inside.

Colonel Kinnick stood near Steele, surveying the map. His ACUs were still mud splattered. His hand sat beneath his chin. "I can't believe you pulled that off against Jackson," he said, staring at the map. He gave Steele a little smirk. "Double envelopment. Nice work."

Eye-patched Master Sergeant Hunter grunted. "Nice little ambush. Didn't save much for us."

Thunder laughed through his gray beard. A red bandana held back his long hair. "Sure didn't. I thought the kid was crazy standing up against that little prick, but he didn't even see it coming. Drove right in through the sandbags." He glanced at the pastor sitting in an old chair near the fireplace, a blanket draped over his legs. The gaunt pastor looked as if he were prepping to give a fireside chat. "The Chosen really strung them along."

The pastor nodded. "My people did what they had to do."

Steele glanced at him. The pastor's bearing was impossibly frail, his face bruised and his body battered. "They held much longer than I asked."

"God was with us on that line."

Steele gulped and met his eyes. The Chosen had lost almost one hundred men and women in the battle.

"Once the last Humvees had passed the sandbags, me and my ol' girl Red Clare opened up on them. The rear vehicles never saw us coming. I took a lieutenant's head off with my Benelli in the first thirty seconds."

Red Clare coughed a smoker's cough and narrowed her eyes at Thunder. "Pretty sure the Seven Sisters did the brunt of the fightin' while you and the Stripes farted around in the trees."

"Now, now, Clare. Me and my boys did plenty," Thunder said, patronizing her.

"Ha," Red Clare laughed. She gave Thunder a sly smile beneath wrinkled lips.

Steele rested his left hand on the head of his tomahawk. "This had a lot of moving pieces. If anyone of you had failed to do your part, we wouldn't have succeeded." He glanced at everyone in the room. His eyes passed from War Child with his bandaged head to Gwen and her grandfather John to Tess, and finally to the badger of a man Frank.

Kinnick nodded his head in confirmation. "Unfortunately, we don't have much time to celebrate or hunt for Jackson and his renegades. There is a greater task at hand."

Steele met his gray eyes. "What do you need from us?"

Kinnick took a deep breath. "Well, everything."

A small smile settled onto Steele's face. "Colonel, I don't think there's been a time when you haven't asked for everything."

Kinnick gave a short chuckle. "I ask on behalf of what remains of our nation, however many few of us there are."

"We will do what we must."

Kinnick eyed him for a moment almost as if he were going to ask something and thought better of it. He cleared his throat. "I will say that I was surprised to find you here and with so many capable people under your command. More of a blessing than anything else."

"We're not here by chance."

Kinnick looked around the room. "Neither are we. The road's been long to reach here, and unfortunately, I can't offer much. Our operation is massive and our front spans the entirety of the United States. I am to rally the northern portion of the western front."

"For what?" Steele asked, but he already knew the answer. He knew it was only a matter of time before the armies of the dead reached them.

"To hold against the dead," Kinnick said. He studied the people in the parlor. "I'm not going to sugarcoat it. Millions of infected are marching this way, and we need to hold out until the military can get established enough to do what they were meant to do and take the fight to the bastards."

"When can we expect military relief?" Steele asked.

Kinnick sighed. "I don't know. I wish I could give you something, but don't plan on soon."

Steele nodded. *Hold against all odds for an infinite amount of time. Sounds about right.*

Kinnick placed a hand on the map spread over the card table that originally had a chessboard on it. "I've been deploying partial ODAs and rifle squads of Marines all along the Mississippi River in an effort to train and set up a militarized civilian front to fight the infected. You being here has changed what I've been asked to do. To have a reliable fighting force sitting in the center of our line is huge for us." He looked up at Steele. "This means I can speed up to the next sector and I don't have to deploy my Marines and Special Forces units along the rest of Iowa. You made my life a little bit easier." Kinnick gave Steele a happy nod.

Steele stared at the map. Iowa shared an over three-hundred-mile long border along the Mississippi River. Steele had at most a thousand fighters and he was willing to bet the Iowans were entrenched and unwilling to leave their homes. Tall orders from Kinnick.

"That's a long area of responsibility. What's in it for us?" Steele asked. He met Kinnick's eyes.

Kinnick licked his lips, his eyes dead serious. "A vaccine."

His answer sucked the air out of the room. Only the soft crackle of the fire reached out. Steele's breath went shallow in his chest as he digested the information. Gwen and Tess exchanged a glance. Thunder beamed. They could hardly fathom the idea of surviving a bite from the infected.

"That's wonderful," Gwen gushed. She wrapped an arm around Steele.

"You can't be serious?" Steele said.

Kinnick smiled with a slight nod. "Dead serious. You can thank Joseph. He was the mastermind behind it all."

Steele stifled a laugh. "Damn, that egghead. Glad we saved his skinny ass now."

Kinnick smiled. "Putting you on that flight to Kinshasa was the best decision I unknowingly made."

Steele blinked. *Not for Andrea and Wheeler.* "At least it meant something."

"It did." Kinnick's eyes asked Steele to question his conclusion. He looked back down to the map. "I left Marine Captain Heath in charge of the Northern Iowa AOR. He has Marines and Green Berets under his command from Lansing to Clinton." His eyes flashed at Steele and went back down to the map. His finger ran up and down the border of Iowa. "I would have you command the Southern Iowa AOR. The border from Davenport to Keokuk will fall to you under a direct military commission." He glanced up at Steele. "That is if you choose to take it, but I will tell you right now. This is coming. Whether or not you want to play along doesn't matter, because either way, you're gonna fight."

The colonel said what Steele already knew. Steele sucked in air through his nose, looking up at Kinnick. The colonel appeared worn-out, but still held a level of confidence. He believed in his mission.

"Citizens of the towns that participate will be the first ones to receive the vaccine."

Steele nodded. "Again, Colonel. You ask so much, yet I don't think I have much of a choice. If there is a vaccine, I want to make sure my people get it. I accept your commission."

"Excellent," Kinnick said with a grim smile that quickly faded. "Technically, I'm enlisting you and giving you a field promotion all at once with no training. Not sure that's ever happened in our nation's history." He glanced at Hunter. "This will give you legitimacy in our military structure." The eye-patched master sergeant kept his face flat.

Kinnick glanced back at the map. "I am going to rejoin the split ODA in Davenport because it's a larger town, and my personal unit is headed south to St. Louis." His eyes went back to the map. "Those units were initially for either Hacklebarney, Keokuk, or Burlington. Garrisoning those towns will be up to you now. Do you understand?"

"I do."

"Good. I'm going to consider all of your units as militia, but the ODA and Marine squads in your AOR will report directly to you."

Steele was taken aback. "Report to me?" He understood his units reporting to him, but not regular soldiers and Marines.

Kinnick looked back at Steele. "Yes. Luckily, your commission fixes that. I'll make you a captain, but for all practical purposes, you would be a lieutenant colonel with this much responsibility. I can't send you to any schools so all of your experience will come from the field."

Steele gave him a nasty look and shook his head in disbelief.

Kinnick twisted his head in confusion. "Is that a problem?"

Gwen laughed. Her smile, caring and genuine, displayed her white teeth. "People around here have been calling him that for weeks and he hates it."

Kinnick raised his eyebrows. "Well, I could make you a major or light colonel?" Can't go higher than me though. General Daugherty would have to do that."

"No, I don't want that. Captain is fine," Steele said. *Jesus Christ. There will be no stopping them from calling me that now.* He gave Gwen a side-glance. "Don't get any ideas."

"Whatever you say, Captain Steele," she said.

"Goddammit," he cursed under his breath.

Kinnick laughed and his face grew serious. "Captain Steele, I hereby place you in command of the Southern Iowa area of responsibility. Take any actions offensive or defensive as you see fit to defend the Mississippi River line and the United States of America."

Steele absorbed the man's words for a minute. He read the colonel's hazel-gray eyes. The colonel had been honest enough in the past. He had delivered Joseph and Patient Zero to the government and had been generous with Steele when they departed, but it wasn't the man that worried Steele. It was who he worked for: the United States Government. He was wary of any promise they made even if it was in his best interest.

Kinnick put out his hand. Steele took it. "Welcome aboard, Captain."

"Thank you. We will hold as long as you need, Colonel." Steele leaned closer. "Just make sure that vaccine comes our way."

Kinnick nodded. "Your command will be the first." They released hands. "That leads me to the next task at hand. The military prisoners."

Almost five hundred soldiers were dead or would be dead by the week's end. The rest were prisoners. Jackson and a few of his men had escaped, but they were so few that Steele didn't consider them an actual threat. As he stared at the map, he knew a much more deadly threat lurked across the river.

Kinnick eyed him. "We need them to hold this front. Every gun means something. Every trained gun something even more." A weird expression settled on his face as if he couldn't figure him out.

Steele clenched his jaw. "They will be given a choice. Life or death."

Kinnick's eyes grew wide. "I assure you, Captain, I of all people understand these men's betrayal to their country, but we have to look beyond that." He jabbed a finger at the map on the table. "We have to hold here. If the infected cross the Mississippi, we will be overrun."

Steele studied the map. "Colonel, I will not have men fighting for me that are just as likely to shoot me as the enemy. They will be given a choice. What they do with it is their own journey."

"Let me take them with me. I can garrison them along the river," Kinnick said. He frowned as he watched Steele.

Steele gently shook his head in contemplation. "No."

Eye-patched Master Sergeant Hunter chewed his beard, staring at Steele. "Gettin' a little big for our britches now, ain't we? Kinnick is your commanding officer."

Steele exhaled. "I know exactly what he is, but he showed up about ten minutes late to the fight and these are my prisoners. He can take the commission back for all the good it does me."

Kinnick and Hunter exchanged a glance and Kinnick continued. "Those prisoners are United States Army. They would fall under military justice laws."

"I will do with them as I see fit, and the way I see it, is you need us more than we need you, sir." His eyes were unwavering blocks of ice.

Hunter stretched his shoulders backward. Kinnick waved his prize fighter off.

"You're correct, Captain Steele. We do need you and desperately. Just think about what I said. Those men could be of immediate help if pointed in the right direction."

"We shall see."

Kinnick nodded gravely. "We're going to stop here in Keokuk, then all the way to Portage des Sioux to rejoin Captain Boucher's forces."

"Wouldn't bother much in Keokuk," Gwen said. "Heard there wasn't many people left there, but there's a bridge."

Kinnick shifted his stance and tapped the map. "We'll take care of the bridge on the way through."

"Thank you. What about Jackson?" Steele said.

Kinnick glanced up. "We'll have no problem cleaning him up if he shows his ugly face again."

"I got a bone to pick with him for Lewis and Gibson," Hunter said.

Steele nodded. "As do I." *For Kevin, Ahmed, and Mauser.*

Hunter and Steele shared a hard gaze. Two hunters on the hunt for their very own white whale. Whoever got it would be the victor in more ways than one.

Steele's eyes fell back to the map. His stare bounced from place to place. There were so many avenues for the dead. *Too many.* "I will try to pull in the villages west of here. Gwen, how many are there?"

"There are eleven villages in Van Buren County. Plenty of farmers between here and there too."

Steele nodded. He could count on maybe another thousand people to support him. Not many compared to the dead. A ton when compared with the living.

"When can we expect to get the vaccine?"

"I'm not sure. Aside from those of us they sent to the front line, they will inoculate the armed forces and the populations surrounding the Golden Triangle first."

435

"Gives you the shits for about a week," Hunter said and pushed the huge wad of chew deeper into his lower left lip.

A short smile cracked Steele's face. "I'll take the shits over death, but shouldn't they start on the front line? We're going to be the ones taking the brunt of the combat."

Kinnick gave him an apologetic look. "Not my plan. They will get it out as fast as they can."

Steele made sure there was no question to his words. "We will hold. It's part of our contract with them."

Kinnick nodded with a grim smile. His eyes were weary. "We're good for it."

KINNICK
Reynolds Farm, IA

Kinnick stepped down off the long farmhouse porch followed by Hunter, Washington, and Hawkins. Their boots crunched through loose gravel back to the river. He made it down to an old wooden dock.

Hamilton One bobbed in the frigid muddy waters of the Mississippi River. Marines sat in the machine gun turrets surveying the river farmlands.

Kinnick's boots thumped the old wood and it groaned in response. He turned around and observed the old farmhouse for a minute.

The farmhouse was white with black shutters that were a bit faded and needed a touch-up. The porch needed to be entirely repainted. The white paint was peeling away to reveal gray wood underneath.

Steele stood on the porch, leaning on a wooden pillar with a gaggle of followers. His one arm hung loose at his side, the other propped underneath his chin as if he were in deep thought. A sidearm and tomahawk hung at his belt. Gwen wrapped an arm around him with her other hand resting on her swollen belly.

Her grandfather stood behind her, watching him.

Next to Steele stood an overweight biker with long hair and a bandana, his beard gray, and on his right was a wrinkled female biker with permanently puckered lips. A stout biker stood next to her along with a short black-haired woman he at first had mistaken for a teenage boy. A faint smirk lined her face letting him know she knew a snarky secret that he could never find out.

Farthest away from them all lingered the tall clergyman with his broad companion and another with wavy hair and a dashing smile. The clergyman's eyes were critical as if he held scales and weighed Kinnick's every move.

These are the people I've entrusted with holding the eastern front of the United States. This motley crew of bikers, farmers, fighters, and rebels. Kinnick blinked as he stared at them from afar.

"Forget something, boss?" Hunter asked. His single eye scrutinized the farmhouse. "He's a bit meaner than the last time we met him. I like him."

"He is." *Did I make the right choice by giving him control of this AOR? Or have I created a warlord in the power vacuum of a collapsing nation?* "There's something about him. I can't put my finger on it."

"Some things are better left uncovered. He'll keep his word." Hunter pulled out a can of chew and placed a wad of black tobacco in his mouth. "He's fought in the past and he'll do it again. That's all he knows and that's all we need to know."

"I wonder if I've made too many assumptions about the man." Kinnick eyed his one-eyed master sergeant.

Hunter licked his lips, shoving tobacco down with his tongue inside his mouth. "What's that? He's fought Jackson twice now. Once to help us escape and once in an all-out battle. He helped us find Patient Zero. Killed plenty of the dead. He's an ally we not only want but we need."

"You're right, but he was different than before. Look at him up there. He's practically a king." Kinnick shook his head, not understanding the entirety of the situation.

Steele raised a hand in a short wave. Kinnick waved back.

Have I created something that can't be stopped? How many times have we armed one group of rebels only to fight them ten years down the road?

"We can worry about it later. As long as he holds, we've got a shot."

Hunter spit into the water. The tobacco plopped and disappeared from the surface.

"Where's the next fight?"

Is it here? Kinnick looked at the flowing water. "Downriver."

"You know what they say?"

"What's that?"

Hunter smirked beneath his thick brown beard. "My grandma always used to say if you're facing the right direction, all you need to do is walk."

Hunter spit again and used the gunwale to hop into the Hamilton One. He smiled and gave Kinnick a hand, helping him on board.

Kinnick nodded his thanks. "That's good advice, Master Sergeant."

Hunter peered out with his single eye. "I reckon it is, isn't it."

A Message from the Author

Thank you for reading *The Departing*, Book 4 of The End Time Saga. I truly hope you enjoyed this installment. I had so much fun putting this one together for you. If you have the time, please consider writing a review.

Reviews are important tools that I use to hone my craft. They help me identify what I'm getting right and what needs work in my writing. Reviews also help potential readers decide whether or not to purchase and read my work. I take them very seriously and appreciate your time.

If you do take the time to write a review, reach out to me on my website *DanielGreeneBooks.com* or email me at *DanielGreeneBooks@gmail.com*. I would like to take the time to thank you personally for your feedback and support. Don't be afraid to reach out. I love meeting new readers!

The Greene Army Newsletter List: *Click here to sign up*
Facebook: *Daniel Greene Books*
Website: *DanielGreeneBooks.com*
Email: *DanielGreeneBooks@gmail.com*

The End Time Saga doesn't end here. *The Holding*, Book 5 of The End Time Saga is coming…

A Note

I have a few notes on the places depicted in this novel. Oddly enough, Hacklebarney is a real place in Southeast Iowa. It is a small place, probably only known by the people that live there or have lived there. You will never find it on map. I have been fortunate enough to know some of these great people. They have shared their stories with me, so I decided to honor them by giving Hacklebarney a place on the map as Gwen's hometown. I took their tiny section of Iowa and turned it into a town on the Mississippi River. So, if while you're cruising in Southeast Iowa, you hope to find a town sign that reads "*Hacklebarney: If it ain't Heaven, it's close*," I'm sorry, but unless you pull up a rocking chair to listen to some anecdote from a couple of nonagenarians (and I recommend you do), you're probably not going to find it. If you do find Hacklebarney, take a million pictures and send them my way!

What you will find along the Iowa banks of the Mississippi River are some of the nicest folks you'll meet in the United States. I've fictionalized them for the sake of my novel, but it is a beautiful part of the Midwest country filled with some of the best people I know. They have good reason to be so proud of their little corner of the world.

The same holds true for the quaint lake towns in northern Michigan. I've spent quite a bit of time in northern Michigan or "Up North," as we call it, and the summers are some of the best I've ever experienced. It's almost magical and certainly beautiful, especially if you are coming from concrete jungles of the city. There are small inland lakes around every corner, and of course, the big lakes are like freshwater oceans. It's also an excellent place to visit if you are interested in craft beer. I feel like it's one of the best-kept secrets in the United States, but then there are the winters…

As with the other novels, the military units have been fictionalized. The Marine units, ODAs, and Jackson's Legion are all made up. I have so much respect for those who serve and the dedication it takes to keep us not only safe but also free. A special thanks goes to them. I hope I was able to make this novel realistic enough for your enjoyment.

Every day I make progress on *The Holding*, Book 5 of The End Time Saga. Those of you who love Joseph, do not despair. He is making his slightly nerdy comeback in *The Holding*. He had to take a back burner in *The Departing* to give some of the other characters room to grow. I hope that you can live without him until Book 5.

You may also be wondering, how long is this series going to be? How will our downtrodden heroes survive in an apocalyptic landscape with so much danger? Can the hordes be overcome or is it a countdown to extinction? Will there be anyone left to rebuild? You'll have to keep reading to find out. However, there is an end in sight.

Right now, there are six books planned for this series. I want to make sure that the characters and stories within make their full arcs but don't want to lead you on a never-ending tale, rehashing the same threats and stories over and over. If I feel that the series needs more, I will make sure that happens, but at this point, I am only planning on six. Whether or not this happens, may be out of my hands and with my creative psyche or the Nine Greek Muses who throw a story my way every now and then. Either way, I can't wait to share new novels with you in the future.

- Daniel Greene
10/30/2018

Special Thanks

Writing may be a solitary endeavor, but so much more goes into a book than just sitting down at a keyboard. Without my gang of allies—some motley, some holy, some dirty, some noble, but all my crew—these books might not exist. Thank you all for sharing in this project with me.

To my Beta readers and contributors (you know who you are): Thank you for your valuable feedback and responses to my endless questions. Your steadfast input has elevated this novel above what it originally was.

To my editor (Lisa): With every pass you make over my novel, you remind me of how important your work is. Thank you for polishing my novel. Please see her services here: *Lisa's Editing Services*

To my cover artist (Tim): I am thrilled with your ability to capture this novel in a single image. I commend you for your excellent work.

To my photographer (Justin): You're a master of the lens. Thank you for taking the time to ensure our images were done well. I know you made Tim's life a lot easier.

To my family, friends, and readers: Thank you for pushing me along on this journey as an author. Your support means the world to me. As long as you keep reading, I will keep writing.

About the Author

Daniel Greene is the award-winning debut author of the growing apocalyptic thriller series The End Time Saga. He is an avid traveler and physical fitness enthusiast with a deep passion for history. He is inspired by the works of George R.R. Martin, Steven Pressfield, Bernard Cornwell, and George Romero. Although he is a Midwesterner for life, he now lives on the East Coast.

Books by Daniel Greene

The End Time Saga
End Time
The Breaking
The Rising
The Departing
The Holding (Coming 2019)

Made in the USA
Coppell, TX
24 January 2021

48737617R00252